D1266752

The Giant of the North

VIEW FROM CAPE CHAOS—PAGE 94

The Giant of the North

Pokings Round the Pole

by

R.M. BALLANTYNE

Author of
Red Rooney, Blue Lights,
The Pirate City, etc., etc.

THE VISION FORUM, INC.
San Antonio, Texas

Reprinted from the 1881 Classic by R.M. Ballantyne

SECOND PRINTING

Copyright © 2007 The Vision Forum, Inc.
All Rights Reserved.

"Where there is no vision, the people perish."

www.visionforum.com

ISBN-10 1-934554-05-7
ISBN-13 978-1-934554-05-0

The cloth covers in this series are color-coded to represent the geographic region of each story. The regions and their respective colors are as follows:

NORTH AMERICA—*Forest Green*   SOUTH AMERICA—*Wheat*
SOUTH PACIFIC—*Light Blue*   ARCTIC REGIONS—*Grey*
EUROPE—*Navy Blue*   AFRICA—*Sienna*
ASIA—*Red*

PRINTED IN THE UNITED STATES OF AMERICA

 The "Scotch Thistle," the floral emblem of Scotland, serves as the emblem of the R.M. Ballantyne Series published by Vision Forum.

PREFACE

THE DISCOVERY of the North Pole has been delayed too long.

To settle this question, and relieve men's minds of further anxiety and speculation in regard to the circumjacent regions, I lately sent an old friend on a voyage of discovery to the Arctic regions. My friend, though not a "special correspondent," has been successful. He has discovered the North Pole.

This volume lays the results and romantic details of his expedition before the reader.

R.M.B.
Harrow-on-the-Hill, 1881

CONTENTS

Chapter I

The Giant was an Eskimo of the Arctic regions. At the beginning of his career he was known among his kindred by the name of Skreekinbroot, or the howler, because he howled oftener and more furiously than any infant that had ever been born in Arctic land. His proper name, however, was Chingatok, though his familiars still ventured occasionally to style him Skreekinbroot.

Now it must not be supposed that our giant was one of those ridiculous myths of the nursery, with monstrous heads and savage hearts, who live on human flesh, and finally receive their deserts at the hands of famous giant-killing Jacks. No! Chingatok was a real man of moderate size—not more than seven feet two in his sealskin boots—with a lithe, handsome figure, immense chest and shoulders, a gentle disposition, and a fine, though flattish countenance, which was sometimes grave with thought, at other times rippling with fun.

We mention the howling characteristic of his babyhood because it was, in early life, the only indication of the grand spirit that dwelt within him— the solitary evidence of the tremendous energy with which he was endowed. At first he was no bigger than an ordinary infant. He was, perhaps, a little fatter, but *not* larger, and there was not an oily man or woman of the tribe to which he belonged who would have noticed anything peculiar about him if he had only kept moderately quiet; but this he would not or could not do. His mouth was his safety-valve. His spirit seemed to have been born big at once. It was far too large for his infant body, and could only find relief from the little plump dwelling in which it was at first enshrined by rushing out at the mouth. The shrieks of pigs were trifles to the yelling of that Eskimo child's impatience. The caterwauling of cats was as nothing to the growls of his disgust. The angry voice of the Polar bear was a mere chirp compared with the furious howling of his disappointment, and the barking of a mad walrus was music to the roaring of his wrath.

Every one, except his mother, wished him dead and buried in the centre of an iceberg or at the bottom of the Polar Sea. His mother—squat, solid, pleasant-faced, and mild—alone put up with his ways with that long-suffering endurance which is characteristic of mothers. Nothing could disturb the serenity of Toolooha. When the young giant, (that was to be), roared, she fondled him; if that was ineffectual, she gave him a walrus tusk or a seal's flipper to play with; if that did not suffice, she handed him a lump of blubber to suck; if that failed, as was sometimes the case, she gambolled with him on the floor of her snow-hut, and rubbed his oily visage lovingly over her not less oleaginous countenance. Need we enlarge on this point? Have not all mothers acted thus, or similarly, in all times and climes?

> From pole to pole a mother's soul
>   Is tender, strong, and true;
> Whether the loved be good or bad—
>   White, yellow, black, or blue.

But Toolooha's love was wise as well as strong. If all else failed, she was wont to apply corporal punishment, and whacked her baby with her tail. Be not shocked, reader. We refer to the tail of her coat, which was so long that it trailed on the ground, and had a flap at the end which produced surprising results when properly applied.

But the howling condition of life did not last long.

At the age of five years little Chingatok began to grow unusually fast, and when he reached the age of seven, the tribe took note of him as a more than promising youth. Then the grand spirit, which had hitherto sought to vent itself in yells and murderous assaults on its doting mother, spent its energies in more noble action. All the little boys of his size, although much older than himself, began to look up to him as a champion. None went so boldly into mimic warfare with the walrus and the bear as Chingatok. No one could make toy sledges out of inferior and scanty materials so well as he. If any little one wanted a succourer in distress, Skreekinbroot was the lad to whom he, or she, turned. If a broken toy had to be mended, Chingatok could do it better than any other boy. And so it went on until he became a man and a giant.

When he was merely a big boy—that is, bigger than the largest man of his tribe—he went out with the other braves to hunt and fish, and signalised himself by the reckless manner in which he would attack the polar bear single-handed; but when he reached his full height and breadth he gave up reckless acts, restrained his tendency to display his great strength, and became unusually modest and thoughtful, even pensive, for an Eskimo.

The superiority of Chingatok's mind, as well as his body, soon became manifest. Even among savages, intellectual power commands respect. When coupled with physical force it elicits reverence. The young giant soon became an oracle and a leading man in his tribe. Those who had wished him dead, and in the centre of an iceberg or at the bottom of the Polar Sea, came to wish that there were only a few more men like him.

Of course he had one or two enemies. Who has not? There were a few who envied him his physical powers. There were some who envied him his moral influence. None envied him his intellectual superiority, for they did not understand it. There was one who not only envied but hated him. This was Eemerk, a mean-spirited, narrow-minded fellow, who could not bear to play what is styled second fiddle.

Eemerk was big enough—over six feet—but he wanted to be bigger. He was stout enough, but wanted to be stouter. He was influential too, but wanted to reign supreme. This, of course, was not possible while there existed a taller, stouter, and cleverer man than himself. Even if Eemerk had been the equal of Chingatok in all these respects, there would still have remained one difference of character which would have rendered equality impossible.

It was this: our young giant was unselfish and modest. Eemerk was selfish and vain-glorious. When the latter killed a seal he always kept the tit-bits for himself. Chingatok gave them to his mother, or to any one else who had a mind to have them. And so in regard to everything.

Chingatok was not a native of the region in which we introduce him to the reader. He and the tribe, or rather part of the tribe, to which he belonged, had travelled from the far north; so far north that nobody knew the name of the land from which they had come. Even Chingatok himself did not know it. Being unacquainted with geography, he knew no more about his position on the face of this globe than a field-mouse or a sparrow.

But the young giant had heard a strange rumour, while in his far-off country, which had caused his strong intellect to ponder, and his huge heart to beat high. Tribes who dwelt far to the south of his northern home had told him that other tribes, still further south, had declared that the people who dwelt to the south of them had met with a race of men who came to them over the sea on floating islands; that these islands had something like trees growing out of them, and wings which moved about, which folded and expanded somewhat like the wings of the sea-gull; that these men's faces were whiter than Eskimo faces; that they wore skins of a much more curious kind than sealskins, and that they were amazingly clever with their hands, talked a language that no one could understand, and did many wonderful things that nobody could comprehend.

A longing, wistful expression used to steal over Chingatok's face as he gazed at the southern horizon while listening to these strange rumours, and a very slight smile of incredulity had glimmered on his visage, when it was told him that one of the floating islands of these Kablunets, or white men, had been seen with a burning mountain in the middle of it, which vomited forth smoke and fire, and sometimes uttered a furious hissing or shrieking sound, not unlike his own voice when he was a Skreekinbroot.

The giant said little about these and other subjects, but thought deeply. His mind, as we have said, was far ahead of his time and condition. Let us listen to some of the disjointed thoughts that perplexed this man.

"Who made me?" he asked in a low tone, when floating alone one day in his kayak, or skin canoe, "whence came I? whither go I? What is this great sea on which I float? that land on which I tread? No sledge, no spear, no kayak, no snow-hut makes itself!

Who made all that which I behold?"

Chingatok looked around him, but no audible answer came from Nature. He looked up, but the glorious sun only dazzled his eyes.

"There *must* be One," he continued in a lower tone, "who made all things; but who made *Him*? No one? It is impossible! The Maker must have ever been. *Ever been*!" He repeated this once or twice with a look of perplexed gravity.

The northern savage had grasped the grand mystery, and, like all true philosophers savage or civilised who have gone before him, relapsed into silence.

At last he resolved to travel south, until he should arrive at the coasts where these strange sights before described were said to have been seen.

Having made up his mind, Chingatok began his arrangements without delay; persuaded a few families of his tribe to accompany him, and reached the north-western shores of Greenland after a long and trying journey by water and ice.

Here he spent the winter. When spring came, he continued his journey south, and at last began to look out, with sanguine expectation, for the floating islands with wings, and the larger island with the burning mountain on it, about which he had heard.

Of course, on his way south, our giant fell in with some members of the tribes through whom the rumours that puzzled him had been transmitted to the far north; and, as he advanced, these rumours took a more definite, also a more correct, form. In time he came to understand that the floating islands were gigantic kayaks, or canoes, with masts and sails, instead of trees and wings. The burning mountain, however, remained an unmodified mystery, which he was still inclined to disbelieve. But these more correct views did not in the least abate Chingatok's eager desire to behold, with his own eyes, the strange men from the unknown south.

Eemerk formed one of the party who had volunteered to join Chingatok on this journey. Not that Eemerk was influenced by large-minded views or a thirst for knowledge, but he could not bear the thought that his rival should have all the honour of going forth on a long journey of exploration to the mysterious south, a journey which was sure to be full of adventure, and the successful accomplishment of which would unquestionably raise him very much in the estimation of his tribe.

Eemerk had volunteered to go, not as second in command, but as an independent member of the party—a sort of free-lance. Chingatok did not quite relish having Eemerk for a companion, but, being a good-humoured, easy-going fellow, he made no objection to his going. Eemerk took his wife with him. Chingatok took his mother and little sister; also a young woman named Tekkona, who was his wife's sister. These were the only females of the exploring party. Chingatok had left his wife behind him, because she was not robust at that time; besides, she was very small—as is usually the case with giants' wives—and he was remarkably fond of her, and feared to expose her to severe fatigue and danger.

The completed party of explorers numbered twenty souls, with their respective bodies, some of which latter were large, some small, but all strong and healthy. Four of the men were friends of Eemerk, whom he had induced to join because he knew them to be kindred spirits who would support him.

"I go to the ice-cliff to look upon the sea," said Chingatok one morning, drawing himself up to his full height, and unconsciously brushing some of the lamp-black off the roof of his hut with the hood of his sealskin coat.

At this point it may be well to explain, once for all, that our giant did not speak English, and as it is highly improbable that the reader understands the Eskimo tongue, we will translate as literally as possible—merely remarking that Chingatok's language, like his mind, was of a superior cast.

"Why goes my son to the ice-cliff?" asked Toolooha in a slightly reproachful tone. "Are not the floes nearer? Can he not look on the great salt lake from the hummocks? The sun has been hot a long time now. The ice-cliffs are dangerous. Their edges split off every day. If my son goes often to them, he will one day come tumbling down upon the floes and be crushed flat, and men will carry him to his mother's feet like a mass of shapeless blubber."

It is interesting to note how strong a resemblance there is in sentiment and modes of thought between different members of the human family. This untutored savage, this Polar giant, replied, in the Eskimo tongue, words which may be freely translated—"Never fear, mother, I know how to take care of myself."

Had he been an Englishman, he could not have expressed himself more naturally. He smiled as he looked down at his stout and genial mother, while she stooped and drew forth a choice morsel of walrus flesh from one of her boots. Eskimo ladies wear enormous sealskin boots the whole length of their legs. The tops of these boots are made extremely wide, for the purpose of stowing away blubber, or babies, or other odd articles that might encumber their hands.

Chingatok seemed the personification of savage dignity as he stood there, leaning on a short walrus spear. Evidently his little mother doted on him. So did Oblooria, a pretty little girl of about sixteen, who was his only sister, and the counterpart of her mother, hairy coat and tail included, only a few sizes smaller.

But Chingatok's dignity was marred somewhat when he went down on his hands and knees, in order to crawl through the low snow-tunnel which was the only mode of egress from the snow-hut.

Emerging at the outer end of the tunnel, he stood up, drew the hood of his sealskin coat over his head, shouldered his spear, and went off with huge and rapid strides over the frozen billows of the Arctic Sea.

Spring was far advanced at the time of which we write, and the sun shone not only with dazzling brilliancy, but with intense power on the fields of ice which still held the ocean in their cold unyielding embrace. The previous winter had been unusually severe, and the ice showed little or no sign of breaking up, except at a great distance from land, where the heaving of the waves had cracked it up into large fields. These were gradually parting from the main body, and drifting away with surface-currents to southern waters, there to be liquefied and re-united to their parent sea.

The particular part of the Greenland coast to which the giant went in his ramble is marked by tremendous cliffs descending perpendicularly into the water. These, at one part, are divided by a valley tilled with a great glacier, which flows from the mountains of the interior with a steep declivity to the sea, into which it thrusts its tongue, or extreme end. This mighty river of ice completely fills the valley from side to side, being more than two miles in width and many hundred feet thick. It seems as solid and motionless as the rocks that hem it in, nevertheless the markings on the surface resemble the currents and eddies of a stream which has been suddenly frozen in the act of flowing, and if you were to watch it narrowly, day by day, and week by week, you would perceive, by the changed position of objects on its surface, that it does actually advance or flow towards the sea. A further proof of this advance is, that although the tongue is constantly shedding off large icebergs, it is never much decreased in extent, being pushed out continuously by the ice which is behind. In fact, it is this pushing process which causes the end of the tongue to shed its bergs, because, when the point is thrust into deep water and floats, the motion of the sea cracks the floating mass off from that pail which is still aground, and lets it drift away.

Now it was to these ice-cliffs that the somewhat reckless giant betook himself. Although not well acquainted with that region, or fully alive to the extent of the danger incurred, his knowledge was sufficient to render him cautious in the selection of the position which should form his outlook.

And a magnificent sight indeed presented itself when he took his stand among the glittering pinnacles. Far as the eye could reach, the sea lay stretched in the sunshine, calm as a mill-pond, and sparkling with ice-jewels of every shape and size. An Arctic haze, dry and sunny, seemed to float over all like golden gauze. Not only was the sun encircled by a beautiful halo, but also by those lovely lights of the Arctic regions known as parhelia, or mock-suns. Four of these made no mean display in emulation of their great original. On the horizon, refraction caused the ice-floes and bergs to present endless variety of fantastic forms, and in the immediate foreground—at the giant's feet— tremendous precipices of ice went sheer down into the deep water, while, away to the right, where a bay still retained its winter grasp of an ice-field, could be seen, like white bee-hives, the temporary snow-huts of these wandering Eskimos.

Well might the eye, as well as the head, of the so-called savage rise upwards while he pondered the great mystery of the Maker of all! As he stood on the giddy ledge, rapt in contemplation, an event occurred which was fitted to deepen the solemnity of his thoughts. Not twenty yards from the point on which he stood, a great ice-cliff—the size of an average house—snapped off with a rending crash, and went thundering down into the deep, which seemed to boil and heave with sentient emotion as it received the mass, and swallowed it in a turmoil indescribable.

Chingatok sprang from his post and sought a safer but not less lofty outlook, while the new-born berg, rising from the sea, swayed majestically to and fro in its new-found cradle.

"It is not understandable," muttered the giant as he took up his new position and gazed with feelings of awe upon the grand scene. "I wonder if the pale-faced men in the floating islands think much about these things. Perhaps they dwell in a land which is still more wonderful than this, and hunt the walrus and the seal like us. It is said they come for nothing else but to see our land and find out what is in it. Why should I not go to see their land? My kayak is large, though it has no wings. The land may be far off, but am I not strong? They are pale-faced; perhaps the reason is that they are starved. That must be so, else they would not leave their home. I might bring some of the poor creatures to this happy land of ours, where there is always plenty to eat. They might send messengers for their relations to come and dwell with us. I will speak to mother about that; she is wise!"

Like a dutiful son, the giant turned on his heel, descended the cliffs, and went straight home to consult with his mother.

Chapter II

"Mother, I have been thinking," said Chingatok, as he crept into his hut and sat down on a raised bench of moss.

"That is not news, my son; you think much. You are not like other men. They think little and eat much."

The stout little woman looked up through the smoke of her cooking-lamp and smiled, but her big son was too much absorbed in his thoughts to observe her pleasantry, so she continued the cooking of a walrus chop in silence.

"The Kablunets are not to be seen, mother," resumed Chingatok. "I have looked for them every day for a long time, and begin to weary. My thought is now to launch my kayak when we come to open water, load it with meat, take four spears and more lines than a strong hunter needs for a whole season, then paddle away south to discover the land of the Kablunets. They must be poor; they may be starving. I will guide them to our home, and show them this land of plenty."

He paused abruptly, and looked at his mother with solemn anxiety, for he was well aware that he had given her food for profound reflection.

We feel tempted here to repeat our remark about the strong resemblance between different members of the human family, but refrain.

This untutored woman of the Arctic lands met her son's proposition with the well-known reply of many civilised persons.

"Of what use would it be, my son? No good can come of searching out these poor lands. You cannot benefit the miserable Kablunets. Perhaps they are savage and fierce; and you are sure to meet with dangers by the way. Worse—you may die!"

"Mother," returned Chingatok, "when the white bear stands up with his claws above my head and his mouth a-gape, does my hand tremble or my spear fail?"

"No, my son."

"Then why do you speak to me of danger and death?"

Toolooha was not gifted with argumentative powers. She relapsed into silence and lamp-smoke.

But her son was not to be so easily dissuaded. He adopted a line of reasoning which never failed.

"Mother," he said, sadly, "it may be that you are right, and I am of too fearful a spirit to venture far away from you by myself; I will remain here if you think me a coward."

"Don't say so, Chingatok. You know what I think. Go, if you must go, but who will hunt for your poor old mother when you are gone?"

This was an appeal which the astute little woman knew to be very powerful with her son. She buried her head in the smoke again, and left the question to simmer.

Chingatok was tender-hearted. He said nothing, but, as usual, he thought much, as he gazed in a contemplative manner at his oily parent, and there is no saying to what lengths of self-sacrifice he would have gone if he had not been aroused, and his thoughts scattered to the winds, by a yell so tremendous that it might well have petrified him on the spot. But it did nothing of the kind. It only caused him to drop on his knees, dart through the tunnel like an eel, spring into the open air like an electrified rabbit from its burrow, and stand up with a look of blazing interrogation on his huge countenance.

The cry had been uttered by his bosom friend and former playmate, Oolichuk, who came running towards him with frantic gesticulations.

"The Kablunets!" he gasped, "the white-faces have come!—on a floating island!—alive!—smoking!—it is all true!"

"Where?" demanded our giant, whose face blazed up at once.

"There!" cried Oolichuk, pointing seaward towards the ice-hummocks with both hands and glaring up at his friend.

Without another word Chingatok ran off in the

direction pointed out, followed hotly by his friend.

Oolichuk was a large and powerful man, but, his legs were remarkably short. His pace, compared with that of Chingatok, was as that of a sparrow to an ostrich. Nevertheless he kept up, for he was agile and vigorous.

"Have you seen them—have you spoken?" asked the giant, abruptly.

"Yes, all the tribe was there."

"No one killed?"

"No, but terribly frightened; they made me run home to fetch you."

Chingatok increased his speed. So did Oolichuk.

While they run, let us leap a little ahead of them, reader, and see what had caused all the excitement.

The whole party had gone off that morning, with the exception of Chingatok and his mother, to spear seals in a neighbouring bay, where these animals had been discovered in great numbers. Dogs and sledges had been taken, because a successful hunt was expected, and the ice was sufficiently firm.

The bay was very large. At its distant southern extremity there rose a great promontory which jutted far out into the sea. While the men were busy there making preparations to begin the hunt, Oblooria, Chingatok's little sister, amused herself by mounting a hummock of ice about thirty feet high.

When there, she chanced to look towards the promontory. Instantly she opened her eyes and mouth and uttered a squeal that brought her friends running to her side.

Oolichuk was the first to reach her. He had no need to ask questions. Oblooria's gaze directed his, and there, coming round the promontory, he beheld an object which had never before filled his wondering eyes. It was, apparently, a monstrous creature with a dark body and towering wings, and a black thing in its middle, from which were vomited volumes of smoke.

"Kablunets! white men!" he yelled.

"Kablunets!—huk! huk!" echoed the whole tribe, as they scrambled up the ice-hill one after another.

And they were right. A vessel of the pale-faces had penetrated these northern solitudes, and was advancing swiftly before a light breeze under sail and steam.

Despite the preparation their minds had received, and the fact that they were out in search of these very people, this sudden appearance of them filled most of the Eskimos with alarm—some of them with absolute terror, insomuch that the term "pale-face" became most appropriate to themselves.

"What shall we do?" exclaimed Akeetolik, one of the men.

"Fly!" cried Ivitchuk, another of the men, whose natural courage was not high.

"No; let us stay and behold!" said Oolichuk, with a look of contempt at his timid comrade.

"Yes, stay and see," said Eemerk sternly.

"But they will kill us," faltered the young woman, whom we have already mentioned by the name of Tekkona.

"No—no one would kill *you*," said Eemerk gallantly;

"they would only carry you off and keep you."

While they conversed with eager, anxious looks, the steam yacht—for such she was—advanced rapidly, threading her way among the ice-fields and floes with graceful rapidity and ease, to the unutterable amazement of the natives. Although her sails were spread to catch the light breeze, her chief motive power at the time was a screw-propeller.

"Yes, it must be alive," said Oolichuk to Akeetolik, with a look of solemn awe. "The white men do not paddle. They could not lift paddles big enough to move such a great oomiak,[1] and the wind is not strong; it could not blow them so fast. See, the oomiak has a tail—and wags it!"

"Oh! *do* let us run away!" whispered the trembling Oblooria, as she took shelter behind Tekkona.

"No, no," said the latter, who was brave as well as pretty, "we need not fear. Our men will take care of us."

"I wish that Chingatok was here!" whimpered poor little Oblooria, nestling closer to Tekkona and grasping her tail, "he fears nothing and nobody."

"Ay," assented Tekkona with a peculiar smile, "and is brave enough to fight everything and everybody."

"Does Oblooria think that no one can fight but the giant?" whispered Oolichuk, who stood nearest to the little maid.

---

1. The oomiak is the open boat of skin used by Eskimo women, and is capable of holding several persons. The kayak, or man's canoe, holds only one.

He drew a knife made of bone from his boot, where it usually lay concealed, and flourished it, with a broad grin. The girl laughed, blushed slightly, and, looking down, toyed with the sleeve of Tekkona's fur coat.

Meanwhile the yacht drew near to the floe on which our Eskimos were grouped. The ice was cracked right across, leaving a lane of open water about ten feet wide between its inner edge and the shore ice. The Eskimos stood on the land side of this crack, a hundred yards or so from it. On nearing the floe the strange vessel checked her speed.

"It moves its wings!" exclaimed Eemerk.

"And turns its side to us," said Akeetolik.

"And wags its tail no more," cried Oolichuk.

"Oh! do, *do* let us run away," gasped Oblooria.

"No, no, we will not run," said Tekkona.

At that moment a white cloud burst from the side of the yacht.

"Hi! hee! huk!" shouted the whole tribe in amazement.

A crash followed which not only rattled like thunder among the surrounding cliffs, but went like electric fire to the central marrow of each Eskimo. With a united yell of terror, they leaped three feet into the air—more or less—turned about, and fled. Tekkona, who was active as a young deer, herself took the lead; and Oblooria, whose limbs trembled so that she could hardly run, held on to Oolichuk, who gallantly dragged her along. The terror was increased by a prolonged screech from the steam-whistle. It was a wild scramble in sudden panic. The Eskimos reached their sledges, harnessed their teams, left their spears on the ice, cracked their whips, which caused the dogs to join in the yelling chorus, and made for the land at a furious gallop.

But their fear began to evaporate in a few minutes, and Oolichuk was the first to check his pace.

"Ho! stop," he cried.

Eemerk looked back, saw that they were not pursued, and pulled up. The others followed suit, and soon the fugitives were seen by those on board the yacht grouped together and gazing intently at them from the top of another ice-hummock.

The effect of the cannon-shot on board the yacht itself was somewhat startling. The gun had been loaded on the other side of the promontory for the purpose of being fired if Eskimos were not visible on the coast beyond, in order to attract them from the interior, if they should chance to be there. When, however, the natives were discovered on the ice, the gun was, of course, unnecessary, and had been forgotten. It therefore burst upon the crew with a shock of surprise, and caused the Captain, who was in the cabin at the moment, to shoot up from the hatchway like a Jack-in-the-box.

"Who did that?" he demanded, looking round sternly.

The crew, who had been gazing intently at the natives, did not know.

"I really cannot tell, sir," said the chief mate, touching his cap.

Two strapping youths—one about sixteen, the other

eighteen—leaned over the side and paid no regard to the question; but it was obvious, from the heaving motion of their shoulders, that they were not so much absorbed in contemplation as they pretended to be.

"Come, Leo, Alf, you know something about this."

The Captain was a large powerful man of about forty, with bushy iron-grey curls, a huge beard, and an aquiline nose. The two youths turned to him at once, and Leo, the eldest, said respectfully, "We did not see it done, uncle, but—but we think—"

"Well, what do you think?"

At that moment a delicate-looking, slender lad, about twelve years of age, with fair curly hair, and flashing blue eyes, stepped out from behind the funnel, which had hitherto concealed him, and said boldly, though blushingly—

"I did it, father."

"Ha! just like you; why did you do it? eh!"

"I can hardly tell, father," said the boy, endeavouring to choke a laugh, "but the Eskimos looked so funny, and I—I had a box of matches in my pocket, and—and—I thought a shot would make them look so very much funnier, and—and—I was right!"

"Well, Benjamin, you may go below, and remain there till further orders."

When Captain Vane called his son "Benjamin," he was seriously displeased. At other times he called him Benjy.

"Yes, father," replied the boy, with a very bad grace, and down he went in a state of rebellious despair, for he was wildly anxious to witness all that went on.

His despair was abated, however, when, in the course of a few minutes, the yacht swung round so as to present her stern to the shore, and remained in that position, enabling him to observe proceedings from the cabin windows almost as well as if he had been on deck. He was not aware that his father, knowing his son's nature, and wishing to temper discipline with mercy, had placed the vessel in that position for his special benefit!

The difficulty now was, how to attract the natives, and inspire them with confidence in the good intentions of their visitors. In any case this would have been a difficult matter, but the firing of that unlucky gun had increased the difficulty tenfold. When, however, Captain Vane saw the natives cease their mad flight, and turn to gaze at the vessel, his hopes revived, and he set about a series of ingenious efforts to attain his end.

First of all, he sent a boat in charge of his two nephews, Leonard and Alphonse Vandervell, to set up a small table on the ice, on which were temptingly arranged various presents, consisting of knives, beads, looking-glasses, and articles of clothing. Having done this, they retired, like wary anglers, to watch for a bite. But the fish would not rise, though they observed the proceedings with profound attention from the distant hummock. After waiting a couple of hours, the navigators removed the table and left an Eskimo dog in its place, with a string of blue beads tied round its neck. But this bait also failed.

"Try something emblematic, uncle," suggested

Leonard, the elder of the brothers before mentioned.

"And get Benjy to manufacture it," said Alphonse.

As Benjy was possessed of the most fertile imagination on board, he was released from punishment and brought on deck. The result of his effort of genius was the creation of a huge white calico flag, on which were painted roughly the figure of a sailor and an Eskimo sitting on an iceberg, with a kettle of soup between them. On one side were a pair of hands clasped together; on the other a sprig of heath, the only shrub that could be seen on the shore.

"Splendid!" exclaimed Leo and Alf in the same breath, as they held the flag up to view.

"You'll become a Royal Academician if you cultivate your talents, Benjy," said the Captain, who was proud, as well as fond, of this his only child.

The boy said nothing, but a pleased expression and a twinkle in his eyes proved that he was susceptible to flattery, though not carried off his legs by it.

The banner with the strange device was fixed to a pole which was erected on an ice-hummock between the ship and the shore, and a bag containing presents was hung at the foot of it.

Still these Eskimo fish would not bite, though they "rose" at the flag.

Oolichuk's curiosity had become so intense that he could not resist it. He advanced alone, very warily, and looked at it, but did not dare to touch it. Soon he was joined by Eemerk and the others. Seeing this, Captain Vane sent to meet them an interpreter whom he had procured at one of the Greenland settlements in passing. Just as this man, whose name was Anders, stepped into the boat alongside, it occurred to the Eskimos that their leader should be sent for. Oolichuk undertook to fetch him; he ran back to the sledges, harnessed a small team, and set off like the wind. Thus it came to pass that Chingatok and his mother were startled by a yell, as before mentioned.

Meanwhile Anders was put on the ice, and advanced alone and unarmed towards the canal, or chasm, which separated the parties. He carried a small white flag and a bag containing presents. Innocent-looking and defenceless though he was, however, the Eskimos approached him with hesitating and slow steps, regarding every motion of the interpreter with suspicion, and frequently stooping to thrust their hands into their boots, in which they all carried knives.

At last, when within hearing, Anders shouted a peaceful message, and there was much hallooing and gesticulation among the natives, but nothing comprehensible came of it. After a time Anders thought he recognised words of a dialect with which he was acquainted, and to his satisfaction found that they understood him.

"Kakeite! kakeite!—come on, come on," he cried, holding up the present.

"Nakrie! nakrie!—no, no, go away—you want to kill us," answered the doubtful natives.

Thereupon Anders protested that nothing was further from his thoughts, that he was a man and a friend, and had a mother like themselves, and that he wanted to please them.

At this, Eemerk approached to the edge of the canal, and, drawing a knife from his boot, said, "Go away! I can kill you."

Nothing daunted, Anders said he was not afraid, and taking a good English knife from his bag threw it across the canal.

Eemerk picked it up, and was so pleased that he exclaimed, "Heigh-yaw! heigh-yaw!" joyously, and pulled his nose several times. Anders, understanding this to be a sign of friendship, immediately pulled his own nose, smiled, and threw several trinkets and articles of clothing to the other natives, who had by that time drawn together in a group, and were chattering in great surprise at the things presented. Ivitchuk was perhaps the most excited among them. He chanced to get hold of a round box, in the lid of which was a mirror. On beholding himself looking at himself, he made such an awful face that he dropt the glass and sprang backward, tripping up poor Oblooria in the act, and tumbling over her.

This was greeted with a shout of laughter, and Anders, now believing that friendly relations had been established, went to the boat for a plank to bridge the chasm. As Leo and Alf assisted him to carry the plank, the natives again became grave and anxious.

"Stop!" shouted Eemerk, "you want to kill us. What great creature is that? Does it come from the moon or the sun? Does it eat fire and smoke?"

"No, it is only a dead thing. It is a wooden house."

"You lie!" cried the polite Eemerk, "it shakes its wings. It vomits fire and smoke. It has a tail, and wags it."

While speaking he slowly retreated, for the plank was being placed in position, and the other natives were showing symptoms of an intention to fly.

Just then a shout was heard landwards. Turning round they saw a dog-sledge flying over the ice towards them, with Oolichuk flourishing the long-lashed whip, and the huge form of their leader beside him.

In a few seconds they dashed up, and Chingatok sprang upon the ice. Without a moment's hesitation he strode towards the plank and crossed it. Walking up to Anders he pulled his own nose. The interpreter was not slow to return the salutation, as he looked up at the giant with surprise, not unmingled with awe. In addition, he grasped his huge hand, squeezed, and shook it.

Chingatok smiled blandly, and returned the squeeze so as to cause the interpreter to wince. Then, perceiving at once that he had got possession of a key to the affections of the strangers, he offered to shake hands with Leonard and his brother, stooping with regal urbanity to them as he did so. By this time the Captain and first mate, with Benjy and several of the crew, were approaching. Instead of exhibiting fear, Chingatok advanced to meet them, and shook hands all round. He gazed at Captain Vane with a look of admiration which was not at first quite accountable, until he laid his hand gently on the Captain's magnificent beard, and stroked it.

The Captain laughed, and again grasped the hand of the Eskimo. They both squeezed, but neither could make the other wince, for Captain Vane was remarkably powerful, though comparatively short of limb.

"Well, you *are* a good fellow in every way," exclaimed the Captain.

"Heigh, yah!" returned Chingatok, who no doubt meant to be complimentary, though we confess our inability to translate. It was obvious that two sympathetic souls had met.

"Come across," shouted Chingatok, turning abruptly to his companions, who had been gazing at his proceedings in open-mouthed wonder.

The whole tribe at once obeyed the order, and in a few minutes they were in the seventh heaven of delight and good-will, receiving gifts and handshakings, each pulling his own nose frequently by way of expressing satisfaction or friendship, and otherwise exchanging compliments with the no less amiable and gratified crew of the steam yacht *Whitebear*.

Chapter III

SHOWS HOW THE ESKIMOS WERE
ENTERTAINED BY THE WHITE MEN.

The *Whitebear* steam yacht, owned and commanded by Captain Jacob Vane, had sailed from England, and was bound for the North Pole.

"I'll find it—I'm bound to find it," was the Captain's usual mode of expressing himself to his intimates on the subject, "if there's a North Pole in the world at all, and my nephews Leo and Alf will help me. Leo's a doctor, *almost*, and Alf's a scientific Jack-of-all-trades, so we can't fail. I'll take my boy Benjy for the benefit of his health, and see if we don't bring home a chip o' the Pole big enough to set up beside Cleopatra's Needle on the Thames embankment."

There was tremendous energy in Captain Vane, and indomitable resolution; but energy and resolution cannot achieve all things. There are other factors in the life of man which help to mould his destiny.

Short and sad and terrible—ay, we might even say tremendous—was the *Whitebear's* wild career.

Up to the time of her meeting with the Eskimos, all had gone well. Fair weather and favouring winds had blown her across the Atlantic. Sunshine and success had received her, as it were, in the Arctic regions. The sea was unusually free of ice. Upernavik, the last of the Greenland settlements touched at, was reached early in the season, and the native interpreter Anders secured. The dreaded "middle passage," near the head of Baffin's Bay, was made in the remarkably short space of fifty hours, and, passing Cape York into the North Water, they entered Smith's Sound without having received more than a passing bump—an Arctic kiss as it were—from the Polar ice.

In Smith's Sound fortune still favoured them. These resolute intending discoverers of the North Pole passed in succession the various "farthests" of previous explorers, and the stout brothers Vandervell, with their cousin Benjy Vane, gazed eagerly over the bulwarks at the swiftly-passing headlands, while the Captain pointed out the places of interest, and kept up a running commentary on the brave deeds and high aspirations of such well-known men as Frobisher, Davis, Hudson, Ross, Parry, Franklin, Kane, McClure, Rae, McClintock, Hayes, Hall, Nares, Markham, and all the other heroes of Arctic story.

It was an era in the career of those three youths that stood out bright and fresh—never to be forgotten— this first burst of the realities of the Arctic world on minds which had been previously well informed by books. The climax was reached on the day when the Eskimos of the far north were met with.

But from that time a change took place in their experience. Fortune seemed to frown from that memorable day. We say "seemed," because knitted brows do not always or necessarily indicate what is meant by a frown.

After the first fears of the Eskimos had been allayed, a party of them were invited to go on board the ship. They accepted the invitation and went, headed by Chingatok.

That noble savage required no persuasion. From the first he had shown himself to be utterly devoid of fear. He felt that the grand craving of his nature—a thirst for knowledge—was about to be gratified, and that would have encouraged him to risk anything, even if he had been much less of a hero than he was.

But if fear had no influence over our giant, the same cannot be said of his companions. Oolichuk, indeed, was almost as bold, though he exhibited a considerable amount of caution in his looks and movements; but Eemerk, and one or two of his friends, betrayed their craven spirits in frequent startled looks and changing colour. Ivitchuk was a strange compound of nervousness and courage, while Akeetolik appeared to have lost the power of expressing every feeling but one—that of blank amazement. Indeed, surprise at what they saw on board the steam yacht was the predominant feeling amongst these children of nature. Their eyebrows seemed to have gone up and fixed themselves in the middle of their foreheads, and their eyes and mouths to have opened wide permanently. None of the women accepted the invitation to go aboard except Tekkona, and Oblooria followed her, not because she was courageous, but because she seemed to cling to the stronger nature as a protection from undefined and mysterious dangers.

"Tell them," said Captain Vane to Anders, the Eskimo interpreter, "that these are the machines that drive the ship along when there is no wind."

He pointed down the hatchway, where the complication of rods and cranks glistened in the hold.

"Huk!" exclaimed the Eskimos. They sometimes exclaimed, "Hi! ho! hoy! and hah!" as things were pointed out to them, but did not venture on language more intelligible at first.

"Let 'em hear the steam-whistle," suggested the mate.

Before the Captain could countermand the order, Benjy had touched the handle and let off a short, sharp *skirl*. The effect on the natives was powerful.

They leaped, with a simultaneous yell, at least a foot off the deck, with the exception of Chingatok, though even he was visibly startled, while Oblooria seized Tekkona round the waist, and buried her face in her friend's jacket.

A brief explanation soon restored them to equanimity, and they were about to pass on to some other object of interest, when both the steam-whistle and the escape-valve were suddenly opened to their full extent, and there issued from the engine a hissing yell so prolonged and deafening that even the Captain's angry shout was not heard.

A yard at least was the leap into the air made by the weakest of the Eskimos—except our giant, who seemed, however, to shrink into himself, while he grasped his knife and looked cautiously round, as if to guard himself from any foe that might appear. Eemerk fairly turned and fled to the stern of the yacht, over which he would certainly have plunged had he not been forcibly restrained by two stout seamen. The others, trembling violently, stood still, because they knew not what to do, and poor Oblooria fell flat on the deck, catching Tekkona by the tail, and pulling her down beside her.

"You scoundrel!" exclaimed the Captain, when the din ceased, "I—I—go down, sir, to—"

"Oh! father, don't be hard on me," pleaded Benjy, with a gleefully horrified look, "I really could *not* resist it. The—the temptation was too strong!"

"The temptation to give you a rope's-ending is almost too strong for *me*, Benjamin," returned the Captain sternly, but there was a twinkle in his eye notwithstanding, as he turned to explain to Chingatok that his son had, by way of jest, allowed part of the mighty Power imprisoned in the machinery to escape.

The Eskimo received the explanation with dignified gravity, and a faint smile played on his lips as he glanced approvingly at Benjy, for he loved a jest, and was keenly alive to a touch of humour.

"What power is imprisoned in the machinery?"

asked our Eskimo through the interpreter.

"What power?" repeated the Captain with a puzzled look, "why, it's boiling water—steam." Here he tried to give a clear account of the nature and power and application of steam, but, not being gifted with capacity for lucid explanation, and the mind of Anders being unaccustomed to such matters, the result was that the brain of Chingatok was filled with ideas that were fitted rather to amaze than to instruct him.

After making the tour of the vessel, the party again passed the engine hatch. Chingatok touched the interpreter quietly, and said in a low, grave tone, "Tell Blackbeard," (thus he styled the Captain), "to let the Power yell again!"

Anders glanced up in the giant's grave countenance with a look of amused surprise. He understood him, and whispered to the Captain, who smiled intelligently, and, turning to his son, said—

"Do it again, Benjy. Give it 'em strong."

Never before did that lad obey his father with such joyous alacrity. In another instant the whistle shrieked, and the escape-valve hissed ten times more furiously than before. Up went the Eskimo—three feet or more—as if in convulsions, and away went Eemerk to the stern, over which he dived, swam to the floe, leaped on his sledge, cracked his whip, and made for home on the wings of terror. Doubtless an evil conscience helped his cowardice.

Meanwhile Chingatok laughed, despite his struggles to be grave. This revealed the trick to some of his quick-witted and humour-loving companions, who at once burst into loud laughter. Even Oblooria dismissed her fears and smiled. In this restored condition they were taken down to the cabin and fed sumptuously.

That night, as Chingatok sat beside his mother, busy with a seal's rib, he gradually revealed to her the wonders he had seen.

"The white men are very wise, mother."

"So you have said four times, my son."

"But you cannot understand it."

"But my son can make me understand," said Toolooha, helping the amiable giant to a second rib.

Chingatok gazed at his little mother with a look of solemnity that evidently perplexed her. She became restless under it, and wiped her forehead uneasily with the flap at the end of her tail. The youth seemed about to speak, but he only sighed and addressed himself to the second rib, over which he continued to gaze while he masticated.

"My thoughts are big, mother," he said, laying down the bare bone.

"That may well be, for so is your head, my son," she replied, gently.

"I know not how to begin, mother."

"Another rib may open your lips, perhaps," suggested the old woman, softly.

"True; give me one," said Chingatok.

The third rib seemed to have the desired effect, for, while busy with it, he began to give his parent a graphic account of the yacht and its crew, and it was really interesting to note how correctly he described all that he understood of what he had seen. But some of the things he had partly failed to comprehend, and about these he was vague.

"And they have a—a Power, mother, shut up in a hard thing, so that it can't get out unless they let it, and it drives the big canoe through the water. It is very strong—terrible!"

"Is it a devil?" asked Toolooha.

"No, it is not alive. It is dead. It is *that*," he pointed with emphasis to a pot hanging over the lamp out of which a little steam was issuing, and looked at his mother with awful solemnity. She returned the look with something of incredulity.

"Yes, mother, the Power is not a beast. It lives not, yet it drives the white man's canoe, which is as big as a little iceberg, and it whistles; it shrieks; it yells!"

A slightly sorrowful look rested for a moment on Toolooha's benign countenance. It was evident that she suspected her son either of derangement, or having forsaken the paths of truth. But it passed like a summer cloud.

"Tell me more," she said, laying her hand affectionately on the huge arm of Chingatok, who had fallen into a contemplative mood, and, with hands clasped over one knee, sat gazing upwards.

Before he could reply the heart of Toolooha was made to bound by a shriek more terrible than she had ever before heard or imagined.

Chingatok caught her by the wrist, held up a finger as if to impose silence, smiled brightly, and listened.

Again the shriek was repeated with prolonged power.

"Tell me, my son," gasped Toolooha, "is Oblooria—are the people safe? Why came you to me alone?"

"The little sister and the people are safe. I came alone to prevent your being taken by surprise. Did I not say that it could shriek and yell? This is the white man's big canoe."

Dropping the old woman's hand as he spoke, Chingatok darted into the open air with the agility of a Polar bear, and Toolooha followed with the speed of an Arctic hare.

Chapter IV

Two days after her arrival at the temporary residence of the northern Eskimos, the steam yacht *Whitebear*, while close to the shore, was beset by ice, so that she could neither advance nor retreat. Everywhere, as far as the eye could reach, the sea was covered with hummocks and bergs and fields of ice, so closely packed that there was not a piece of open water to be seen, with the exception of one small basin a few yards ahead of the lead or lane of water in which the vessel had been imprisoned.

"No chance of escaping from this, I fear, for a long time," said Alf Vandervell to his brother, as they stood near the wheel, looking at the desolate prospect.

"It seems quite hopeless," said Leo, with, however, a look of confidence that ill accorded with his words.

"I do believe we are frozen in for the winter," said

Benjy Vane, coming up at the moment.

"There speaks ignorance," said the Captain, whose head appeared at the cabin hatchway. "If any of you had been in these regions before, you would have learned that nothing is so uncertain as the action of pack ice. At one time you may be hard and fast, so that you couldn't move an inch. A few hours after, the set of the currents may loosen the pack, and open up lanes of water through which you may easily make your escape. Sometimes it opens up so as to leave almost a clear sea in a few hours."

"But it is pretty tight packed just now, father, and looks wintry-like, doesn't it?" said Benjy in a desponding tone.

"Looks! boy, ay, but things are not what they seem hereaway. You saw four mock-suns round the real one yesterday, didn't you? and the day before you saw icebergs floating in the air, eh?"

"True, father, but these appearances were deceptive, whereas this ice, which looks so tightly packed, is a reality."

"That is so, lad, but it is not set fast for the winter, though it looks like it. Well, doctor," added the Captain, turning towards a tall cadaverous man who came on deck just then with the air and tread of an invalid, "how goes it with you? Better, I hope?"

He asked this with kindly interest as he laid his strong hand on the sick man's shoulder; but the doctor shook his head and smiled sadly.

"It is a great misfortune to an expedition, Captain, when the doctor himself falls sick," he said, sitting down on the skylight with a sigh.

"Come, come, cheer up, doctor," returned the Captain, heartily, "don't be cast down; we'll all turn doctors for the occasion, and nurse you well in spite of yourself."

"I'll keep up all heart, Captain, you may depend on't, as long as two of my bones will stick together, but—well, to change the subject; what are you going to do now?"

"Just all that can be done in the circumstances," replied the Captain. "You see, we cannot advance over ice either with sail or steam, but there's a basin just ahead which seems a little more secure than that in which we lie. I'll try to get into it. There is nothing but a neck of ice between us and it, which I think I could cut by charging in under full steam, and there seems a faint gleam of something far ahead, which encourages me. Tell the steward to fetch my glasses, Benjy."

"Butterface!" shouted the boy.

"Yis, massa."

"Fetch the Captain's glasses, please."

"Yis, massa."

A pair of large binoculars were brought up by a huge negro, whose name was pre-eminently unsuggestive of his appearance.

After a long steady gaze at the horizon, the Captain shut up the glass with an air of determination, and ordered the engineer to get up full steam, and the crew to be ready with the ice-poles.

There was a large berg at the extremity of the lakelet of open water into which Captain Vane wished to break. It was necessary to keep well out of the way of that berg. The Captain trusted chiefly to his screw, but got out the ice-poles in case they should be required.

When all the men were stationed, the order was given to go ahead full steam. The gallant little yacht charged the neck of ice like a living creature, hit it fair, cut right through, and scattered the fragments right and left as she sailed majestically into the lakelet beyond. The shock was severe, but no harm was done, everything on board having been made as strong as possible, and of the very best material, for a voyage in ice-laden seas.

An unforeseen event followed, however, which ended in a series of most terrible catastrophes. The neck of ice through which they had broken had acted as a check on the pressure of the great body of the floe, and it was no sooner removed than the heavy mass began to close in with slow but irresistible power, compelling the little vessel to steam close up to the iceberg—so close that some of the upper parts actually overhung the deck.

They were slowly forced into this dangerous position. With breathless anxiety the Captain and crew watched the apparently gentle, but really tremendous grinding of the ice against the vessel's side. Even the youngest on board could realise the danger. No one moved, for nothing whatever could be done.

"Everything depends, under God, on the ice easing off before we are crushed," said the Captain.

As he spoke, the timbers of the yacht seemed to groan under the pressure; then there was a succession of loud cracks, and the vessel was thrust bodily up the sloping sides of the berg. While in this position, with the bow high and dry, a mass of ice was forced against the stern-post, and the screw-propeller was snapped off as if it had been made of glass.

Poor Captain Vane's heart sank as if he had received his death-blow, for he knew that the yacht was now, even in the event of escaping, reduced to an ordinary vessel dependent on its sails. The shock seemed to have shaken the berg itself, for at that moment a crashing sound was heard overhead. The terror-stricken crew looked up, and for one moment a pinnacle like a church spire was seen to flash through the air right above them. It fell with an indescribable roar close alongside, deluging the decks with water. There was a momentary sigh of relief, which, however, was chased away by a succession of falling masses, varying from a pound to a ton in weight, which came down on the deck like cannon-shots, breaking the topmasts, and cutting to pieces much of the rigging. Strange to say, none of the men were seriously injured, though many received bruises more or less severe.

During this brief but thrilling period, the brothers Vandervell and Benjy Vane crouched close together beside the port bulwarks, partially screened from the falling ice by the mizzen shrouds. The Captain stood on the quarter-deck, quite exposed, and apparently unconscious of danger, the picture of despair.

"It can't last long," sighed poor Benjy, looking solemnly up at the vast mass of the bluish-white berg, which hung above them as if ready to fall.

Presently the pressure ceased, then the ice eased off, and in a few minutes the *Whitebear* slid back into the sea, a pitiable wreck! Now had come the time for action.

"Out poles, my lads, and shove her off the berg!" was the sharp order.

Every one strained as if for life at the ice-poles, and slowly forced the yacht away from the dreaded berg. It mattered not that they were forcing her towards a rocky shore. Any fate would be better than being crushed under a mountain of ice.

But the danger was not yet past. No sooner had they cleared the berg, and escaped from that form of destruction, than the ice began again to close in, and this time the vessel was "nipped" with such severity, that some of her principal timbers gave way. Finally, her back was broken, and the bottom forced in.

"So," exclaimed the Captain, with a look of profound grief, "our voyage in the *Whitebear*, lads, has come to an end. All that we can do now is to get the boats and provisions, and as much of the cargo as we can, safe on the ice. And sharp's the word, for when the floes ease off, the poor little yacht will certainly go to the bottom."

"No, massa," said the negro steward, stepping on deck at that moment, "we can't go to de bottom, cause we's dare a-ready!"

"What d'ye mean, Butterface?"

"Jus' what me say," replied the steward, with a look of calm resignation. "I's bin b'low, an' seed de rocks stickin' troo de bottom. Der's one de size ob a jolly-boat's bow comed right troo my pantry, an' knock all de crockery to smash, an' de best teapot, he's so flat he wouldn't know hisself in a lookin'-glass."

It turned out to be as Butterface said. The pack had actually thrust the little vessel on a shoal, which extended out from the headland off which the catastrophe occurred, and there was therefore no fear of her sinking.

"Well, we've reason to be thankful for that, at all events," said the Captain, with an attempt to look cheerful; "come, lads, let's to work. Whatever our future course is to be, our first business is to get the boats and cargo out of danger."

With tremendous energy—because action brought relief to their overstrained feelings—the crew of the ill-fated yacht set to work to haul the boats upon the grounded ice. The tide was falling, so that a great part of the most valuable part of the cargo was placed in security before the rising tide interrupted the work.

This was fortunate, for, when the water reached a certain point the ice began to move, and the poor little vessel was so twisted about that they dared not venture on board of her.

That night—if we may call it night in a region where the sun never quite went down—the party encamped on the north-western coast of Greenland, in the lee of a huge cliff just beyond which the tongue of a mighty glacier dipped into the sea. For convenience the party divided into two, with a blazing fire for each, round which the castaways circled, conversing in subdued, sad tones while supper was being prepared.

It was a solemn occasion, and a scene of indescribable grandeur, with the almost eternal glacier of Greenland—the great Humboldt glacier—shedding its bergs into the dark blue sea, the waters of which had by that time been partially cleared to the northward. On the left was the weird pack and its thousand grotesque forms, with the wreck in its iron grasp; on the right the perpendicular cliffs, and the bright sky over all, with the smoke of the campfires rising into it from the foreground.

"Now, my friends," said Captain Vane to the crew when assembled after supper, "I am no longer your commander, for my vessel is a wreck, but as I suppose you still regard me as your leader, I assemble you here for the purpose of considering our position, and deciding on what is best to be done."

Here the Captain said, among other things, it was his opinion that the *Whitebear* was damaged beyond the possibility of repair, that their only chance of escape lay in the boats, and that the distance between the place on which they stood and Upernavik, although great, was not beyond the reach of resolute men.

"Before going further, or expressing a decided opinion," he added, "I would hear what the officers have to say on this subject. Let the first mate speak."

"It's my opinion," said the mate, "that there's only one thing to be done, namely, to start for home as soon and as fast as we can. We have good boats, plenty of provisions, and are all stout and healthy, excepting our doctor, whom we will take good care of, and expect to do no rough work."

"Thanks, mate," said the doctor with a laugh, "I think that, at all events, I shall keep well enough to physic you if you get ill."

"Are you willing to take charge of the party in the event of my deciding to remain here?" asked the Captain of the mate.

"Certainly, sir," he replied, with a look of slight surprise. "You know I am quite able to do so. The second mate, too, is as able as I am. For that matter, most of the men, I think, would find little difficulty in navigating a boat to Upernavik."

"That is well," returned the Captain, "because I do not intend to return with you."

"Not return!" exclaimed the doctor; "surely you don't mean to winter here."

"No, not here, but further north," replied the Captain, with a smile which most of the party returned, for they thought he was jesting.

Benjy Vane, however, did not think so. A gleeful look of triumph caused his face, as it were, to sparkle, and he said, eagerly—

"We'll winter at the North Pole, father, eh?"

This was greeted with a general laugh.

"But seriously, uncle, what do you mean to do?" asked Leonard Vandervell, who, with his brother, was not unhopeful that the Captain meditated something desperate.

"Benjy is not far off the mark. I intend to winter at the Pole, or as near to it as I can manage to get."

"My dear Captain Vane," said the doctor, with an anxious look, "you cannot really mean what you say.

You must be jesting, or mad."

"Well, as to madness," returned the Captain with a peculiar smile, "you ought to know best, for it's a perquisite of your cloth to pronounce people mad or sane, though some of yourselves are as mad as the worst of us; but in regard to jesting, nothing, I assure you, is further from my mind. Listen!"

He rose from the box which had formed his seat, and looked earnestly round on his men. As he stood there, erect, tall, square, powerful, with legs firmly planted, and apart, as if to guard against a lurch of his ship, with his bronzed face flushed, and his dark eye flashing, they all understood that their leader's mind was made up, and that what he had resolved upon, he would certainly attempt to carry out.

"Listen," he repeated; "it was my purpose on leaving England, as you all know, to sail north as far as the ice would let me; to winter where we should stick fast, and organise an over-ice, or overland journey to the Pole with all the appliances of recent scientific discovery, and all the advantages of knowledge acquired by former explorers. It has pleased God to destroy my ship, but my life and my hopes are spared. So are my stores and scientific instruments. I intend, therefore, to carry out my original purpose. I believe that former explorers have erred in some points of their procedure. These errors I shall steer clear of. Former travellers have ignored some facts, and despised some appliances. These facts I will recognise; these appliances I will utilise. With a steam yacht, you, my friends, who have shown so much enthusiasm and courage up to this point, would have been of the utmost service to me. As a party in boats, or on foot, you would only hamper my movements. I mean to prosecute this enterprise almost alone. I shall join myself to the Eskimos."

He paused at this point as if in meditation. Benjy, whose eyes and mouth had been gradually opening to their widest, almost gasped with astonishment as he glanced at his cousins, whose expressive countenances were somewhat similarly affected.

"I have had some long talks," continued the Captain, "with that big Eskimo Chingatok, through our interpreter, and from what he says I believe my chances of success are considerable. I am all the more confirmed in this resolution because of the readiness and ability of my first mate to guide you out of the Arctic regions, and your willingness to trust him. Anders has agreed to go with me as interpreter, and now, all I want is one other man, because—"

"Put me down, father," cried Benjy, in a burst of excitement—"*I'm* your man."

"Hush, lad," said the Captain with a little smile, "of course I shall take you with me and also your two cousins, but I want one other man to complete the party—but he must be a heartily willing man. Who will volunteer?"

There was silence for a few moments. It was broken by the doctor.

"I for one won't volunteer," he said, "for I'm too much shaken by this troublesome illness to think of such an expedition. If I were well it might be otherwise, but perhaps some of the others will offer."

"You can't expect me to do so," said the mate, "for I've got to guide our party home, as agreed on; besides, under any circumstances, I would not join you, for it is simple madness. You'll forgive me, Captain. I mean no disrespect, but I have sailed many years to these seas, and I know from experience that what you propose is beyond the power of man to accomplish."

"Experience!" repeated the Captain, quickly. "Has your experience extended further north than this point?"

"No, sir, I have not been further north than this—nobody has. It is beyond the utmost limit yet reached, so far as I know."

"Well, then, you cannot speak from *experience* about what I propose," said the Captain, turning away. "Come, lads, I have no wish to constrain you, I merely give one of you the chance."

Still no one came forward. Every man of the crew of the *Whitebear* had had more or less personal acquaintance with arctic travel and danger. They would have followed Captain Vane anywhere in the yacht, but evidently they had no taste for what he was about to undertake.

At last one stepped to the front. It was Butterface, the steward. This intensely black negro was a bulky, powerful man, with a modest spirit and a strange disbelief in his own capacities, though, in truth, these were very considerable. He came forward, stooping slightly, and rubbing his hands in a deprecating manner.

"'Scuse me, massa Capting. P'r'aps it bery

presumsheeous in dis yer chile for to speak afore his betters, but as no oder man 'pears to want to volunteer, I's willin' to go in an' win. I's a willin' negro, an' kin do a few small tings—cook de grub, wash up de cups an' sarsers, pull a oar, clean yer boots, fight de Eskimos if you wants me to, an' ginrally to scrimmage around a'most anything. Moreover, I eats no more dan a babby—'sep wen I's hungry—an' I'll foller you, massa, troo tick and tin—to de Nort Pole, or de Sout Pole, or de East Pole, or de West Pole—or any oder pole wotsomediver—all de same to Butterface, s'long's you'll let 'im stick by you."

The crew could not help giving the negro a cheer as he finished this loyal speech, and the Captain, although he would have preferred one of the other men, gladly accepted his services.

A few days later the boats were ready and provisioned; adieus were said, hats and handkerchiefs waved, and soon after Captain Vane and his son and two nephews, with Anders and Butterface, were left to fight their battles alone, on the margin of an unexplored, mysterious Polar sea.

Chapter V

There are times, probably, in all conditions of life, when men feel a species of desolate sadness creeping over their spirits, which they find it hard to shake off or subdue. Such a time arrived to our Arctic adventurers the night after they had parted from the crew of the wrecked *Whitebear*. Nearly everything around, and much within, them was calculated to foster that feeling.

They were seated on the rocky point on the extremity of which their yacht had been driven. Behind them were the deep ravines, broad valleys, black beetling cliffs, grand mountains, stupendous glaciers, and dreary desolation of Greenland. To right and left, and in front of them, lay the chaotic ice-pack of the Arctic sea, with lanes and pools of water visible here and there like lines and spots of ink. Icebergs innumerable rose against the sky, which at the time was entirely covered with grey and gloomy clouds. Gusts of wind swept over the frozen waste now and then, as if a squall which had recently passed, were sighing at the thought of leaving anything undestroyed behind it. When we add to this, that the wanderers were thinking of the comrades who had just left them—the last link, as it were, with the civilised world from which they were self-exiled, of the unknown dangers and difficulties that lay before them, and of the all but forlorn hope they had undertaken, there need be little wonder that for some time they all looked rather grave, and were disposed to silence.

But life is made up of opposites, light and shade, hard and soft, hot and cold, sweet and sour, for the purpose, no doubt, of placing man between two moral battledores so as to drive the weak and erring shuttlecock of his will right and left, and thus keep it in the middle course of rectitude. No sooner had our adventurers sunk to the profoundest depths of gloom, than the battledore of brighter influences began to play upon them. It did not, however, achieve the end at once.

"I'm in the lowest, bluest, dreariest, grumpiest, and most utterly miserable state of mind I ever was in in all my life," said poor little Benjy Vane, thrusting his hands into his pockets, sitting down on a rock, and gazing round on the waste wilderness, which had only just ceased howling, the very personification of despair.

"So's I, massa," said Butterface, looking up from a

compound of wet coal and driftwood which he had been vainly trying to coax into a flame for cooking purposes; "I's most 'orribly miserable!"

There was a beaming grin on the negro's visage that gave the lie direct to his words.

"That's always the way with you, Benjy," said the Captain, "either bubblin' over with jollity an' mischief, or down in the deepest blues."

"Blues! father," cried the boy, "don't talk of blues— it's the blacks I'm in, the very blackest of blacks."

"Ha! jus' like me," muttered Butterface, sticking out his thick lips at the unwilling fire, and giving a blow that any grampus might have envied.

The result was that a column of almost solid smoke, which had been for some time rising thicker and thicker from the coals, burst into a bright flame. This was the first of the sweet influences before referred to.

"Mind your wool," cried Benjy, as the negro drew quickly back.

It may be remarked here that the mysterious bond of sympathy which united the spirits of Benjy Vane and the black steward found expression in kindly respect on the part of the man, and in various eccentric courses on the part of the boy—among others, in a habit of patting him on the back, and giving him a choice selection of impromptu names, such as Black-mug, Yellow-eyes, Square-jaws, and the like.

"What have you got in the kettle?" asked Leo Vandervell, who came up with some dry driftwood at the moment.

"Bubble-um-squeak," replied the cook.

"What sort o' squeak is that?" asked Leo, as he bent his tall strong frame over the fire to investigate the contents of the kettle.

"What am it, massa? Why, it am a bit o' salt pork, an' a bit o' dat bear you shooted troo de nose yes'rday, an' a junk o' walrus, an' two puffins, an' some injin corn, a leetil pepper, an' a leetil salt."

"Good, that sounds well," said Leo. "I'll go fetch you some more driftwood, for it'll take a deal of boiling, that will, to make it eatable."

The driftwood referred to was merely some pieces of the yacht which had been cast ashore by the hurly-burly of ice and water that had occurred during the last tide. No other species of driftwood was to be found on that coast, for the neighbouring region was utterly destitute of trees.

"Where has Alf gone to?" asked the Captain, as Leo was moving away.

"Oh, he's looking for plants and shells, as usual," answered Leo, with a smile. "You know his heart is set upon these things."

"He'll have to set his heart on helping wi' the cargo after supper," said the Captain, drawing a small notebook and pencil from his pocket.

A few more of the sweet and reviving influences of life now began to circle round the wanderers. Among them was the savoury odour that arose from the pot of bubble-um-squeak, also the improved appearance of the sky.

It was night, almost midnight, nevertheless the sun was blazing in the heavens, and as the storm-clouds had rolled away like a dark curtain, his cheering rays were by that time gilding the icebergs, and rendering the land-cliffs ruddily. The travellers had enjoyed perpetual daylight for several weeks already, and at that high latitude they could count on many more to come. By the time supper was ready, the depressing influences were gone, and the spirits of all had recovered their wonted tone. Indeed it was not to the discredit of the party that they were so much cast down on that occasion, for the parting, perhaps for ever, from the friends with whom they had hitherto voyaged, had much more to do with their sadness than surrounding circumstances or future trials.

"What plan do you intend to follow out, uncle?" asked Alphonse Vandervell, as they sat at supper that night round the kettle.

"That depends on many things, lad," replied the Captain, laying down his spoon, and leaning his back against a convenient rock. "If the ice moves off, I shall adopt one course; if it holds fast I shall try another. Then, if you insist on gathering and carrying along with you such pocket-loads of specimens, plants, rocks, etcetera, as you've brought in this evening, I'll have to build a sort of Noah's ark, or omnibus on sledge-runners, to carry them."

"And suppose I don't insist on carrying these things, what then?"

"Well," replied the Captain, "in that case I would— well, let me see—a little more of the bubble, Benjy."

"Wouldn't you rather some of the squeak?" asked the boy.

"Both, lad, both—some of everything. Well, as I was saying—and you've a right to know what's running in my head, seeing that you have to help me carry out the plans—I'll give you a rough notion of 'em."

The Captain became more serious as he explained his plans. "The Eskimos, you know," he continued, "have gone by what I may call the shore ice, two days' journey in advance of this spot, taking our dogs along with them. It was my intention to have proceeded to the same point in our yacht, and there, if the sea was open, to have taken on board that magnificent Eskimo giant, Chingatok, with his family, and steered away due north. In the event of the pack being impassable, I had intended to have laid the yacht up in some safe harbour; hunted and fished until we had a stock of dried and salted provisions, enough to last us two years, and then to have started northward in sledges, under the guidance of Chingatok, with a few picked men, leaving the rest and the yacht in charge of the mate. The wreck of the *Whitebear* has, however, forced me to modify these plans. I shall now secure as much of our cargo as we have been able to save, and leave it here *en cache*—"

"What sort of cash is that, father?" asked Benjy.

"You are the best linguist among us, Leo, tell him," said the Captain, turning to his nephew.

"'*En cache*' is French for 'in hiding,'" returned Leo, with a laugh.

"Why do you speak French to Englishmen, father?" said Benjy in a pathetic tone, but with a pert look.

"'Cause the expression is a common one on this side

the Atlantic, lad, and you ought to know it. Now, don't interrupt me again. Well, having placed the cargo in security," ("*En cache*," muttered Benjy with a glance at Butterface), "I shall rig up the sledges brought from England, load them with what we require, and follow up the Eskimos. You're sure, Anders, that you understood Chingatok's description of the place?"

The interpreter declared that he was quite sure.

"After that," resumed the Captain, "I'll act according to the information the said Eskimos can give me. D'ye know, I have a strong suspicion that our Arctic giant Chingatok is a philosopher, if I may judge from one or two questions he put and observations he made when we first met. He says he has come from a fine country which lies far—very far—to the north of this; so far that I feel quite interested and hopeful about it. I expect to have more talk with him soon on the subject. A little more o' the bubble, lad; really, Butterface, your powers in the way of cookery are wonderful."

"Chingatok seems to me quite a remarkable fellow for an Eskimo," observed Leo, scraping the bottom of the kettle with his spoon, and looking inquiringly into it. "I, too, had some talk with him—through Anders—when we first met, and from what he said I can't help thinking that he has come from the remote north solely on a voyage of discovery into what must be to him the unknown regions of the south. Evidently he has an inquiring mind."

"Much like yourself, Leo, to judge from the way you peer into that kettle," said Benjy; "please don't scrape the bottom out of it. There's not much tin to mend it with, you know, in these regions."

"Brass will do quite as well," retorted Leo, "and there can be no lack of that while you are here."

"Come now, Benjy," said Alf, "that insolent remark should put you on your mettle."

"So it does, but I won't open my lips, because I feel that I should speak ironically if I were to reply," returned the boy, gazing dreamily into the quiet countenance of the steward. "What are *you* thinking of?"

"Me, massa? me tink dere 'pears to be room for more wittles inside ob me; but as all de grub's eated up, p'r'aps it would be as well to be goin' an' tacklin' suffin' else now."

"You're right, Butterface," cried the Captain, rousing himself from a reverie. "What say you, comrades? Shall we turn in an' have a nap? It's past midnight."

"I'm not inclined for sleep," said Alf, looking up from some of the botanical specimens he had collected.

"No more am I," said Leo, lifting up his arms and stretching his stalwart frame, which, notwithstanding his youth, had already developed to almost the full proportions of a powerful man.

"I vote that we sit up all night," said Benjy, "the sun does it, and why shouldn't we?"

"Well, I've no objection," rejoined the Captain, "but we must work if we don't sleep—so, come along."

Setting the example, Captain Vane began to shoulder the bags and boxes which lay scattered around with the energy of an enthusiastic railway porter. The other members of the party were not a whit behind him in diligence and energy. Even Benjy, delicate-looking though he was, did the work of an average man, besides enlivening the proceedings with snatches of song and a flow of small talk of a humorous and slightly insolent nature.

Chapter VI

FUTURE PLANS DISCUSSED AND DECIDED.

Away to the northward of the spot where the *Whitebear* had been wrecked there stretched a point of land far out into the Arctic Ocean. It was about thirty miles distant, and loomed hugely bluff and grand against the brilliant sky, as if it were the forefront of the northern world. No civilised eyes had ever beheld that land before. Captain Vane knew that, because it lay in latitude 83 north, which was a little beyond the furthest point yet reached by Arctic navigators. He therefore named it Cape Newhope. Benjy thought that it should have been named Butterface-beak, because the steward had been the first to observe it, but his father thought otherwise.

About three miles to the northward of this point of land the Eskimos were encamped. According to arrangement with the white men they had gone there,

as we have said, in charge of the dogs brought by
Captain Vane from Upernavik, as these animals, it was
thought, stood much in need of exercise.

Here the natives had found and taken possession of
a number of deserted Eskimo huts.

These rude buildings were the abodes to which
the good people migrated when summer heat
became so great as to render their snow-huts sloppily
disagreeable.

In one of the huts sat Chingatok, his arms resting on
his knees, his huge hands clasped, and his intelligent
eyes fixed dreamily on the lamp-flame, over which his
culinary mother was bending in busy sincerity. There
were many points of character in which this remarkable
mother and son resembled each other. Both were
earnest—intensely so—and each was enthusiastically
eager about small matters as well as great. In short,
they both possessed great though uncultivated minds.

The hut they occupied was in some respects as
remarkable as themselves. It measured about six feet
in height and ten in diameter. The walls were made of
flattish stones, moss, and the bones of seals, whales,
narwhals, and other Arctic creatures. The stones were
laid so that each overlapped the one below it, a very
little inwards, and thus the walls approached each
other gradually as they rose from the foundation; the
top being finally closed by slabs of slate-stone. Similar
stones covered the floor—one half of which floor was
raised a foot or so above the other, and this raised half
served for a seat by day as well as a couch by night. On
it were spread a thick layer of dried moss, and several

seal, dog, and bear skins. Smaller elevations in the corners near the entrance served for seats. The door was a curtain of sealskin. Above it was a small window, glazed, so to speak, with strips of semi-transparent dried intestines sewed together.

Toolooha's cooking-lamp was made of soapstone, formed like a clam-shell, and about eight inches in diameter; the fuel was seal-oil, and the wick was of moss. It smoked considerably, but Eskimos are smoke-proof. The pot above it, suspended from the roof, was also made of soapstone. Sealskins hung about the walls drying; oily mittens, socks and boots were suspended about on pegs and racks of rib-bones. Lumps of blubber hung and lay about miscellaneously. Odours, not savoury, were therefore prevalent—but Eskimos are smell-proof.

"Mother," said the giant, raising his eyes from the flame to his parent's smoke-encircled visage, "they are a most wonderful people, these Kablunets. Blackbeard is a great man—a grand man—but I think he is—"

Chingatok paused, shook his head, and touched his forehead with a look of significance worthy of a white man.

"Why think you so, my son?" asked the old woman, sneezing, as a denser cloud than usual went up her nose.

"Because he has come here to search for *nothing.*"

"Nothing, my son?"

"Yes—at least that is what he tried to explain to me. Perhaps the interpreter could not explain. He is not a smart man, that interpreter. He resembles a walrus with his brain scooped out. He spoke much, but I could not understand."

"Could not understand?" repeated Toolooha, with an incredulous look, "let not Chingatok say so. Is there *anything* that passes the lips of man which he cannot understand?"

"Truly, mother, I once thought there was not," replied the giant, with a modest look, "but I am mistaken. The Kablunets make me stare and feel foolish."

"But it is not possible to search for *nothing*," urged Toolooha.

"So I said," replied her son, "but Blackbeard only laughed at me."

"Did he?" cried the mother, with a much relieved expression, "then let your mind rest, my son, for Blackbeard must be a fool if he laughed at *you*."

"Blackbeard is no fool," replied Chingatok.

"Has he not come to search for new lands *here*, as you went to search for them *there*?" asked Toolooha, pointing alternately north and south.

"No—if I have understood him. Perhaps the brainless walrus translated his words wrongly."

"Is the thing he searches for something to eat?"

"Something to drink or wear?"

"No, I tell you. It is *nothing*! Yet he gives it a name. He calls it *Nort Pole*!"

Perhaps it is needless to remind the reader that Chingatok and his mother conversed in their native tongue, which we have rendered as literally as possible, and that the last two words were his broken English for "North Pole!"

"Nort Pole!" repeated Toolooha once or twice contemplatively. "Well, he may search for nothing if he will, but that he cannot find."

"Nay, mother," returned the giant with a soft smile, "if he will search for nothing he is sure to find it!"

Chingatok sighed, for his mother did not see the joke.

"Blackbeard," he continued with a grave, puzzled manner, "said that this world on which we stand floats in the air like a bird, and spins round!"

"Then Blackbeard is a liar," said Toolooha quietly, though without a thought of being rude. She merely meant what she said, and said what she meant, being a naturally candid woman.

"That may be so, mother, but I think not."

"How can the world float without wings?" demanded the old woman indignantly. "If it spinned should we not feel the spinning, and grow giddy?"

"And Blackbeard says," continued the giant, regardless of the questions propounded, "that it spins round upon this *Nort Pole*, which he says is not a real thing, but only nothing. I asked Blackbeard—How can a world spin upon nothing?"

"And what said he to that?" demanded Toolooha quickly.

"He only laughed. They all laughed when the brainless walrus put my question. There is one little boy—the son I think of Blackbeard—who laughed more than all the rest. He lay down on the ice to laugh, and rolled about as if he had the bowel-twist."

"That son of Blackbeard must be a fool more than

his father," said Toolooha, casting a look of indignation at her innocent kettle.

"Perhaps; but he is not like his father," returned Chingatok meekly. "There are two other chiefs among the Kablunets who seem to me fine men. They are very young and wise. They have learned a little of our tongue from the Brainless One, and asked me some questions about the rocks, and the moss, and the flowers. They are tall and strong. One of them is very grave and seems to think much, like myself. He also spoke of this Nothing—this Nort Pole. They are all mad, I think, about that thing—that Nothing!"

The conversation was interrupted at this point by the sudden entrance of the giant's little sister with the news that the Kablunets were observed coming round the great cape, dragging a sledge.

"Is not the big oomiak with them?" asked her brother, rising quickly.

"No, we see no oomiak—no wings—no fire," answered Oblooria, "only six men dragging a sledge."

Chingatok went out immediately, and Oblooria was about to follow when her mother recalled her.

"Come here, little one. There is a bit of blubber for you to suck. Tell me, saw you any sign of madness in these white men when they were talking with your brother about this—this—Nort Pole."

"No, mother, no," answered Oblooria thoughtfully, "I saw not madness. They laughed much, it is true—but not more than Oolichuk laughs sometimes. Yes—I think again! There was one who seems mad—the small boy, whom brother thinks to be the son of

Blackbeard—Benjay, they call him."

"Hah! I thought so," exclaimed Toolooha, evidently pleased at her penetration on this point. "Go, child, I cannot quit the lamp. Bring me news of what they say and do."

Oblooria obeyed with alacrity, bolting her strip of half-cooked blubber as she ran; her mother meanwhile gave her undivided attention to the duties of the lamp.

The white men and all the members of the Eskimo band were standing by the sledge engaged in earnest conversation when the little girl came forward. Captain Vane was speaking.

"Yes, Chingatok," he said, looking up at the tall savage, who stood erect in frame but with bent head and his hands clasped before him, like a modest chief, which in truth he was. "Yes, if you will guide me to your home in the northern lands, I will pay you well—for I have much iron and wood and such things as I think you wish for and value, and you shall also have my best thanks and gratitude. The latter may not indeed be worth much, but, nevertheless, you could not purchase it with all the wealth of the Polar regions."

Chingatok looked with penetrating gaze at Anders while he translated, and, considering the nature of the communication, the so-called Brainless One proved himself a better man than the giant gave him credit for.

"Does Blackbeard," asked Chingatok, after a few seconds' thought, "expect to find this Nothing—this Nort Pole, in my country?"

"Well, I cannot exactly say that I do," replied the Captain; "you see, I'm not quite sure, from what you tell me, where your country is. It may not reach to the Pole, but it is enough for me that it lies in that direction, and that you tell me there is much open water there. Men of my nation have been in these regions before now, and some of them have said that the Polar Sea is open, others that it is covered always with ice so thick that it never melts. Some have said it is a 'sea of ancient ice' so rough that no man can travel over it, and that it is not possible to reach the North Pole. I don't agree with that. I had been led to expect to fall in with this sea of ancient ice before I had got thus far, but it is not to be found. The sea indeed is partly blocked with ordinary ice, but there is nothing to be seen of this vast collection of mighty blocks, some of them thirty feet high—this wild chaos of ice which so effectually stopped some of those who went before me."

This speech put such brains as the Brainless One possessed to a severe test, and, after all, he failed to convey its full meaning to Chingatok, who, however, promptly replied to such portions as he understood.

"What Blackbeard calls the sea of old ice does exist," he said; "I have seen it. No man could travel on it, only the birds can cross it. But ice is not land. It changes place. It is here to-day; it is there to-morrow. Next day it is gone. We cannot tell where it goes to or when it will come back. The *very* old ice comes back again and again. It is slow to become like your Nort Pole—nothing. But it melts at last and more comes in its place—growing old slowly and vanishing slowly. It is full of wonder—like the stars; like the jumping flames; like the sun and moon, which we cannot understand."

Chingatok paused and looked upwards with a solemn expression. His mind had wandered into its favourite channels, and for the moment he forgot the main subject of conversation, while the white men regarded him with some surprise, his comrades with feelings of interest not unmingled with awe.

"But," he continued, "I know where the sea of ancient ice-blocks is just now. I came past it in my kayak, and can guide you to it by the same way."

"That is just what I want, Chingatok," said the Captain with a joyful look, "only aid me in this matter, and I will reward you well. I've already told you that my ship is wrecked, and that the crew, except those you see here, have left me; but I have saved all the cargo and buried it in a place of security with the exception of those things which I need for my expedition. One half of these things are on this sledge,—the other half on a sledge left behind and ready packed near the wreck. Now, I want you to send men to fetch that sledge here."

"That shall be done," said Chingatok. "Thanks, thanks, my good fellow," returned the Captain, "and we must set about it at once, for the summer is advancing, and you know as well as I do that the hot season is but a short one in these regions."

"A moment more shall not be lost," said the giant.

He turned to Oolichuk, who had been leaning on

a short spear, and gazing open-mouthed, eyed, and eared, during the foregoing conversation, and said a few words to him and to the other Eskimos in a low tone.

Oolichuk merely nodded his head, said "Yah!" or something similarly significant, shouldered his spear and went off in the direction of the Cape of Newhope, followed by nearly all the men of the party.

"Stay, not quite so fast," cried Captain Vane.

"Stop!" shouted Chingatok.

Oolichuk and his men paused.

"One of us had better go with them," said the Captain, "to show the place where the sledge has been left."

"I will go, uncle, if you'll allow me," said Leo Vandervell.

"Oh! let me go too, father," pleaded Benjy, "I'm not a bit tired; do."

"You may both go. Take a rifle with you, Leo. There's no saying what you may meet on the way."

In half-an-hour the party under Oolichuk had reached the extremity of the cape, and Captain Vane observed that his volatile son mounted to the top of an ice-block to wave a farewell. He looked like a black speck, or a crow, in the far distance. Another moment, and the speck had disappeared among the hummocks of the ice-locked sea.

Chapter VII

DIFFICULTIES ENCOUNTERED AND FACED.

They had not quite doubled the Cape of Newhope, and were about to round the point which concealed the spot that had been named Wreck Bay, when they suddenly found themselves face to face with a Polar bear!

Bruin was evidently out for an evening stroll, for he seemed to have nothing particular to do.

Surprise lit up alike the countenances of the men and the visage of the bear. It was an unexpected meeting on both sides. The distance between them was not more than thirty feet. Leo was the only one of the party who carried a rifle. More than once during the voyage had Leo seen and shot a bear. The sight was not new to him, but never before had he come so suddenly, or so very close, upon this king of the Arctic Seas. He chanced at the time to be walking a few yards in advance of the party in company with Oolichuk and Benjy.

The three stopped, stared, and stood as if petrified.

For one moment, then they uttered a united and half involuntary roar.

Right royally did that bear accept the challenge. It rose, according to custom, on its hind legs, and immediately began that slow, but deadly war-dance with which the race is wont to preface an attack, while its upper lip curled in apparent derision, exposing its terrible fangs.

Leo recovered self-possession instantly. The rifle leaped to his shoulder, the centre of the bear's breast was covered, and the trigger pulled.

Only a snap resulted. Leo had forgotten to load! Benjy gasped with anxiety. Oolichuk, who had held himself back with a sparkling smile of expectation at the prospect of seeing the Kablunet use his thunder-weapon, looked surprised and disappointed, but went into action promptly with his spear, accompanied by Akeetolik. Leo's rifle, being a breech-loader, was quickly re-charged, but as the rest of the party stood leaning on their spears with the evident intention of merely watching the combat, the youth resolved to hold his hand, despite Benjy's earnest recommendation to put one ball between the bear's eyes, and the other into his stomach.

It was but a brief though decisive battle. Those Eskimos were well used to such warfare.

Running towards the animal with levelled spears,

the two men separated on coming close, so that Bruin was forced to a state of indecision as to which enemy he would assail first. Akeetolik settled the point for him by giving him a prick on the right side, thus, as it were, drawing the enemy's fire on himself. The bear turned towards him with a fierce growl, and in so doing, exposed his left side to attack. Oolichuk was not slow to seize the opportunity. He leaped close up, and drove his spear deep into the animal's heart—killing it on the spot.

Next day the party returned to the Eskimo camp with the sledge-load of goods, and the bear on the top.

While steaks of the same were being prepared by Toolooha, Captain Vane and his new allies were busy discussing the details of the advance.

"I know that the difficulties will be great," he said, in reply to a remark from the interpreter, "but I mean to face and overcome them."

"Ah!" exclaimed Alf, who was rather fond of poetry:—

"To dare unknown dangers in a noble cause,
Despite an adverse Nature and her tiresome Laws."

"Just so, Alf, my boy, stick at nothing; never give in; victory or death, that's my way of expressing the same sentiment. But there's one thing that I must impress once more upon you all—namely, that each man must reduce his kit to the very lowest point of size and weight. No extras allowed."

"What, not even a box of paper collars?" asked Benjy.

"Not one, my boy, but you may take a strait-waistcoat in your box if you choose, for you'll be sure to need it."

"Oh! father," returned the boy, remonstratively, "you are severe. However, I will take one, if you agree to leave your woollen comforter behind. You won't need that, you see, as long as I am with you."

"Of course," said Alf, "you will allow us to carry small libraries with us?"

"Certainly not, my lad, only one book each, and that must be a small one."

"The only book I possess is my Bible," said Leo, "and that won't take up much room, for it's an uncommonly small one."

"If I only had my Robinson Crusoe here," cried Benjy, "I'd take it, for there's enough of adventure in that book to carry a man over half the world."

"Ay," said Alf, "and enough of mind to carry him over the other half. For my part, if we must be content with one book each, I shall take Buzzby's poems."

"Oh! horrible!" cried Benjy, "why, he's no better than a maudlin', dawdlin', drawlin', caterwaulin'—"

"Come, Benjy, don't be insolent; he's second only to Tennyson. Just listen to this *morceau* by Buzzby. It is an Ode to Courage—

"'High! hot! hillarious compound of—'"

"Stop! stop! man, don't begin when we're in the middle of our plans," interrupted Benjy, "let us hear what book Butterface means to take."

"I not take no book, massa, only take my flute. Music is wot's de matter wid me. Dat is de ting what hab charms to soove de savage beast."

"I wouldn't advise you try to soothe a Polar bear with it," said Leo, "unless you have a rifle handy."

"Yes—and especially an unloaded one, which is very effective against Polar bears," put in the Captain, with a sly look. "Ah, Leo, I could hardly have believed it of you—and you the sportsman of our party, too; our chief huntsman. Oh, fie!"

"Come, uncle, don't be too hard on that little mistake," said Leo, with a slight blush, for he was really annoyed by the unsportsmanlike oversight hinted at; "but pray, may I ask," he added, turning sharply on the Captain, "what is inside of these three enormous boxes of yours which take up so much space on the sledges?"

"You may ask, Leo, but you may not expect an answer. That is my secret, and I mean to keep it as a sort of stimulus to your spirits when the hardships of the way begin to tell on you. Ask Chingatok, Anders," continued the Captain, turning to the interpreter, "if he thinks we have enough provisions collected for the journey. I wish to start immediately."

"We have enough," answered Chingatok, who had been sitting a silent, but deeply interested observer— so to speak—of the foregoing conversation.

"Tell him, then, to arrange with his party, and be prepared to set out by noon to-morrow."

That night, by the light of the midnight sun, the Eskimos sat round their kettles of bear-chops, and went into the *pros* and *cons* of the proposed expedition. Some were enthusiastically in favour of casting in their lot with the white men, others were decidedly against it, and a few were undecided. Among the latter was Akeetolik.

"These ignorant men," said that bold savage, "are foolish and useless. They cannot kill bears. The one named Lo, (thus was Leonard's name reduced to its lowest denomination), is big enough, and looks very fine, but when he sees bear he only stares, makes a little click with his thunder-weapon, and looks stupid."

"Blackbeard explained that," said Oolichuk; "Lo made some mistake."

"That may be so," retorted Akeetolik, "but if you and me had not been there, the *bear* would not make a mistake."

"I will not go with these Kablunets," said Eemerk with a frown, "they are only savages. They are not taught. No doubt they had a wonderful boat, but they have not been able to keep their boat. They cannot kill bears; perhaps they cannot kill seals or walruses, and they ask us to help them to travel—to show them the way! They can do nothing. They must be led like children. My advice is to kill them all, since they are so useless, and take their goods."

This speech was received with marks of decided approval by those of the party who were in the habit of siding with Eemerk, but the rest were silent. In a few moments Chingatok said, in a low, quiet, but impressive tone: "The Kablunets are not foolish or ignorant. They are wise—far beyond the wisdom of the Eskimos. It is Eemerk who is like a walrus without brains. He thinks that his little mind is outside of everything, and so he has not eyes to perceive that he is ignorant as well as foolish, and that other men are wise."

This was the severest rebuke that the good-natured Chingatok had yet administered to Eemerk, but the latter, foolish though he was, had wisdom enough not to resent it openly. He sat in moody silence, with his eyes fixed on the ground.

Of course Oolichuk was decidedly in favour of joining the white men, and so was Ivitchuk, who soon brought round his hesitating friend Akeetolik, and several of the others. Oblooria, being timid, would gladly have sided with Eemerk, but she hated the man, and, besides, would in any case have cast in her lot with her mother and brother, even if free to do otherwise.

The fair Tekkona, whose courage and faith were naturally strong, had only one idea, and that was to follow cheerfully wherever Chingatok led; but she was very modest, and gave no opinion. She merely remarked: "The Kablunets are handsome men, and seem good."

As for Toolooha, she had enough to do to attend to the serious duties of the lamp, and always left the settlement of less important matters to the men.

"You and yours are free to do what you please," said Chingatok to Eemerk, when the discussion drew to a close. "I go with the white men to-morrow."

"What says Oblooria?" whispered Oolichuk when the rest of the party were listening to Eemerk's reply.

"Oblooria goes with her brother and mother," answered that young lady, toying coquettishly with her sealskin tail.

Oolichuk's good-humoured visage beamed with satisfaction, and his flat nose curled up—as much as it was possible for such a feature to curl—with contempt, as he glanced at Eemerk and said—

"I have heard many tales from Anders—the white man's mouthpiece—since we met. He tells me the white men are very brave and fond of running into danger for nothing but fun. Those who do not like the fun of danger should join Eemerk. Those who are fond of fun and danger should come with our great chief Chingatok—huk! Let us divide."

Without more palaver the band divided, and it was found that only eight sided with Eemerk. All the rest cast in their lot with our giant, after which this Arctic House of Commons adjourned, and its members went to rest.

A few days after that, Captain Vane and his Eskimo allies, having left the camp with Eemerk and his friends far behind them, came suddenly one fine morning on a barrier which threatened effectually to arrest their further progress northward. This was nothing less than that tremendous sea of "ancient ice" which had baffled previous navigators and sledging parties.

"Chaos! absolute chaos!" exclaimed Alf Vandervell, who was first to recover from the shock of surprise, not to say consternation, with which the party beheld the scene on turning a high cape.

"It looks bad," said Captain Vane, gravely, "but things often look worse at a first glance than they really are."

"I hope it may be so in this case," said Leo, in a low tone.

"Good-bye to the North Pole!" said Benjy, with a look of despondency so deep that the rest of the party laughed in spite of themselves.

The truth was that poor Benjy had suffered much during the sledge journey which they had begun, for although he rode, like the rest of them, on one of the Eskimo sledges, the ice over which they had travelled along shore had been sufficiently rugged to necessitate constant getting off and on, as well as much scrambling over hummocks and broken ice. We have already said that Benjy was not very robust, though courageous and full of spirit, so that he was prone to leap from the deepest depths of despair to the highest heights of hope at a moment's notice—or *vice versa.* Not having become inured to ice-travel, he was naturally much cast down when the chaos above-mentioned met his gaze.

"Strange," said the Captain, after a long silent look at the barrier, "strange that we should find it here. The experience of former travellers placed it considerably to the south and west of this."

"But you know," said Leo, "Chingatok told us that the old ice drifts about just as the more recently formed does. Who knows but we may find the end of it not far off, and perhaps may reach open water beyond, where we can make skin canoes, and launch forth on a voyage of discovery."

"I vote that we climb the cliffs and try to see over the top of this horrid ice-jumble," said Benjy.

"Not a bad suggestion, lad. Let us do so. We will encamp here, Anders. Let all the people have a good feed, and tell Chingatok to follow us. You will come along with him."

A few hours later, and the Captain, Leo, Alf, Benjy, Chingatok, and the interpreter stood on the extreme summit of the promontory which they had named Cape Chaos, and from which they had a splendid bird's-eye view of the whole region.

It was indeed a tremendous and never-to-be-forgotten scene.

As far as the eye could reach, the ocean was covered with ice heaped together in some places in the wildest confusion, and so firmly wedged in appearance that it seemed as if it had lain there in a solid mass from the first day of creation. Elsewhere the ice was more level and less compact. In the midst of this rugged scene, hundreds of giant icebergs rose conspicuously above the rest, towering upwards in every shape and of all sizes, from which the bright sun was flashed back in rich variety of form, from the sharp gleam that trickled down an edge of ice to the refulgent blaze on a glassy face which almost rivalled the sun himself in brilliancy. These icebergs, extending as they did to the horizon, where they mingled with and were lost in the pearl-grey sky, gave an impression of vast illimitable perspective. Although no sign of an open sea was at first observed, there was no lack of water to enliven the scene, for here and there, and everywhere, were pools and ponds, and even lakes of goodly size, which had been formed on the surface by the melting ice. In these the picturesque masses were faithfully reflected, and over them vast flocks of gulls, eider-ducks, puffins, and other wild-fowl of the north, disported themselves in garrulous felicity.

On the edge of the rocky precipice, from which they had a bird's-eye view of the scene, our discoverers stood silent for some time, absorbed in contemplation, with feelings of mingled awe and wonder. Then exclamations of surprise and admiration broke forth.

"The wonderful works of God!" said the Captain, in a tone of profound reverence.

"Beautiful, beyond belief!" murmured Alf.

"But it seems an effectual check to our advance," said the practical Leo, who, however, was by no means insensible to the extreme beauty of the scene.

"Not effectual, lad; not effectual," returned the Captain, stretching out his hand and turning to the interpreter; "look, Anders, d'ye see nothing on the horizon away to the nor'ard? Isn't that a bit of water-sky over there?"

"Ya," replied the interpreter, gazing intently, "there be watter-sky over there. Ya. But not possobubble for go there. Ice too big an' brokkin up."

"Ask Chingatok what he thinks," returned the Captain.

Chingatok's opinion was that the water-sky indicated the open sea. He knew that sea well—had often paddled over it, and his own country lay in it.

"But how ever did he cross that ice?" asked the Captain; "what says he to that, Anders?"

"I did not cross it," answered the Eskimo, through Anders. "When I came here with my party the ice was not there; it was far off yonder."

He pointed to the eastward.

"Just so," returned the Captain, with a satisfied nod, "that confirms my opinion. You see, boys, that the coast here trends off to the East'ard in a very decided manner. Now, if that was only the shore of a bay, and the land again ran off to the nor'ard, it would not be possible for such a sea of ice to have come from *that* direction. I therefore conclude that we are standing on the most northern cape of Greenland; that Greenland itself is a huge island, unconnected with the Polar lands; that we are now on the shores of the great Polar basin, in which, somewhere not very far from the Pole itself, lies the home of our friend Chingatok—at least so I judge from what he has said. Moreover, I feel sure that the water-sky we see over there indicates the commencement of that 'open sea' which, I hold, in common with many learned men, lies around the North Pole, and which I am determined to float upon before many days go by."

"We'd better spread our wings then, father, and be off at once," said Benjy; "for it's quite certain that we'll never manage to scramble over that ice-jumble with sledges."

"Nevertheless, I will try, Benjy."

"But how, uncle?" asked Leo.

"Ay, how?" repeated Alf, "*that* is the question."

"Come, come, Alf, let Shakespeare alone," said the pert Benjy; "if you *must* quote, confine yourself to Buzzby."

"Nay, Benjy, be not so severe. It was but a slip. Besides, our leader has not forbidden our carrying a whole library in our heads, so long as we take only one book in our pockets. But, uncle, you have not yet told us how you intend to cross that amazing barrier which Benjy has appropriately styled an ice-jumble."

"How, boy?" returned the Captain, who had been gazing eagerly in all directions while they talked, "it is impossible for me to say how. All that I can speak of with certainty as to our future movements is, that the road by which we have come to the top of this cliff will lead us to the bottom again, where Toolooha is preparing for us an excellent supper of bear-steaks and tea. One step at a time, lads, is my motto; when that is taken we shall see clearly how and where to take the next."

A sound sleep was the step which the whole party took after that which led to the bear-steaks. Then Captain Vane arose, ordered the dogs to be harnessed to the sledges, and, laying his course due north, steered straight out upon the sea of ancient ice.

Chapter VIII

DIFFICULTIES AND DANGERS INCREASE, AND
THE CAPTAIN EXPOUNDS HIS VIEWS.

The first part of the journey over the rugged ice was not so difficult as had been anticipated, because they found a number of openings—narrow lanes, as it were—winding between the masses, most of which were wide enough to permit of the passage of the sledges; and when they chanced to come on a gap that was too narrow, they easily widened it with their hatchets and ice-chisels.

There was, however, some danger connected with this process, for some of the mighty blocks of ice amongst which they moved were piled in such positions that it only required a few choppings at their base to bring them down in ruins on their heads. One instance of this kind sufficed to warn them effectually.

Captain Vane's dog-sledge was leading the way at the time. Leo drove it, for by that time the Eskimos had taught him how to use the short-handled whip with the lash full fifteen feet long, and Leo was an apt pupil in every athletic and manly exercise. Beside him sat the Captain, Alf, Benjy, and Butterface—the black visage of the latter absolutely shining with delight at the novelty of the situation. Behind came the sledge of Chingatok, which, besides being laden with bear-rugs, sealskins, junks of meat, and a host of indescribable Eskimo implements, carried himself and the precious persons of Toolooha and Tekkona. Next came the sledge of the laughter-loving Oolichuk, with the timid Oblooria and another woman. Then followed the sledges of Ivitchuk and Akeetolik, laden with the rest of the Eskimo women and goods, and last of all came Captain Vane's two English-made sledges, heavily-laden with the goods and provisions of the explorers. These latter sledges, although made in England, had been constructed on the principle of the native sledge, namely, with the parts fastened by means of walrus-sinew lashings instead of nails, which last would have snapped like glass in the winter frosts of the Polar regions, besides being incapable of standing the twistings and shocks of ice-travel.

All the dogs being fresh, and the floor of the lanes not too rough, the strangely-assorted party trotted merrily along, causing the echoes among the great ice-blocks, spires, and obelisks, to ring to the music of their chatting, and the cracks of their powerful whips. Suddenly, a shout at the front, and an abrupt pull up, brought the whole column to a halt. The Captain's dogs had broken into a gallop. On turning suddenly round a spur of a glacier about as big as Saint Paul's

Cathedral, they went swish into a shallow pond which had been formed on the ice. It was not deep, but there was sufficient water in it to send a deluge of spray over the travellers.

A burst of laughter greeted the incident as they sprang off the sledge, and waded to the dry ice a few yards ahead.

"No damage done," exclaimed the Captain, as he assisted the dogs to haul the sledge out of the water.

"No damage!" repeated Benjy, with a rueful look, "why, I'm soaked from top to toe!"

"Yes, you've got the worst of it," said Leo, with a laugh; "that comes of being forward, Benjy. You would insist on sitting in front."

"Well, it is some comfort," retorted Benjy, squeezing the water from his garments, "that *Alf* is as wet as myself, for that gives us an opportunity of sympathising with each other. Eh, *Alf?* Does Buzzby offer no consolatory remarks for such an occasion as this?"

"O yes," replied Alf; "in his beautiful poem on Melancholy, sixth canto, Buzzby says:—

> "'When trouble, like a curtain spread,
>   Obscures the clouded brain,
> And worries on the weary head
>   Descend like soaking rain—
> Lift up th'umbrella of the heart,
>   Stride manfully along;
> Defy depression's dreary dart,
>   And shout in gleeful song.'"

"Come, Alf, clap on to this tow-rope, an' stop

your nonsense," said Captain Vane, who was not in a poetical frame of mind just then.

"Dat is mos' boosiful potry!" exclaimed Butterface, with an immense display of eyes and teeth, as he lent a willing hand to haul out the sledge. "Mos' boosiful. But he's rader a strong rem'dy, massa, don' you tink? Not bery easy to git up a gleefoo' shout when one's down in de mout' bery bad, eh!"

Alf's reply was checked by the necessity for remounting the sledge and resuming the journey. Those in rear avoided the pond by going round it.

"The weather's warm, anyhow, and that's a comfort," remarked Benjy, as he settled down in his wet garments. "We can't freeze in summer, you know, and—"

He stopped abruptly, for it became apparent just then that the opening close ahead of them was too narrow for the sledge to pass. It was narrowed by a buttress, or projection, of the cathedral-berg, which jutted up close to a vast obelisk of ice about forty feet high, if not higher.

"Nothing for it, boys, but to cut through," said the Captain, jumping out, and seizing an axe, as the sledge was jammed between the masses. The dogs lay down to rest and pant while the men were at work.

"It's cut an' come again in dem regins," muttered the negro steward, also seizing an axe, and attacking the base of the obelisk.

A sudden cry of alarm from the whole party caused him to desist and look up. He echoed the cry and sprang back swiftly, for the huge mass of ice having been just on the balance, one slash at its base had destroyed the equilibrium, and it was leaning slowly over with a deep grinding sound. A moment later the motion was swift, and it fell with a terrible crash, bursting into a thousand fragments, scattering lumps and glittering morsels far and wide, and causing the whole ice-field to tremble. The concussion overturned several other masses, which had been in the same nicely-balanced condition, some near at hand, others out of sight, though within earshot, and, for a moment, the travellers felt as if the surrounding pack were disrupting everywhere and falling into utter ruin, but in a few seconds the sounds ceased, and again all was quiet.

Fortunately, the obelisk which had been overturned fell towards the north—away from the party; but although it thus narrowly missed crushing them all in one icy tomb, it blocked up their path so completely that the remainder of that day had to be spent in cutting a passage through it.

Need we say that, after this, they were careful how they used their axes and ice-chisels?

Soon after the occurrence of this incident, the labyrinths among the ice became more broken, tortuous, and bewildering. At last they ceased altogether, and the travellers were compelled to take an almost straight course right over everything, for blocks, masses, and drifts on a gigantic scale were heaved up in such dire confusion, that nothing having the faintest resemblance to a track or passage could be found.

"It's hard work, this," remarked the Captain to Leo

one evening, seating himself on a mass of ice which he had just chopped from an obstruction, and wiping the perspiration from his brow.

"Hard, indeed," said Leo, sitting down beside him, "I fear it begins to tell upon poor Benjy. You should really order him to rest more than he does, uncle."

A grim smile of satisfaction played for a minute on the Captain's rugged face, as he glanced at his son, who, a short distance ahead, was hacking at the ice with a pick-axe, in company with Alf and Butterface and the Eskimo men.

"It'll do him good, lad," replied the Captain. "Hard work is just what my Benjy needs. He's not very stout, to be sure, but there is nothing wrong with his constitution, and he's got plenty of spirit."

This was indeed true. Benjy had too much spirit for his somewhat slender frame, but his father, being a herculean man, did not quite perceive that what was good for himself might be too much for his son. Captain Vane was, however, the reverse of a harsh man. He pondered what Leo had said, and soon afterwards went up to his son.

"Benjy, my lad."

"Yes, father," said the boy, dropping the head of his pick-axe on the ice, resting his hands on the haft, and looking up with a flushed countenance.

"You should rest a bit now and then, Benjy. You'll knock yourself up if you don't."

"Rest a bit, father! Why, I've just had a rest, and I'm not tired—that is, not very. Ain't it fun, father? And the ice cuts up so easily, and flies about so splendidly—see here."

With flashing eyes our little hero raised his pick and drove it into the ice at which he had been working, with all his force, so that a great rent was made, and a mass the size of a dressing-table sprang from the side of a berg, and, falling down, burst into a shower of sparkling gems. But this was not all. To Benjy's intense delight, a mass of many tons in weight was loosened by the fall of the smaller lump, and rolled down with a thunderous roar, causing Butterface, who was too near it, to jump out of the way with an amount of agility that threw the whole party into fits of laughter.

"What d'ye think o' that, father?"

"I think it's somewhat dangerous," answered the Captain, recovering his gravity and re-shouldering his axe. "However, as long as you enjoy the work, it can't hurt you, so go ahead, my boy; it'll be a long time before you cut away too much o' the Polar ice!"

Reaching a slightly open space beyond this point, the dogs were harnessed, and the party advanced for a mile or so, when they came to another obstruction worse than that which they had previously passed.

"There's a deal of ice-rubbish in these regions," remarked Benjy, eyeing the wildly heaped masses with a grave face, and heaving a deep sigh.

"Yes, Massa Benjy, bery too much altogidder," said Butterface, echoing the sigh.

"Come, we won't cut through this," cried Captain Vane in a cheery voice; "we'll try to go over it. There is a considerable drift of old snow that seems to offer a sort of track. What says Chingatok?"

The easy-going Eskimo said that it would be as well

to go over it as through it, perhaps better!

So, over it they went, but they soon began to wish they had tried any other plan, for the snow-track quickly came to an end, and then the difficulty of passing even the empty sledges from one ice mass to another was very great, while the process of carrying forward the goods on the shoulders of the men was exceedingly laborious. The poor dogs, too, were constantly falling between masses, and dragging each other down, so that they gave more trouble at last than they were worth.

In all these trying circumstances, the Eskimo women were almost as useful as the men. Indeed they would have been quite as useful if they had been as strong, and they bore the fatigues and trials of the journey with the placid good humour, and apparent, if not real, humility of their race.

At last, one afternoon, our discoverers came suddenly to the edge of this great barrier of ancient ice, and beheld, from an elevated plateau to which they had climbed, a scene which was calculated to rouse in their breasts feelings at once of admiration and despair, for there, stretching away below them for several miles, lay a sea of comparatively level ice, and beyond it a chain of stupendous glaciers, which presented an apparently impassable barrier—a huge continuous wall of ice that seemed to rise into the very sky.

This chain bore all the evidences of being very old ice—compared to which that of the so-called "ancient sea" was absolutely juvenile. On the ice-plain, which was apparently illimitable to the right and left, were hundreds of pools of water in which the icebergs, the golden clouds, the sun, and the blue sky were reflected, and on the surface of which myriads of Arctic wild-fowl were sporting about, making the air vocal with their plaintive cries, and ruffling the glassy surfaces of the lakes with their dipping wings. The heads of seals were also observed here and there.

"These will stop us at last," said Alf, pointing to the bergs with a profound sigh.

"No, they won't," remarked the Captain quietly. "*Nothing* will stop us!"

"That's true, anyhow, uncle," returned Alf; "for if it be, as Chingatok thinks, that we are in search of nothing, of course when we find nothing, nothing will stop us!"

"Why, Alf," said Leo, "I wonder that you, who are usually in an enthusiastic and poetical frame of mind, should be depressed by distant difficulties, instead of admiring such a splendid sight of birds and beasts enjoying themselves in what I may style an Arctic heaven. You should take example by Benjy."

That youth did indeed afford a bright example of rapt enthusiasm just then, for, standing a little apart by himself, he gazed at the scene with flushed face, open mouth, and glittering eyes, in speechless delight.

"Ask Chingatok if he ever saw this range before," said the Captain to Anders, on recovering from his first feeling of surprise.

No, Chingatok had never seen it, except, indeed, the tops of the bergs—at sea, in the far distance—but he had often heard of it from some of his countrymen, who, like himself, were fond of exploring. But that sea of ice was not there, he said, when he had passed on his journey southward. It had drifted there, since that time, from the great sea.

"Ah! the great sea that he speaks of is just what we must find and cross over," muttered the Captain to himself.

"But how are we to cross over it, uncle?" asked Leo.

The Captain replied with one of his quiet glances. His followers had long become accustomed to this silent method of declining to reply, and forbore to press the subject.

"Come now, boys, get ready to descend to the plain. We'll have to do it with caution."

There was, indeed, ground for caution. We have said that they had climbed to an elevated plateau on one of the small bergs which formed the outside margin of the rugged ice. The side of this berg was a steep slope of hard snow, so steep that they thought it unwise to attempt the descent by what in Switzerland is termed glissading.

"We'll have to zig-zag down, I think," continued the Captain, settling himself on his sledge; but the Captain's dogs thought otherwise. Under a sudden impulse of reckless free-will, the whole team, giving vent to a howl of mingled glee and fear, dashed down the slope at full gallop. Of course they were overtaken in a few seconds by the sledge, which not only ran into them, but sent them sprawling on their backs right and left. Then it met a slight obstruction, and itself upset, sending Captain Vane and his companions, with its other contents, into the midst of the struggling dogs. With momentarily increasing speed this avalanche of mixed dead and living matter went sliding, hurtling, swinging, shouting, struggling, and yelling to the bottom. Fortunately, there was no obstruction there, else had destruction been inevitable. The slope merged gradually into the level plain, over which the avalanche swept for a considerable distance before the momentum of their flight was expended.

When at length they stopped, and disentangled themselves from the knot into which the traces had tied them, it was found that no one was materially hurt. Looking up at the height down which they had come, they beheld the Eskimos standing at the top with outstretched arms in the attitude of men who glare in speechless horror. But these did not stand thus long. Descending by a more circuitous route, they soon rejoined the Captain's party, and then, as the night was far advanced, they encamped on the edge of the ice-plain, on a part that was bathed in the beams of the ever-circling sun.

That night at supper Captain Vane was unusually thoughtful and silent.

"You're not losing heart, are you, uncle?" asked Leo, during a pause.

"No, lad, certainly not," replied the Captain, dreamily.

"You've not been bumped very badly in the tumble, father, have you?" asked Benjy with an anxious look.

"Bumped? no; what makes you think so?"

"Because you're gazing at Toolooha's lamp as if you saw a ghost in it."

"Well, perhaps I do see a ghost there," returned the Captain with an effort to rouse his attention to things going on around him. "I see the ghost of things to come. I am looking through Toolooha's lamp into futurity."

"And what does futurity look like?" asked Alf. "Bright or dark?"

"Black—black as me," muttered Butterface, as he approached and laid fresh viands before the party.

It ought to be told that Butterface had suffered rather severely in the recent glissade on the snow-slope, which will account for the gloomy view he took of the future at that time.

"Listen," said the Captain, with a look of sudden earnestness; "as it is highly probable that a day or two more will decide the question of our success or failure, I think it right to reveal to you more fully my thoughts, my plans, and the prospects that lie before us. You all know very well that there is much difference of opinion about the condition of the sea around the North Pole. Some think it must be cumbered with eternal ice, others that it is comparatively free from ice, and that it enjoys a somewhat milder climate than those parts of the Arctic regions with which we have hitherto been doing battle. I hold entirely with the latter view—with those who believe in an open Polar basin. I won't weary you with the grounds of my belief in detail, but here are a few of my reasons—

"It is an admitted fact that there is constant circulation of the water in the ocean. That wise and painstaking philosopher, Maury, of the US navy, has proved to my mind that this grand circulation of the sea-water round the world is the cause of all the oceanic streams, hot and cold, with which we have been so long acquainted.

"This circulation is a necessity as well as a fact. At the Equator the water is extremely warm and salt, besides lime-laden, in consequence of excessive evaporation. At the Poles it is extremely cold and fresh. Mixing is therefore a necessity. The hot salt-waters of the Equator flow to the Poles to get freshened and cooled. Those of the Poles flow to the Equator to get salted, limed, and warmed. They do this continuously in two grand currents, north and south, all round the world. But the land comes in as a disturbing element; it diverts the water into streams variously modified in force and direction, and the streams also change places variously, sometimes the hot currents travelling north as under-currents with the cold currents above, sometimes the reverse. One branch of the current comes from the Equator round the Cape of Good Hope, turns up the west coast of Africa, and is deflected into the Gulf of Mexico, round which it sweeps, and then shoots across the Atlantic to England and Norway. It is known as our Gulf Stream.

"Now, the equatorial warm and salt current enters Baffin's Bay as a submarine current, while the cold and comparatively fresh waters of the Polar regions descend as a surface-current, bearing the great ice-fields of the

Arctic seas to the southward. One thing that goes far to prove this, is the fact that the enormous icebergs thrown off from the northern glaciers have been frequently seen by navigators travelling northward, right *against* the current flowing south. These huge ice-mountains, floating as they do with seven or eight parts of their bulk beneath the surface, are carried thus forcibly up stream by the under-current until their bases are worn off by the warm waters below, thus allowing the upper current to gain the mastery, and hurry them south again to their final dissolution in the Atlantic.

"Now, lads," continued the Captain, with the air of a man who propounds a self-evident proposition; "is it not clear that if the warm waters of the south flow into the Polar basin as an *under* current, they must come up *somewhere*, to take the place of the cold waters that are for ever flowing away from the Pole to the Equator? Can anything be clearer than that—except the nose on Benjy's face? Well then, that being so, the waters round the Pole *must* be comparatively warm waters, and also, comparatively, free from ice, so that if we could only manage to cross this ice-barrier and get into them, we might sail right away to the North Pole."

"But, father," said Benjy, "since you have taken the liberty to trifle with my nose, I feel entitled to remark that we can't sail in waters, either hot or cold, without a ship."

"That's true, boy," rejoined the Captain. "However," he added, with a half-humorous curl of his black moustache, "you know I'm not given to stick at trifles. Time will show. Meanwhile I am strongly of opinion that this is the last ice-barrier we shall meet with on our way to the Pole."

"Is there not some tradition of a mild climate in the furthest north among the Eskimos?" asked Alf.

"Of course there is. It has long been known that the Greenland Eskimos have a tradition of an island in an iceless sea, lying away in the far north, where there are many musk-oxen, and, from what I have been told by our friend Chingatok, I am disposed to think that he and his kindred inhabit this island, or group of islands, in the Polar basin—not far, perhaps, from the Pole itself. He says there are musk-oxen there. But there is another creature, and a much bigger one than any Eskimo, bigger even than Chingatok, who bears his testimony to an open Polar sea, namely, the Greenland whale. It has been ascertained that the 'right' whale does not, and cannot, enter the tropical regions of the Ocean. They are to him as a sea of fire, a wall of adamant, so that it is impossible for him to swim south, double Cape Horn, and proceed to the North Pacific; yet the very same kind of whale found in Baffin's Bay is found at Behring Straits. Now, the question is, how did he get there?"

"Was born there, no doubt," answered Benjy, "and had no occasion to make such a long voyage!"

"Ah! my boy, but we have the strongest evidence that he was *not* born there, for you must know that some whalers have a habit of marking their harpoons with date and name of ship; and as we have been told by that good and true man Dr. Scoresby, there have been several instances where whales have been captured near Behring Straits with harpoons in them bearing the stamp of ships that were known to cruise on the Baffin's Bay side of America. Moreover, in one or two instances a very short time had elapsed between the date of harpooning on the Atlantic and capturing on the Pacific side. These facts prove, at all events, a 'North-west Passage' for whales, and, as whales cannot travel far under ice without breathing, they also tend to prove an open Polar sea.

"Another argument in favour of this basin is the migration of birds to the northward at certain seasons. Birds do not migrate to frozen regions, and such migrations northward have been observed by those who, like ourselves, have reached the highest latitudes.

"Captain Nares of the *Alert*, in May 1876, when only a little to the southward of this, saw ptarmigan flying in pairs to the north-west, seeking for better feeding-grounds. Ducks and geese also passed northward early in June, indicating plainly the existence of suitable feeding-grounds in the undiscovered and mysterious North.

"We have now passed beyond the point reached by Captain Nares. My last observation placed us in parallel 84° 40 minutes, the highest that has yet been reached by civilised man."

"The highest, uncle?" interrupted Leo. "Yes—the highest. Scoresby reached 81° 50 minutes in 1806, Parry 82° 45 minutes in 1827—with sledges. That unfortunate and heroic American, Captain Hall, ran his vessel, the *Polaris*, in the shortest space of time on record, up to latitude 82° 16 minutes. Captain Nares reached a higher latitude than had previously been attained by ships, and Captain Markham, of Captain Nares' expedition, travelled over this very 'sea of ancient ice' with sledges to latitude 83° 20.4 minutes— about 400 miles from the Pole, and the highest yet reached, as I have said. So, you see, we have beaten them all! Moreover, I strongly incline to the belief that the open Polar Sea lies just beyond that range of huge icebergs which we see before us."

The Captain rose as he spoke, and pointed to the gigantic chain, behind one of which the sun was just about to dip, causing its jagged peaks to glow as with intense fire.

"But how are we ever to pass that barrier, uncle?" asked Alf, who was by nature the least sanguine of the party in regard to overcoming difficulties of a geographical nature, although by far the most enthusiastic in the effort to acquire knowledge.

"You shall see, to-morrow," answered the Captain; "at present we must turn in and rest. See, the Eskimos have already set us the example."

Chapter IX

THE CAPTAIN MAKES A STUPENDOUS EFFORT.
DISAPPOINTMENTS AND DISCOVERIES.

Next morning the ice-plain was crossed at a swinging gallop. Indeed, the dogs were so fresh and frisky after a good rest and a hearty meal that they ran away more than once, and it became a matter of extreme difficulty to check them. At last the great chain was reached, and the party came to an abrupt halt at the base of one of the largest of the bergs. Captain Vane gazed up at it as Napoleon the First may be supposed to have gazed at the Alps he had resolved to scale and cross.

The resemblance to alpine scenery was not confined to mere form—such as towering peaks and mighty precipices—for there were lakelets and ponds here and there up among the crystal heights, from which rivulets trickled, streams brawled, and cataracts thundered.

It was evident, however, that the old giant that

frowned on them was verging towards dissolution, for he was honey-combed in all directions.

"Impossible to scale that," said Alf, with a solemn look.

Even Leo's sanguine temperament was dashed for a moment. "We dare not attempt to cut through it," he said, "for masses are falling about here and there in a very dangerous fashion."

As he spoke, a tall spire was seen to slip from its position, topple over, and go crashing down into a dark blue gulf of ice below it.

"No chance of success *now*," said Benjamin Vane, gloomily.

"None wotsomediver," muttered Butterface, his broad black visage absolutely elongated by sympathetic despair. For, you must know, as far as his own feelings were concerned, sympathy alone influenced him. Personally, he was supremely indifferent about reaching the North Pole. In fact he did not believe in it at all, and made no scruple of saying so, when asked, but he seldom volunteered his opinion, being an extremely modest and polite man.

During these desponding remarks Captain Vane did not seem to be much depressed.

"Anders," he said, turning abruptly to the interpreter, "ask Chingatok what he thinks. Can we pass this barrier, and, if not, what would he advise us to do?"

It was observed that the other Eskimos drew near with anxious looks to hear the opinion of their chief.

Toolooha and Tekkona, however, seemed quite

devoid of anxiety. They evidently had perfect confidence in the giant, and poor little Oblooria glanced up in the face of her friend as if to gather consolation from her looks.

Chingatok, after a short pause, said:—

"The ice-mountains cannot be passed. The white men have not wings; they cannot fly. They must return to land, and travel for many days to the open water near the far-off land—there."

He pointed direct to the northward.

Captain Vane made no reply. He merely turned and gave orders that the lashings of one of the large sledges which conveyed the baggage should be cast loose. Selecting a box from this, he opened it, and took therefrom a small instrument made partly of brass, partly of glass, and partly of wood.

"You have often wondered, Benjy," he said, "what I meant to do with this electrical machine. You shall soon see. Help me to arrange it, boy, and do you, Leo, uncoil part of this copper wire. Here, Alf, carry this little box to the foot of the berg, and lay it in front of yon blue cavern."

"Which? That one close to the waterfall or—"

"No, the big cavern, just under the most solid part of the berg—the one that seems to grow bluer and bluer until it becomes quite black in its heart. And have a care, Alf. The box you carry is dangerous. Don't let it fall. Lay it down gently, and come back at once. Anders," he added, turning round, "let all the people go back with dogs and sledges for a quarter of a mile."

There was something so peremptory and abrupt in

their leader's manner that no one thought of asking him a question, though all were filled with surprise and curiosity as to what he meant to do.

"Come here, Leo," he said, after his orders had been obeyed. "Hold this coil, and pay it out as I walk to the berg with the end in my hand."

The coil was one of extremely fine copper wire. Leo let it run as the Captain walked off. A minute or two later he was seen to enter the dark blue cavern and disappear.

"My dear dad is reckless," exclaimed Benjy, in some anxiety, "what if the roof o' that cave should fall in. There are bits of ice dropping about everywhere. What *can* he be going to do?"

As he spoke, the Captain issued from the cave, and walked smartly towards them.

"Now then, it's all right," he said, "give me the coil, Leo, and come back, all of you. Fetch the machine, Alf."

In a few minutes the whole party had retired a considerable distance from the huge berg, the Captain uncoiling the wire as he went.

"Surely you're not going to try to blow it up piecemeal?" said Leo.

"No, lad, I'm not going to do that, or anything so slow," returned the Captain, stopping and arranging the instrument.

"But if the box contains gunpowder," persisted Leo, "there's not enough to—"

"It contains dynamite," said the Captain, affixing the coil to the machine, and giving it a sharp turn.

If a volcano had suddenly opened fire under the iceberg the effect could not have been more tremendous. Thunder itself is not more deep than was the crash which reverberated among the ice-cliffs. Smoke burst in a huge volume from the heart of the berg. Masses, fragments, domes, and pinnacles were hurled into the air, and fell back to mingle with the blue precipices that tumbled, slid, or plunged in horrible confusion. Only a portion, indeed, of the mighty mass had been actually disrupted, but the shock to the surrounding ice was so shattering that the entire berg subsided.

"Stu-pendous!" exclaimed Alf, with a look of awe-stricken wonder.

Benjy, after venting his feelings in a shriek of joyful surprise, seemed to be struck dumb. Anders and Butterface stood still,—speechless. As for the Eskimos, they turned with one hideous yell, and fled from the spot like maniacs—excepting Chingatok, who, although startled, stood his ground in an attitude expressive of superlative surprise.

"So,—it has not disappointed me," remarked the Captain, when the hideous din had ceased, "dynamite is indeed a powerful agent when properly applied: immeasurably more effective than powder."

"But it seems to me," said Leo, beginning to recover himself, "that although you have brought the berg down you have not rendered it much more passable."

"That's true, lad," answered the Captain with a somewhat rueful expression. "It does seem a lumpy sort of heap after all; but there may be found some practicable bits when we examine it more closely. Come, we'll go see."

On closer inspection it was found that the ruined berg still presented an absolutely insurmountable obstacle to the explorers, who, being finally compelled to admit that even dynamite had failed, left the place in search of a natural opening.

Travelling along the chain for a considerable time, in the hope of succeeding, they came at last to a succession of comparatively level floes, which conducted them to the extreme northern end of the chain, and there they found that the floes continued onwards in an unbroken plain to what appeared to be the open sea.

"That is a water-sky, for certain," exclaimed Captain Vane, eagerly, on the evening when this discovery was made. "The open ocean cannot now be far off."

"There's a very dark cloud there, father," said Benjy, who, as we have before said, possessed the keenest sight of the party.

"A cloud, boy! where? Um—Yes, I see something—"

"It is land," said Chingatok, in a low voice.

"Land!" exclaimed the Captain, "are you sure?"

"Yes, I know it well. I passed it on my journey here. We left our canoes and oomiaks there, and took to sledges because the floes were unbroken. But these ice-mountains were not here at that time. They have come down since we passed from the great sea."

"There!" said the Captain, turning to Leo with a look of triumph, "he still speaks of the great sea! If these bergs came from it, we *must* have reached it, lad."

"But the land puzzles me," said Leo. "Can it be part of Greenland?"

"Scarcely, for Greenland lies far to the east'ard, and the latest discoveries made on the north of that land show that the coast turns still more decidedly east—tending to the conclusion that Greenland is an island. This land, therefore, must be entirely new land—an island—a continent perhaps."

"But it may be a cape, father," interposed Benjy. "You know that capes have a queer way of sticking out suddenly from land, just as men's noses stick out from their faces."

"True, Benjy, true, but your simile is not perfect, for men's noses don't always stick out from their faces—witness the nose of Butterface, which, you know, is well aft of his lips and chin. However, this *may* be Greenland's nose—who knows? We shall go and find out ere long. Come, use your whip, Leo. Ho! Chingatok, tell your hairy kinsmen to clap on all sail and make for the land."

"Hold on, uncle!" cried Alf, "I think I see a splendid specimen of—"

The crack of Leo's whip, and the yelping of the team, drowned the rest of the sentence, and Alf was whirled away from his splendid specimen, (whatever it was), for ever!

"It is a piece of great good fortune," said the Captain, as they swept along over the hard and level snow, "that the Eskimos have left their boats on this land, for now I shall have two strings to my bow."

"What is the other string?" asked Leo, as he administered a flip to the flank of a lazy dog.

"Ah, that remains to be seen, lad," replied the Captain.

"Why, what a tyrant you are, uncle!" exclaimed Alf, who had recovered from his disappointment about the splendid specimen. "You won't tell us anything, almost. Who ever before heard of the men of an expedition to the North Pole being kept in ignorance of the means by which they were to get there?"

The Captain's reply was only a twinkle of the eye.

"Father wants to fill you with bliss, Alf," said Benjy, "according to your own notions of that sort of thing."

"What do you mean, Ben?"

"Why, have we not all heard you often quote the words:— 'Where ignorance is bliss, 'tis folly to be wise.'"

"Hear, hear! That's it, Benjy," said the Captain, with a nod and a short laugh, while his son assumed the satisfied gravity of look appropriate to one who has made a hit; "I won't decrease his bliss by removing his ignorance yet awhile."

"Hain't Buzzby got nuffin' to say on that 'ere pint?" whispered Butterface to Benjy, who sat just in front of him.

"Ah! to be sure. I say, Alf," said the boy with an earnest look, "hasn't your favourite author got something to say about the bliss of ignorance? I'm almost sure I heard you muttering something in your dreams on that subject the other day."

"Of course he has. He has a long poem on that subject. Here is a bit of it."

Alf, whose memory was good, immediately recited the following:

"How sweet is ignorance! How soothing to the mind,
To search for treasures in the brain, and nothing find!
Consider. When the memory is richly stored,
How apt the victim of redundant knowledge to be bored!
When Nothing fills the chambers of the heart and brain,
Then negative enjoyment comes with pleasures in her train!
Descending on the clods of sense like summer rain.

"Knowledge, 'tis said, gives power, and so it often does;
Knowledge makes sorrow, too, around our pillows buzz.
In debt I am, with little cash; I know it—and am sad.
Of course, if I were ignorant of this—how glad!
A loving friend, whom once I knew in glowing health,
Has broken down, and also, somehow, lost his wealth.
How sad the knowledge makes me! Better far
In ignorance to live, than hear of things that jar,
And think of things that are not,—not of things that are.

"'If ignorance is bliss,' the poet saith—why 'if'?
Why doubt a fact so clearly proven, stubborn, stiff?
The heavy griefs and burdens of the world around,
The hideous tyranny by which mankind is ground,
The earthquake, tempest, rush of war, and wail of woe,
Are all as though they were not—if I do not know!
Wrapped in my robe of ignorance, what can I miss?
Am I not saved from all—and more than all—of this?
Do I not revel in a regal realm of bliss?"

"Bravo! Buzzby," cried the Captain, "but, I say, Alf, don't it seem to smack rather too much of selfishness?"

"Of course it does, uncle. I do not think Buzzby always sound in principle, and, like many poets, he is sometimes confused in his logic."

"You're right, Benjy, the land is clear enough now," remarked the Captain, whose interest in Buzzby was not profound, and whose feelings towards logic bordered on the contemptuous, as is often the case with half-educated men, and, strange to say, sometimes with highly-educated men, as well as with the totally ignorant—so true is it that extremes meet!

In the course of a couple of hours the sledges drew near to the island, which proved to be a large but comparatively low one, rising not more than a hundred feet in any part. It was barren and ragged, with patches of reindeer moss growing in some parts, and dwarf willows in others. Myriads of sea-birds made it their home, and these received the invaders with clamorous cries, as if they knew that white men were a dangerous novelty, and objected to the innovation.

Despite their remonstrances, the party landed, and the Eskimos hurried over the rocks to that part of the island where they had left their kayaks and women's boats in charge of a party of natives who were resident on the island at the time they passed, and from whom they had borrowed the dogs and sledges with which they had travelled south.

Meanwhile the white men took to rambling; Leo to shoot wild-fowl for supper, Alf to search for "specimens," and Benjy to scramble among the rocks in search of anything that might "turn up." Butterface assisted the latter in his explorations. While the rest were thus engaged, the Captain extemporised a flag-staff out of two spears lashed together with a small block at the top for the purpose of running up a flag, and formally taking possession of the island when they should re-assemble. This done, he wrote a brief outline of his recent doings, which he inserted in a ginger-beer bottle brought for that very purpose. Then he assisted Anders in making the encampment and preparing supper.

The two were yet in the midst of the latter operation when a shout was heard in the distance. Looking in the direction whence it came they saw Chingatok striding over the rocks towards them with unusual haste. He was followed by the other Eskimos, who came forward gesticulating violently.

"My countrymen have left the island," said Chingatok when he came up.

"And taken the kayaks with them?" asked Captain Vane anxiously.

"Every one," replied the giant.

This was depressing news to the Captain, who had counted much on making use of the Eskimo canoes in the event of his own appliances failing.

"Where have they gone, think you?" he asked.

"Tell Blackbeard," replied Chingatok, turning to Anders, "that no one knows. Since they went away the lanes of open water have closed, and the ice is solid everywhere."

"But where the kayak and the oomiak cannot float the sledge may go," said the Captain.

"That is true; tell the pale chief he is wise, yet he

knows not all things. Let him think. When he comes to the great open sea what will he do without canoes?"

"Huk!" exclaimed Oolichuk, with that look and tone which intimated his belief that the pale chief had received a "clincher."

The chattering of the other Eskimos ceased for a moment or two as they awaited eagerly the Captain's answer, but the Captain disappointed them. He merely said, "Well, we shall see. I may not know all things, Chingatok, nevertheless I know a deal more than you can guess at. Come now, let's have supper, Anders; we can't wait for the wanderers."

As he spoke, three of the wanderers came into camp, namely Leo, Benjy, and Butterface.

"What's come of Alf?" asked the Captain.

Neither Leo nor Benjy had seen him since they parted, a quarter of an hour after starting, and both had expected to find him in camp, but Butterface had seen him.

"Sawd him runnin'," said the sable steward, "runnin' like a mad kangaroo arter a smallish brute like a mouse. Nebber sawd nuffin' like Massa Alf for runnin'."

"Well, we can't wait for him," said the Captain, "I want to take possession of the island before supper. What shall we call it?"

"Disappointment Isle," said Leo, "seeing that the Eskimos have failed us."

"No—I won't be ungrateful," returned the Captain, "considering the successes already achieved."

"Call it Content Isle, then," suggested Benjy.

"But I am not content with partial success. Come, Butterface, haven't you got a suggestion to make."

The negro shook his woolly head. "No," he said, "I's 'orrible stoopid. Nebber could get nuffin' to come out o' my brain—sep w'en it's knocked out by accident. You's hard to please, massa. S'pose you mix de two,— dis'pintment an' content,—an' call 'im Half-an'-half Island."

"Home is in sight now," said Chingatok, who had taken no interest in the above discussion, as it was carried on in English. "A few days more and we should be there if we only had our kayaks."

"There's the name," exclaimed the Captain eagerly when this was translated, "'Home-in-sight,' that will do."

Rising quickly, he bent a Union Jack to the halyards of his primitive flag-staff, ran it up, and in the name of Queen Victoria took possession of *Home-in-sight Island.* After having given three hearty British cheers, in which the Eskimos tried to join, with but partial success, they buried the ginger-beer bottle under a heap of stones, a wooden cross was fixed on the top of the cairn, and then the party sat down to supper, while the Captain made a careful note of the latitude and longitude, which he had previously ascertained. This latest addition to Her Majesty's dominions was put down by him in latitude 85° 32 minutes, or about 288 geographical miles from the North Pole.

Chapter X

The first night on Home-in-sight Island was not so
undisturbed as might have been expected. The
noisy gulls did indeed go to sleep at their proper bed-
time, which, by the way, they must have ascertained by
instinct, for the sun could be no certain guide, seeing
that he shone all night as well as all day, and it would
be too much to expect that gulls had sufficient powers
of observation to note the great luminary's exact
relation to the horizon. Polar bears, like the Eskimo,
had forsaken the spot. All nature, indeed, animate
and inanimate, favoured the idea of repose when the
explorers lay down to sleep on a mossy couch that
was quite as soft as a feather bed, and much more
springy.

The cause of disturbance was the prolonged
absence of Alf Vandervell. That enthusiastic naturalist's

failure to appear at supper was nothing uncommon. His non-appearance when they lay down did indeed cause some surprise, but little or no anxiety, and they all dropped into a sound sleep which lasted till considerably beyond midnight. Then the Captain awoke with a feeling of uneasiness, started up on one elbow, yawned, and gazed dreamily around. The sun, which had just kissed his hand to the disappointed horizon and begun to re-ascend the sky, blinded the Captain with his beams, but did not prevent him from observing that Alf's place was still vacant.

"Very odd," he muttered, "Alf didn't use to-to-w'at's 'is name in—this—way—"

The Captain's head dropped, his elbow relaxed, and he returned to the land of Nod for another half-hour.

Again he awoke with a start, and sat upright.

"This'll never do," he exclaimed, with a fierce yawn, "something *must* be wrong. Ho! Benjy!"

"Umph!" replied the boy, who, though personally light, was a heavy sleeper.

"Rouse up, Ben, Alf's not come back. Where did you leave him?"

"Don' know, Burrerface saw 'im las'—." Benjy dropped off with a sigh, but was re-aroused by a rough shake from his father, who lay close to him.

"Come, Ben, stir up Butterface! We must go look for Alf."

Butterface lay on the other side of Benjy, who, only half alive to what he was doing, raised his hand and let it fall heavily on the negro's nose, by way of stirring him up.

"Hallo! massa Benjamin! You's dreamin' drefful strong dis mornin'."

"Yer up, ol' ebony!" groaned the boy.

In a few minutes the whole camp was roused; sleep was quickly banished by anxiety about the missing one; guns and rifles were loaded, and a regular search-expedition was hastily organised. They started off in groups in different directions, leaving the Eskimo women in charge of the camp.

The Captain headed one party, Chingatok another, and Leo with Benjy a third, while a few of the natives went off independently, in couples or alone.

"I was sure Alf would get into trouble," said Benjy, as he trotted beside Leo, who strode over the ground in anxious haste. "That way he has of getting so absorbed in things that he forgets where he is, won't make him a good explorer."

"Not so sure of that, Ben," returned Leo; "he can discover things that men who are less absorbed, like you, might fail to note. Let us go round this hillock on separate sides. We might pass him if we went together. Keep your eyes open as you go. He may have stumbled over one of those low precipices and broken a leg. Keep your ears cocked also, and give a shout now and then."

We have said that the island was a low one, nevertheless it was extremely rugged, with little ridges and hollows everywhere, like miniature hills and valleys. Through one of these latter Benjy hurried, glancing from side to side as he went, like a red Indian on the war-path—which character, indeed, he thought of, and tried to imitate.

The little vale did not, however, as Leo had imagined, lead round the hillock. It diverged gradually to the right, and ascended towards the higher parts of the island. The path was so obstructed by rocks and boulders which had evidently been at one time under the pressure of ice, that the boy could not see far in any direction, except by mounting one of these. He had not gone far when, on turning the corner of a cliff which opened up another gorge to view, he beheld a sight which caused him to open mouth and eyes to their widest.

For there, seated on an eminence, with his back to a low precipice, not more than three or four hundred yards off, sat the missing explorer, with book on knees and pencil in hand—sketching; and there, seated on the top of the precipice, looking over the edge at the artist, skulked a huge Polar bear, taking as it were, a surreptitious lesson in drawing! The bear, probably supposing Alf to be a wandering seal, had dogged him to that position just as Benjy Vane discovered him, and then, finding the precipice too high for a leap perhaps, or doubting the character of his intended victim, he had paused in uncertainty on the edge.

The boy's first impulse was to utter a shout of warning, for he had no gun wherewith to shoot the brute, but fear lest that might precipitate an attack restrained him. Benjy, however, was quick-witted. He saw that the leap was probably too much even for a Polar bear, and that the nature of the ground would necessitate a detour before it could get at the artist.

These and other thoughts passed through his brain like the lightning flash, and he was on the point of turning to run back and give the alarm to Leo, when a rattling of stones occurred behind him—just beyond the point of rocks round which he had turned. In the tension of his excited nerves he felt as if he had suddenly become red hot. Could this be another bear? If so, what was he to do, whither to fly? A moment more would settle the question, for the rattle of stones continued as the steps advanced. The boy felt the hair rising on his head. Round came the unknown monster in the form of—a man!

"Ah, Benjy, I—"

But the appearance of Benjy's countenance caused Leo to stop abruptly, both in walk and talk. He had found out his mistake about sending the boy round the hillock, and, turning back, had followed him.

"Ah! look there," said Benjy, pointing at the *tableau vivant* on the hill-top.

Leo's ready rifle leaped from his shoulder to his left palm, and a grim smile played on his lips, for long service in a volunteer corps had made him a good judge of distance as well as a sure and deadly shot.

"Stand back, Benjy, behind this boulder," he whispered. "I'll lean on it to make more certain."

He was deliberately arranging the rifle while speaking, but never for one instant took his eye off the bear, which still stood motionless, with one paw raised, as if petrified with amazement at what it saw. As for Alf, he went on intently with his work, lifting and lowering his eyes continuously, putting in bold dashes here, or tender touches there; holding out the book occasionally at arm's length to regard his work, with head first on one side, then on the other, and, in short, going through all those graceful and familiar little evolutions of artistic procedure which arouse one's home feelings so powerfully everywhere—even in the Arctic regions! Little did the artist know who was his uninvited pupil on that sunny summer night!

With one knee resting on a rock, and his rifle on the boulder, Leo took a steady, somewhat lengthened aim, and fired. The result was stupendous! Not only did the shot reverberate with crashing echoes among surrounding cliffs and boulders, but a dying howl from the bear burst over the island, like the thunder of a heavy gun, and went booming over the frozen sea. No wonder that the horrified Alf leapt nearly his own height into the air and scattered his drawing-materials right and left like chaff. He threw up his arms, and wheeled frantically round just in time to receive the murdered bear into his very bosom! They rolled down a small slope together, and then, falling apart, lay prone and apparently dead upon the ground.

You may be sure that Leo soon had his brother's head on his knee, and was calling to him in an agony of fear, quite regardless of the fact that the bear lay at his elbow, giving a few terrific kicks as its huge life oozed out through a bullet-hole in its heart, while Benjy, half weeping with sympathy, half laughing with glee, ran to a neighbouring pool to fetch water in his cap.

A little of the refreshing liquid dashed on his face and poured down his throat soon restored Alf, who

ALF AND HIS POLAR PUPIL—Page 136

had only been stunned by the fall.

"What induced you to keep on sketching all night?" asked Leo, after the first explanations were over.

"All night?" repeated Alf in surprise, "have I been away all night? What time is it?"

"Three o'clock in the morning at the very least," said Leo. "The sun is pretty high, as you might have seen if you had looked at it."

"But he never looked at it," said Benjy, whose eyes were not yet quite dry, "he never looks at anything, or thinks of anything, when he goes sketching."

"Surely you must allow that at least I look at and think of my work," said Alf, rising from the ground and sitting down on the rock from which he had been so rudely roused; "but you are half right, Benjy. The sun was at my back, you see, hid from me by the cliff over which the bear tumbled, and I had no thoughts for time, or eyes for nature, except the portion I was busy with—by the way, where is it?"

"What, your sketch?"

"Ay, and the colours. I wouldn't lose these for a sight of the Pole itself. Look for them, Ben, my boy, I still feel somewhat giddy."

In a few minutes the sketch and drawing-materials were collected, undamaged, and the three returned to camp, Alf leaning on Leo's arm. On the way thither they met the Captain's party, and afterwards the band led by Chingatok. The latter was mightily amused by the adventure, and continued for a considerable time afterwards to upheave his huge shoulders with suppressed laughter.

When the whole party was re-assembled the hour was so late, and they had all been so thoroughly excited, that no one felt inclined to sleep again. It was resolved, therefore, at once to commence the operations of a new day. Butterface was set to prepare coffee, and the Eskimos began breakfast with strips of raw blubber, while steaks of Leo's bear were being cooked.

Meanwhile Chingatok expressed a wish to see the drawing which had so nearly cost the artist his life.

Alf was delighted to exhibit and explain it.

For some time the giant gazed at it in silence. Then he rested his forehead in his huge hand as if in meditation.

It was truly a clever sketch of a surpassingly lovely scene. In the foreground was part of the island with its pearl-grey rocks, red-brown earth, and green mosses, in the midst of which lay a calm pool, like the island's eye looking up to heaven and reflecting the bright indescribable blue of the midnight sky. Further on was a mass of cold grey rocks. Beyond lay the northern ice-pack, which extended in chaotic confusion away to the distant horizon, but the chaos was somewhat relieved by the presence of lakelets which shone here and there over its surface like shields of glittering azure and burnished gold.

"Ask him what he thinks of it," said Leo to Anders, a little surprised at Chingatok's prolonged silence.

"I cannot speak," answered the giant, "my mind is bursting and my heart is full. With my finger I have drawn faces on the snow. I have seen men put wonderful things on flat rocks with a piece of stone, but this!—this is my country made little. It looks as if I could walk in it, yet it is flat!"

"The giant is rather complimentary," laughed Benjy, when this was translated; "to my eye your sketch is little better than a daub."

"It is a daub that causes me much anxiety," said the Captain, who now looked at the drawing for the first time. "D'you mean to tell me, Alf, that you've been true to nature when you sketched that pack?"

"As true as I could make it, uncle."

"I'll answer for its truth," said Leo, "and so will Benjy, for we both saw the view from the top of the island, though we paid little heed to it, being too much occupied with Alf and the bear at the time. The pack is even more rugged than he has drawn it, and it extends quite unbroken to the horizon."

The Captain's usually hopeful expression forsook him for a little as he commented on his bad fortune.

"The season advances, you see," he said, "and it's never very long at the best. I had hoped we were done with this troublesome 'sea of ancient ice,' but it seems to turn up everywhere, and from past experience we know that the crossing of it is slow work, as well as hard. However, we mustn't lose heart. 'Nebber say die,' as Butterface is fond of remarking."

"Yis, Massa, nebber say die, but allers say 'lib, to de top ob your bent.' Dems my 'pinions w'en dey's wanted. Also 'go a-hid.' Dat's a grand sent'ment—was borned 'mong de Yankees, an' I stoled it w'en I left ole Virginny."

"What says Chingatok?" asked the Captain of the Eskimo, who was still seated with the sketch on his knees in profound meditation.

"Blackbeard has trouble before him," answered the uncompromising giant, without removing his eyes from the paper. "There," he said, pointing to the pack, "you have three days' hard work. After that three days' easy and swift work. After that no more go on. Must come back."

"He speaks in riddles, Anders. What does he mean by the three days of hard work coming to an end?"

"I mean," said Chingatok, "that the ice was loose when I came to this island. It is now closed. The white men must toil, toil, toil—very slow over the ice for three days, then they will come to smooth ice, where the dogs may run for three days. Then they will come to another island, like this one, on the far-off side of which there is no ice—nothing but sea, sea, sea. Our kayaks are gone," continued the giant, sadly, "we must come back and travel many days before we find things to make new ones."

While he was speaking, Captain Vane's face brightened up.

"Are you sure of what you say, Chingatok?"

"Chingatok is sure," replied the Eskimo quietly.

"Then we'll conquer our difficulties after all. Come, boys, let's waste no more time in idle talk, but harness the dogs, and be off at once."

Of course the party had to travel round the island, for there was neither ice nor snow on it. When the other side was reached the real difficulties of the journey were fully realised. During the whole of that day and the next they were almost continuously engaged in dragging the sledges over masses of ice, some of which rose to thirty feet above the general level. If the reader will try to imagine a very small ant or beetle dragging its property over a newly macadamised road, he will have a faint conception of the nature of the work. To some extent the dogs were a hindrance rather than a help, especially when passing over broken fragments, for they were always tumbling into holes and cracks, out of which they had to be dragged, and were much given to venting their ill-humour on each other, sometimes going in for a free fight, in the course of which they tied their traces into indescribable knots, and drove their Eskimo masters furious. On such occasions the whips—both lash and handle—were applied with unsparing vigour until the creatures were cowed.

Danger, also, as well as toil, was encountered during the journey. On the evening of the second day the sledge driven by Oolichuk diverged a little from the line of march towards what seemed an easier passage over the hummocks. They had just gained the top of an ice-block, which, unknown to the driver, overhung its base. When the dogs reached the edge of the mass, it suddenly gave way. Down went the team with a united howl of despair. Their weight jerked the sledge forward, another mass of the ice gave way, and over went the whole affair. In the fall the lashings broke, and Oolichuk, with several of his kindred, including poor little Oblooria, went down in a shower of skins, packages, bags, and Eskimo cooking utensils.

Fortunately, they dropped on a slope of ice which broke their fall, and, as it were, shunted them all safely,

THE SEA OF ANCIENT ICE—Page 142

though violently, to the lower level of the pack.

Beyond a few scratches and bruises, no evil resulted from this accident to these hardy natives of the north.

That night they all encamped, as on the previous night, in the midst of the pack, spreading their skins and furs on the flattest ice they could find, and keeping as far from overhanging lumps as possible.

"What does Blackbeard mean by coming here?" asked Chingatok of Anders, as they lay side by side, gazing up at the blue sky awaiting sleep. "We cannot swim over the sea, and we have no boats."

"I don't know," answered the interpreter. "Our chief is a wonderful man. He does things that seem to be all wrong, but they turn out mostly to be all right."

"Does he ever speak of a Great Spirit?" asked the giant in a solemn tone.

"Not to me," replied the other, "but I hear him sometimes speaking to his little boy about his God."

"Then he must know his God," returned Chingatok. "Has he seen him—spoken to him?"

Anders was a good deal surprised as well as puzzled by the questions put by his new friend. His extremely commonplace mind had never been exercised by such ideas. "I never asked him about that," he said, "and he never told me. Perhaps he will tell you if you ask him."

The interpreter turned on his side with a sigh and went to sleep. The giant lay on his back gazing long and steadily with a wistful look at the unbroken vault of sky, whose vast profundity seemed to thrust him mercilessly back. As he gazed, a little cloud, light as a puff of eider-down, and golden as the sun from which its lustre came, floated into the range of his vision. He smiled, for the thought that light may suddenly arise when all around seems blank gave his inquiring spirit rest, and he soon joined the slumbering band who lay upon the ice around him.

According to Chingatok's prophecy, on the third day the fagged and weary discoverers surmounted their first difficulty, and came upon comparatively smooth ice, the surface of which resembled hard-trodden snow, and was sufficiently free from obstructing lumps to admit of rapid sledge travelling. It was late when they reached it, but as they could now all sit on the sledges and leave the hard work to the dogs, the leader resolved to continue the advance without resting.

"It's time enough to stop when we're stopped," he remarked to Leo, while making preparations to start. "We will sleep at the first obstruction we meet with, if it's a sufficiently troublesome one. See that the things are well lashed on all the sledges, Alf. Remember that I hold you responsible for lost articles."

"And what am I responsible for, father?" asked Benjy with a pert look.

"For keeping out of mischief, Ben. That's the most I can expect of you."

"You are only a sort of negative blessing to us, you see, Benjy," said Alf, as he stooped to tighten a rope. "It's not so much what you do, as what you don't do, that rejoices us."

"I'm glad of that," retorted the boy, arranging himself comfortably on his father's sledge, "because

I won't do anything at all for some hours to come, which ought to fill you all with perfect felicity. Awake me, Leo, if we chance to upset."

"Now then, all ready?" cried the Captain. "Off you go, then—clap on all sail!"

Crack went the mighty whips, howl went the dogs, and the sledges were soon skimming over the sea at the rate of ten miles an hour. Of course they did not keep that pace up very long. It became necessary to rest at times, also, to give the dogs a little food. When this latter process had been completed, the teams became so lively that they tried to runaway.

"Let them run," said the Captain to Leo.

"And help them on," added Benjy.

Leo took the advice of both, applied the lash, and increased the speed so much that the sledge swung from side to side on the smooth places, sometimes catching on a lump of ice, and all but throwing out its occupants. The Eskimos entered into the spirit of their leaders. They also plied their lashes, and, being more dexterous than Leo, soon converted the journey into a race, in which Chingatok—his giant arm flourishing an appropriately huge whip—was rapidly coming to the front when a tremendous shout in the rear caused them to pull up. Looking back, Alf's sledge was seen inverted and mixed, as it were, with the team, while Alf himself and his Eskimo friends were sprawling around on the ice. No damage was done to life or limb, but a sledge-runner had been partially broken, and could not be mended,—so said Oolichuk—in less than an hour.

"This, then," said the Captain, "is our first obstruction, so here we will make our beds for the night."

Chapter XI

As Chingatok had predicted, on the sixth day from Home-in-sight Island the party came to another island, where the great pack abruptly terminated. It was not large, probably ten or twelve miles in length, from the Eskimo account, but the ends of it could not be seen from the spot where they landed. At that point it was only two miles wide, and on the opposite side its shores were laved by an open sea, which was quite free from ice, with the exception of a few scattered floes and bergs—a sea whose waves fell in slow regular cadence on a pebbly beach, and whose horizon was an unbroken line barely distinguishable from the sky.

Close to it a few black rocks showed above the water, around which great numbers of gulls, puffins, and other sea-birds disported themselves in clamorous joy;

sometimes flying to the shore as if to have a look at the newcomers, and then sheering off with a scream—it might be a laugh—to tell their comrades what they had seen.

"Here, then, at last, is the open Polar Sea," said Captain Vane, after the first long silent gaze of joy and admiration. "I have no doubt of it whatever. And now we shall proceed, I hope without interruption, to the Pole!"

"Of course you do not intend that we should swim there, do you, uncle?" said Leo.

"Of course not, my boy. In those big cases, which have cost us so much labour to bring here, I have three large and stout india-rubber boats—"

"Ha! I guessed as much," exclaimed Alf.

"No doubt," returned the Captain, "but you did not guess all."

"I hope not," said Leo, "for to say truth I don't much relish the idea of rowing over an unknown sea an unknown distance at the rate of three or four miles an hour. I hope you have a patent steam-engine that will drive us along somewhat faster."

"No, lad, no, I have no such steam-engine or any other miraculous contrivance that sets the laws of nature at defiance, and appears only in nursery tales. This expedition has been undertaken on no haphazard or insane plan. It was all cut and dry before we left Old England, and it is much simpler than you suppose."

"What, then, is to be your motive power, if not oars or sails—which last would not work well, I fear, in an india-rubber boat?" asked Leo.

"Kites," replied the Captain.

"Kites!" repeated both Alf and Leo in surprise.

"Not paper ones, surely," said Benjy, in a tone of disappointment, not unmingled with contempt.

"No, Ben, not paper ones," said the Captain, "but you shall see. Let the boxes be unlashed and carried into yonder cave. I'll unpack them presently. Meanwhile, Anders, I want you to interpret for me. Go, tell Chingatok I wish to have a talk with him."

While the brothers went to obey their leader's order, and Benjy to superintend the pitching of the camp, Captain Vane walked along the shore with Anders and the giant.

"Are you sure, Chingatok, that there is no more ice in this sea?" asked the Captain.

"No more great packs; only a little here and there, and a few ice-mountains." answered the Eskimo.

"And no more islands?"

"No more islands till you come to the land where I and my people dwell. There are more islands beyond that with people on them—people who are not friendly to us."

"How far off, now, is your land from this island?" continued the Captain, with a grave nod to Leo, who joined them at the moment.

"About three days with a kayak."

The Captain pondered for a few minutes.

"Leo," he said, "the observation which I took yesterday enables me to place this island in latitude 86° 40 minutes. I judge that a kayak may travel at the rate of three miles an hour, which, making allowance for sleep and rests, gives the distance of this island from Chingatok's native land approximately at about 100 miles, so that the home of this giant and his tribe is actually in the near neighbourhood of the Pole itself. If this be so, we may consider that our success, wind, weather, etcetera, permitting, is absolutely certain."

The Captain spoke in the deep earnest tones of one under the influence of powerful but suppressed enthusiasm.

"Now then, Leo," he continued, "we will go and take formal possession of this new discovery. What shall we call it? Good Hope is too familiar as a cape."

"Why not Great Hope?" asked Leo.

"Good! That will do well."

So Captain Vane took possession of Great Hope Island; having fixed its position in latitude 86° 40 minutes north, and longitude 60° west.

After that he proceeded to open the cases which had so long been objects of interest to his own party, and objects of intense curiosity to the Eskimos, who crowded round the entrance of the shallow cavern with eager looks, while their leader went to work with hammer and chisel on the copper fastenings.

"Wugh! Huk! hi! hosh! ho!" were something like the exclamations uttered by the Eskimos when the lid of the first case flew up and revealed only a mass of brown paper wrappings.

It was interesting to observe the utter self-oblivion of these children of nature! Of course the eyes and mouths of all opened wider and wider while the work went on. We can understand this, for it is characteristic of the simple in all nations, but it was not so easy to understand why shoulders should slowly rise and elbows be slightly bent, and the ten fingers gradually expand like claws. Anxiety might account for the way in which some of them softly lifted one foot and then the other; but why did little Oblooria raise her left foot by imperceptible degrees, and remain poised upon the other as if she were a bird, except on the supposition that she was unconsciously imitating Tekkona, who was doing the same thing?

It was interesting, also, to note the slight substratum of consciousness that displayed itself in Oolichuk, who, while regarding the Captain in glaring expectancy, put his arm, inadvertently as it were, round Oblooria's waist—also the complete absence of consciousness in the latter, who was so engrossed with the Captain, that she did not appear to feel the touch of Oolichuk! These little peculiarities, however, although extremely interesting, were not observed by any of the actors on that occasion—except, perhaps, by Benjy, who, being sharp-witted, had a knack of seeing round a corner at times!

When the contents of the case were turned out, they proved to consist of several coils of rope, and a large square bundle. The uncording of the latter intensified the expectation of the Eskimo to boiling point, and when the brown paper was removed, and a roll of something with a strange, not to say bad, smell was displayed, they boiled over in a series of exclamations to which the former "huks" and "hos" were mere child's play. But when the roll was unrolled, and assumed a flat shape not unlike the skin of a huge walrus, they gave a shout. Then, when the Captain, opening a smaller package, displayed a pair of bellows like a concertina, they gave a gasp. When he applied these to a hole in the flat object, and caused it slowly to swell, they uttered a roar, and when, finally, they saw the flat thing transformed into a goodly-sized boat, they absolutely squealed with delight, and began to caper about in childlike joy.

In this manner, three cases were opened, and three boats produced. Then the Magician, who went about his work in perfect silence, with a knowing smile on his lips, opened several longish boxes, which Leo had guessed to be filled with fishing-rods or spare rifles, but which, it turned out, contained oars for the india-rubber boats. After that, the Captain opened another large case, which roused the surprise of his white followers as much as that of the natives.

"It looks like one of mother's silk dresses," remarked Benjy, as the new wonder was dragged forth.

"Too voluminous for that," said Alf.

"A balloon!" exclaimed Leo.

"No, boys, it's only a kite," said the Captain, unfolding it. "I confess it does not look very like one, but its appearance will change by and by."

And its appearance did change remarkably as it was opened out and put together.

The construction of this kite was peculiar. In the first place, it was square in form, or, rather, diamond-shaped, and its size, when fully distended, was eighteen feet by fourteen.

"The simplicity of it, you see," said the Captain, as he put it together, "is its great recommendation."

He ceased to speak for a few moments, while engaged with a troublesome joint, and Benjy took advantage of the pause to express a hope that simplicity was not its *greatest* recommendation, because he had never heard of any one attempting to reach the Pole on the strength of simplicity.

Without noticing this remark, the Captain went on—

"You see it would be troublesome to carry distending sticks of great length, because they would be in the way, and apt to get broken. Each stick, therefore, has a joint in the middle like that of a fishing-rod. There are four such sticks, fastened to, or radiating from, a strong steel central hinge, so that they can be folded together, or opened out into the form of a cross. A small but very strong cross of bamboo fits on the machine, behind the central hinge, and locks it in a distended position, after the silk has been placed on it. Strong cords run round the outer edges of the silk, and there are loops at the corners to attach it to the distenders. Thus, you see, the kite can be put up, or folded into a portable form like an umbrella, though not of course as quickly, nor yet as easily, owing to its great size."

While he was speaking, the Captain was busily putting the several parts of the kite together.

As he concluded, he laid the machine on its face, locked it with the little bamboo cross, and then held it up in triumph, to the delight of his white observers, and the blank astonishment of the Eskimos. We say blank, because, unlike the boat, the nature of which they understood before it had been quite inflated, this machine was to them an absolute mystery, and seemed to be of no use at all.

Their opinion of it was not improved when a sudden puff of wind blew it flat on the ground, causing the Captain to fall on the top of it.

"It's a little awkward in handling," he growled, unlocking the centre-cross. "Hold the points down, lads, till I drag it into the umbrella form. There; it's all safe now. The truth is, unmanageableness when in hand is the only fault of my kite. Once in the air, it's as tractable as a lamb; getting it up is the chief difficulty, but that is not too great to be overcome."

"Besides, you know, nothing's perfect in this world, father," said Benjy, with a wink at Butterface, who, having acute risible tendencies, exploded. Some of the Eskimos, whose sympathies were strong, joined in the laugh by way of relief to their feelings.

When the Captain had wound a strap round the closed kite, to restrain its volatile nature, he opened another large case which contained several reels of strong cord, somewhat resembling log-lines, but with this peculiarity, that, alongside of each thick cord there ran a thin red line of twine, connected with though not bound to the other by means of little loops or rings of twine fixed about six feet apart throughout its entire length.

"These are the cords to fly the kites," said the Captain, taking up one of the reels, which was as large as a man's hat. "You see I have three sets of silk in that box, and six sets of reels and sticks, besides a few spare pieces of the latter, so that we can afford to suffer a little damage. Now, the use of this peculiar sort of double line will be clear when in action, but I may as well explain it. The end of this stout line is to be made fast to the band which you saw on the kite, and the end of this thin red line to the top of its upright stick. You remember well enough how independent ordinary kites are. You cannot cause them to descend except by hauling them in by main force, and you cannot moderate their pull. This kite of mine is capable of exerting a pull equal to six horses, with a sufficiently strong wind. So, you see, it would be impossible for a dozen men to hold it without some check on its power. This check is supplied by the thin red line, which is made of the strongest silk. By pulling it gently you bend the head of the kite forward, so that it ceases to present a flat surface to the wind, which flies off it more or less at the tail. By pulling still more on the red line, the traction-power is still further reduced, and, with a good pull, the kite can be made to present its head altogether to the wind, and thus to lie flat on it, when, of course, it will descend slowly to the ground, waving from side to side, like a dropped sheet of paper."

"Are you going to try it, father?" asked Benjy eagerly.

The Captain looked up at the clouds with a critical glance. "There's hardly enough of wind to-day, boy. Nevertheless we will try."

In a very short time the kite was again extended,

the centre locked, the thick cord fixed to a loop in the band, and the thin cord to the head of the main stick. While this was being done, the corners were held down by Leo, Benjy, Anders, and Butterface.

"How about a tail, father?" asked Benjy, with sudden animation.

"Ha! I forgot the tail. I've got several tails. It's well you reminded me."

"It is indeed," responded the boy, "for I remember well that when my kites lost their tails they used to whirl wildly about until they dashed their heads on the ground. This kite would be little better than a mad elephant without its tail!"

A short tail, made of the strongest cat-gut, was now fixed to the lower extremity of the kite. It had a bag at the end, to be weighted with stones as required.

"Now, then, Alf, do you carry the reel away fifty yards or so, and pay out the line as you go. Make a dozen of the Eskimos hold on with you till I come and regulate the pull. I must remain here to set it off."

Alf did as he was ordered. When he was far enough out, the Captain and Leo raised the aerial monster with caution, grasping it by the shoulders, while Benjy held on to the tail. Their great care was to keep it flat, so that it presented nothing but its thin head to the wind, but this was a difficulty, for it kept fluttering as if anxious to get away, catching a slant of wind underneath now and then, which caused both Leo and the Captain to stagger.

"Don't hold down the tail, Benjy," cried the Captain, looking anxiously over his shoulder.

Unfortunately Ben did not hear the "don't." Not only did he hold on with increased vigour, but he gave the tail an energetic pull downwards. The result was that the wind got fairly underneath, and the head was jerked upward. Leo, fearing to tear the silk, let go, and the Captain was thrown violently off. Benjy alone stood to his guns—or to his tail—with loyal heroism for a moment, but when he felt himself lifted off the ground a few inches, a feeling of horror seized him. He let go, and came down with a whack.

Free at last, the huge kite shot upwards like a rocket, and a terrible howl from the Eskimo showed that all was not right at their end of the line. The truth was that none of them were impressed with the importance of the duty required of them. The sudden strain jerked the line out of the hands of some, and threw others to the ground, and Alf, who had for greater security taken a turn of the line round his right arm, was dragged forward at full racing speed. Indeed he was beginning to take those tremendous bounds called "giant strides," which were sure to terminate in his being dragged along the ground.

Captain Vane saw the danger, and was equal to the occasion. There was little time for thought or action. Another moment and Alf would be off the beach into the sea.

"Let go! Alf; let go!" cried Leo, in an agony of alarm.

"No, no! hold on!" shouted the Captain.

Poor Alf could not help holding on. The turns of the line round his arm held him fast.

Another moment, and he was abreast of the Captain

who sprang at him as he passed like a leopard on his prey and held on. But the pace was little checked with this additional weight. It was beyond the Captain's running powers, and both he and Alf would have been thrown violently to the ground had it not happened that they had reached the water, into which they plunged with a tremendous splash. They were dragged through it, however, only for a few seconds, for by that time the Captain had succeeded in getting hold of the red line and pulling it separately. The result was immediate and satisfactory. The head of the kite was thrown forward, acting somewhat as a sail does when a ship is thrown into the wind, and the two unfortunates came to an anchor in four feet of water.

"We must not let it into the water, Alf," gasped the Captain, clearing the water from his eyes.

"How can we prevent it?" spluttered Alf, shaking the wet hair off his face.

"Ease your fingers a bit. There; hold on." As he spoke the Captain gave a slight pull on the regulating line. The kite at once caught the wind and soared, giving the two operators an awful tug, which nearly overturned them again.

"Too much," growled the Captain. "You see it takes some experience to regulate the excitable thing properly. There, now, haul away for the shore."

By this time they were joined by Leo and Chingatok, who ran into the water and aided them in dragging the refractory machine ashore.

"That's a vigorous beginning, father," remarked Benjy as they came to land.

"It is, my boy. Go and fetch me dry clothes while we haul in the kite and make her snug."

"When do you mean to start?" asked Leo, as he coiled away the slack of the line on the reel.

"The first steady fair wind that blows from the south," answered the Captain, "but we must have one or two experimental trials of the kites and boats together, before we set out on the real voyage."

"It's a capital idea," returned Leo enthusiastically. "There's a sort of neck-or-nothing dash about it that quite suits me. But, uncle, what of the Eskimos? The three boats won't carry the half of them."

"I know that, lad, and shall get over the difficulty by leaving some of them behind. Chingatok says they are quite able to take care of themselves; can easily regain the Greenland shore, find their canoes, or make new ones, and return to their own land if they choose."

"But, uncle," said Alf, who was by no means as reckless as his brother, "don't you think it's rather risky to go off into an unknown sea in open boats, for no one knows how long, to go no one knows exactly where?"

"Why, Alf," returned the Captain with a laugh, "if you were as stupid about your scientific pursuits as you are about geographical affairs, you would not be worth your salt. A sea's a sea, isn't it, whether known or unknown, and the laws that affect all seas are pretty much alike. Of course it is risky. So is going on a forlorn hope. So is shooting with a set of fellows who don't know how to manage their guns. So is getting on a horse, for it may kick you off or run away. So is eating fish, for you may choke yourself. Everything, almost, is more or less risky. You *must* risk something if you'd discover the North Pole, which has baffled adventurers from the days of Adam till now. And you are wrong in saying that we shall go off for no one knows how long. The distance from this island to the Pole is pretty nearly 200 miles. If our kites carry us along at the rate of ten miles an hour, we shall cover the distance in 20 hours. If we have calms or contrary winds we may take 20 days. If storms come, we have not much to fear, for the weather is warm,—so, too,—is the water. Then, our boats are lifeboats—they cannot sink. As to not knowing where exactly we are going, why, man, we're going to the North Pole. Everybody knows where that is, and we are going to the home of Chingatok, which cannot be very far from it."

"There, Alf, I hope you are sufficiently answered," said Leo, as he undid the locking-gear of the kite, which by that time lay prone on its face, as peaceful as a lamb.

The next three days were spent in flying the other kites, tying them on the boats, acquiring experience, and making preparations for the voyage. It was found that, with a moderate breeze, the kites towed the boats at the rate of ten miles an hour, which was beyond the most sanguine hopes of the Captain. Of course they could not beat to windward with them, but they could sail with a considerable slant, and they prevented the boats, while thus advancing, from making much leeway by means of deep *leeboards*, such as are used even at the present day by Dutch ships.

"But I can't understand," said Benjy, after several trials had been made, "why you should not have fitted sails to the boats, instead of kites."

"Because a sail only a quarter the size of a kite would upset the boat," said the Captain, "and one small enough to suit it would be little better than a pair of oars. This kite system is like fitting a gigantic sail to a lilliputian boat, d'ye see?"

"I see, father. But I wish it had been a balloon. It would have been greater fun to have gone to the Pole in a balloon!"

"A balloon will never go there, nor anywhere else, Benjy, except where the wind carries it, for a balloon cannot be steered. It's impossible in the nature of things—as much so as that dream of the visionary, perpetual motion."

On the fourth day after their arrival at Great Hope Island the wind blew strong and steady from the south, and the explorers prepared to start. The Eskimos had been told that they were to remain behind and shift for themselves—a piece of news which did not seem to affect them at all, one way or other. Those who were selected to go with the explorers were perfectly willing to do so. Chingatok, of course, was particularly ready. So were his corpulent mother and Tekkona and Oblooria; so also were Oolichuk, Ivitchuk, and Akeetolik.

It was a splendid sunny afternoon when the kites were finally flown and attached to the three boats which were commanded respectively by the Captain Leo, and Alf. These three sat at the bow of each boat manipulating the regulators, and keeping the kites fluttering, while the goods and provisions were put on board. Then the Eskimo women and crews stepped in, and the stern ropes were cast loose.

"Let go the check-strings!" shouted the Captain.

This was done. The huge kites began to strain at once, and the india-rubber boats went rushing out to sea, leaving the remainder of the Eskimo band speechless on the shore. They stood there motionless, with open mouths and eyes, the very embodiment of unbelieving wonder, till the boats had disappeared on the horizon.

Chapter XII

THE OPEN POLAR BASIN AT LAST!
ALF WASHES HIMSELF IN IT.

Who can imagine or describe the feelings of Captain Vane and his young relatives on finding themselves sweeping at such a magnificent rate over the great Polar basin?—that mysterious sea, which some believe to be a sea of thick-ribbed ice, and others suppose to be no sea at all, but dry land covered with eternal snows. One theorist even goes the length of saying that the region immediately around the Pole is absolutely nothing at all!—only empty space caused by the whirling of the earth,—a space which extends through its centre from pole to pole!

Much amusement did the Captain derive from the contemplation of these theories as he crossed over the grand and boundless ocean, and chatted pleasantly with his son, or Chingatok, or Toolooha, who formed the crew of his little boat.

The party consisted of thirteen, all told. These were distributed as follows:—

In the Captain's boat were the three just mentioned.

In Leo's boat were Butterface, Oolichuk, and Oblooria. How it came to pass that Oolichuk and Oblooria were put into the same boat no one seemed to know, or indeed to care, except Oolichuk himself, who, to judge from the expression of his fat face, was much pleased. As for Oblooria, her mild visage always betokened contentment or resignation—save when overshadowed by timidity.

In Alf's boat were Anders, Ivitchuk, Akeetolik, and Tekkona. The interpreter had been given to Alf because he was not quite so muscular or energetic as the Captain or his brother, while Anders was eminently strong and practical. The Eskimo women counted as men, being as expert with oar and paddle as they, and very nearly as strong as most ordinary men.

What added to the romance of the first day's experience was the fact that, a few hours after they started, a dead calm settled down over the sea, which soon became like a great sheet of undulating glass, in which the rich, white clouds, the clear sky, and the boats with their crews, were reflected as in a moving, oily mirror; yet, strange to say, the kites kept steady, and the pace of ten or twelve miles an hour did not abate for a considerable time. This, of course, was owing to the fact that there was a continuous current blowing northward in the higher regions of the atmosphere. The sun, meantime, glowed overhead with four

VOYAGING ON THE OPEN POLAR SEA—Page 166

mock-suns around him, nevertheless the heat was not oppressive, partly because the voyagers were sitting at rest, and partly because a slight current of cool air, the creation of their own progress, fanned their cheeks. Still further to add to the charm, flocks of sea-birds circling in the air or dipping in the water, a berg or two floating in the distance, a porpoise showing its back fin now and then, a seal or a walrus coming up to stare in surprise and going down to meditate, perhaps in wonder, with an occasional puff from a lazy whale,— all this tended to prevent monotony, and gave life to the lovely scene.

"Is it not the most glorious and altogether astonishing state of things you ever heard or dreamed of, father?" asked Benjy, breaking a prolonged silence.

"Out o' sight, my boy, out o' sight," replied the Captain. "Never heard nor saw nor dreamed of anything like it before."

"P'raps it *is* a dream!" said Benjy, with a slightly distressed look. "How are we ever to know that we're *not* dreaming?"

The boy finished his question with a sharp cry and leaped up.

"Steady, boy, steady! Have a care, or you'll upset the boat," said the Captain.

"What did you do *that* for, father?"

"What, my boy?"

"Pinch me so hard! Surely you didn't do it on purpose?"

"Indeed I did, Ben," replied the Captain with a laugh. "You asked how you were to know you were not dreaming. If you had been dreaming that would have wakened you—wouldn't it?"

"I dare say it would, father," returned the boy, resuming his seat, "but I'm convinced now. Don't do it again, please. I wish I knew what Chingatok thinks of it. Try to ask him, father. I'm sure you've had considerable experience in his lingo by this time."

Benjy referred here, not only to the numerous conversations which his father had of late carried on with the giant through the interpreter, but to the fact that, having been a whaler in years past, Captain Vane had previously picked up a smattering of various Eskimo dialects. Up to that day he had conversed entirely through the medium of Anders, but as that useful man was now in Alf's boat, the Captain was left to his own resources, and got on much better than he had expected.

Chingatok turned his eyes from the horizon on which they had been fixed, and looked dreamily at the Captain when asked what he was thinking about.

"I have been thinking," said he, "of home, _my_ home over there." He lifted his huge right arm and pointed to the north. "And I have been thinking," he continued, "that there must be another home up there." He raised his hand and pointed to the sky.

"Why do you think so?" asked the Captain in some surprise.

"Because it is so beautiful, so wonderful, so full of light and peace," replied the Eskimo. "Sometimes the clouds, and the wind, and the rain, come and cover it; but they pass away, and there it is, just the same, always calm, and bright, and beautiful. Could such a place have been made for nothing? Is there no one up there? not even the Maker of it? and if there is, does he stay there alone? Men and women die, but surely there is something in us that does not die. If there is no spirit in us that lives, of what use was it to make us at all? I think we shall have a home up there."

Chingatok had again turned his eyes to the horizon, and spoke the concluding words as if he were thinking aloud. The Captain looked at him earnestly for some time in silence.

"You are right, Chingatok," he said at length, or at least attempted to say as best he could—"you are right. My religion teaches me that we have spirits; that God—your God and mine—dwells up there in what we call heaven, and that His people shall dwell with him after death."

"His people!" repeated the Eskimo with a perplexed look. "Are some men his people and some not?"

"Undoubtedly," replied the Captain, "men who obey a chief's commands are *his* men—his friends. Those who refuse to obey, and do every kind of wickedness, are *not* his friends, but his enemies. God has given us free-wills, and we may reject him—we may choose to be his enemies."

It must not be supposed that Captain Vane expressed himself thus clearly, but the above is the substance of what he attempted by many a strange and complicated sentence to convey. That he had made his meaning to some extent plain, was proved by Chingatok's reply.

"But I do not know God's commands; how then can I obey them?"

"You may not know them by book," replied the Captain promptly; "for you have no books, but there is such a thing as the commands or law of God written in the heart, and it strikes me, Chingatok, that you both know and obey more of your Maker's laws than many men who have His word."

To this the Eskimo made no answer, for he did not rightly understand it, and as the Captain found extreme difficulty in expressing his meaning on such questions, he was quite willing to drop the conversation. Nevertheless his respect for Chingatok was immensely increased from that day forward.

He tried to explain what had been said to Benjy, and as that youth's mind was of an inquiring turn he listened with great interest, but at last was forced to confess that it was too deep for him. Thereafter he fell into a mood of unusual silence, and pondered the matter for a long time.

Awaking from his reverie at last, he said, abruptly, "How's her head, father?"

"Due north, Benjy."

He pulled out a pocket-compass about the size of an ordinary watch, which instrument it was his habit to guard with the most anxious care.

"North!" repeated the boy, glancing at the instrument with a look of surprise, "why, we're steering almost due east!"

"Ah! Ben, that comes of your judging from appearances without knowledge, not an uncommon state of mind in man and boy, to say nothing of woman. Don't you know what variation of the compass is?"

"No, father."

"What! have you been so long at sea with me and never heard yet about the magnetic pole?"

"Never a word, father. It seems to me that poles are multiplying as we get further north."

"Oh, Benjy, for shame—fie! fie!"

"Maybe if you had told me about it I might have had less to be shamed of, and you too, father."

"That's true, Benjy. That's true. You're a sharp boy for your age. But don't be disrespectful to your father, Ben; no good can ever come o' that. Whatever you are, be respectful to your old father. Come, I'll tell you about it now."

It will have been observed by this time that little Benjamin Vane was somewhat free in his converse with his father, but it must not therefore be supposed that he was really insolent. All his freedom of speech was vented in good humour, and the Captain knew that. There was, indeed, a powerful bond not only of affection but of sympathy between the little delicate boy and the big strong man. They thoroughly understood each other, and between those who understand each other there may be much freedom without offence, as everybody knows.

"You must understand," began the Captain, "that although the needle of the mariner's compass is said to point to the north with its head and to the south with its tail, it does not do so exactly, because the magnetic poles do not coincide exactly with the geographical poles. There are two magnetic poles just as there are two geographical poles, one in the southern hemisphere, the other in the northern. D'ye understand?"

"Clear as daylight, father."

"Well, Benjy, the famous Arctic discoverer, Sir James Ross, in 1832, discovered that the northern magnetic pole was situated in the island of Boothia Felix, in latitude 70° 5 seconds and longitude 96° 46 seconds West. It was discovered by means of an instrument called the dipping needle, which is just a magnetised needle made for dipping perpendicularly instead of going round horizontally like the mariner's compass. A graduated arc is fitted to it so that the amount of dip at any place on the earth's surface can be ascertained. At the magnetic equator there is no dip at all, because the needle, being equally distant from the north and south magnetic poles, remains horizontal. As you travel north the needle dips more and more until it reaches the region of the north magnetic pole when it is almost perpendicular—pointing straight down.

"Now, it is only on a very few places of the earth's surface that the horizontal needle points to the true north and south, and its deviation from the *earth's* pole in its determination to point to the *magnetic* pole is called the variation of the compass. This variation is greater or less of course at different places, and must be allowed for in estimating one's exact course. In our present explorations we have got so far beyond the beaten track of travel that greater allowance than usual has to be made. In fact we have got considerably to the north of the magnetic pole. At the same time we are a good way to the east'ard of it, so that when I see the compass with its letter N pointing to what I know to be the magnetic north, I take our geographical position into account and steer almost due east by *compass*, for the purpose of advancing due north. D'ye see?"

"I'm not so sure that I do, father. It seems to me something like the Irishman's pig which you pull one way when you want him to go another. However, I'll take your word for it."

"That's right, my boy; when a man can't understand, he must act on faith, if he *can*, for there's no forcing our beliefs, you know. Anyhow he must be content to follow till he does understand; always supposing that he can trust his leader."

"I'm out of my depths altogether now, father. P'r'aps we'd better change the subject. What d'ye say to try a race with Leo? His boat seems to be overhauling us."

"No, no, Ben; no racing. Let us advance into the great unknown north with suitable solemnity."

"We appear to sail rather better than you do, uncle," shouted Leo, as his boat drew near.

"That's because you're not so heavily-laden," replied the Captain, looking back; "you haven't got giants aboard, you see; moreover there's one o' you rather light-headed."

"Hallo! uncle; evil communications, eh? You'd better change Benjy for Oblooria. She's quite quiet, and never jokes. I say, may I go ahead of you?"

"No, lad, you mayn't. Take a reef in your regulator, and drop into your proper place."

Obedient to orders, Leo pulled the regulator or check-string until the kite's position was altered so as to present less resistance to the wind, and dropped astern of the *Faith*, which was the name given by Benjy to his father's boat, the other two being named respectively the *Hope* and the *Charity*.

The prosperous advance did not, however, last very long. Towards evening the three kites suddenly, and without any previous warning, began to dive, soar, flutter, and tumble about in a manner that would have been highly diverting if it had not been dangerous. This no doubt was the effect of various counter-currents of air into which they had flown. The order was at once given to haul on the regulators and coil up the towing lines. It was promptly obeyed, but before a few fathoms had been coiled in, the kites again became as steady as before, with this change, however, that they travelled in a north-westerly direction.

The value of the leeboards now became apparent.

These were hinged down the middle so as to fold and become small enough to stow in the bottom of each boat when not in use. When unfolded and hung over the side, they presented a surface of resistance to the water much greater than that of an ordinary boat's keel, so that very little leeway indeed was made. By means of the steering-oar Captain Vane kept his boat advancing straight northward, while the kite was puffing in a north-westerly direction. The kite was thus compelled by the boat also to travel due north, though of course it did so in a sidelong manner.

Thus far the advance continued prosperously, the pace being but little checked and the course unaltered, but when, an hour or two later, the wind again shifted so as to carry the kites further to the west, the pace became much slower, and the leeway, or drift to leeward, considerable. Ultimately the wind blew straight to the west, and the boats ceased to advance. "This won't do, uncle," said Leo, who was close astern of the *Faith*, "I'm drifting bodily to leeward, and making no headway at all."

"Down with the tops,—I mean, the kites," shouted the Captain. "Pass the word to Alf."

Accordingly, the kites were reeled in, the regulators being so pulled and eased off that they were kept just fluttering without tugging during the operation. When, however, they passed out of the wind-stratum into the region of calm which still prevailed immediately above the sea, the kites descended in an alarming manner, swaying to and fro with occasional wild swoops, which rendered it necessary to haul in on the lines and reel up with the utmost speed.

Captain Vane was very successful in this rather difficult operation. While he hauled in the line Benjy reeled it up with exemplary speed, and the kite was finally made to descend on the boat like a cloud. When secured the locking-cross was removed, the distending-rods were folded inwards, the restraining, or what we may term the waist-band was applied, and the whole affair was changed into a gigantic Mrs. Gamp umbrella. Being placed in the bow of the boat, projecting over the water, it formed a not ungraceful though peculiar bowsprit, and was well out of the way.

Leo and Butterface were equally successful, but poor Alf was not so fortunate. The too eager pursuit of knowledge was the cause of Alf's failure as has often been the case with others! He took on himself, as chief of his boat, the difficult and responsible task of hauling in the line,—which involved also the occasional and judicious manipulation of the regulating cord, when a sudden puff of wind should tend to send the kite soaring upwards with six or eight horse-power into the sky. To Ivitchuk was assigned the easy task of gathering in the "slack" and holding on to Alf if a sudden jerk should threaten to pull him overboard. Anders reeled up.

Just as the kite was passing out of the windy region above into the calm region below Alf beheld floating near the boat a beautiful, and to him entirely new, species of marine creature of the jelly-fish kind. With a wild desire to possess it he leaned over the boat's edge to the uttermost and stretched out his left hand, while with his right he held on to the kite! Need we say that the kite assisted him?—assisted him overboard altogether, and sent him with a heavy plunge into the sea!

Ivitchuk dropped his line and stretched out both arms towards the spot where the "Kablunet" had gone down. Akeetolik roared. Anders howled, and dropped his reel. Left to itself, the kite, with characteristic indecision, made an awful swoop towards the North Pole with its right shoulder. Changing its mind, it then made a stupendous rush with its left to the south-east. Losing presence of mind it suddenly tossed up its tail, and, coming down head foremost, went with fatal facility into the deep sea.

When Alf rose and was dragged panting into the boat, his first glance was upwards,—but not in thankfulness for his preservation!

"Gone!" he groaned, rising to his feet.

But the kite was not gone. The word had barely left his lips when it rose half its length out of the water, and then fell, in melancholy inaptitude for further mischief, flat upon the sea.

"Anything damaged?" asked the Captain, as he and Leo rowed their boats towards the *Charity*.

"Nothing," replied Alf with a guilty look, "the stick and things seem to be all right, but it has got *awfully* wet."

"No matter," said the Captain, laughing at Alf's forlorn look, "the sun will soon dry it. So long as nothing is broken or torn, we'll get on very well. But now, boys, we must go to work with oars. There must be no flagging in this dash for the Pole. It's a neck-or-nothing business. Now, mark my orders. Although we've got four oars apiece, we must only work two at a time. I know that young bloods like you are prone to go straining yourselves at first, an' then bein' fit for nothing afterwards. We must keep it up steadily. Two in each boat will pull at a time for one hour, while the other two rest or sleep, and so on, shift about; till another breeze springs up. Don't fold it up tight, Alf. Leave it pretty slack till it is dry, and then put on its belt."

"Don't you think we might have supper before taking to the oars?" suggested Leo.

"I second that motion," cried Benjy.

"And I support it," said Alf.

"Very good, get out the prog; an' we'll lay ourselves alongside, three abreast, as Nelson did at the Battle o' the Nile," said the Captain.

Their food was simple but sufficient. Pemmican— a solid greasy nutricious compound—was the foundation. Hard biscuit, chocolate, and sugar formed the superstructure. In default of fire, these articles could be eaten cold, but while their supply of spirits of wine lasted, a patent Vesuvian of the most complete and almost miraculous nature could provide a hot meal in ten minutes. Of fresh water they had a two-weeks' supply in casks, but this was economised by means of excellent water procured from a pond in a passing berg—from which also a lump of clear ice had been hewn, wrapped in a blanket, and carried into the Captain's boat as a supply of fresh water in solid form.

Laying the oars across the boats to keep them together, they floated thus pleasantly on the glassy sea, bathed in midnight sunshine. And while they feasted in comfort inexpressible—to the surprise, no doubt, of surrounding gulls and puffins—Benjamin Vane once again gave utterance to the opinion that it was the most glorious and altogether astonishing state of things that he had ever heard or dreamed of since the world began!

Chapter XIII

A GALE AND A NARROW ESCAPE.

This is a world of alternations. We need not turn aside to prove that. The calm with which the voyage of our discoverers began lasted about four days and nights, during which period they advanced sometimes slowly under oars, sometimes more or less rapidly under kites—if we may so express it—according to the state of the wind.

And, during all that time the discipline of two and two—at watch, or at sleep, if not at work—was rigidly kept up. For none knew better than Captain Vane the benefit of discipline, and the demoralising effect of its absence, especially in trying circumstances. It is but just to add that he had no difficulty in enforcing his laws. It is right also to state that the women were not required to conform, even although they were accustomed to hard labour and willing to work as much as required.

In all three boats the bow was set apart as the women's quarters, and when Toolooha, Oblooria or Tekkona showed symptoms of a desire to go to sleep—(there was no retiring for the night in these latitudes)—a blanket stretched on two oars cut their quarters off from those of the men, and maintained the dignity of the sex.

But soon the serene aspect of nature changed. Grey clouds overspread the hitherto sunny sky. Gusts of wind came sweeping over the sea from time to time, and signs of coming storm became so evident that the Captain gave orders to make all snug and prepare for dirty weather.

"You see, lads," he said, when the three boats were abreast, and the kites had been furled, "we don't know what may happen to us now. Nobody in the world has had any experience of these latitudes. It may come on to blow twenty-ton Armstrongs instead of great guns, for all we know to the contrary. The lightning may be sheet and fork mixed instead of separate for any light we've got on the subject, and it may rain whales and walruses instead of cats and dogs; so it behoves us to be ready."

"That's true, father," said Benjy, "but it matters little to me, for I've made my will. Only I forgot to leave the top with the broken peg and the rusty penknife to Rumty Swillpipe; so if you survive me and get home on a whale's back—or otherwise—you'll know what to do."

"This is not a time for jesting, Ben," said Alf rather seriously.

"Did I say it was?" inquired Ben, with a surprised look.

Alf deigned no reply, and Butterface laughed, while he and the others set about executing the Captain's orders.

The arrangements made in these india-rubber boats for bad weather were very simple and complete. After the lading in each had been snugly arranged, so as to present as flat a surface on the top as possible, a waterproof sheet was drawn over all, and its edges made fast to the sides of the boat, by means of tags and loops which were easily fastened and detached. As each sheet overhung its boat, any water that might fall upon it was at once run off. This, of course, was merely put on to protect the cargo and any one who chose to take shelter under it. The boat being filled with air required no such sheet, because if filled to overflowing it would still have floated. All round this sheet ran a strong cord for the crew, who sat outside of it as on a raft, to lay hold of if the waves should threaten to wash them off. There were also various other ropes attached to it for the same purpose, and loops of rope served for rowlocks.

When all had been arranged, those whose duty it was to rest leaned comfortably against the lumps caused by inequalities of the cargo, while the others took to their oars.

"It's coming!" cried Benjy, about half-an-hour after all had been prepared.

And unquestionably it *was* coming. The boy's quick eyes had detected a line on the southern horizon, which became gradually broader and darker as it rose until it covered the heavens. At the same time the indigo ripple caused by a rushing mighty wind crept steadily over the sea. As it neared the boats the white crests of breaking waves were seen gleaming sharply in the midst of the dark blue.

"Clap the women under hatches," shouted the Captain, with more good sense than refinement.

Benjy, Butterface, and Anders at the word lifted a corner of their respective sheets. Obedient Toolooha, Oblooria, and Tekkona bent their meek heads and disappeared: The sheets were refastened, and the men, taking their places, held on to the cords or life-lines. It was an anxious moment. No one could guess how the boats would behave under the approaching trial.

"Oars out," cried the Captain, "we must run before it."

A hiss, which had been gradually increasing as the squall drew near, broke into a kind of roar, and wind and waves rushed upon them as the men bent their backs to the oars with all their might.

It was soon found that the boats had so little hold of the water that the wind and oars combined carried them forward so fast as to decrease considerably the danger of being whelmed by a falling wave. These waves increased every moment in size, and their crests were so broken and cut off by the gale that the three boats, instead of appearing as they had hitherto done the only solid objects in the scene, were almost lost to sight in the chaos of black waves and driving foam. Although they tried their best to keep close together they failed, and each soon became ignorant of the position of the others. The last that they saw of Alf's boat was in the hollow between two seas like a vanishing cormorant or a northern diver. Leo was visible some time longer. He was wielding the steering-oar in an attitude of vigorous caution, while his Eskimos were pulling as if for their lives. An enormous wave rose behind them, curled over their heads and appeared ready to overwhelm them, but the sturdy rowers sent the boat forward, and the broken crest passed under them. The next billow was still larger. Taken up though he was with his own boat the Captain found time to glance at them with horror.

"They're gone!" he cried, as the top of the billow fell, and nothing was seen save the heads of the four men like dark spots on the foam. The boat had in truth been overwhelmed and sunk, but, like a true lifeboat it rose to the surface like a cork the instant the weight of water was removed, and her crew, who had held on to the life-lines and oars, were still safe.

"Well done the little *Hope*!" cried the Captain, while Benjy gave vent to his feelings in a cheer, which was evidently heard by Leo, for he was seen to wave his hand in reply. Next moment another wave hid the *Hope* from view, and it was seen no more at that time.

"I feel easier now, Benjy, thank God, after *that*. Alf is a fair steersman, and our boats are evidently able to stand rough usage."

Benjy made no reply. He was rubbing the water out of his eyes, and anxiously looking through the thick air in the hope of seeing Leo's boat again. The poor boy was grave enough now. When the might and majesty of the Creator are manifested in the storm and the raging sea, the merely humorous fancies of man are apt to be held in check.

The Captain's boat went rushing thus wildly onwards, still, fortunately, in the right direction; and for some hours there was no decrease in the force of the gale. Then, instead of abating, as might have been expected, it suddenly increased to such an extent that speedy destruction appeared to be inevitable.

"No sort o' craft could live long in *this*," muttered the Captain, as if to himself rather than to his son, who sat with a firm expression on his somewhat pale countenance, looking wistfully towards the northern horizon. Perhaps he was wondering whether it was worth while to risk so much for such an end. Suddenly he shaded his eyes with his hand and gazed intently.

"Land!" he exclaimed in a low eager tone.

"Whereaway, boy? Ay, so there is something there. What say you, Chingatok? Is it land?"

The giant, who, during all this time, had calmly plied a pair of oars with strength equal almost to that of four men, looked over his shoulder without, however, relaxing his efforts.

"No," he said, turning round again, "it is an ice-hill."

"A berg!" exclaimed the Captain. "We will make for it. Tie your handkerchief, Benjy, to the end of an oar and hold it up. It will serve as a guide to our comrades."

In a wonderfully short space of time the berg which

Benjy had seen as a mere speck on the horizon rose sharp, rugged, and white against the black sky. It was a very large one—so large that it had no visible motion, but seemed as firm as a rock, while the billows of the Arctic Ocean broke in thunder on its glassy shore.

"We'll get shelter behind it, Ben, my boy," said the Captain, "hold the oar well up, and don't let the rag clap round the blade. Shake it out so. God grant that they may see it."

"Amen," ejaculated Benjy to the prayer with heartfelt intensity.

There was danger as well as safety in the near vicinity to this berg, for many of its pinnacles seemed ready to fall, and there was always the possibility of a mass being broken off under water, which might destroy the equilibrium of the whole berg, and cause it to revolve with awfully destructive power.

However, there was one favourable point—the base was broad, and the ice-cliffs that bordered the sea were not high.

In a few more minutes the western end of the berg was passed. Its last cape was rounded, and the *Faith* was swept by the united efforts of Chingatok, Benjy, and Toolooha, (who *would* not remain under cover), into the comparatively still water on the lee, or northern side of the berg.

"Hurrah!" shouted Benjy in a tone that was too energetic and peculiar to have been called forth by the mere fact of his own escape from danger.

Captain Vane looked in the direction indicated by the boy's glistening eyes—glistening with the salt tears of joy as well as with salt sea spray—and there beheld the other two boats coming dancing in like wild things on the crests of the heaving waves. They had seen the signal of the handkerchief, understood and followed it, and, in a few minutes more, were under the lee of the ice-cliffs, thanking God and congratulating each other on their deliverance.

A sheltered cove was soon found, far enough removed from cliffs and pinnacles to insure moderate safety. Into this they ran, and there they spent the night, serenaded by the roaring gale, and lullabied by the crash of falling spires and the groans of rending ice.

Chapter XIV

RECORDS A WONDERFUL APPARITION
BUT A FURIOUS NIGHT.

When the storm had passed, a profound calm once more settled down on the face of nature, as if the elements had been utterly exhausted by the conflict. Once more the sea became like a sheet of undulating glass, in which clouds and sun and boats were reflected vividly, and once again our voyagers found themselves advancing towards the north, abreast of each other, and rowing sociably together at the rate of about four miles an hour.

When advancing under oars they went thus abreast so as to converse freely, but when proceeding under kites they kept in single file, so as to give scope for swerving, in the event of sudden change of wind, and to prevent the risk of the entanglement of lines.

"What is that?" exclaimed Benjy, pointing suddenly to an object ahead which appeared at regular intervals on the surface of the water.

"A whale, I think," said Leo.

"A whale usually spouts on coming up, doesn't it?" said Alf.

Chingatok uttered an unpronounceable Eskimo word which did not throw light on the subject.

"What is it, Anders?" shouted the Captain.

"What you say?" asked the interpreter from Alf's boat, which was on the other side of the *Hope*.

"If these squawkin' things would hold their noise, you'd hear better," growled the Captain before repeating the question.

His uncourteous remark had reference to a cloud of gulls which circled round and followed the boats with remonstrative cries and astonished looks.

"It's beast," shouted Anders, "not knows his name in Ingliss."

"Humph! a man with half an eye might see it is 'beast,'" retorted the Captain in an undertone.

As he spoke, the "beast" changed its course and bore down upon them. As it drew near the Englishmen became excited, for the size of the creature seemed beyond anything they had yet seen. Strange to say, the Eskimos looked at it with their wonted gaze of calm indifference.

"It's the great sea-serpent at last," said Benjy, with something like awe on his countenance.

"It does look uncommon like it," replied the Captain, with a perplexed expression on his rugged visage. "Get out the rifles, lad! It's as well to be ready. D'ye know what it is, Chingatok?"

Again the giant uttered the unpronounceable name, while Benjy got out the fire-arms with eager haste.

"Load 'em all, Ben, load 'em all, an' cram the Winchester to the muzzle," said the Captain. "There's no sayin' what we may have to encounter; though I *have* heard of a gigantic bit of seaweed bein' mistaken for the great sea-serpent before now."

"That may be, father," said Benjy, with increasing excitement, "but nobody ever saw a bit of seaweed swim with the activity of a gigantic eel like *that*. Why, I have counted its coils as they rise and sink, and I'm quite sure it's a hundred and fifty yards long if it's an inch."

Those in the other boats were following the Captain's example,—getting out and charging the fire-arms,—and truly there seemed some ground for their alarm, for the creature, which approached at a rapid rate, appeared most formidable. Yet, strange to say, the Eskimos paid little attention to it, and seemed more taken up with the excitement of the white men.

When the creature had approached to within a quarter of a mile, it diverged a little to the left, and passed the boats at the distance of a few hundred yards. Then Captain Vane burst into a sudden laugh, and shouted:—

"Grampuses!"

"What?" cried Leo.

"Grampuses!" repeated the Captain. "Why, it's only a shoal of grampuses following each other in single file, that we've mistaken for one creature!"

Never before was man or boy smitten with heavier disappointment than was poor Benjy Vane on that trying occasion.

"Why, what's wrong with you, Benjy?" asked his father, as he looked at his woeful countenance.

"To think," said the poor boy, slowly, "that I've come all the way to the North Pole for *this*! Why I've believed in the great sea-serpent since ever I could think, I've seen pictures of it twisting its coils round three-masted ships, and goin' over the ocean with a mane like a lion, and its head fifty feet out o' the water! Oh! it's too bad, I'd have given my ears to have seen the great sea-serpent."

"There wouldn't have been much of you left, Benjy, if you had given *them*."

"Well, well," continued the boy, not noticing his father's remark, "it's some comfort to know that I've all *but* seen the great sea-serpent."

It is some comfort to us, reader, to be able to record the fact that Benjy Vane was not doomed to total disappointment on that memorable day, for, on the same evening, the voyagers had an encounter with walruses which more than made up for the previous misfortune.

It happened thus:—

The three boats were proceeding abreast, slowly but steadily over the still calm sea, when their attention was attracted by a sudden and tremendous splash or upheaval of water, just off what the Captain styled his "port bow." At the same moment the head of a walrus appeared on the surface like a gigantic black bladder. It seemed to be as large as the head of a small elephant, and its ivory tusks were not less than two feet long. There was a square bluntness about the creature's head, and a savage look about its little bloodshot eyes, which gave to it a very hideous aspect. Its bristling moustache, each hair of which was six inches long, and as thick as a crow quill, dripped with brine, and it raised itself high out of the water, turning its head from side to side with a rapidity and litheness of action that one would not have expected in an animal so unwieldy. Evidently it was looking eagerly for something.

Catching sight of the three boats, it seemed to have found what it looked for, and made straight at them. Leo quietly got ready his Winchester repeater, a rifle which, as the reader probably knows, can discharge a dozen or more shots in rapid succession; the cartridges being contained in a case resembling a thick ram-rod under the barrel, from which they are thrust almost instantaneously into their places.

But before the creature gained the boats, a second great upheaval of water took place, and another walrus appeared. This was the real enemy of whom he had been in quest. Both were bulls of the largest and most ferocious description. No sooner did they behold each other, than, with a roar, something betwixt a bark and a bellow, they collided, and a furious fight began. The sea was churned into foam around them as they rolled, reared, spurned, and drove their tusks into each other's skulls and shoulders.

The boats lay quietly by, their occupants looking on

with interest. The Eskimos were particularly excited, but no one spoke or acted. They all seemed fascinated by the fight.

Soon one and another and another walrus-head came up out of the sea, and then it was understood that a number of cow walruses had come to witness the combat! But the human audience paid little regard to these, so much were they engrossed by the chief actors.

It might have been thought, from the position of their tusks, which are simply an enlargement and prolongation of the canine teeth, that these combatants could only strike with them in a downward direction, but this was not so. On the contrary, they turned their thick necks with so much ease and rapidity that they could strike in all directions with equal force, and numerous were the wounds inflicted on either side, as the blood-red foam soon testified.

We have said that the human spectators of the scene remained inactive, but, at the first pause, the Captain said he thought they might as well put a stop to the fight, and advised Leo to give one of them a shot.

"We'll not be the worse for a fresh steak," he added to Benjy, as Leo was taking aim.

The effect of the shot was very unexpected. One of the bulls was hit, but evidently not in a deadly manner, for the motion of the boat had disturbed Leo's aim. Each combatant turned with a look of wild surprise at the interruptor, and, as not unfrequently happens in cases of interference with fights, both made a furious rush at him. At the same moment, all the cows seemed to be smitten with pugnacity, and joined in the attack. There was barely time to get ready, when the furious animals were upon them. Guns and rifles were pointed, axes and spears grasped, and oars gripped. Even the women seized each a spear, and stood on the defensive. A simultaneous volley checked the enemy for a moment, and sent one of the cows to the bottom; but with a furious bellow they charged again.

The great anxiety of the defenders was to prevent the monsters from getting close to the boats, so as to hook on to them with their tusks, which would probably have overturned them, or penetrated the inflated sides. In either case, destruction would have been inevitable, and it was only by the active use of oar, axe, and spear that this was prevented.

Twice did one of the bulls charge the Captain's boat, and on both occasions he was met by the tremendous might of Chingatok, who planted the end of an oar on his blunt nose, and thrust him off. On each occasion, also, he received a shot from the double barrel of Benjy, who fired the first time into his open mouth, and the second time into his eye, but an angry cough from the one, and a wink from the other showed that he did not mind it much. Meantime the Captain, with the Winchester repeater, was endeavouring—but vainly, owing to the motions of the giant, and the swaying of the boat—to get a shot at the beast, while Toolooha, with an axe, was coquetting with a somewhat timid cow near the stern.

At last an opportunity offered. Captain Vane poured half a dozen balls as quick as he could fire into the head of the bull, which immediately sank.

Not less vigorously did the occupants of the other boats receive the charge. Leo, being more active than the Captain, as well as more expert with his repeater, slew his male opponent in shorter time, and with less expenditure of ammunition. Butterface, too, gained much credit by the prompt manner in which he split the skull of one animal with an axe. Even Oblooria, the timid, rose to the occasion, and displayed unlooked-for heroism. With a barbed seal-spear she stood up and invited a baby walrus to come on—by looks, not by words. The baby accepted the invitation—perhaps, being a pugnacious baby, it was coming on at any rate—and Oblooria gave it a vigorous dab on the nose. It resented the insult by shaking its head fiercely, and endeavouring to back off, but the barb had sunk into the wound and held on. Oblooria also held on. Oolichuk, having just driven off a cow walrus, happened to observe the situation, and held on to Oblooria. The baby walrus was secured, and, almost as soon as the old bull was slain, had a line attached to it, and was made fast to the stern.

"Well done, little girl!" exclaimed Oolichuk in admiration, "you're almost as good as a man."

Among civilised people this might have been deemed a doubtful compliment, but it was not so in Eskimo-land. The little maid was evidently much pleased, and the title of the Timid One, which Oolichuk was wont to give her when in a specially endearing frame of mind, was changed for the Brave One from that day. In a few more minutes the last charge of the enemy was repulsed, and those of them that remained alive dived back to that native home into which the slain had already sunk.

Thus ended that notable fight with walruses.

After consummating the victory with three cheers and congratulating each other, the conquerors proceeded to examine into the extent of damage received. It was found that, beyond a few scratches, the *Faith* and the *Hope* had escaped scathless, but the *Charity* had suffered considerably. Besides a bad rip in the upper part of the gunwale, a small hole had been poked in her side below water, and her air-chamber was filling rapidly.

"Come here, quick, uncle," cried Alf, in consternation, when he discovered this.

To his surprise the Captain was not so much alarmed as he had expected.

"It won't sink you, Alf, so keep your mind easy," he said, while examining the injury. "You see I took care to have the boats made in compartments. It will only make you go lop-sided like a lame duck till I can repair the damage."

"Repair it, uncle! how can—"

"Never mind just now, hand out a blanket, quick; I'll explain after; we must undergird her and keep out as much water as we can."

This operation was soon accomplished. The blanket was passed under the boat and made fast. By pressing against the injured part it checked the inflow of water. Then the cargo was shifted, and part of it was transferred to the other boats, and soon they were advancing as pleasantly, though not as quickly as before, while the Captain explained that he had brought a solution of gutta-percha for the express purpose of repairing damages to the boats, but that it was impossible to use it until they could disembark either on land or on an iceberg.

"We'll come to another berg ere long, no doubt, shan't we, Chingatok?" he asked.

The Eskimo shook his head and said he thought not, but there was a small rocky islet not far from where they were, though it lay somewhat out of their course.

On hearing this the Captain changed his course immediately, and rowed in the direction pointed out.

"There's wind enough up there, Benjy," remarked his father, looking up to the sky, where the higher clouds were seen rapidly passing the lower strata to the northward, "but how to get the kites set up in a dead calm is more than I can tell."

"There is a way out of the difficulty, father," said Benjy, pointing behind them.

He referred to a slight breeze which was ruffling the sea into what are called cat's paws far astern.

"Right boy, right. Prepare to hoist your tops'ls, lads," shouted the Captain.

In a few minutes the kites were expanded and the tow-lines attached. When the light breeze came up they all soared, heavily, it is true, but majestically, into the sky. Soon reaching the upper regions, they caught the steady breeze there, and towed the boats along at the rate of eight or ten miles an hour.

In two hours they sighted the islet which Chingatok

had mentioned, and, soon afterwards, had landed and taken possession of it, in the usual manner, under the name of Refuge Island.

Chapter XV

The islet, or rock, for it was little more, which the explorers had reached, was low and extremely barren. Nevertheless it had on it a large colony of sea-fowl, which received the strangers with their wonted clamour of indignation—if not of welcome.

As it was near noon at the time, the Captain and Leo went with their sextants to the highest part of the island to ascertain its position; the Eskimos set about making an encampment, unloading the boats, etcetera, and Alf, with hammer and botanical box, set off on a short ramble along the coast, accompanied by Benjy and Butterface.

Sometimes these three kept together and chatted, at other times they separated a little, each attracted by some object of interest, or following the lead, it might have been, of wayward fancy. But they never lost sight of each other, and, after a couple of hours, converged, as if by tacit consent, until they met and sat down to rest on a ledge of rock.

"Well, I *do* like this sort o' thing," remarked Benjy, as he wiped his heated brow. "There is something to me so pleasant and peaceful about a low rocky shore with the sun blazing overhead and the great sea stretching out flat and white in a dead calm with just ripple enough to let you know it is all alive and hearty—only resting, like a good-humoured and sleepy giant."

"Why, Ben, I declare you are becoming poetical," said Alf with a smile; "your conceptions correspond with those of Buzzby, who writes:—

> "'Great Ocean, slumb'ring in majestic calm,
> Lies like a mighty—a mighty—'

"I—I fear I've forgotten. Let me see:—

> "'Great Ocean, slumb'ring in majestic calm,
> Lies like a mighty—'"

"Giant in a dwalm," suggested Benjy.

"We'll change the subject," said Alf, opening his botanical box and taking out several specimens of plants and rocks. "See, here are some bits of rock of a kind that are quite new to me."

"What's de use ob dem?" inquired Butterface with a look of earnest simplicity.

"The use?" said Benjy, taking on himself to reply; "why, you, don't you know that these bits of rock are made for the express purpose of being carried home, identified, classified, labelled, stuck up in a museum, and stared at by wondering ignoramuses, who care nothing whatever about them, and know less. Geologists are constantly going about the world with their little hammers keeping up the supply."

"Yes, Butterface," said Alf, "Benjy is partly correct; such specimens will be treated as he describes, and be stared at in blank stupidity by hundreds of fellows like himself, but they will also be examined and understood by geologists, who from their profound knowledge of the plans which our Creator seems to have had in arranging the materials of the earth, are able to point out many interesting and useful facts which are not visible to the naked and unscientific eye, such, for instance, as the localities where coal and other precious things may be found."

"Kin dey tell whar' gold is to be found, massa Alf?"

"O yes, they can tell that."

"Den it's dis yer chile as wishes," said Butterface with a sigh, "dat he was a jollygist."

"Oh! Butterface, you're a jolly goose at all events," said Benjy; "wouldn't it be fun to go and discover a gold mine, and dig up as much as would keep us in happy idleness all the rest of our lives? But I say, Alf, have you nothing better than geological specimens in your box—no grubological specimens, eh?"

Alf replied by producing from his box a paper parcel which contained some of the required specimens in the shape of biscuit and pemmican.

"Capital! Well, you are a good fellow, Alf. Let us make a table-cloth of the paper—now, you undisciplined black, don't glare so at the victuals, else you'll grow too hungry for a moderate supply."

When the trio were in the full swing of vigorous feeding, the negro paused, with his mouth full, to ask Alf what would be the use of the North Pole when it was discovered.

"Make matches or firewood of it," said Benjy just as he was about to stop up his impudent mouth with a lump of pemmican.

"Truly, of what use the Pole itself may be—supposing it to exist in the form of a thing," said Alf, "I cannot tell, but it has already been of great use in creating expeditions to the Polar regions. You know well enough, Butterface, for you've been round the Capes of Good Hope and Horn often enough, what a long long voyage it is to the eastern seas, on the other side of the world, and what a saving of time and expense it would be if we could find a shorter route to those regions, from which so many of our necessaries and luxuries come. Now, if we could only discover an open sea in the Arctic regions which would allow our ships to sail in a straight line from England across the North Pole to Behring's Straits, the voyage to the East would be reduced to only about 5000 miles, and we should be able to reach Japan in three or four weeks. Just think what an advantage that would be to commerce!"

"Tea at twopence a pound an' sugar to match—not to mention molasses and baccy, you ignorant negro!" said Benjy;—"pass the biscuits."

"An' now, massa Alf," said Butterface with an eager look, "we's diskivered dis open sea—eh!"

"Well, it seems as if we had."

"But what good will it do us," argued Benjy, becoming more earnest in the discussion, "if it's all surrounded by a ring of ice such as we have passed over on sledges."

"If," repeated Alf, "in that 'if' lies the whole question. No doubt Enterprise has fought heroically for centuries to overleap this supposed ring of ice, and science has stood expectant on the edge, looking eagerly for the day when human perseverance shall reveal the secrets of the Far North. It is true, also, that *we* at last appear to have penetrated into the great unknown, but who shall say that the so-called ice-ring has been fully examined? Our explorations have been hitherto confined to one or two parts of it. We may yet find an ever-open entrance to this open Polar sea, and our ships may yet be seen sailing regularly to and fro over the North Pole."

"Just so," said Benjy, "a North Pole steam line once a month to Japan and back—first class accommodation for second class fares. Walrus and white bear parties dropped on the way at the Pole Star Hotel, an easy trip from the Pole itself, which may be made in Eskimo cabs in summer and reindeer sleighs in winter. Return tickets available for six months—touching at China, India, Nova Zembla, Kamtschatka, and Iceland. Splendid view of Hecla and the great Mer de Glace of Greenland—fogs permitting.—Don't eat so much, Butterface, else bu'stin' will surely be your doom."

"Your picture is perhaps a little overdrawn, Ben," rejoined Alf with a smile.

"So would the ancients have said," retorted Benjy, "if

you had prophesied that in the nineteenth century our steamers would pass through the Straits of Hercules, up the Mediterranean, and over the land to India; or that our cousins' steam cars would go rattling across the great prairies of America, through the vast forests, over and under the Rocky Mountains from the States to California, in seven days; or that the telephone or electric light should ever come into being."

"Well, you see, Butterface," said Alf, "there is a great deal to be said in favour of Arctic exploration, even at the present day, and despite all the rebuffs that we have received. Sir Edward Sabine, one of the greatest Arctic authorities, says of the route from the Atlantic to the Pacific, that it is the greatest geographical achievement which can be attempted, and that it will be the crowning enterprise of those Arctic researches in which England has hitherto had the pre-eminence. Why, Butterface," continued Alf, warming with his subject, while the enthusiastic negro listened as it were with every feature of his expressive face, and even the volatile Benjy became attentive, "why, there is no telling what might be the advantages that would arise from systematic exploration of these unknown regions, which cover a space of not less than two million, five hundred thousand square miles. It would advance the science of hydrography, and help to solve some of the difficult problems connected with Equatorial and Polar currents. It would enable us, it is said, by a series of pendulum observations at or near the Pole, to render essential service to the science of geology, to form a mathematical theory of the physical condition of the earth, and to ascertain its exact conformation. It would probably throw light on the wonderful phenomena of magnetism and atmospheric electricity and the mysterious Aurora Borealis—to say nothing of the flora of these regions and the animal life on the land and in the sea."

"Why, Alf," exclaimed Benjy in surprise, "I had no idea you were so deeply learned on these subjects."

"Deeply learned!" echoed Alf with a laugh, "why, I have only a smattering of them. Just knowledge enough to enable me in some small degree to appreciate the vast amount of knowledge which I have yet to acquire."

While Alf was speaking, Leo and the Captain were seen approaching, and the three rose to meet them. There was a grave solemnity in the Captain's look which alarmed them.

"Nothing wrong I hope, uncle?" said Alf.

"Wrong! no, lad, there's nothing wrong. On the contrary, everything is right. Why, where do you think we have got to?"

"A hundred and fifty miles from the Pole," said Alf.

"Less, less," said Leo, with an excited look.

"We are not more," said the Captain slowly, as he took off his hat and wiped his brow, "not more than a hundred and forty miles from it."

"Then we could be there in three days or sooner, with a good breeze," cried Benjy, whose enthusiasm was aroused.

"Ay, Ben, if there was nothing in the way; but it's

quite clear from what Chingatok says, that we are drawing near to his native land, which cannot be more than fifty miles distant, if so much. You remember he has told us his home is one of a group of islands, some of which are large and some small; some mountainous and others flat and swampy, affording food and shelter to myriads of wild-fowl; so, you see, after we get there our progress northward through such a country, without roads or vehicles, won't be at the rate of ten miles an hour by any means."

"Besides," added Leo, "it would not be polite to Chingatok's countrymen if we were to leave them immediately after arriving. Perhaps they would not let us go, so I fear that we shan't gain the end of our journey yet a while, but that does not matter much, for we're sure to make it out at last."

"What makes the matter more uncertain," resumed the Captain, as they sauntered back to camp, "is the fact that this northern archipelago is peopled by different tribes of Eskimos, some of whom are of a warlike spirit and frequently give the others trouble. However, Chingatok says we shall have no difficulty in reaching this Nothing—as he will insist on styling the Pole, ever since I explained to him that it was not a real but an imaginary point."

"I wonder how Anders ever got him to understand what an imaginary point is," said Benjy.

"That has puzzled me too," returned the Captain, "but he did get it screwed into him somehow, and the result is—Nothing!"

"Out of nothing nothing comes," remarked Leo,

as the giant suddenly appeared from behind a rock, "but assuredly *nothing* can beat Chingatok in size or magnificence, which is more than anything else can."

The Eskimo had been searching for the absentees to announce that dinner was ready, and that Toolooha was impatient to begin; they all therefore quickened their pace, and soon after came within scent of the savoury mess which had been prepared for them by the giant's squat but amiable mother.

Chapter XVI

Fortune, which had hitherto proved favourable to our brave explorers, did not desert them at the eleventh hour.

Soon after their arrival at Refuge Island a fair wind sprang up from the south, and when the *Charity* had been carefully patched and repaired, the kites were sent up and the voyage was continued. That day and night they spent again upon the boundless sea, for the island was soon left out of sight behind them, though the wind was not very fresh.

Towards morning it fell calm altogether, obliging them to haul down the kites and take to the oars.

"It can't be far off now, Chingatok," said the Captain, who became rather impatient as the end drew near.

"Not far," was the brief reply.

"Land ho!" shouted Benjy, about half-an-hour after that.

But Benjy was forced to admit that anxiety had caused him to take an iceberg on the horizon for land.

"Well, anyhow you must admit," said Benjy, on approaching the berg, "that it's big enough for a fellow to mistake it for a mountain. I wonder what it's doing here without any brothers or sisters to keep it company."

"Under-currents brought it here, lad," said the Captain. "You see, such a monster as that must go very deep down, and the warm under-current has not yet melted away enough of his base to permit the surface-current to carry him south like the smaller members of his family. He is still travelling north, but that won't last long. He'll soon become small enough to put about and go the other way. I never saw a bigger fellow than that, Benjy. Hayes, the American, mentions one which he measured, about 315 feet high, and nearly a mile long. It had been grounded for two years. He calculated that there must have been seven times as much of it below water as there was above, so that it was stranded in nearly half-a-mile depth of water. This berg cannot be far short of that one in size."

"Hm! probably then his little brothers and sisters are being now crushed to bits in Baffin's Bay," said Benjy.

"Not unlikely, Ben, if they've not already been melted in the Atlantic, which will be this one's fate at last—sooner or later."

From a pool on this berg they obtained a supply of pure fresh water.

When our explorers did at last sight the land it came upon them unexpectedly, in the form of an island so low that they were quite close before observing it. The number of gulls hovering above it might have suggested its presence, but as these birds frequently hover in large flocks over shoals of small fish, little attention was paid to them.

"Is this your native land, Chingatok?" asked the Captain, quickly.

"No, it is over there," said the Eskimo, pointing to the distant horizon; "this is the first of the islands."

As they gazed they perceived a mountain-shaped cloud so faint and far away that it had almost escaped observation. Advancing slowly, this cloud was seen to take definite form and colour.

"I *knew* it was!" said Benjy, "but was afraid of making another mistake."

Had the boy or his father looked attentively at the giant just then, they would have seen that his colour deepened, his eyes glittered, and his great chest heaved a little more than was its wont, as he looked over his shoulder while labouring at the oars. Perhaps we should have said played with the oars, for they were mere toys in his grasp. Chingatok's little mother also was evidently affected by the sight of home. But the Captain and his son saw it not—they were too much occupied with their own thoughts and feelings. To the Englishmen the sight of land roused only one great all-engrossing thought—the North Pole! which, despite the absurdity of the idea, *would* present itself in the form of an upright post of terrific magnitude—

a worthy axle-tree, as it were, for the world to revolve upon. To the big Eskimo land presented itself in the form of a palatial stone edifice measuring fifteen feet by twelve, with a dear pretty little wife choking herself in the smoke of a cooking-lamp, and a darling little boy choking himself with a mass of walrus blubber. Thus the same object, when presented to different minds, suggested ideas that were:

> "Diverse as calm from thunder,
> Wide as the poles asunder."

It was midnight when the boats drew near to land. The island in which stood the giant's humble home seemed to Captain Vane not more than eight or ten miles in extent, and rose to a moderate height— apparently about five or six hundred feet. It was picturesque in form and composed of rugged rocks, the marks on which, and the innumerable boulders everywhere, showed that at some remote period of the world's history, it had been subjected to the influence of glacial action. No glacier was visible now, however— only, on the rocky summit lay a patch or two of the last winter's snow-drift, which was too deep for the summer sun to melt away. From this storehouse of water gushed numerous tiny rivulets which brawled cheerily rather than noisily among the rocks, watering the rich green mosses and grasses which abounded in patches everywhere, and giving life to countless wild-flowers and berries which decked and enriched the land.

Just off the island—which by a strange coincidence

the inhabitants had named Poloe—there were hundreds of other islets of every shape and size, but nearly all of them low, and many flat and swampy—the breeding-grounds of myriads of waterfowl. There were lakelets in many of these isles, in the midst of which were still more diminutive islets, whose moss-covered rocks and fringing sedges were reflected in the crystal water. Under a cliff on the main island stood the Eskimo village, a collection of stone huts, bathed in the slanting light of the midnight sun.

But no sound issued from these huts or from the neighbouring islands. It was the period of rest for man and bird. Air, earth, and water were locked in profound silence and repose.

"We've got to Paradise at last, father," was the first sound that broke the silence, if we except the gentle dip of the oars and the rippling water on the bow.

"Looks like it, Benjy," replied the Captain.

A wakeful dog on shore was the first to scent the coming strangers. He gave vent to a low growl. It was the keynote to the canine choir, which immediately sent up a howl of discord. Forthwith from every hut there leaped armed men, anxious women, and terrified children, which latter rushed towards the cliffs or took refuge among the rocks.

"Hallo! Chingatok, your relations are not to be taken by surprise," said the Captain—or something to that effect—in Eskimo.

The giant shook his head somewhat gravely.

"They must be at war," he said.

"At war! whom with?"

"With the Neerdoowulls," replied Chingatok with a frown. "They are always giving us trouble."

"Not badly named, father," said Benjy; "one would almost think they must be of Scotch extraction."

At that moment the natives—who had been gesticulating wildly and brandishing spears and bone knives with expressions of fury that denoted a strong desire on their part to carve out the hearts and transfix the livers of the newcomers—suddenly gave vent to a shout of surprise, which was succeeded by a scream of joy. Chingatok had stood up in the boat and been recognised. The giant's dog—an appropriately large one—had been the first to observe him, and expressed its feelings by wagging its tail to such an extent that its hind legs had difficulty in keeping the ground.

Immediately on landing, the party was surrounded by a clamorous crew, who, to do them justice, took very little notice of the strangers, so overjoyed were they at the return of their big countryman.

Soon a little pleasant though flattish-faced woman pushed through the crowd and seized the giant. This was his wife Pingasuk, or Pretty One. She was *petite*— not much larger than Oblooria the timid. The better to get at her, Chingatok went down on his knees, seized her by the shoulders, and rubbed her nose against his so vigorously that the smaller nose bid fair to come off altogether. He had to stoop still lower when a stout urchin of about five years of age came up behind him and tried to reach his face.

"Meltik!" exclaimed the giant, rubbing noses gently for fear of damaging him, "you are stout and fat, my son, you have been eating much blubber—good."

At that moment Chingatok's eyes fell on an object which had hitherto escaped his observation. It was a little round yellow head in his wife's hood, with a pair of small black eyes which stared at him in blank surprise. He made a snatch at it and drew forth—a naked baby!

"Our girlie," said the wife, with a pleased but anxious look; "don't squeeze. She is very young and tender—like a baby seal."

The glad father tried to fold the creature to his bosom; nearly dropped it in his excess of tender caution; thrust it hastily back into his wife's hood, and rose to give a respectful greeting to an aged man with a scrubby white beard, who came forward at the moment.

"Who are these, my son?" asked the old man, pointing to the Englishmen, who, standing in a group with amused expressions, watched the meeting above described.

"These are the Kablunets, father. I met them, as I expected, in the far-off land. The poor creatures were wandering about in a great kayak, which they have lost, searching for *nothing*!"

"Searching for nothing! my son, that cannot be. It is not possible to search for nothing—at least it is not possible to find it."

"But that is what they come here for," persisted Chingatok; "they call it the Nort Pole."

"And what is the Nort Pole, my son?"

"It is nothing, father."

The old man looked at his stately son with something of anxiety mingled with his surprise.

"Has Chingatok become a fool, like the Kablunets, since he left home?" he asked in a low voice.

"Chingatok is not sure," replied the giant, gravely. "He has seen so much to puzzle him since he went away, that he sometimes feels foolish."

The old Eskimo looked steadily at his son for a few moments, and shook his head.

"I will speak to these men—these foolish men," he said. "Do they understand our language?"

"Some of them understand and speak a little, father, but they have with them one named Unders, who interprets. Come here, Unders."

Anders promptly stepped to the front and interpreted, while the old Eskimo put Captain Vane through an examination of uncommon length and severity. At the close of it he shook his head with profound gravity, and turned again to his son.

"You have indeed brought to us a set of fools, Chingatok. Your voyage to the far-off lands has not been very successful. These men want something that they do not understand; that they could not see if it was before them; that they cannot describe when they talk about it, and that they could not lay hold of if they had it."

"Yes, father," sighed Chingatok, "it is as I told you— nothing; only the Nort Pole—a mere name."

A new light seemed to break in on Chingatok as he said this, for he added quickly, "But, father, a name is *something*—my name, Chingatok, is something, yet it is nothing. You cannot see it, you do not lay hold of it, yet it is there."

"Toohoo! my son, that is so, no doubt, but your name describes *you*, and you are something. No one ever goes to a far-off land to search for a *name*. If this Nort Pole is only a name and not a *thing*, how can it *be*?" exclaimed the old man, turning on his heel and marching off in a paroxysm of metaphysical disgust.

He appeared to change his mind, however, for, turning abruptly back, he said to Anders, "Tell these strangers that I am glad to see them; that a house and food shall be given to them, and that they are welcome to Poloe. Perhaps their land—the far-off land—is a poor one; they may not have enough to eat. If so, they may stay in this rich land of mine to hunt and fish as long as they please. But tell them that the Eskimos love wise men, and do not care for foolishness. They must not talk any more about this search after nothing—this Nort Pole—this nonsense—huk!"

Having delivered himself of these sentiments with much dignity, the old man again turned on his heel with a regal wave of the hand, and marched up to his hut.

"That must be the King of Poloe," whispered Captain Vane to Leo, endeavouring to suppress a smile at the concluding caution, as they followed Anders and one of the natives to the hut set apart for them.

The Captain was only half right. Amalatok was indeed the chief of the island, but the respect and deference shown to him by the tribe were owing more to the man's age and personal worth, than to his rank. He had succeeded his father as chief of the tribe, and, during a long life, had led his people in council, at the hunt, and in war, with consummate ability and success. Although old, he still held the reins of power, chiefly because his eldest son and rightful successor— Chingatok's elder brother—was a weak-minded man of little capacity and somewhat malignant disposition. If our giant had been his eldest, he would have resigned cheerfully long ago. As it was, he did not see his way to change the customs of the land, though he could not tell when, or by whom, or under what circumstances, the order of succession had been established. Probably, like many other antiquated customs, it had been originally the result of despotism on the part of men in power, and of stupid acquiescence on the part of an unthinking people.

On reaching his hut the old chief sat down, and, leaning carelessly against the wall, he toyed with a bit of walrus rib, as an Englishman might with a pair of nut-crackers at dessert.

"Why did you bring these barbarians here?"

"I did not bring them, father, they brought me," said the son with a deprecating glance.

"Huk!" exclaimed the chief, after which he added, "hum!"

It was evident that he had received new light, and was meditating thereon.

"My son," continued Amalatok, "these Kablunets seem to be stout-bodied fellows; can they fight—are they brave?"

"They are brave, father, very brave. Even the little one, whom they call Bunjay, is brave—also, he is funny. I have never seen the Kablunets fight with men, but they fight well with the bear and the walrus and the ice. They are not such fools as you seem to think. True, about this nothing—this Nort Pole—they are quite mad, but in other matters they are very wise and knowing, as you shall see before long."

"Good, good," remarked the old chief, flinging the walrus rib at an intrusive dog with signal success, "I am glad to hear you say that, because I may want their help."

Amalatok showed one symptom of true greatness— a readiness to divest himself of prejudice.

"For what do you require their help, father?" asked Chingatok.

Instead of answering, the old chief wrenched off another walrus rib from its native backbone, and began to gnaw it growlingly, as if it were his enemy and he a dog.

"My father is disturbed in his mind," said the giant in a sympathising tone.

Even a less observant man than Chingatok might have seen that the old chief was not only disturbed in mind, but also in body, for his features twitched convulsively, and his face grew red as he thought of his wrongs.

"Listen," said Amalatok, flinging the rib at another intrusive dog, again with success, and laying his hand impressively on his son's arm. "My enemy, Grabantak— that bellowing walrus, that sly seal, that empty-skulled puffin, that porpoise, cormorant, narwhal—s–s–sus!"

The old man set his teeth and hissed.

"Well, my father?"

"It is not well, my son. It is all ill. That marrowless

bear is stirring up his people, and there is no doubt that we shall soon be again engaged in a bloody—a *useless* war."

"What is it all about, father?"

"About!—about nothing."

"Huk! about Nort Pole—nothing," murmured Chingatok—his thoughts diverted by the word.

"No, it is worse than Nort Pole, worse than nothing," returned the chief sternly; "it is a small island—very small—so small that a seal would not have it for a breathing-place. Nothing on it; no moss, no grass. Birds won't stay there—only fly over it and wink with contempt. Yet Grabantak says he must have it—it is within the bounds of *his* land!"

"Well, let him have it, if it be so worthless," said Chingatok, mildly.

"Let him have it!" shouted the chief, starting up with such violence as to overturn the cooking-lamp—to which he paid no regard whatever—and striding about the small hut savagely, "no, never! I will fight him to the last gasp; kill all his men; slay his women; drown his children; level his huts; burn up his meat—"

Amalatok paused and glared, apparently uncertain about the propriety of wasting good meat. The pause gave his wrath time to cool.

"At all events," he continued, sitting down again and wrenching off another rib, "we must call a council and have a talk, for we may expect him soon. When you arrived we took you for our enemies."

"And you were ready for us," said Chingatok, with an approving smile.

"Huk!" returned the chief with a responsive nod. "Go, Chingatok, call a council of my braves for to—night, and see that these miserable starving Kablunets have enough of blubber wherewith to stuff themselves."

Our giant did not deem it worth while to explain to his rather petulant father that the Englishmen were the reverse of starving, but he felt the importance of raising them in the old chief's opinion without delay, and took measures accordingly.

"Blackbeard," he said, entering the Captain's hut and sitting down with a troubled air, "my father does not think much of you. Tell him that, Unders."

"I understand you well enough, Chingatok; go on, and let me know why the old man does not think well of me."

"He thinks you are a fool," returned the plain spoken Eskimo.

"H'm! I'm not altogether surprised at that, lad. I've sometimes thought so myself. Well, I suppose you've come to give me some good advice to make me wiser—eh! Chingatok?"

"Yes, that is what I come for. Do what I tell you, and my father will begin to think you wise."

"Ah, yes, the old story," remarked Benjy, who was an amused listener—for his father translated in a low tone for the benefit of his companions as the conversation proceeded—"the same here as everywhere—Do as I tell you and all will be well!"

"Hold your tongue, Ben," whispered Alf.

"Well, what am I to do?" asked the Captain.

"Invite my father to a feast," said Chingatok eagerly, "and me too, and my mother too; also my wife, and some of the braves with their wives. And you must give us biskit an'—what do you call that brown stuff?"

"Coffee," suggested the Captain.

"Yes, cuffy, also tee, and shoogre, and seal st– ate— what?"

"Steak—eh?"

"Yes, stik, and cook them all in the strange lamp. You must ask us to see the feast cooked, and then we will eat it."

It will be observed that when Chingatok interpolated English words in his discourse his pronunciation was not perfect.

"Well, you are the coolest fellow I've met with for many a day! To order a feast, invite yourself to it, name the rest of the company, as well as the victuals, and insist on seeing the cooking of the same," said the Captain in English; then, in Eskimo,—"Well, Chingatok, I will do as you wish. When would you like supper?"

"Now," replied the giant, with decision.

"You hear, Butterface," said the Captain when he had translated, "go to work and get your pots and pans ready. See that you put your best foot foremost. It will be a turning-point, this feast, I see."

Need we say that the feast was a great success? The wives, highly pleased at the attention paid them by the strangers, were won over at once. The whole party, when assembled in the hut, watched with the most indescribable astonishment the proceedings of the negro—himself a living miracle—as he manipulated a machine which, in separate compartments, cooked steaks and boiled tea, coffee, or anything else, by means of a spirit lamp in a few minutes. On first tasting the hot liquids they looked at each other suspiciously; then as the sugar tickled their palates, they smiled, tilted their pannikins, drained them to the dregs, and asked for more!

The feast lasted long, and was highly appreciated. When the company retired—which did not happen until the Captain declared he had nothing more to give them, and turned the cooking apparatus upside down to prove what he said—there was not a man or woman among them who did not hold and even loudly assert that the Kablunets were wise men.

After the feast the council of war was held and the strangers were allowed to be present. There was a great deal of talk—probably some of it was not much to the point, but there was no interruption or undignified confusion. There was a peace-party, of course, and a war-party, but the latter prevailed. It too often does so in human affairs. Chingatok was understood to favour the peace-party, but as his sire was on the other side, respect kept him tongue-tied.

"These Eskimos reverence age and are respectful to women," whispered Leo to Alf, "so we may not call them savages."

The old chief spoke last, summing up the arguments, as it were, on both sides, and giving his reasons for favouring war.

"The island is of no use," he said; "it is not worth a seal's nose, yet Grabantak wishes to tear it from us—us who have possessed it since the forgotten times. Why is this? because he wishes to insult us," ("huk!" from the audience). "Shall we submit to insult? shall we sit down like frightened birds and see the black-livered cormorant steal what is ours? shall the courage of the Poloes be questioned by all the surrounding tribes? Never! while we have knives in our boots and spears in our hands. We will fight till we conquer or till we are all dead—till our wives are husbandless and our children fatherless, and all our stores of meat and oil are gone!" ("huk! huk!") "Then shall it be said by surrounding tribes, 'Behold! how brave were the Poloes! they died and left their wives and little children to perish, or mourn in slavery, rather than submit to insult!'"

The "huks" that greeted the conclusion of the speech were so loud and numerous that the unfortunate peace-makers were forced to hide their diminished heads.

Thus did Amalatok resolve to go to war for "worse than Nort Pole—for nothing"[1]—rather than submit to insult!

---

1. It may not be inappropriate here to point out that Eskimo savages are sometimes equalled, if not surpassed, in this respect, by civilised and even Christian nations.

Chapter XVII

THE EFFECT OF PERSUASION ON DIVERSE CHARACTERS.

The warlike tendencies of Grabantak, the northern savage, had the effect of compelling Captain Vane and his party to delay for a considerable time their efforts to reach the Pole. This was all the more distressing that they had by that time approached so very near to it. A carefully made observation placed the island of Poloe in latitude 88° 30 minutes 10 seconds, about 90 geographical, or 104 English statute miles from the Pole.

There was no help for it, however. To have ventured on Grabantak's territory while war was impending would have been to court destruction. Captain Vane saw therefore that the only way of advancing his own cause was to promote peace between the tribes. With a view to this he sought an interview with the old chief Amalatok.

"Why do you wish to go to war?" he asked.

"I do not wish to go to war," answered the chief, frowning fiercely.

"Why do you go then?" said the Captain in a soothing tone, for he was very anxious not to rouse the chief's anger; but he was unsuccessful, for the question seemed to set the old man on fire. He started up, grinding his teeth and striding about his hut, knocking over pots, oil cans, and cooking-lamps somewhat like that famous bull which got into a china shop. Finding the space too small for him he suddenly dropped on his knees, crept through the low entrance, sprang up, and began to stride about more comfortably.

The open air calmed him a little. He ceased to grind his teeth, and stopping in front of the Captain, who had followed him, said in a low growl, "Do you think I will submit to insult?"

"Some men have occasionally done so with advantage," answered the Captain.

"Kablunets may do so, Eskimos *never*!" returned the old man, resuming his hurried walk to and fro, and the grinding of his teeth again.

"If Amalatok were to kill all his enemies—all the men, women and children," said the Captain, raising a fierce gleam of satisfaction in the old man's face at the mere suggestion, "and if he were to knock down all their huts, and burn up all their kayaks and oomiaks, the insult would still remain, because an insult can only be wiped out by one's enemy confessing his sin and repenting."

For a few seconds Amalatok stood silent; his eyes

fixed on the ground as if he were puzzled.

"The white man is right," he said at length, "but if I killed them all I should be avenged."

"Vengeance is mine, saith the Lord," leaped naturally to the Captain's mind; but, reflecting that the man before him was a heathen who would not admit the value of the quotation, he paused a moment or two.

"And what," he then said, "if Grabantak should kill Amalatok and all his men, and carry away the women and children into slavery, would the insult be wiped out in that case? Would it not rather be deepened?"

"True, it would; but then we should all be dead—we should not care."

"The *men* would all be dead, truly," returned the Captain, "but perhaps the women and children left behind might care. They would also suffer."

"Go, go," said the Eskimo chief, losing temper as he lost ground in the argument; "what can Kablunets know about such matters? You tell me you are men of peace; that your religion is a religion of peace. Of course, then, you understand nothing about war. Go, I have been insulted, and I *must* fight."

Seeing that it would be fruitless talking to the old chief while he was in this frame of mind, Captain Vane left him and returned to his own hut, where he found Chingatok and Leo engaged in earnest conversation—Alf and Benjy being silent listeners.

"I'm glad you've come, uncle," said Leo, making room for him on the turf seat, "because Chingatok and I are discussing the subject of war; and—"

"A strange coincidence," interrupted the Captain. "I have just been discussing the same subject with old Amalatok. I hope that in showing the evils of war you are coming better speed with the son than I did with the father."

"As to that," said Leo, "I have no difficulty in showing Chingatok the evils of war. He sees them clearly enough already. The trouble I have with him is to explain the Bible on that subject. You see he has got a very troublesome inquiring sort of mind, and ever since I have told him that the Bible is the Word of God he won't listen to my explanations about anything. He said to me in the quietest way possible, just now, 'Why do you give me *your* reasons when you tell me the Great Spirit has given His? I want to know what *He* says.' Well, now, you know, it is puzzling to be brought to book like that, and I doubt if Anders translates well. You understand and speak the language, uncle, better than he does, I think, so I want you to help me."

"I'll try, Leo, though I am ashamed to say I am not so well read in the Word myself as I ought to be. What does Chingatok want to know?"

"He wants to *reconcile* things, of course. That is always the way. Now I told him that the Great Spirit is good, and does not wish men to go to war, and that He has written for us a law, namely, that we should 'live peaceably with all men.' Chingatok liked this very much, but then I had told him before, that the Great Spirit had told His ancient people the Jews to go and fight His enemies, and take possession of their lands. Now he regards this as a contradiction. He says—How can a man live peaceably with all men, and at the same time go to war with some men, kill them, and take their lands?"

"Ah! Leo, my boy, your difficulty in answering the Eskimo lies in your own *partial* quotation of Scripture," said the Captain. Then, turning to Chingatok, he added, "My young friend did not give you the whole law—only part of it. The word is written thus:— 'if it be *possible*, as much as lieth in you, live peaceably with all men.' Some times it is *not* possible, Chingatok; then we must fight. But the law says keep from fighting '*as much as you can*.' Mind that, Chingatok, and if you are ever induced to go to war for the sake of a little island—for the sake of a little insult,—don't flatter yourself that you are keeping out of it as much as lieth in you."

"Good, good," said the giant, earnestly; "Blackbeard's words are wise."

"As to the people of God in the long past," continued the Captain, "God told them to go to war, so they went; but that does not authorise men to go to war at their own bidding. What is right in the Great Father of all may be very wrong in the children. God kills men every day, and we do not blame Him, but if man kills his fellow we hunt him down as a murderer. In the long past time the Great Father spoke to His children by His wise and holy men, and sometimes He saw fit to tell them to fight. With His reasons we have nothing to do. Now, the Great Father speaks to us by His Book. In it He tells us to live in peace with all men—if *possible*."

"Good," said the giant with an approving nod,

though a perplexed expression still lingered on his face. "But the Great Father has never before spoken to me by His Book—never at all to my forefathers."

"He may, however, have spoken by His Spirit within you, Chingatok, I cannot tell," returned the Captain with a meditative air. "You have desires for peace and a tendency to forgive. This could not be the work of the spirit of evil. It must have been that of the Good Spirit."

This seemed to break upon the Eskimo as a new light, and he relapsed into silence as he thought of the wonderful idea that within his breast the Great Spirit might have been working in time past although he knew it not. Then he thought of the many times he had in the past resisted what he had hitherto only thought of as good feelings; and the sudden perception that at such times he had been resisting the Father of all impressed him for the first time with a sensation of guiltiness. It was some time before the need of a Saviour from sin entered into his mind, but the ice had been broken, and at last, through Leo's Bible, as read by him and explained by Captain Vane, Jesus, the Sun of Righteousness, rose upon his soul and sent in the light for which he had thirsted so long.

But, as we have said, this effect was not immediate, and he remained in a state of uncertainty and sadness while the warlike councils and preparations went on.

Meanwhile Captain Vane set himself earnestly to work to hit on some plan by which, if possible, to turn the feeling of the Eskimo community in favour of peace. At first he thought of going alone and unarmed, with Anders as interpreter, to the land of Grabantak to dissuade that savage potentate from attacking the Poloes, but the Eskimos pointed out that the danger of this plan was so great that he might as well kill himself at once. His own party, also, objected to it so strongly that he gave it up, and resolved in the meantime to strengthen his position and increase his influence with the natives among whom his lot was cast, by some exhibitions of the powers with which science and art had invested him.

Chapter XVIII

It will be remembered that the party of Englishmen arrived at Poloeland under oars, and although the india-rubber boats had been gazed at, and gently touched, with intense wonder by the natives, they had not yet seen the process of disinflation, or the expansion of the kites.

Of course, Chingatok and their other Eskimo fellow-travellers had given their friends graphic descriptions of everything, but this only served to whet the desire to see the wonderful oomiaks in action. Several times, during the first few days, the old chief had expressed a wish to see the Kablunets go through the water in their boats, but as the calm still prevailed, and the Captain knew his influence over the natives would depend very much on the effect with which his various proceedings were carried out, he put him off with the assurance that when the proper time for action came, he would let him know.

One night a gentle breeze sprang up and blew directly off shore. As it seemed likely to last, the Captain waited till the whole community was asleep, and then quietly roused his son.

"Lend a hand here, Ben," he whispered, "and make no noise."

Benjy arose and followed his father in a very sleepy frame of mind.

They went to the place where the india-rubber boats lay, close behind the Englishmen's hut, and, unscrewing the brass heads that closed the air-holes, began to press out the air.

"That's it, Ben, but don't squeeze too hard, lest the hissing should rouse some of 'em."

"What'r 'ee doin' this for—ee—yaou?" asked Benjy, yawning.

"You'll see that to-morrow, lad."

"Hum! goin' t'squeeze'm all?"

"Yes, all three, and put 'em in their boxes."

The conversation lagged at this point, and the rest of the operation was performed in silence.

Next morning, after breakfast, seeing that the breeze still held, the Captain sent a formal message to Amalatok, that he was prepared to exhibit his oomiaks.

The news spread like wild-fire, and the entire community soon assembled—to the number of several hundreds—in front of the Englishmen's hut, where the Captain was seen calmly seated on a packing-case, with a solemn expression on his face. The rest of his party had been warned to behave with dignity. Even Benjy's round face was drawn into something of an oval, and Butterface made such superhuman attempts to appear grave, that the rest of the party almost broke down at the sight of him.

Great was the surprise among the natives when they perceived that the three oomiaks had disappeared.

"My friends," said the Captain, rising, "I will now show you the manner in which we Englishmen use our oomiaks."

A soft sigh of expectation ran through the group of eager natives, as they pressed round their chief and Chingatok who stood looking on in dignified silence, while the Captain and his companions went to work. Many of the women occupied a little eminence close at hand, whence they could see over the heads of the men, and some of the younger women and children clambered to the top of the hut, the better to witness the great sight.

Numerous and characteristic were the sighs, "huks," grunts, growls, and other exclamations; all of which were in keeping with the more or less intense glaring of eyes, and opening of mouths, and slight bending of knees and elbows, and spreading of fingers, and raising of hands, as the operators slowly unrolled the india-rubber mass, attached the bellows, gradually inflated the first boat, fixed the thwarts and stretchers, and, as it were, constructed a perfect oomiak in little more than ten minutes.

Then there was a shout of delight when the Captain and Leo, one at the bow, the other at the stern, lifted the boat as if it had been a feather, and, carrying it down the beach, placed it gently in the sea.

But the excitement culminated when Chingatok, stepping lightly into it, sat down on the seat, seized the little oars, and rowed away.

We should have said, attempted to row away, for, though he rowed lustily, the boat did not move, owing to Anders, who, like Eskimos in general, dearly loved a practical joke. Holding fast by the tail-line a few seconds, he suddenly let go, and the boat shot away, while Anders, throwing a handful of water after it, said, "Go off, bad boy, and don't come back; we can do without you." A roar of laughter burst forth. Some of the small boys and girls leaped into the air with delight, causing the tails of the latter to wriggle behind them.

The Captain gave them plenty of time to blow off the steam of surprise. When they had calmed down considerably, he proceeded to open out and arrange one of the kites.

Of course this threw them back into the open-eyed and mouthed, and finger-spreading condition, and, if possible, called forth more surprise than before. When the kite soared into the sky, they shouted; when it was being attached to the bow of the boat, they held their breath with expectation, many of them standing on one leg; and when at last the boat, with four persons in it, shot away to sea at the rate of eight or ten miles an hour, they roared with ecstasy; accompanying the yells with contortions of frame and visage which were so indescribable that we gladly leave it all to the reader's imagination.

There can be no doubt of the fact that the Captain placed himself and his countrymen that day on a pedestal from which there was no fear of their being afterwards dislodged.

"Did not I tell you," said Chingatok to his sire that night, in the privacy of his hut, "that the Kablunets are great men?"

"You did, my son. Chingatok is wise, and his father is a fool!"

No doubt the northern savage meant this self-condemning speech to be understood much in the same way in which it is understood by civilised people.

"When the oomiak swelled I thought it was going to burst," added the chief.

"So did I, when I first saw it," said Chingatok. Father and son paused a few minutes. They usually did so between each sentence. Evidently they pondered what they said.

"Have these men got wives?" asked the chief.

"The old one has, and Bunjay is his son. The other ones—no. The black man may have a wife: I know not, but I should think that no woman would have him."

"What made him black?"

"I know not."

"Was he always black?"

"The Kablunets say he was—from so big."

Chingatok measured off the half of his left hand by way of explaining how big.

"Is he black under the clothes?"

"Yes; black all over."

Again the couple paused.

"It is strange," said the old man, shaking his head. "Perhaps he was made black because his father was wicked."

"Not so," returned the young giant. "I have heard him say his father was a very good man."

"Strange," repeated the chief, with a solemn look. Tell me, my son, where do the Kablunets live? Do they hunt the walrus or the seal?"

"Blackbeard has told me much, father, that I do not understand. His people do not hunt much—only a very few of them do."

"Wah! they are lazy! The few hunt to keep the rest in meat, I suppose."

"No, father, that is not the way. The few hunt for fun. The great many spend their time in changing one thing for another. They seem to be never satisfied—always changing, changing—every day, and all day. Getting and giving, and never satisfied."

"Poor things!" said the chief.

"And they have no walruses, no white bears, no whales, nothing!" added the son.

"Miserables! Perhaps that is why they come here to search for *nothing!*"

"But, father, if they have got nothing at home, why come here to search for it?"

"What do they eat?" asked Amalatok, quickly, as if he were afraid of recurring to the puzzling question that had once already taken him out of his mental depth.

"They eat all sorts of things. Many of them eat things that are nasty—things that grow out of the ground; things that are very hot and burn the tongue; things that are poison and make them ill. They eat fish too, like us, and other people bring them their meat in great oomiaks from far-off lands. They seem to be so poor that they cannot find enough in their own country to feed themselves."

"Wretched creatures!" said the old man, pitifully.

"Yes, and they drink too. Drink waters so hot and so terrible that they burn their mouths and their insides, and so they go mad."

"Did I not say that they were fools?" said Amalatok, indignantly.

"But the strangest thing of all," continued Chingatok, lowering his voice, and looking at his sire in a species of wonder, "is that they fill their mouths with smoke!"

"What? Eat smoke?" said Amalatok in amazement.

"No, they spit it out."

"Did Blackbeard tell you that?"

"Yes."

"Then Blackbeard is a liar!"

Chingatok did not appear to be shocked by the old man's plain speaking, but he did not agree with him.

"No, father," said he, after a pause. "Blackbeard is not a liar. He is good and wise, and speaks the truth. I have seen the Kablunets do it myself. In the big oomiak that they lost, some of the men did it, so—puff, pull, puff, puff—is it not funny?"

Both father and son burst into laughter at this, and then, becoming suddenly grave, remained staring at the smoke of their cooking-lamp, silently meditating on these things.

While thus engaged, a man entered the low doorway in the only possible manner, on hands and knees, and, rising, displayed the face of Anders.

"Blackbeard sends a message to the great old chief," said the interpreter. "He wishes him to pay the Kablunets a visit. He has something to show to the great old chief."

"Tell him I come," said the chief, with a toss of the head which meant, "be off!"

"I wonder," said Amalatok slowly, as Anders crept out, "whether Blackbeard means to show us some of his wisdom or some of his foolishness. The white men appear to have much of both."

"Let us go see," said Chingatok.

They went, and found the Captain seated in front of the door of his hut with his friends round him—all except Benjy, who was absent. They were very grave, as usual, desiring to be impressive.

"Chief," began the Captain, in that solemn tone in which ghosts are supposed to address mankind, "I wish to show you that I can make the stoutest and most obstinate warrior of Poloeland tremble and jump without touching him."

"That is not very difficult," said the old man, who had still a lurking dislike to acknowledge the Englishmen his superiors. "I can make any one of them tremble and jump by throwing a spear at him."

A slight titter from the assembly testified to the success of this reply.

"But," rejoined the Captain, with deepening

solemnity, "I will do it without throwing a spear."

"So will I, by suddenly howling at him in the dark," said Amalatok.

At this his men laughed outright.

"But I will not howl or move," said the Captain.

"That will be clever," returned the chief, solemnised in spite of himself. "Let Blackbeard proceed."

"Order one of your braves to stand before me on that piece of flat skin," said the Captain.

Amalatok looked round, and, observing a huge ungainly man with a cod-fishy expression of face, who seemed to shrink from notoriety, ordered him to step forward. The man did so with obvious trepidation, but he dared not refuse. The Captain fixed his eyes on him sternly, and, in a low growling voice, muttered in English: "Now, Benjy, give it a good turn."

Cod-fishiness vanished as if by magic, and, with a look of wild horror, the man sprang into the air, tumbled on his back, rose up, and ran away!

It is difficult to say whether surprise or amusement predominated among the spectators. Many of them laughed heartily, while the Captain, still as grave as a judge, said in a low growling tone as if speaking to himself:—

"Not quite so stiff, Benjy, not quite so stiff. Be more gentle next time. Don't do it all at once, boy; jerk it, Benjy, a turn or so at a time."

It is perhaps needless to inform the reader that the Captain was practising on the Eskimos with his electrical machine, and that Benjy was secretly turning the handle inside the hut. The machine was connected, by means of wires, with the piece of skin on which the patients stood. These wires had been laid underground, not, indeed, in the darkness, but, during the secrecy and silence of the previous night.

After witnessing the effect on the first warrior, no other brave seemed inclined to venture on the skin, and the women, who enjoyed the fun greatly, were beginning to taunt them with cowardice, when Oolichuk strode forward. He believed intensely, and justifiably, in his own courage. No man, he felt quite sure, had the power to stare *him* into a nervous condition—not even the fiercest of the Kablunets. Let Blackbeard try, and do his worst!

Animated by these stern and self-reliant sentiments, he stepped upon the mat.

Benjy, being quick in apprehension, perceived his previous error, and proceeded this time with caution. He gave the handle of the machine a gentle half-turn and stopped, peeping through a crevice in the wall to observe the effect.

"Ha! ha! ho! ho!—hi! huk!" laughed Oolichuk, as a tickling sensation thrilled through all his nervous system. The laugh was irresistibly echoed by the assembled community.

Benjy waited a few seconds, and then gave the handle another and slightly stronger turn.

The laugh this time was longer and more ferocious, while the gallant Eskimo drew himself together, determined to resist the strange and subtle influence; at the same time frowning defiance at the Captain, who never for a moment took his coal-black eye off him!

Again Benjy turned the handle gently. He evidently possessed something of the ancient Inquisitor spirit, and gloated over the pains of his victim! The result was that Oolichuk not only quivered from head to foot, but gave a little jump and anything but a little yell. Benjy's powers of self-restraint were by that time exhausted. He sent the handle round with a whirr and Oolichuk, tumbling backwards off the mat, rent the air with a shriek of demoniac laughter.

Of course the delight of the Eskimos—especially of the children—was beyond all bounds, and eager were the efforts made to induce another warrior to go upon the mysterious mat, but not one would venture. They would rather have faced their natural enemy, the great Grabantak, unarmed, any day!

In this difficulty an idea occurred to Amalatok. Seizing a huge dog by the neck he dragged it to the mat, and bade it lie down. The dog crouched and looked sheepishly round. Next moment he was in the air wriggling. Then he came to the ground, over which he rushed with a prolonged howl, and disappeared among the rocks on the hill side.

It is said that that poor dog was never again seen, but Benjy asserts most positively that, a week afterwards, he saw it sneaking into the village with its tail very much between its legs, and an expression of the deepest humility on its countenance.

"You'd better give them a taste of dynamite, father," said Benjy that evening, as they all sat round their supper-kettle.

"No, no, boy. It is bad policy to fire off all your

ammunition in a hurry. We'll give it 'em bit by bit."

"Just so, impress them by degrees," said Alf.

"De fust warrior was nigh bu'sted by degrees," said Butterface, with a broad grin, as he stirred the kettle. "You gib it 'im a'most too strong, Massa Benjee."

"Blackbeard must be the bad spirit," remarked Amalatok to his son that same night as they held converse together—according to custom—before going to bed.

"The bad spirit is *never* kind or good," replied Chingatok, after a pause.

"No," said the old man, "never."

"But Blackbeard is always good and kind," returned the giant.

This argument seemed unanswerable. At all events the old man did not answer it, but sat frowning at the cooking-lamp under the influence of intense thought.

After a prolonged meditation—during the course of which father and son each consumed the tit-bits of a walrus rib and a seal's flipper—Chingatok remarked that the white men were totally beyond his comprehension. To which, after another pause, his father replied that he could not understand them at all.

Then, retiring to their respective couches, they calmly went to sleep—"perchance to dream!"

Chapter XIX

A SHOOTING TRIP TO PARADISE ISLE, AND FURTHER
DISPLAY OF THE CAPTAIN'S CONTRIVANCES.

While our explorers were thus reduced to a state of forced inaction as regarded the main object of their expedition, they did not by any means waste their time in idleness. On the contrary, each of the party went zealously to work in the way that was most suitable to his inclination.

After going over the main island of Poloe as a united party, and ascertaining its size, productions, and general features, the Captain told them they might now do as they pleased. For his part he meant to spend a good deal of his time in taking notes and observations, questioning the chief men as to the lands lying to the northward, repairing and improving the hut, and helping the natives miscellaneously so as to gain their regard.

Of course Leo spent much of his time with his rifle,

for the natives were not such expert hunters but that occasionally they were badly off for food. Of course, also, Alf shouldered his botanical box and sallied forth hammer in hand, to "break stones," as Butterface put it. Benjy sometimes followed Alf—more frequently Leo, and always carried his father's double-barrelled shot-gun. He preferred that, because his powers with the rifle were not yet developed. Sometimes he went with Toolooha, or Tekkona, or Oblooria, in one of the native oomiaks to fish. At other times he practised paddling in the native kayak, so that he might accompany Chingatok on his excursions to the neighbouring islands after seals and wild-fowl.

In the excursions by water Leo preferred one of the india-rubber boats—partly because he was strong and could row it easily, and partly because it was capable of holding more game than the kayak.

These expeditions to the outlying islands were particularly delightful. There was something so peaceful, yet so wild, so romantic and so strange about the region, that the young men felt as if they had passed into a new world altogether. It is scarcely surprising that they should feel thus, when it is remembered that profound calms usually prevailed at that season, causing the sea to appear like another heaven below them; that the sun never went down, but circled round and round the horizon—dipping, indeed, a little more and more towards it each night, but not yet disappearing; that myriads of wild birds filled the air with plaintive cries; that whales, and sea-unicorns, and walruses sported around; that icebergs were only numerous enough to give a certain strangeness of aspect to the scene—a strangeness which was increased by the frequent appearance of arctic phenomena, such as several mock-suns rivalling the real one, and objects being enveloped in a golden haze, or turned upside down by changes in atmospheric temperature.

"No wonder that arctic voyagers are always hankering after the far north," said Leo to Benjy, one magnificent morning, as they rowed towards the outlying islands over the golden sea.

Captain Vane was with them that morning, and it was easy to see that the Captain was in a peculiar frame of mind. A certain twinkle in his eyes and an occasional smile, apparently at nothing, showed that his thoughts, whatever they might be, were busy.

Now, it cannot have failed by this time to strike the intelligent reader, that Captain Vane was a man given to mystery, and rather fond of taking by surprise not only Eskimos but his own companions. On the bright morning referred to he took with him in the boat a small flat box, or packing-case, measuring about three feet square, and not more than four inches deep.

As they drew near to Leo's favourite sporting-ground,—a long flat island with several small lakes on it which were bordered by tall reeds and sedges, where myriads of ducks, geese, gulls, plover, puffins, and other birds revelled in abject felicity,—Benjy asked his father what he had got in the box.

"I've got somethin' in it, Benjy,—somethin'."

"Why, daddy," returned the boy with a laugh, "if I were an absolute lunatic you could not treat me with greater contempt. Do you suppose I am so weak as to imagine that you would bring a packing-case all the way from England to the North Pole with nothing in it?"

"You're a funny boy, Benjy," said the Captain, regarding his son with a placid look.

"You're a funny father, daddy," answered the son with a shake of the head; "and it's fortunate for you that I'm good as well as funny, else I'd give you some trouble."

"You've got a good opinion of yourself, Ben, anyhow," said Leo, looking over his shoulder as he rowed. "Just change the subject and make yourself useful. Jump into the bow and have the boat-hook ready; the water shoals rather fast here, and I don't want to risk scraping a hole in our little craft."

The island they were approaching formed part of the extensive archipelago of which Poloe was the main or central island. Paradise Isle, as Leo had named it, lay about two miles from Poloe. The boat soon touched its shingly beach, but before it could scrape thereon its occupants stepped into the water and carefully carried it on shore.

"Now, Benjy, hand me the rifle and cartridges," said Leo, after the boat was placed in the shadow of a low bank, "and fetch the game-bag. What! you don't intend to carry the packing-case, uncle, do you?"

"I think I'd better do it," answered the Captain, lifting the case by its cord in a careless way; "it might take a fancy to have a swim on its own account, you know. Come along, the birds are growing impatient, don't you see?"

With a short laugh, Leo shouldered his rifle, and

marched towards the first of a chain of little lakes, followed by Benjy with the game-bag, and the Captain with the case.

Soon a splendid grey wild-goose was seen swimming at a considerable distance beyond the reeds.

"There's your chance, now, Leo," said the Captain. But Leo shook his head. "No use," he said; "if I were to shoot that one I'd never be able to get it; the mud is too deep for wading, and the reeds too thick for swimming amongst. It's a pity to kill birds that we cannot get hold of, so, you see, I must walk along the margin of the lake until I see a bird in a good position to be got at, and then pot him."

"But isn't that slow work, lad?" asked the Captain.

"It might be slow if I missed often or wounded my birds," replied Leo, "but I don't often miss."

The youth might with truth have said he never missed, for his eye was as true and his hand as sure as that of any Leatherstocking or Robin Hood that ever lived.

"Why don't you launch the boat on the lake?" asked the Captain.

"Because I don't like to run the risk of damaging it by hauling it about among mud and sticks and overland. Besides, that would be a cumbersome way of hunting. I prefer to tramp about the margin as you see, and just take what comes in my way. There are plenty of birds, and I seldom walk far without getting a goodish—hist! There's one!"

As he spoke another large grey goose was seen stretching its long neck amongst the reeds at a distance of about two hundred yards. The crack of the rifle was followed by the instant death of the goose. At the same moment several companions of the bird rose trumpeting into the air amid a cloud of other birds. Again the rifle's crack was heard, and one of the geese on the wing dropped beside its comrade.

As Leo carried his repeating rifle, he might easily have shot another, but he refrained, as the bird would have been too far out to be easily picked up.

"Now, Benjy, are you to go in, or am I?" asked the sportsman with a sly look.

"Oh! I suppose *I* must," said the boy with an affectation of being martyred, though, in truth, nothing charmed him so much as to act the part of a water-dog.

A few seconds more, and he was stripped, for his garments consisted only of shirt and trousers. But it was more than a few seconds before he returned to land, swimming on his back and trailing a goose by the neck with each hand, for the reeds were thick and the mud softish, and the second bird had been further out than he expected.

"It's glorious fun," said Benjy, panting vehemently as he pulled on his clothes.

"It's gloriously knocked up you'll be before long at that rate," said the Captain.

"Oh! but, uncle," said Leo, quickly, "you must not suppose that I give him all the hard work. We share it between us, you know. Benjy sometimes shoots and then I do the retrieving. You've no idea how good a shot he is becoming."

"Indeed, let me see you do it, my boy. D'ye see

that goose over there?"

"What, the one near the middle of the lake, about four hundred yards off?"

"Ay, Benjy, I want that goose. You shoot it, my boy."

"But you'll never be able to get it, uncle," said Leo.

"Benjy, I want that goose. You shoot it." There was no disobeying this peremptory command. Leo handed the rifle to the boy.

"Down on one knee, Ben, Hythe position, my boy," said the Captain, in the tone of a disciplinarian. Benjy obeyed, took a long steady aim, and fired.

"Bravo!" shouted the Captain as the bird turned breast up. "There's that goose's brother comin' to see what's the matter with him; just cook *his* goose too, Benjy."

The boy aimed again, fired, and missed.

"Again!" cried the Captain, "look sharp!"

Again the boy fired, and this time wounded the bird as it was rising on the wing.

Although wounded, the goose was quite able to swim, and made rapidly towards the reeds on the other side.

"What! am I to lose that goose?" cried the Captain indignantly.

Leo seized the rifle. Almost without taking time to aim, he fired and shot the bird dead.

"There," said he, laughing, "but I suspect it is a lost goose after all. It will be hard work to get either of these birds, uncle. However, I'll try."

Leo was proceeding to strip when the Captain forbade him.

"Don't trouble yourself, lad," he said, "I'll go for them myself."

"You, uncle?"

"Ay, me. D'ye suppose that nobody can swim but you and Benjy? Here, help me to open this box."

In silent wonder and expectation Leo and Benjy did as they were bid. When the mysterious packing-case was opened, there was displayed to view a mass of waterproof material. Tumbling this out and unrolling it, the Captain displayed a pair of trousers and boots in one piece attached to something like an oval life-buoy. Thrusting his legs down into the trousers and boots, he drew the buoy—which was covered with india-rubber cloth—up to his waist and fixed it there. Then, putting the end of an india-rubber tube to his mouth, he began to blow, and the buoy round his waist began to extend until it took the form of an oval.

"Now, boys," said the Captain, with profound gravity, "I'm about ready to go to sea. Here, you observe, is a pair o' pants that won't let in water. At the feet you'll notice two flaps which expand when driven backward, and collapse when moved forward. These are propellers—human web-feet—to enable me to walk ahead, d'ye see? and here are two small paddles with a joint which I can fix together—so—and thus make one double-bladed paddle of 'em, about four feet long. It will help the feet, you understand, but I'm not dependent on it, for I can walk without the paddles at the rate of two or three miles an hour."

As he spoke Captain Vane walked quietly into the water, to the wild delight of Benjy, and the amazement of his nephew.

When he was about waist-deep the buoy floated him. Continuing to walk, though his feet no longer touched ground, he was enabled by the propellers to move on. When he had got out a hundred yards or so, he turned round, took off his hat, and shouted—"land ho!"

"Ship ahoy!" shrieked Benjy, in an ecstasy.

"Mind your weather eye!" shouted the Captain, resuming his walk with a facetious swagger, while, with the paddles, he increased his speed. Soon after, he returned to land with the two geese.

"Well now, daddy," said his son, while he and Leo examined the dress with minute interest, "I wish you'd make a clean breast of it, and let us know how many more surprises and contrivances of this sort you've got in store for us."

"I fear this is the last one, Benjy, though there's no end to the applications of these contrivances. You'd better apply this one to yourself now, and see how you get on in it."

Of course Benjy was more than willing, though, as he remarked, the dress was far too big for him.

"Never mind that, my boy. A tight fit ain't needful, and nobody will find fault with the cut in these regions."

"Where ever did you get it, father?" asked the boy, as the fastenings were being secured round him.

"I got it from an ingenious friend, who says he's goin' to bring it out soon. Mayhap it's in the shops of old England by this time. There, now, off you go, but don't be too risky, Ben. Keep her full, and mind your helm."[1]

Thus encouraged, the eager boy waded into the water, but, in his haste, tripped and fell, sending a volume of water over himself. He rose, however, without difficulty, and, proceeding with greater caution, soon walked off into deep water. Here he paddled about in a state of exuberant glee. The dress kept him perfectly dry, although he splashed the water about in reckless fashion, and did not return to land till quite exhausted.

Benjamin Vane from that day devoted himself to that machine. He became so enamoured of the "water-tramp," as he styled it—not knowing its proper name at the time—that he went about the lakelets in it continually, sometimes fishing, at other times shooting. He even ventured a short distance out to sea in it, to the amazement of the Eskimos, the orbits of whose eyes were being decidedly enlarged, Benjy said, and their eyebrows permanently raised, by the constant succession of astonishment-fits into which they were thrown from day to day by their white visitors.

---

1. Lest it should be supposed that the "pedomotive" here described is the mere creature of the author's brain, it may be well to state that he has seen it in the establishment of the patentees, Messrs. Thornton and Company of Edinburgh.

Chapter XX

One pleasant morning, towards the end of summer, Benjamin Vane went out with his gun in the water-tramp on the large lake of Paradise Isle.

Leo and he had reached the isle in one of the india-rubber boats. They had taken Anders with them to carry their game, and little Oblooria to prepare their dinner while they were away shooting; for they disliked the delay of personal attention to cooking when they were ravenous! After landing Benjy, and seeing him busy getting himself into the aquatic dress, Leo said he would pull off to a group of walruses, which were sporting about off shore, and shoot one. Provisions of fowl and fish were plentiful enough just then at the Eskimo village, but he knew that walrus beef was greatly prized by the natives, and none of the huge creatures had been killed for some weeks past.

About this time the threatened war with the northern Eskimos had unfortunately commenced.

The insatiable Grabantak had made a descent on one of Amalatok's smaller islands, killed the warriors, and carried off the women and children, with everything else he could lay hands on. Of course Amalatok made reprisals; attacked a small island belonging to Grabantak, and did as much general mischief as he could. The paltry islet about which the war began was not worthy either of attack or defence!

Then Amalatok, burning with the righteous indignation of the man who did not begin the quarrel, got up a grand muster of his forces, and went with a great fleet of kayaks to attack Grabantak in his strongholds.

But Grabantak's strongholds were remarkably strong. A good deal of killing was done, and some destruction of property accomplished, but that did not effect the conquest of the great northern Savage. Neither did it prove either party to be right or wrong! Grabantak retired to impregnable fastnesses, and Amalatok returned to Poloeland "covered with glory,"—some of his followers also covered with wounds, a few of which had fallen to his own share. The success, however, was not decided. On the whole, the result was rather disappointing, but Amalatok was brave and high-spirited, as some people would say. *He* was not going to give in; not he! He would fight as long as a man was left to back him, and bring Grabantak to his knees—or die! Either event would, of course, have been of immense advantage to both nations. He ground his teeth and glared when he announced this determination, and also shook his fist, but a sharp twinge of pain in one of his unhealed wounds caused him to cease frowning abruptly.

There was a sound, too, in the air, which caused him to sit down and reflect. It was a mixed and half-stifled sound, as if of women groaning and little children wailing. Some of his braves, of course, had fallen in the recent conflicts—fallen honourably with their faces to the foe. Their young widows and their little ones mourned them, and refused to be comforted, because they were not. It was highly unpatriotic, no doubt, but natural.

Amalatok had asked the white men to join him in the fight, but they had refused. They would help him to defend his country, if attacked, they said, but they would not go out to war. Amalatok had once threatened Blackbeard if he refused to go, but Blackbeard had smiled, and threatened to retaliate by making him "jump!" Whereupon the old chief became suddenly meek.

This, then, was the state of affairs when Benjy and Leo went shooting, on the morning to which we have referred.

But who can hope to describe, with adequate force, the joyful feelings of Benjamin Vane as he moved slily about the lakelets of Paradise Isle in the water-tramp? The novelty of the situation was so great. The surrounding circumstances were so peculiar. The prolonged calms of the circumpolar basin, at that period of the year, were so new to one accustomed to the variable skies of England; the perpetual sunshine, the absence of any necessity to consider time, in a land from which night seemed to have finally fled; the glassy repose of lake and sea, so suggestive of peace; the cheery bustle of animal life, so suggestive of pleasure—all these influences together filled the boy's breast with a strong romantic joy which was far too powerful to seek or find relief in those boisterous leaps and shouts which were his usual safety-valves.

Although not much given to serious thought, except when conversing with his father, Benjy became meditative as he moved quietly about at the edge of the reeds, and began to wonder whether the paradise above *could* exceed this paradise below!

Events occurred that day which proved to him that the sublunary paradise was, at least, woefully uncertain in its nature.

"Now, just keep still, will you, for one moment," muttered Benjy, advancing cautiously through the outer margin of reeds, among the stems of which he peered earnestly while he cocked his gun.

The individual to whom he spoke made no reply, because it was a goose—would that it were thus with all geese! It was a grey goose of the largest size. It had caught a glimpse of the new and strange creature that was paddling about its home, and was wisely making for the shelter of a spot where the reeds were more dense, and where Benjy would not have dared to follow. For, it must be remembered that our young sportsman was sunk to his waist in water, and that the reeds rose high over his head, so that if once lost in the heart of them, he might have found it extremely difficult to find his way out again.

Anxious not to lose his chance, he gave vent to a loud shout. This had the effect of setting up innumerable flocks of wild-fowl, which, although unseen, had been lurking listeners to the strange though gentle sound of the water-tramp. Among them rose the grey goose with one or two unexpected comrades.

Benjy had not at that time acquired the power of self-restraint necessary to good shooting. He fired hastily, and missed with the first barrel. Discharging the second in hotter haste, he missed again, but brought down one of the comrades by accident. This was sufficiently gratifying. Picking it up, he placed it on the boat-buoy in front of him to balance several ducks which already lay on the part in rear. He might have carried a dozen geese on his novel hunting-dress, if there had been room for them, for its floating power was sufficient to have borne up himself, and at least four, if not five, men.

Pursuing his way cautiously and gently, by means of the webbed feet alone, the young sportsman moved about like a sly water-spirit among the reeds, sometimes addressing a few pleasant words, such as, "how d'ye do, old boy," or, "don't alarm yourself, my tulip," to a water-hen or a coot, or some such bird which crossed his path, but was unworthy of his shot; at other times stopping to gaze contemplatively through the reed stems, or to float and rest in placid enjoyment, while he tried to imagine himself in a forest of water-trees.

Everywhere the feathered tribes first gazed at him

in mute surprise; then hurried, with every variety of squeak, and quack, and fluttering wing, from his frightful presence.

Suddenly he came in sight of a bird so large that his heart gave a violent leap, and the gun went almost of its own accord to his shoulder, but the creature disappeared among the reeds before he could take aim. Another opening, however, again revealed it fully to view! It was a swan—a hyperborean wild swan!

Just as he made this discovery, the great bird, having observed Benjy, spread its enormous wings and made off with an amazing splutter.

Bang! went Benjy's gun, both barrels in quick succession, and down fell the swan quite dead, with its head in the water and its feet pointing to the sky.

"What a feast the Eskimos will have to-night!" was Benjy's first thought as he tramped vehemently towards his prize.

But his overflowing joy was rudely checked, for, having laid his gun down in front of him, for the purpose of using the paddle with both hands, it slipped to one side, tilted up, and, disappearing like an arrow in the lake, went to the bottom.

The sinking of Benjy's heart was not less complete. He had the presence of mind, however, to seize the reeds near him and check his progress at the exact spot. Leaning over the side of his little craft, he beheld his weapon quivering, as it were, at the bottom, in about eight feet of water. What was to be done? The energetic youth was not long in making up his mind on that point. He would dive for it. But diving in the water-tramp was out of the question. Knowing that it was all but impossible to make his way to the shore through the reeds, he resolved to reach the opposite shore, which was in some places free from vegetation. Seizing one of the reeds, he forced it down, and tied it into a knot to mark the spot where his loss had happened. He treated several more reeds in this way till he gained the open water outside, thus marking his path. Then he paddled across the lake, landed, undressed, and swam out again, pushing the empty dress before him, intending to use it as a resting-place.

On reaching the spot, he dived with a degree of vigour and agility worthy of a duck, but found it hard to reach the bottom, as he was not much accustomed to diving. For the same reason he found it difficult to open his eyes under water, so as to look for the gun. While trying to do so, a desperate desire to breathe caused him to leap to the surface, where he found that he had struggled somewhat away from the exact spot. After a few minutes' rest, he took a long breath and again went down; but found, to his dismay, that in his first dive he had disturbed the mud, and thus made the water thick. Groping about rendered it thicker, and he came to the surface the second time with feelings approaching to despair. Besides which, his powers were being rapidly exhausted.

But Benjy was full of pluck as well as perseverance. Feeling that he could not hold out much longer, he resolved to make the next attempt with more care—a resolve, it may be remarked, which it would have been better to have made at first.

He swam to the knotted reed, considered well the position he had occupied when his loss occurred, took an aim at a definite spot with his head, and went down. The result was that his hands grasped the stock of the gun the moment they reached the bottom.

Inflated with joy he leaped with it to the surface like a bladder; laid it carefully on the water-dress, and pushing the latter before him soon succeeded in getting hold of the dead swan. The bird was too heavy to be lifted on the float, he therefore grasped its neck with his teeth, and thus, heavily weighted, made for the shore.

It will not surprise the reader to be told that Benjy felt hungry as well as tired after these achievements, and this induced him to look anxiously for Leo, and to wonder why the smoke of Oblooria's cooking-lamp was not to be seen anywhere.

The engrossing nature of the events just described had prevented our little hero from observing that a smart breeze had sprung up, and that heavy clouds had begun to drive across the hitherto blue sky, while appearances of a very squally nature were gathering on the windward horizon. Moreover, while engaged in paddling among the reeds he had not felt the breeze.

It was while taking off the water-tramp that he became fully alive to these facts.

"That's it," he muttered to himself. "They've been caught by this breeze and been delayed by having had to pull against it, or perhaps the walruses gave them more trouble than they expected."

Appeasing his appetite as well as he could with this

reflection, he left the water-tramp on the ground, with the dripping gun beside it, and hurried to the highest part of the island. Although not much of an elevation, it enabled him to see all round, and a feeling of anxiety filled his breast as he observed that the once glassy sea was ruffled to the colour of indigo, while wavelets flecked it everywhere, and no boat was visible!

"They may have got behind some of the islands," he thought, and continued his look-out for some time, with growing anxiety and impatience, however, because the breeze was by that time freshening to a gale.

When an hour had passed away the poor boy became thoroughly alarmed.

"Can anything have happened to the boat?" he said to himself. "The india-rubber is easily cut. Perhaps they may have been blown out to sea!"

This latter thought caused an involuntary shudder. Looking round, he observed that the depression of the sun towards the horizon indicated that night had set in.

"This will never do," he suddenly exclaimed aloud. "Leo will be lost. I *must* risk it!"

Turning as he spoke, he ran back to the spot where he had left the water-dress, which he immediately put on. Then, leaving gun and game on the beach, he boldly entered the sea, and struck out with feet and paddle for Poloeland.

Although sorely buffeted by the rising waves, and several times overwhelmed, his waterproof costume proved well able to bear him up, and with comparatively little fatigue he reached the land in less than two hours. Without waiting to take the dress off, he ran up to the Eskimo village and gave the alarm.

While these events were going on among the islets, Captain Vane and Alphonse Vandervell had been far otherwise engaged.

"Come, Alf," said the Captain, that same morning, after Leo and his party had started on their expedition, "let you and me go off on a scientific excursion,—on what we may style a botanico-geologico-meteorological survey."

"With all my heart, uncle, and let us take Butterface with us, and Oolichuk."

"Ay, lad, and Ivitchuk and Akeetolik too, and Chingatok if you will, for I've fixed on a spot whereon to pitch an observatory, and we must set to work on it without further delay. Indeed I would have got it into working order long ago if it had not been for my hope that the cessation of this miserable war would have enabled us to get nearer the North Pole this summer."

The party soon started for the highest peak of the island of Poloe—or Poloeland, as Alf preferred to call it. Oolichuk carried on his broad shoulders one of those mysterious cases out of which the Captain was so fond of taking machines wherewith to astonish the natives.

Indeed it was plain to see that the natives who accompanied them on this occasion expected some sort of surprise, despite the Captain's earnest assurance that there was nothing in the box except a few meteorological instruments. How the Captain translated to the Eskimos the word meteorological we have never been able to ascertain. His own explanation is that he did it in a roundabout manner which they failed to comprehend, and which he himself could not elucidate.

On the way up the hill, Alf made several interesting discoveries of plants which were quite new to him.

"Ho! stop, I say, uncle," he exclaimed for the twentieth time that day, as he picked up some object of interest.

"What now, lad?" said the Captain, stopping and wiping his heated brow.

"Here is another specimen of these petrifactions—look!"

"He means a vegetable o' some sort turned to stone, Chingatok," explained the Captain, as he examined the specimen with an interested though unscientific eye.

"You remember, uncle, the explanation I gave you some time ago," said the enthusiastic Alf, "about Professor Heer of Zurich, who came to the conclusion that primeval forests once existed in these now treeless Arctic regions, from the fossils of oak, elm, pine, and maple leaves discovered there. Well, I found a fossil of a plane leaf the other day,—not a very good one, to be sure—and now, here is a splendid specimen of a petrified oak-leaf. Don't you trace it quite plainly?"

"Well, lad," returned the Captain, frowning at the specimen, "I do believe you're right. There does seem to be the mark of a leaf there, and there is some ground for your theory that this land may have been once covered with trees, though it's hard to believe that when we look at it."

"An evidence, uncle, that we should not be too ready to judge by appearances," said Alf, as they resumed their upward march.

The top gained, a space was quickly selected and cleared, and a simple hut of flat stones begun, while the Captain unpacked his box. It contained a barometer, a maximum and minimum self-registering thermometer, wet and dry bulb, also a black bulb thermometer, a one-eighth-inch rain-gauge, and several other instruments.

"I have another box of similar instruments, Alf, down below," said the Captain, as he laid them carefully out, "and I hope, by comparing the results obtained up here with those obtained at the level of the sea, to carry home a series of notes which will be of considerable value to science."

When the Captain had finished laying them out, the Eskimos retired to a little distance, and regarded them for some minutes with anxious expectancy; but, as the strange things did not burst, or go up like sky-rockets, they soon returned with a somewhat disappointed look to their hut-building.

The work was quickly completed, for Eskimos are expert builders in their way, and the instruments had been carefully set up under shelter when the first symptoms of the storm began.

"I hope the sportsmen have returned," said the Captain, looking gravely round the horizon.

"No doubt they have," said Alf, preparing to descend the mountain. "Leo is not naturally reckless, and if he were, the cautious Anders would be a drag on him."

An hour later they regained the Eskimo village, just as Benjy came running, in a state of dripping consternation, from the sea.

Need it be said that an instant and vigorous search was instituted? Not only did a band of the stoutest warriors, headed by Chingatok, set off in a fleet of kayaks, but the Captain and his companions started without delay in the two remaining india-rubber boats, and, flying their kites, despite the risk of doing so in a gale, went away in eager haste over the foaming billows.

After exerting themselves to the uttermost, they failed to discover the slightest trace of the lost boat. The storm passed quickly, and a calm succeeded, enabling them to prosecute the search more effectively with oar and paddle, but with no better result.

Day after day passed, and still no member of the band—Englishman or Eskimo—would relax his efforts, or admit that hope was sinking. But they had to admit it at last, and, after three weeks of unremitting toil, they were compelled to give up in absolute despair. The most sanguine was driven to the terrible conclusion that Leo, Anders, and timid little Oblooria were lost.

It was an awful blow. What cared Alf or the Captain now for discovery, or scientific investigation! The poor negro, who had never at any time cared for plants, rocks, or Poles, was sunk in the profoundest depths of sorrow. Benjy's gay spirit was utterly broken.

Oolichuk's hearty laugh was silenced, and a cloud of settled melancholy descended over the entire village of Poloe.

Chapter XXI

FATE OF THE LOST ONES.

Leo, Anders, and timid little Oblooria, however, were not lost! Their case was bad enough, but it had not quite come to that.

On parting from Benjy, as described in the last chapter, these three went after a walrus, which coquetted with them instead of attacking, and drew them a considerable distance away from the island. This would have been a matter of trifling import if the weather had remained calm, but, as we have seen, a sudden and violent gale arose.

When the coming squall was first observed the boat was far to leeward of Paradise Isle, and as that island happened to be one of the most northerly of the group over which Amalatok ruled, they were thus far to leeward of any land with the exception of a solitary sugar-loaf rock near the horizon. Still Leo and his companions were not impressed with any sense of danger. They had been so long accustomed to calms, and to moving about in the india-rubber boats by means of paddles with perfect ease and security, that they had half forgotten the force of wind. Besides, the walrus was still playing with them provokingly—keeping just out of rifle-shot as if he had studied fire-arms and knew their range exactly.

"The rascal!" exclaimed Leo at last, losing patience, "he will never let us come an inch nearer."

"Try 'im once more," said Anders, who was a keen sportsman, "push him, paddle strong. Ho! Oblooria, paddle hard and queek."

Although the interpreter, being in a facetious mood, addressed Oblooria in English, she quite understood his significant gestures, and bent to her work with a degree of energy and power quite surprising in one apparently so fragile. Leo also used his oars, (for they had both oars and paddles), with such good-will that the boat skimmed over the Arctic sea like a northern diver, and the distance between them and the walrus was perceptibly lessened.

"I don't like the looks o' the southern sky," said Leo, regarding the horizon with knitted brows.

"Hims black 'nough—any'ow," said Anders.

"Hold. I'll have a farewell shot at the brute, and give up the chase," said Leo, laying down the oars and grasping his rifle.

The ball seemed to take effect, for the walrus dived immediately with a violent splutter, and was seen no more.

By this time the squall was hissing towards them

so fast that the hunters, giving up all thought of the walrus, turned at once and made for the land, but land by that time lay far off on the southern horizon with a dark foam-flecked sea between it and them.

"There's no fear of the boat, Oblooria," said Leo, glancing over his shoulder at the girl, who sat crouching to meet the first burst of the coming storm, "but you must hold on tight to the life-lines."

There was no need to caution Anders. That worthy was already on his knees embracing a thwart—his teeth clenched as he gazed over the bow.

On it came like a whirlwind of the tropics, and rushed right over the low round gunwale of the boat, sweeping loose articles overboard, and carrying her bodily to leeward. Leo had taken a turn of the life-lines round both thighs, and held manfully to his oars. These, after stooping to the first rush of wind and water, he plied with all his might, and was ably seconded by Oblooria as well as by the interpreter, but a very few minutes of effort sufficed to convince them that they laboured in vain. They did not even "hold their own," as sailors have it, but drifted slowly, yet steadily, to the north.

"It's impossible to make head against *this*," said Leo, suddenly ceasing his efforts, "and I count it a piece of good fortune, for which we cannot be too thankful, that there is still land to leeward of us."

He pointed to the sugar-loaf rock before mentioned, towards which they were now rapidly drifting.

"Nothing to eat dere. Nothing to drink," said Anders, gloomily.

"Oh! that won't matter much. A squall like this can't last long. We shall soon be able to start again for home, no doubt. I say, Anders, what are these creatures off the point there? They seem too large and black for sea-birds, and not the shape of seals or walruses."

The interpreter gazed earnestly at the objects in question for some moments without answering. The rock which they were quickly nearing was rugged, barren, and steep on its southern face, against which the waves were by that time dashing with extreme violence, so that landing there would have been an impossibility. On its lee or northern side, however they might count on quiet water.

"We have nothing to fear," said Leo, observing that Oblooria was much agitated; "tell her so, Anders; we are sure to find a sheltered creek of some sort on the other side."

"I fear not the rocks or storm," replied the Eskimo girl to Anders. "It is Grabantak, the chief of Flatland, that I fear."

"Grabantak!" exclaimed Anders and Leo in the same breath.

"Grabantak is coming with his men!"

Poor little Oblooria, whose face had paled while her whole frame trembled, pointed towards the dark objects which had already attracted their attention. They were by that time near enough to be distinguished, and as they came, one after another, round the western point of Sugarloaf rock, it was all too evident that the girl was right, and that the fleet of kayaks was probably bearing the northern savage and his men to attack the inhabitants of Poloe.

Leo's first impulse was to seize his repeating rifle and fill its cartridge-chamber quite full. It may be well to observe here that the cartridges, being carried in a tight waterproof case, had not been affected by the seas which had so recently overwhelmed them.

"What's de use?" asked Anders, in an unusually sulky tone, as he watched the youth's action. "Two men not can fight all de mans of Flatland."

"No, but I can pick off a dozen of them, one after another, with my good rifle, and then the rest will fly. Grabantak will fall first, and his best men after him."

This was no idle boast on the part of Leo. He knew that he could accomplish what he threatened long before the Eskimos could get within spear-throwing distance of his boat.

"No use," repeated Anders, firmly, still shaking his head in a sulky manner. "When you's bullets be done, more an' more inimies come on. Then dey kill you, an' me, an' Oblooria."

Leo laid down his weapon. The resolve to die fighting to the last was the result of a mere impulse of animal courage. Second thoughts cooled him, and the reference to Oblooria's fate decided him.

"You are right, Anders. If by fighting to the death I could save Oblooria, it would be my duty as well as my pleasure to fight; but I see that I haven't the ghost of a chance against such a host as is approaching, and it would be simply revengeful to send as many as I can into the next world before going there myself. Besides, it would exasperate the savages, and make them harder on the poor girl."

In saying this Leo was rather arguing out the point with himself than talking to the interpreter, who did not indeed understand much of what he said. Having made up his mind how to act, Leo stowed his precious rifle and ammunition in a small bag placed for that purpose under one of the thwarts, and, resuming the oars, prepared to meet his fate, whatever it should be, peacefully and unarmed.

While thus drifting in silence before the gale, the thought suddenly occurred to Leo, "How strange it is that I, who am a Christian—in name at least—should feel as if it were absurd to pray for God's help at such a time as this! Surely He who made me and these Eskimos is capable of guarding us? The very least we can do is to ask Him to guide us!"

The youth was surprised at the thought. It had flashed upon him like a ray of light. It was not the first time that he had been in even more imminent danger than the present, yet he had never before thought of the necessity of asking help from God, as if He were really present and able as well as willing to succour. Before the thought had passed he acted on it. He had no time for formal prayer. He looked up! It was prayer without words. In a few minutes more the boat was surrounded by the fleet of kayaks. There were hundreds of these tiny vessels of the north, each with its solitary occupant, using his double-bladed paddle vigorously.

Need we say that the strangers were at first gazed on with speechless wonder? and that the Eskimos kept for some time hovering round them at a respectful distance, as if uncertain how to act, but with their war-spears ready? All the time the whole party drifted before the gale towards the island-rock.

"Anders," said Leo, while the natives remained in this state of indecision, "my mind is made up as to our course of action. We will offer no resistance whatever to these fellows. We must be absolutely submissive, unless, indeed, they attempt to ill-treat Oblooria, in which case of course we will defend her. Do you hear?"

This was said with such quiet decision, and the concluding question was put in such a tone, that the interpreter replied, "Yis, sar," promptly.

As Leo made no sign of any kind, but continued to guide the boat steadily with the oars, as if his sole anxiety was to round the western point of the island and get into a place of shelter, the natives turned their kayaks and advanced along with him. Naturally they fell into the position of an escort—a part of the fleet paddling on each side of the captives, (for such they now were), while the rest brought up the rear.

"What ails Oblooria, Anders?" asked Leo in a low tone.

"What is the matter?" asked the interpreter, turning to the girl, who, ever since the approach of the Eskimos, had crouched like a bundle in the bottom of the boat with her face buried in her hands. "There is no fear. Grabantak is a man, not a bear. He will not eat you."

"Grabantak knows me," answered the poor girl, without lifting her head; "he came to Poloe once, before the war, and wanted me to be the wife of his son. I want not his son. I want Oolichuk!"

The simplicity and candour of this confession caused Leo to laugh in spite of himself, while poor little Oblooria, who thought it no laughing matter, burst into tears.

Of course the men of Flatland kept their eyes fixed in wide amazement on Leo, as they paddled along, and this sudden laugh of his impressed them deeply, being apparently without a cause, coupled as it was with an air of absolute indifference to his probable fate, and to the presence of so many foes. Even the ruthless land-hungerer, Grabantak, was solemnised.

In a few minutes the whole party swept round the point of rocks, and proceeded towards the land over the comparatively quiet waters of a little bay which lay under the lee of the Sugar-loaf rock.

During the brief period that had been afforded for thought, Leo had been intently making his plans. He now proceeded to carry them out.

"Hand me the trinket-bundle," he said to Anders.

The interpreter searched in a waterproof pouch in the stern of the boat, and produced a small bundle of such trinkets as are known to be valued by savages. It had been placed and was always kept there by Captain Vane, to be ready for emergencies.

"They will be sure to take everything from us at any rate," remarked Leo, as he divided the trinkets into two separate bundles, "so I shall take the wind out of their sails by giving everything up at once with a good grace."

The Grabantaks, if we may so style them, drew near,

as the fleet approached the shore, with increasing curiosity. When land was reached they leaped out of their kayaks and crowded round the strangers. It is probable that they would have seized them and their possessions at this point, but the tall strapping figure of Leo, and his quiet manner, overawed them. They held back while the india-rubber boat was being carried by Leo and Anders to a position of safety.

Poor Oblooria walked beside them with her head bowed down, shrinking as much as possible out of sight. Everybody was so taken up with the strange white man that no one took any notice of her.

No sooner was the boat laid down than Leo taking one of the bundles of trinkets stepped up to Grabantak, whom he easily distinguished by his air of superiority and the deference paid him by his followers.

Pulling his own nose by way of a friendly token, Leo smiled benignantly in the chief's face, and opened the bundle before him.

It is needless to say that delight mingled with the surprise that had hitherto blazed on the visage of Grabantak.

"Come here, Anders, and bring the other bundle with you. Tell this warrior that I am very glad to meet with him."

"Great and unconquerable warrior," began the interpreter, in the dialect which he had found was understood, by the men of Poloe, "we have come from far-off lands to bring you gifts—"

"Anders," said Leo, whose knowledge of the Eskimo tongue was sufficient, by that time, to enable him in a measure to follow the drift of a speech, "Anders, if you don't tell him *exactly* what I say I'll kick you into the sea!"

As Anders stood on a rock close to the water's edge, and Leo looked unusually stern, he thereafter rendered faithfully what the latter told him to say. The speech was something to the following effect:—

"I am one of a small band of white men who have come here to search out the land. We do not want the land. We only want to see it. We have plenty of land of our own in the far south. We have been staying with the great chief Amalatok in Poloeland."

At the mention of his enemy's name the countenance of Grabantak darkened. Without noticing this, Leo went on:—

"When I was out hunting with my man and a woman, the wind arose and blew us hither. We claim your hospitality, and hope you will help us to get back again to Poloeland. If you do so we will reward you well, for white men are powerful and rich. See, here are gifts for Grabantak, and for his wife."

This latter remark was a sort of inspiration. Leo had observed, while Anders was speaking, that a stout cheerful-faced woman had been pushing aside the men and gradually edging her way toward the Eskimo chief with the air of a privileged person. That he had hit the mark was obvious, for Grabantak turned with a bland smile, and hit his wife a facetious and rather heavy slap on the shoulder. She was evidently accustomed to such treatment, and did not wince.

Taking from his bundle a gorgeous smoking-cap

richly ornamented with brilliant beads, Leo coolly crowned the chief with it. Grabantak drew himself up and tried to look majestic, but a certain twitching of his face, and sparkle in his eyes, betrayed a tendency to laugh with delight. Fortunately, there was another cap of exactly the same pattern in the bundle, which Leo instantly placed on the head of the wife—whose name he afterwards learned was Merkut.

The chief's assumed dignity vanished at this. With that childlike hilarity peculiar to the Eskimo race, he laughed outright, and then, seizing the cap from Merkut's head, put it above his own to the amusement of his grinning followers.

Leo then selected a glittering clasp-knife with two blades, which the chief seized eagerly. It was evidently a great prize—too serious a gift to be lightly laughed at. Then a comb was presented to the wife, and a string of gay beads, and a pair of scissors. Of course the uses of combs and scissors he explained, and deep was the interest manifested during the explanation, and utter the forgetfulness of the whole party for the time being in regard to everything else in the world—Oblooria included, who sat unnoticed on the rocks with her face still buried in her hands.

When Grabantak's possessions were so numerous that the hood of his coat, and the tops of his wife's boots were nearly filled with them, he became generous, and, prince-like, (having more than he knew what to do with), began to distribute things to his followers.

Among these followers was a tall and stalwart son of his own, to whom he was rather stern, and not very liberal. Perhaps the chief wished to train him with Spartan ideas of self-denial. Perhaps he wanted his followers to note his impartiality. Merkut did not, however, act on the same principles, for she quietly passed a number of valuable articles over to her dear son Koyatuk, unobserved by his stern father.

Things had gone on thus pleasantly for some time; the novelty of the gifts, and the interest in their explanation having apparently rendered these people forgetful of the fact that they might take them all at once; when a sudden change in the state of affairs was wrought by the utterance of one word.

"We must not," said Leo to Anders, looking at his follower over the heads of the Eskimos, "forget poor little Oblooria."

"Oblooria!" roared Grabantak with a start, as if he had been electrified.

"Oblooria!" echoed Koyatuk, glaring round.

"Oblooria!" gasped the entire band.

Another moment and Grabantak, bursting through the crowd, leaped towards the crouching girl and raised her face. Recognising her he uttered a yell which probably was meant for a cheer.

Hurrying the frightened girl into the circle through which he had broken, the chief presented her to his son, and, with an air worthy of a civilised courtier, said:—

"Your *wife*, Koyatuk—your Oblooria!—Looria!"

He went over the last syllables several times, as if he doubted his senses, and feared it was too good news to be true.

This formal introduction was greeted by the chief's followers with a series of wild shouts and other demonstrations of extreme joy.

Chapter XXII

A FIGHT IN DEFENCE OF A WOMAN, AND
RIFLE-SHOOTING EXTRAORDINARY.

When the excitement had somewhat abated, Leo stepped to the side of Oblooria, and laying his hand on her shoulder said firmly, through Anders:—

"Pardon me, Grabantak, this girl is *not* the wife of Koyatuk; she is my *sister*!"

The chief frowned, clenched his teeth, and grasped a spear—

"When did Kablunet men begin to have Eskimo sisters?"

"When they took all distressed women under their protection," returned Leo promptly. "Every woman who needs my help is my sister," he added with a look of self-sufficiency which he was far from feeling.

This new doctrine obviously puzzled the chief, who frowned, smiled, and looked at the ground, as if in meditation. It seemed to afford great comfort to

Oblooria, who nestled closer to her champion. As for Koyatuk, he treated the matter with an air of mingled surprise and scorn, but dutifully awaited his father's pleasure.

Koyatuk was physically a fine specimen of a savage, but his spirit was not equal to his body. Like his father he was over six feet high, and firmly knit, being of both larger and stronger build than Leo, whom he now regarded, and of course hated, as his rival—a contemptible one, no doubt; still—a rival.

The warriors watched their chief in breathless suspense. To them it was a thoroughly new and interesting situation. That a white stranger, tall and active, but slender and very young, should dare single-handed to defy not only their chief, but, as it were, the entire tribe, including the royal family, was a state of things in regard to which their previous lives afforded no parallel. They could not understand it at all, and stood, as it were, in eager, open-mouthed, and one-legged expectation.

At last Grabantak looked up, as if smitten by a new idea, and spoke—

"Can Kablunet men fight?" he asked.

"They love peace better than war," answered Leo, "but when they see cause to fight they can do so."

Turning immediately to his son, Grabantak said with a grim smile—

"Behold your wife, take her!"

Koyatuk advanced. Leo placed Oblooria behind him, and, being unarmed, threw himself into a pugilistic posture of defence. The young Eskimo laid one of his strong hands on the Englishman's shoulder, intending to thrust him aside violently. Leo was naturally of a tender disposition. He shrank from dealing a violent blow to one who had not the remotest idea of what was coming, or how to defend himself from the human fist when used as a battering-ram.

But Leo chanced to be, in a sense, doubly armed. During one of his holiday rambles in England he had visited Cornwall, and there had learned that celebrated "throw" which consists in making your haunch a fulcrum, your right arm a lever, and your adversary a shuttlecock. He suddenly grasped his foe round the waist with one arm. Next moment the Grabantaks saw what the most imaginative among them had never till then conceived of—Koyatuk's soles turned to the sky, and his head pointing to the ground! The moment following, he lay flat on his back looking upwards blankly.

The huk! hi! ho! hooroos! that followed may be conceived, but cannot be described. Some of the men burst into laughter, for anything ludicrous is irresistible to an Eskimo of the very far north. A few were petrified. Others there were who resented this indignity to the heir-apparent, and flourished their spears in a threatening manner. These last Grabantak quieted with a look. The incident undoubtedly surprised that stern parent, but also afforded him some amusement. He said it was an insult that must be avenged. Oddly enough he made use of an expression which sounded curiously familiar to Leo's ears, as translated by Anders. "The insult," said Grabantak, "could only be *washed out in blood*!"

Strange, that simple savages of the far north should hold to that ridiculous doctrine. We had imagined that it was confined entirely to those further south, whose minds have been more or less warped by civilised usage.

A ring was immediately formed, and poor Leo now saw that the matter was becoming serious. He was on the eve of fighting an enforced duel in Oblooria's service.

While the savages were preparing the lists, and Koyatuk, having recovered, was engaged in converse with his father, Leo whispered to Anders—

"Perhaps Oblooria has no objection to be the wife of this man?"

But the poor girl had very strong objections. She was, moreover, so emphatic in her expressions of horror, and cast on her champion such a look of entreaty, that he would have been more than mortal had he refused her. It was very perplexing. The idea of killing, or being killed, in such a cause was very repulsive. He tried to reason with Grabantak about the sin of injuring a defenceless woman, and the abstract right of females in general to have some say in the selection of their husbands, but Grabantak was inexorable.

"Is the Kablunet afraid?" he asked, with a glance of scornful surprise.

"Does he *look* afraid?" returned Leo, quietly.

Koyatuk now stepped into the middle of the ring of warriors, with a short spear in his right hand, and half-a-dozen spare ones in his left, whereby Leo perceived that the battle before him was not meant to be a mere "exchange of shots," for the "satisfaction of honour." There was evidently no humbug about these Eskimos.

Two men mounted guard over Anders and Oblooria, who, however, were allowed to remain inside the ring to witness the combat. A warrior now advanced to Leo and presented him with a small bundle of spears. He took them almost mechanically, thanked the giver, and laid them down at his feet without selecting one. Then he stood up, and, crossing his arms on his breast, gazed full at his opponent, who made a hideous face at him and flourished his spear.

It was quite evident that the Eskimos were perplexed by the white youth's conduct, and knew not what to make of it. The truth is that poor Leo was almost beside himself with conflicting emotions and uncertainty as to what he ought to do. Despite all that had taken place, he found it almost impossible to persuade himself that he was actually about to engage in mortal combat. He had not a vestige of angry feeling in his heart against the man whom he was expected to fight with to the death, and the extraordinary nature of the complex faces that Koyatuk was making at him tended to foster the delusion that the whole thing was a farce—or a dream.

Then the knowledge that he could burst through the ring, get hold of his rifle, and sell his life dearly, or, perhaps, cause the whole savage tribe to fly in terror, was a sore temptation to him. All this, coupled with the necessity for taking instant and vigorous action of some sort, was enough to drive an older head distracted. It did drive the blood violently to the youth's face, but, by a powerful effort of self-restraint, he continued to stand perfectly still, like a living statue, facing the Eskimo.

At last Koyatuk became tired of making useless faces at his rival. Suddenly poising his spear, he launched it.

Had Leo's eye been less quick, or his limbs less active, that spear had laid him low for ever. He had barely time to spring aside, when the weapon passed between his side and his left arm, grazing the latter slightly, and drawing blood which trickled to the ends of his fingers.

There could be no further doubt now about the nature of the fight. Catching up a spear from the bundle at his feet he was just in time to receive the Eskimo, who sprang in on him with the intention of coming at once to close quarters. His rush was very furious; probably with a view to make it decisive. But the agile Leo was equal to the occasion. Bending suddenly so low as to be quite under his opponent's desperate thrust, he struck out his right leg firmly. Koyatuk tripped over it, and ploughed the land for some yards with his hands, head, and knees.

Considerably staggered in mind and body by the fall, he sprang up with a roar, and turned to renew the attack. Leo was ready. The Eskimo, by that time mad with pain, humiliation, and rage, exercised no caution in his assault. He rushed at his rival like a mad bull. Our Englishman saw his opportunity. Dropping his own spear he guarded the thrust of his adversary's with his right arm, while, with his left fist, he planted a solid blow on Koyatuk's forehead. The right fist followed the left like the lightning flash, and alighted on Koyatuk's nose, which, flat by nature, was rendered flatter still by art. Indeed it would be the weakest flattery to assert that he had any nose at all after receiving that blow. It was reduced to the shape of a small pancake, from the two holes in which there instantly spouted a stream of blood so copious that it drenched alike its owner and his rival.

After giving him this double salute, Leo stepped quickly aside to let him tumble forward, heels over head, which he did with the only half-checked impetuosity of his onset, and lay prone upon the ground.

"There, Anders," said the victor, turning round as he pointed to his prostrate foe, "surely Grabantak's son has got enough of blood now to wipe out all the insults he ever received, or is likely to receive, from me."

Grabantak appeared to agree to this view of the case. That he saw and relished the jest was obvious, for he burst into an uproarious fit of laughter, in which his amiable warriors joined him, and, advancing to Leo, gave him a hearty slap of approval on the shoulder. At the same time he cast a look of amused scorn on his fallen son, who was being attended to by Merkut.

It may be observed here that Merkut was the only woman of the tribe allowed to go on this war-expedition. Being the chief's wife, she had been allowed to do as she pleased, and it was her pleasure to accompany the party and to travel like the warriors in a kayak, which she managed as well as the best of them.

Grabantak now ordered his men to encamp, and feed till the gale should abate. Then, calling Leo and the interpreter aside, he questioned them closely as to the condition of the Poloese and the numbers of the white men who had recently joined them.

Of course Leo made Anders give him a graphic account of the preparations made by his enemies to receive him, in the hope that he might be induced to give up his intentions, but he had mistaken the spirit of the Eskimo, who merely showed his teeth, frowned, laughed in a diabolic manner, and flourished his spear during the recital of Amalatok's warlike arrangements. He wound up by saying that he was rejoiced to learn all that, because it would be all the more to his credit to make his enemy go down on his knees, lick the dust, crawl in his presence, and otherwise humble himself.

"But tell him, Anders," said Leo, earnestly, "that my white brothers, though few in number, are very strong and brave. They have weapons too which kill far off and make a dreadful noise."

Grabantak laughed contemptuously at this.

"Does the Kablunet," he asked, "think I am afraid to die—afraid of a noise? does he think that none but white men can kill far off?"

As he spoke he suddenly hurled his spear at a gull, which, with many others, was perched on a cliff about thirty yards off, and transfixed it.

"Go to the boat, Anders, and fetch my rifle," said Leo in a low tone.

When the rifle was brought a crowd of Eskimos came with it. They had been closely observing their chief and the stranger during the conference, but remained at a respectful distance until they saw something unusual going on.

"Tell the chief," said Leo, "to look at that peak with the solitary gull standing on it."

He pointed to a detached cone of rock upwards of two hundred yards distant.

When the attention of the whole party was concentrated on the bird in question, Leo took a steady aim and fired.

Need we say that the effect of the shot was wonderful? not only did the braves utter a united yell and give a simultaneous jump, but several of the less brave among them bolted behind rocks, or tumbled in attempting to do so, while myriads of sea-fowl, which clustered among the cliffs, sprang from their perches and went screaming into the air. At the same time echoes innumerable, which had lain dormant since creation, or at best had given but sleepy response to the bark of walruses and the cry of gulls, took up the shot in lively haste and sent it to and fro from cliff to crag in bewildering continuation.

"Wonderful!" exclaimed Grabantak in open-mouthed amazement, when he beheld the shot gull tumbling from its lofty perch, "Do it again."

Leo did it again—all the more readily that another gull, unwarned by its predecessor's fate, flew to the conical rock at the moment, and perched itself on the same peak. It fell, as before, and the echoes were again awakened, while the sea-birds cawed and screamed more violently than ever.

The timid ones among the braves, having recovered from their first shock, stood fast this time, but trembled much and glared horribly. The chief, who was made of sterner stuff than many of his followers; did not move, though his face flushed crimson with suppressed emotion. As to the sea-birds, curiosity seemed to have overcome fear, for they came circling and wheeling overhead in clouds so dense that they almost darkened the sky—many of them swooping close past the Eskimos and then shearing off and up with wild cries.

An idea suddenly flashed into Leo's head. Pointing his rifle upwards he began and continued a rapid fire until all the bullets in it, (ten or twelve), were expended. The result was as he had expected. Travelling through such a dense mass of birds, each ball pierced we know not how many, until it absolutely rained dead and wounded gulls on the heads of the natives, while the rocks sent forth a roar of echoes equal to a continuous fire of musketry. It was stupendous! Nothing like it had occurred in the Polar regions since the world first became a little flattened at the poles! Nothing like it will happen again until the conjunction of a series of similar circumstances occurs. The timid braves lost heart again and dived like the coneys into holes and corners of the rocks. Others stood still with chattering teeth. Even Grabantak wavered for a moment. But it was only for a moment. Recovering himself he uttered a mighty shout; then he yelled; then he howled; then he slapped his breast and thighs; then he seized a smallish brave near him by the neck and hurled him into the sea. Having relieved his feelings thus he burst into a fit of laughter such as has never been equalled by the wildest maniac either before or since.

Suddenly he calmed, stepped up to Leo, and wrenched the rifle from his grasp.

"I will do that!" he cried, and held the weapon out at arms-length in front of his face with both hands; but there was no answering shot.

"Why does it not bark?" he demanded, turning to Leo sternly.

"It will only bark at my bidding," said Leo, with a significant smile.

"Bid it, then," said the chief in a peremptory tone, still holding the rifle out.

"You must treat it in the right way, otherwise it will not bark. I will show you."

Having been shown how to pull the trigger, the chief tried again, but a sharp click was the only reply. Grabantak having expected a shot, he nervously dropped the rifle, but Leo was prepared, and caught it.

"You must not be afraid of it; it cannot work properly if you are afraid. See, look there," he added, pointing to the conical rock on which another infatuated gull had perched himself.

Grabantak looked earnestly. His timid braves began to creep out of their holes, and directed their eyes to the same spot. While their attention was occupied Leo managed to slip a fresh cartridge into the rifle unobserved.

"Now," said he, handing the rifle to the chief, "try again."

Grabantak, who was not quite pleased at the hint about his being afraid, seized the rifle and held it out as before. Resolved to maintain his reputation for coolness, he said to his followers in imitation of Leo:—

"Do you see that gull?"

"Huk!" replied the warriors, with eager looks.

Leo thought of correcting his manner of taking aim, but, reflecting that the result would be a miss in any case, he refrained.

Grabantak raised the rifle slowly, as its owner had done, and frowned along the barrel. In doing so, he drew it back until the butt almost touched his face. Then he fired. There was a repetition of previous results with some differences. The gull flew away from the rock unhurt; one of the braves received the bullet in his thigh and ran off shrieking with agony, while the chief received a blow from the rifle on the nose which all but incorporated that feature with his cheeks, and drew from his eyes the first tears he had ever shed since babyhood.

That night Grabantak sat for hours staring in moody silence at the sea, tenderly caressing his injured nose, and meditating, no doubt, on things past, present, and to come.

Chapter XXIII

The result of Grabantak's meditation was that, considering the nature and wonderful weapons of the men by whom Amalatok had been reinforced, he thought it advisable to return to his own land, which was not far distant, for the purpose of adding to the force with which he meant to subjugate the men of Poloe.

"We are unconquerable," he said, while conversing on the situation with Teyma, his first lieutenant, or prime minister; "everybody knows that we are invincible. It is well-known that neither white men, nor yellow men,—no, nor black men, nor blue men,— can overcome the Flatlanders. We must keep up our name. It will not do to let the ancient belief die down, that one Flatlander is equal to three men of Poloe, or any other land."

"The Poloe men laugh in their boots when they hear us boast in this way," said Teyma gently.

We draw attention to the curious resemblance in this phrase to our more civilised "laughing in the sleeve," while we point out that the prime minister, although of necessity a man of war, was by nature a man of peace. Indeed his name, Teyma, which signifies peace, had been given him because of his pacific tendencies.

"What! would you not have me defend the Flatland name?" demanded Grabantak, fiercely.

"No, I would have you defend only the Flatland property," replied the blunt minister.

"And is not Puiröe my property?" growled Grabantak, referring to the barren rock which was the cause of war.

"So is *that* your property," said Teyma, picking up a stone, "and yet I treat it thus!" (He tossed it contemptuously into the sea.) "Is that worth Flatlander blood? would you kill me for *that?* shall Eskimo wives and mothers weep, and children mourn and starve for a useless rock in the sea."

"You always thwart me, Teyma," said Grabantak, trying to suppress a burst of wrath, which he was well aware his fearless minister did not mind in the least. "It is true this island is not worth the shake of a puffin's tail; but if we allow the Poloe men to take it—"

"To keep it," mildly suggested Teyma, "they have long had it."

"Well, to keep it, if you will," continued the chief testily; "will not other tribes say that the old name of the Flatlanders is dead, that the war-spirit is gone, that they may come and attack us when they please; for we cannot defend our property, and they will try to make us slaves? What! shall Flatlanders become slaves? no never, never, *never!*" cried Grabantak, furiously, though unconsciously quoting the chorus of a well-known song.

"No, *never,*" re-echoed Teyma with an emphatic nod, "yet there are many steps between fighting for a useless rock, and being made slaves."

"Well then," cried Grabantak, replying to the first part of his lieutenant's remark and ignoring the second, "we must fight to prove our courage. As to losing many of our best men, of course we cannot help that. Then we must kill, burn, and destroy right and left in Poloeland, to prove our power. After that we will show the greatness of our forbearance by letting our enemies alone. Perhaps we may even condescend to ask them to become our friends. What an honour that would be to them, and, doubtless, what a joy!"

"Grabantak," said Teyma with a look and tone of solemnity which invariably overawed his chief, and made him uncomfortable, "you have lived a good many years now. Did you ever make a friend of an enemy by beating him?"

"Of course not," said the other with a gesture of impatience.

"Grabantak, you had a father."

"Yes," said the chief, with solemn respect.

"And *he* had a father."

"True."

"And he, too, had a father."

"Well, I suppose he had."

"Of course he had. All fathers have had fathers back and back into the mysterious Longtime. If not, where did our tales and stories come from? There are many stories told by fathers to sons, and fathers to sons, till they have all come down to us, and what do these stories teach us? that all fighting is bad, except what *must* be. Even what *must* be is bad—only, it is better than some things that are worse. Loss of life, loss of country, loss of freedom to hunt, and eat, and sleep, are worse. We must fight for these—but to fight for a bare rock, for a name, for a coast, for a fancy, it is foolish! and when you have got your rock, and recovered your name, and pleased your fancy, do the brave young men that are dead return? Do the maidens that weep rejoice? Do the mothers that pine revive? Of what use have been all the wars of Flatland from Longtime till now? Can you restore the mountain-heaps of kayaks, and oomiaks, and spears, and walrus-lines, from the smoke into which they vanished! Can you recall the great rivers of whale-oil from the sea into which they have been poured, or the blood of men from the earth that swallowed it? Is not war *always* loss, loss, loss, and *never* gain? Why cannot we live at peace with those who will, and fight only with those who insist on war."

"Go, Teyma, stop your mouth with blubber," said the chief, rising; "I am weary of you. I tell you, Amalatok shall die; Puiröe shall be mine. The tribes shall all learn to tremble at the name of Grabantak and to respect the men of Flatland."

"Ay, and to love them too, I suppose," added Teyma with a facetious sneer.

"Boo!" replied his chief, bringing the conversation to an abrupt close by walking away.

In accordance with their chief's resolve, the Grabantak band embarked in their kayaks next morning, the gale having moderated, and with the intention of obtaining reinforcements, paddled back to Flatland, which they reached in a couple of days.

On the voyage Leo confined himself strictly to the oars and paddles, being unwilling to let the Eskimos into the secret of the kite, until he could do so with effect, either in the way of adding to their respect for the white man and his contrivances, or of making his escape.

Now, as has been said or hinted, although Grabantak's son, Koyatuk, was a stout and tall man, he was not gifted with much brain. He possessed even less of that substance than his father, whose energy and power of muscle, coupled with indomitable obstinacy, enabled him to hold the reins of government which were his by hereditary right. Besides being a fearless man, Grabantak was respected as a good leader in war. But Koyatuk had neither the energy of his father, nor his determination. He was vacillating and lazy, as well as selfish. Hence he was not a favourite, and when, after landing at Flatland, he endeavoured to renew his claim to Oblooria, neither his father nor the people encouraged him. The timid one was therefore left with Leo and Anders, who immediately fitted up for her a separate screened-off apartment in the hut which was assigned to them in the native village.

Even Koyatuk's mother did not befriend her son on this occasion. Merkut had her own reasons for proving faithless to her spoilt boy, whom on most occasions she favoured. Knowing his character well, the sturdy wife of Grabantak had made up her mind that Koyatuk should wed a young intelligent, and what you may call lumpy girl named Chukkee, who was very fond of the huge and lazy youth, and who, being herself good-natured and unselfish, would be sure to make him a good wife.

After one or two unavailing efforts, therefore, and a few sighs, the heir-apparent to the throne of Flatland ceased to trouble Oblooria, and devoted himself to his three favourite occupations—hunting, eating, and repose.

"Misser Lo," whispered Anders, on the first night after landing, as they busied themselves with the partition above referred to, "we 'scapes from dis here land very easy."

"How, Anders?"

"W'y, you's on'y got wait for nort' vint, den up kite, launch boat, an'—hup! away."

"True, lad, but I don't want to escape just yet."

"Not want to 'scape?"

"No. You see, Anders, we are now on very friendly terms with this tribe, and it seems to me that if we were to remain for a time and increase our influence, we might induce Grabantak to give up this war on which he seems to have set his heart. I have great hopes of doing something with Teyma. He is evidently a reasonable fellow, and has much power, I think, with the chief—indeed with every one. Pity that he is not to succeed Grabantak instead of that stupid Koyatuk. Besides, now I am here I must explore the land if possible. It is a pity no doubt to leave our friends, even for a short time, in ignorance of our fate, but we can't help that at present. Light the lamp, Anders, and let's see what we're about."

The summer was by that time so far advanced that the sun descended a considerable way below the horizon each night, leaving behind a sweet mellow twilight which deepened almost into darkness inside the Eskimo huts. These latter, like those already described, were made of stone, and the small openings that served for windows did not let in much light at any time.

The hut which had been assigned by Grabantak to his prisoners—or visitors, for as such he now seemed to regard them—was a large roomy one, made chiefly of clay. It stood on a little mound a hundred yards or so apart from the main village of Flatland, and was probably one of the chief's private palaces. It was oval in form—like a huge oven—about fifteen feet in diameter, and six feet in height. One-half of the floor was raised about eight inches, thus forming the "breck," which served for a lounge by day, and a couch by night. Its furniture of skins, cooking-lamp, etcetera, was much the same as that of the Eskimo huts already described, except that the low tunnel-shaped entrance was very long—about twelve feet. Light was admitted by a parchment-covered hole or window, with several rents in it, as well as by various accidental holes in the roof.

When the lamp was lighted, and skins were spread on the breck, and Leo, having finished the partition, was busy making entries in a note-book, and Anders was amusing himself with a tobacco pipe—foolish man! and Oblooria was devoting herself to the lamp, from which various charming sounds and delicious smells emanated—as well as smoke—this northern residence looked far more cheerful and snug than the luxurious dwellers in civilised lands will readily believe.

"I wonder," said Leo, looking up from his book after a prolonged silence, "I wonder what strange sounds are those I hear."

"P'r'aps it's de vint," said Anders, puffing a cloud from his lips in sleepy contentment, and glancing upwards.

When he and Leo looked at the roof of the hut it shook slightly, as if something had fallen on it.

"Strange," muttered Leo, reverting to his notebook, "it did not look like wind when the sun went down. It must be going to blow hard."

After a few minutes of silence Leo again looked up inquiringly.

"Dere's anoder squall," said Anders.

"More like a sneeze than a squall. Listen; that is a queer pattering sound."

They listened, but all was silent. After a minute or so they resumed their occupations.

The sounds were, however, no mystery to those who were in the secret of them. Knowing the extreme curiosity of his countrymen, Grabantak had placed a sentinel over his guests' hut, with orders to let no one go near it. The sentinel entered on his vigil with that stern sense of duty-unto-death that is supposed to animate all sentinels. At first the inhabitants of Flatland kept conscientiously away from the forbidden spot, but as the shades of night toned down the light, some of them could not resist drawing near occasionally and listening with distended eyes, ears, and nostrils, as if they expected to drink in foreign sounds at all these orifices. The sentinel grasped his spear, steeled his heart, and stood in front of the door with a look of grand solemnity worthy of the horse-guards.

At last, however, the sentinel's own curiosity was roused by the eager looks of those—chiefly big boys—who drew ever nearer and nearer. Occasional sounds from the hut quickened his curiosity, and the strange smell of tobacco-smoke at last rendered it unbearable.

Slowly, sternly, as if it were part of his duty to spy, he moved to the torn window and peeped in. He was fascinated at once of course. After gazing for five minutes in rapt admiration, he chanced to withdraw his face for a moment, and then found that nine Eskimos had discovered nine holes or crevices in the hut walls, against which their fat faces were thrust, while at least half-a-dozen others were vainly searching for other peep-holes.

A scarcely audible hiss caused the rapt nine to look up. A terrible frown and a shake of the official spear caused them to retire down the slope that led to the hut.

This was the unaccountable "squall" that had first perplexed Leo and his comrade.

But like tigers who have tasted blood, the Flatlanders could not now be restrained.

"Go!" said the sentinel in a low stern voice to the retreating trespassers, whom he followed to the foot of the slope. "If you come up again I will tell Grabantak, who will have you all speared and turned into whale-buoys."

The boys did not appear to care much for the threat. They were obviously buoyed up with hope.

"Oh! do, *do* let us peep! just once!" entreated several of them in subdued but eager tones.

The sentinel shook his obdurate head and raised his deadly spear.

"We will make no noise," said a youth who was the exact counterpart of Benjamin Vane in all respects except colour and costume—the first being dirty yellow and the latter hairy.

The sentinel frowned worse than ever.

"The Kablunets," said another of the band, entreatingly, "shall hear nothing louder than the falling of a snow-flake or a bit of eider-down."

Still the sentinel was inexorable.

The Eskimos were in despair.

Suddenly Benjy's counterpart turned and fled to the village on light and noiseless toe. He returned immediately with a rich, odorous, steaming piece of blubber in his hand. It was a wise stroke of policy. The sentinel had been placed there without any reference to the fact that he had not had his supper. He was ravenously hungry. Can you blame him for lowering his spear, untying his eyebrows, and smiling blandly as he held out his hand?

"Just one peep, and it is yours," said the counterpart, holding the morsel behind him.

"My life is in danger if I do," remonstrated the sentinel.

"Your supper is in danger if you don't," said the counterpart.

It was too much for him. The sentinel accepted the bribe, and, devouring it, returned with the bribers on tiptoe to the hut, where they gazed in silent wonder to their hearts' content.

"Well, that beats everything," said Leo, laying down his book and pencil, "but I never did hear a gale that panted and snorted as this one does. I'll go out and have a look at it."

He rose and crawled on hands and knees through the tunnel. The spies rolled off the hut with considerable noise and fled, while the sentinel resuming his spear and position, tried to look innocent.

While he was explaining to Anders why he was there, Grabantak himself walked up, accompanied by his lieutenant. They were hospitably entertained, and as Oblooria had by that time prepared a savoury mess, such as she knew the white men loved, the chief and Teyma condescended to sup with their captive-guests.

Leo had not with him the great cooking machine with which his uncle had effected so much in Poloeland, but he had a tin kettle and a couple of pannikins, with some coffee, sugar, and biscuit, which did good service

in the way of conciliating, if not surprising, the chief
of Flatland.

Both he and his lieutenant, moreover, were deeply
interested in Anders's proceedings with the pipe.

At first they supposed he was conducting some
religious ceremony, and looked on with appropriate
solemnity, but, on being informed of the mistake,
Grabantak smiled graciously and requested a "whiff."
He received one, and immediately made such a
hideous face that Anders could not restrain a short
laugh, whereupon the chief hit him over the head
with his empty pannikin, but, after frowning fiercely,
joined in the laugh.

Leo then began to question the chief about the
land over which he ruled, and was told that it was a
group of islands of various sizes, like the group which
belonged to Amalatok, but with more islands in it;
that most of these islands were flat, and covered with
lakes, large and small, in which were to be found many
animals, and birds as numerous almost as the stars.

"Ask him from what direction these birds come,"
said Leo, pulling out his pocket-compass and expecting
that Grabantak would point to the south; but the chief
pointed to the north, then to the south, then to the
east, and then to the west!

"What does he mean? I don't understand him," said
Leo.

"The birds come from *everywhere*—from all round.
They come here to breed," said the chief, spreading
his hands round him and pointing in all directions.
"Then, when the young are strong and the cold season

begins, they spread the wing and go away there—to *every* place—all round."

"Anders," said Leo impressively, "do you know I think we have actually arrived at the immediate region of the North Pole! What the chief says almost settles the question. This, you see, must be the warmest place in the Polar regions; the central spot around the Pole to which migratory birds flock from the south. If voyagers, crossing the Arctic circle at *all* parts, have observed these birds ever flying *north*, it follows that they *must* have some meeting-place near the Pole, where they breed and from which they depart in autumn. Well, according to Grabantak, *this* is the meeting-place, therefore *this* must be near the Pole! How I wish uncle were here!"

Leo had been more than half soliloquising; he now looked up and burst into a laugh, for the interpreter was gazing at him with an expression of blank stupidity.

"You's kite right, Missr Lo," he said at last, with a meek smile, "kite right, no doubt; only you's too clibber for *me*."

"Well, Anders, I'll try not to be quite so clibber in future; but ask Grabantak if he will go with me on an expedition among these islands. I want very much to examine them all."

"Examine them all!" repeated the chief with emphasis when this was translated; "tell the young Kablunet with the hard fist, that the sunless time would come and go, and the sun-season would come again, before he could go over half my lands. Besides, I have more important work to do. I must first go to

Poloeland, to kill and burn and destroy. After that I will travel with Hardfist."

Hardfist, as the chief had styled him in reference to his late pugilistic achievements, felt strongly inclined to use his fists on Grabantak's skull when he mentioned his sanguinary intentions, but recalling Alf's oft-quoted words, "Discretion is the better part of valour," he restrained himself. He also entered into a long argument with the savage, in the hope of converting him to peace principles, but of course in vain. The chief was thoroughly bent on destroying his enemies.

Then, in a state of almost desperate anxiety, Leo sought to turn him from his purpose by telling him about God the Father, and the Prince of Peace, and, pulling out his Bible, began to read and make Anders interpret such passages of the Word as bore most directly on his subject. While acting in this, to him, novel capacity as a teacher of God's Word, Leo more than once lifted up his heart in brief silent prayer that the Spirit might open the heart of the savage to receive the truth. The chief and his lieutenant listened with interest and surprise. Being savages, they also listened with profound respect to the young enthusiast, but Grabantak would not give up his intention. He explained, however, that he meant first to go to the largest and most central island of his dominions, to make inquiry there of the Man of the Valley what would be the best time to set out for the war.

"The Man of the Valley!" asked Leo, "who is that?"

"He is an Eskimo," replied Grabantak, with a sudden

air of solemnity in his manner, "whose first forefather came in the far past longtime, from nobody knows where; but this first forefather never had any father or mother. He settled among the Eskimos and taught them many things. He married one of their women, and his sons and daughters were many and strong. Their descendants inhabit the Great Isle of Flatland at the present day. They are good and strong; great hunters and warriors. The first forefather lived long, till he became white and blind. His power and wisdom lay in a little strange thing which he called 'buk.' How it made him strong or wise no one can tell, but so it was. His name was Makitok. When he died he gave *buk* to his eldest son. It was wrapped up in a piece of sealskin. The eldest son had much talk with his father about this mystery-thing, and was heard to speak much about the Kablunets, but the son would never tell what he said. Neither would he unwrap the mystery-thing, for fear that its power might escape. So he wrapped it up in another piece of sealskin, and gave it to his eldest son, telling him to hand it down from son to son, along with the name Makitok. So *buk* has grown to be a large bundle now, and no one understands it, but every one has great reverence for it, and the Makitok now in possession is a great mystery-man, very wise; we always consult him on important matters."

Here was food for reflection to Leo during the remainder of that night, and for many hours did his sleepless mind puzzle over the mystery of Makitok, the Man of the Valley.

This sleepless condition was, not unpleasantly,

prolonged by the sounds of animal life that entered his oven-like dwelling during great part of the night. Evidently great numbers of the feathered tribes were moving about, either because they meant to retire at dissipatedly late, or had risen at unreasonably early, hours. Among them he clearly distinguished the musical note of the long-tailed duck and the harsh scream of the great northern diver, while the profound calmness of the weather enabled him to hear at intervals the soft blow and the lazy plash of a white whale, turning, it might be, on his other side in his water-bed on the Arctic Sea.

Following the whale's example, Leo turned round at last, buried his face in a reindeer pillow, and took refuge in oblivion.

Chapter XXIV

A GLORIOUS REGION CONTEMPLATED,
AND A GLORIOUS CHASE PLANNED.

Leo did not slumber long. Very early in the morning
he awoke with that sensation about him which told
that at that time further repose was not attainable. He
therefore rose, donned the few garments which he
had put off on lying down, crept through his tunnel,
and emerged into the open air.

And what a vision of glorious beauty met his
enraptured eyes, while the fresh sea-breeze entered,
like life, into his heaving chest! It was still a profound
calm. Earth, air, water, sky, seemed to be uniting in a
silent act of adoration to their great Creator, while the
myriad creatures therein contained were comparatively
quiet in the enjoyment of His rich and varied bounties.
It seemed as if the hour were too early for the strife of
violent passions—too calm for the stirrings of hatred
or revenge. Everything around spoke only of peace.

Sitting down with his back to a sun-bathed rock, and his face to the silver sea, Leo drew out his Bible and proceeded to read the records of the Prince of Peace.

As he lifted his eyes from the words, "marvellous are thy works, and that my soul knoweth right well," to the vision of beauty and life that lay before him, Leo made the words and the thought, for the first time, *his own.*

The prospect embraced innumerable islands of all sizes, studding like gems the gently-heaving sea. Over these, countless millions of sea-birds flew or sailed to and fro; some with the busy fluttering of activity, as if they had something to do and a mind to do it; others loitering idly on the wing, or dipping lightly on the wave, as if to bid their images good-morning. Burgomaster, yellow-legged, and pink-beaked gulls, large and small, wheeled in widening circles round him. Occasional flocks of ptarmigan, in the mixed brown and white plumage of summer, whirred swiftly over him and took refuge among the rocky heights of the interior, none of which heights rose above three hundred feet. Eider-ducks, chattering kittiwakes, and graceful tern, auks, guillemots, puffins, geese, and even swans, swarmed on the islands, far and near, while seals, whales, narwhals, dolphins, and grampuses, revelled in the sea, so that the Arctic world appeared almost overcharged with animal life.

Of course the noise of their cries and evolutions would have been great had not distance lent enchantment to sound as well as view. To Leo there seemed even a sort of restfulness in the voices of the innumerable wild-fowl. They were so far off, most of them, that the sounds fell on his ear like a gentle plaint, and even the thunderous plash of the great Greenland whale was reduced by distance to a ripple like that which fell on the shore at his feet.

While he was meditating, Anders joined him and responded heartily to his salutation, but Anders was not in a poetical frame of mind that morning. His thoughts had been already turned to an eminently practical subject.

"I'm tole," said he, seating himself beside our hero, "dat Grabantak holds a talk 'bout fighting."

"And a council of war," said Leo. "I know what the result of that will be. When leaders like Grabantak and Amalatok decide for war, most of the people follow them like a flock of sheep. Although most of the people never saw this miserable island—this Puiröe—and know, and care, nothing about it, you'll see that the Flatlanders will be quite enthusiastic after the council, and ready to fight for it to the bitter end. A very bitter end it is, indeed, to see men and women make fools of themselves about nothing, and be ready to die for the same! Will Grabantak allow us to be present at the council, think you?"

"Ho yis. He send me to say you muss come."

Leo was right. Nothing could surpass the impetuosity of Grabantak, except the anxiety of many of the Flatlanders to be led by the nose. Was not the point in question one of vital importance to the wellbeing of the community—indeed of the whole Arctic world? Teyma mildly asked them what *was* the point in question, but not a soul could tell, until Grabantak, starting up with furious energy, manufactured a "point," and then explained it in language so intricate, yet so clear, that the whole council stood amazed at their never having seen it before in that light, and then said, more or less emphatically, "There, that's what we thought exactly, only we could not state it so well as the great Grabantak!"

After this there was no chance for Teyma and his party—and he had a party, even among northern savages,—who believed in men working hard at their own affairs and letting other people alone, as far as that was possible. But the peace-party in Arctic land was in a minority at that time, and the council broke up with shouts for Grabantak, and denunciations of death and destruction to the men of Poloeland.

But things do not always turn out as men—even wise men—arrange them. From that day, during the brief period of preparation for the setting out of an expedition to visit Makitok of Great Isle, Leo received daily visits from the Prime Minister, who was deeply interested and inquisitive about the strange "*thing*," as he styled the Bible, which told the Kablunets about God and the Prince of Peace. Of course Leo was willing and happy to give him all the information he desired, and, in doing so, found a new and deep source of pleasure.

Teyma was not the man to hide his light under a bushel. He was a fearless outspoken counsellor, and not only sought to advance the pacific views he held, by talking to the men of his own party in private, but even propounded them in public to Grabantak himself, who, however, could not be moved, though many of his men quietly changed sides.

With all this Teyma was loyal to his chief. Whatever he did was in the way of fair and open argument. He was too loyal to help Leo when he made a certain proposal to him one day.

"Teyma," said Leo, on that occasion, "you have been very friendly to me. Will you do me a great favour? Will you send a young man in a kayak to Poloeland with a message from me to my people? They must think I am dead. I wish them to know that I am here, and well."

"No," replied Teyma promptly; "that would let the men of Poloe know that we talk of going to attack them. I do not love war. I wish to let our enemies alone, but if my chief decides for war, it is my duty to help, not to frustrate him. If we go to war with Poloeland, we must take the men of Poloe by surprise. That could not be if a young man went with your message."

Leo saw the force of this, and respected Teyma's disinterested loyalty to his chief; but felt inclined to argue that, fidelity to the best interests of his country stood higher than loyalty to a chief. He refrained, however, from pressing the matter at that time.

Not so Anders. When that worthy saw that Teyma would not act, and that Leo from some inexplicable reason hesitated, he quietly took the matter into his own hands, and so wrought on the feelings of a weak but amiable youth of the tribe, that he prevailed on him to carry a message to the enemy, explaining to him earnestly that no evil, but the reverse, would result from his mission; that the Kablunets were men of peace, who would immediately come over to Flatland and put everything right in a peaceable and satisfactory manner.

"Tell the white men," said Anders, "that we are prisoners in Flatland—alive and well—but they must come to help us quickly."

No difficulty was experienced in· sending the messenger away. There was unlimited personal freedom in Flatland. Young men frequently went off to hunt for days together at a time, without saying anything about their intentions, unless they chose; so the secret messenger set out. Thus the interpreter lighted the fuse of a mine which was eminently calculated to blow up the plans of Grabantak.

But another fuse had been lighted which, in a still more effectual manner, overturned the plans of that warlike chief.

It chanced at this time that the Flatlanders ran short of meat. Their habit was to go off on a grand hunt, gather as much meat as they could, and then come home to feast and rejoice with their families until scarcity again obliged them to hunt. Of course there were many among them whose natural activity rebelled against this lazy style of life, but the exertions of these did not suffice to keep the whole tribe supplied. Hence it came to pass, that they often began to be in want while in the midst of plenty. A grand hunt was therefore organised.

They were tired, they said, of ducks and geese and swans. They wanted a change from seals and bears, walruses and such small fry. Nothing short of a whale would serve them!

Once stirred up to the point of action, there was no lack of energy among these northern Eskimos. Kayaks, lines, and spears were got ready, and oomiaks were launched; for women and children loved to see the sport, though they did not join in it. Everywhere bustle and excitement reigned, and the hubbub was not a little increased by the agitated dogs, which knew well what was a-foot, and licked their lips in anticipation.

Of course Leo and Anders prepared to go and see the fun. So did Oblooria. It was arranged that Leo and the latter were to go in the india-rubber boat.

That vessel had been the source of deep, absorbing interest and curiosity to the natives. When our travellers landed, it had been conveyed to the side of the hut assigned them, and laid gently on the turf, where it was stared at by successive groups all day. They would have stayed staring at it all night, if they had not been forbidden by Grabantak to approach the Kablunets during the hours of repose. Leo explained its parts to them, but made no reference to its expansive and contractile properties. He also launched it and paddled about to gratify the curiosity of his new friends, but did not show them the kite, which, folded and in its cover, he had stowed away in the hut.

One night, fearing that the sun might injure the boat, Leo had squeezed the air out of it, folded it, and stowed it away in the hut beside the kite. The astonishment of the natives, when they came out next morning to stare and wonder, according to custom, was very great. Leo resolved to make a mystery of it, looked solemn when spoken to on the point, and gave evasive replies.

When, however, the time came for setting off on this grand hunt, he carried his boat, still bundled up in skins, down to the water's edge, where kayaks and oomiaks in hundreds lay ready to be launched.

The news spread like wild-fire that the Kablunet was going to "act wonderfully!"

Every man, woman, and child in the place hurried to the spot.

"It is destroyed!" exclaimed Grabantak, sadly, when he saw the boat unrolled, flat and empty, on the sand.

We shall not describe the scene in detail. It is sufficient to say that Leo did not disappoint the general expectation. He did indeed "act wonderfully," filling the unsophisticated savages with unbounded surprise and admiration, while he filled the boat with air and launched it. He then stepped into it with Anders, gallantly lifted Oblooria on board, and, seizing the oars, rowed gently out to sea.

With shouts of delight the Eskimos jumped into their kayaks and followed. Their admiration was, however, a little calmed by the discovery that the kayaks could beat the Kablunet boat in speed, though the women in their oomiaks could not keep up with it. There was no emulation, however; Leo carefully refrained from racing.

He had been supplied with a long lance and a couple of spears, to which latter were attached, by thongs of walrus hide, two inflated sealskins to act as buoys. These Leo had been previously instructed how to use.

He took the kite with him on this occasion, without, however, having much expectation of being able to use it, as the calm still prevailed. It was folded of course, and fixed in its place in the bow. The natives thought it must be a spear or harpoon of strange form.

It was not long before a whale was sighted. There were plenty of these monsters about, some coming lazily to the surface to blow, others lying quite still, with their backs out of the water as if sunning themselves, or asleep.

Soon the spirit of the hunter filled each Eskimo bosom. What appeared to be an unusually large whale was observed on the horizon. Kablunets, india-rubber boats, and all less important things, were forgotten for the moment; paddles were plied with energy, and the chase began.

Chapter XXV

IN WHICH A GREAT HUNT IS DESCRIBED, A WAR
EXPEDITION FRUSTRATED, AND A HERO ENNOBLED.

Now, in a fit of unwise ambition, Anders the interpreter resolved to signalise himself, and display his valour on the occasion of this hunt. He borrowed a kayak of one of the natives, and went as an independent hunter. Leo, being quite able to row his boat alone, with Oblooria to steer, did not object.

The whale which had been selected was a thorough-going Arctic monster of the largest size, nearly a hundred feet long, which, while on his passage from the Atlantic to the Pacific through Behring Straits, had paused for a nap off the isles of Flatland.

The fleet of kayaks converged towards the fish like a flock of locusts. Despite his utmost efforts, Leo could not do more than keep up in rear of the hunters, for the sharp shuttle-like kayaks shot like arrows over the smooth sea, while his clumsier boat required greater force to propel it.

In a few minutes those Eskimos who were best paddlers crept ahead of the rest. Grabantak and his son took the lead, whether because of right or because of superior strength it was hard to say. Anders, who was a powerful fellow, and an expert canoeman, kept close alongside of them. Not content with this, he attempted to pass them; but they saw his intention, put on what sporting men call a "spurt," and in a few seconds left him several yards behind.

On nearing their victim, Grabantak and Koyatuk checked their speed and got their spears ready. A few minutes later and a dozen of the followers were up and prepared to act, but they all held back—all except the excitable Anders—while the chief and his son glided cautiously towards the fish, one on either side. Suddenly each grasped a spear and drove it with all the force of both arms deep into the whale's flesh. It was a rude awaking! Of course the fish dived instantly. In doing so it flung its tail on high with a superb sweep, sending tons of water, and the impatient Anders, into the air.

The interpreter came down in a cataract of spray, with his kayak doubled up but himself uninjured, while the Eskimos greeted the event with a shout of alarm. This changed into laughter when it was found that the ambitious man was none the worse for his toss; and the women in one of the oomiak; paddling quickly up, hauled the drenched and crestfallen man out of the sea. They also picked up his spear with the sealskin buoy attached. Giving him the place of honour in the bow, they put the spear in his hand, and bade him keep up heart and do better next time.

Meanwhile the whale, having got over its first surprise, and feeling the two large sealskin-floats a somewhat heavy as well as unusual drag, soon came again to the surface, not far from the spot where Leo lay on his oars, an amused as well as interested spectator of the scene.

"Ho!" shrieked Oblooria, whose eager little heart was easily excited. She pointed to the fish, and gazed at Leo with blazing eyes.

You may be sure our hero did not lose time. The india-rubber boat leaped over the water as if it had suddenly been endowed with life. The smart little woman carefully arranged the spear and buoy ready to hand. Several of the kayaks which chanced to be nearest to the whale rushed towards it like sword-fish; but they had no chance, Leo being so near. He did not check his speed on reaching the fish, but allowed the boat to run tilt on its back. The smooth india-rubber glided up on the slippery surface till more than half its length was on the creature's back. It was thus checked without a shock—probably unfelt by the whale.

Leo seized the spear, leaped up, and, with both hands, drove it deep into the flesh, just as the chief and his son had done. The force with which he drove it was so great that it thrust the boat back into the water. This was fortunate, for it enabled them narrowly to escape the vortex that was instantly made by the diving of the now enraged monster; a few back-strokes of the oars took them out of the sea of foam left behind.

The masterly manner in which this was done called forth shouts of admiration from the entire fleet, and it greatly surprised Leo himself, for it was the first time he had attempted to use the harpoon.

"It *must* have been chance," he muttered to himself as he again lay on his oars awaiting the whale's reappearance, "a sort of happy accident. I feel convinced I could not do it so well a second time."

The fish took a longer dive on this occasion, and when he retained to the surface for another breath of air, was at a considerable distance from all parts of the fleet. The instant he was seen, however, every paddle flashed into the sea, and the kayaks darted away in pursuit. They soon came up with their victim, and another spear, with its accompanying sealskin buoy, was fixed in its side. Down it went a third time, and reappeared in quite an opposite direction from that in which it had been looked for.

This uncertainty in the movements of the whale was a matter of small moment to the occupiers of the light kayaks, but it told rather heavily on Leo in his clumsier boat. He therefore resolved to paddle gently about, take things easy, watch the progress of the chase, and trust to the chapter of accidents giving him another chance.

"You see, Oblooria," he said in the Eskimo tongue, which he was picking up rapidly, "it's of no use my pulling wildly about in all directions, blowing myself for nothing; so we'll just hang off-and-on here and watch them."

As this remark called for no direct reply, Oblooria merely smiled—indeed she more than smiled—but said nothing. It is just possible that Leo's rendering of the phrase "off-and-on" into Eskimo may have sounded ridiculous.

However this may be, the two sat there for some time, absorbed and silent spectators of the chase.

"How long will they take to kill it?" asked Leo when he saw Grabantak thrust somewhere about the thirty-fifth spear into the victim.

"All day," answered Oblooria.

"All day!" repeated Leo in surprise.

"If they could lance him far in," said the girl, "he would die soon, but his flesh is thick and his life is deep down."

Leo relapsed into silence. The idea of remaining a mere spectator all day was distasteful to his active mind and body. He had almost made up his mind to ask one of the natives to lend him a kayak and change places, when a puff of wind sent a few cats-paws over the hitherto glassy sea.

He looked quickly in the direction whence it came, and observed a blue line on the horizon. It was a coming breeze. Ere long it touched them, blowing gently, indeed, but steadily. A glance upwards showed that it was steadier and stronger in the upper regions, and blew towards the south-east, in which direction the chase was being prosecuted with unflagging activity.

"If there was only enough," muttered Leo, "to take the kite up, I'd soon be alongside of the whale; come, I'll try. Lend a hand, Oblooria."

The Eskimo girl had, during her voyage to Flatland, become so well acquainted with the operation of extending and setting up the kite, that she was able to lend effective assistance. In less than ten minutes it was expanded, and although Leo was nearly pulled into the water before he got fair hold of the regulator, while Oblooria was thrown down by an eccentric whisk of the tail, they managed at last to get it fairly over their heads, and soon sent it shooting upwards into the stronger air current above. Of course they began to rush over the sea at a pace that would have quickly left the best kayak in the fleet far astern, but Leo did not wish to act precipitately. He sat down in the bow to attend to the regulator, while Oblooria held the steering-oar.

"Keep her away a bit, Oblooria; starboard—I mean to *that* side. So, we won't spoil their sport too soon."

He pulled the regulator as he spoke, and eased the pace, while the Eskimo girl, with eyes glittering from expectancy and hope, turned the boat off to the right.

Leo seemed to be meditative at first, as if uncertain how to proceed. Soon this condition of mind passed. He let go the regulator, and, taking up the long whale lance with which he had been provided, examined its blade and point. The full force of the breeze filled the kite and carried them along at not less than ten miles an hour.

Hitherto the Eskimos had been so intent on their prey that they had no eyes for anything else. Again and again had the whale been pierced by the stinging harpoons, and the number of inflated sealskins which he was obliged by that time to drag down into the deep was so great that his dives had become more frequent and much shorter. It was obvious that the perseverance of his little foes would in the end overcome his mighty strength. It was equally evident, however, that there was still a great deal of fighting power left in him, and as some of the harpoons had come out while several of the floats had broken loose, there was just a possibility that he might yet escape if not vigorously followed up.

Suddenly one of the Eskimos was seen to drop his paddle and point with both hands to the sky, uttering at the same time a cry of surprise and alarm. There was no mistaking the cry. Every paddle ceased to dip, and every eye was turned to the sky. Of course every voice gave forth a howl!

"A mystery!" shouted Grabantak.

"An evil spirit!" cried Koyatuk.

"A new kind of bird!" roared Teyma.

At that moment a cry louder than ever arose. Leo's boat was observed coming like a narwhal over the sea, with the foam flying from its bows!

The "new kind of bird," so they at first imagined, had let down a long thin tail, caught the boat of the white man, and was flying away with it!

Into the midst of them the boat rushed. They dashed aside right and left. Leo was standing in the bow. He moved not, spoke not, looked at no one, but stood up, bent a little forward, with a stern frown on his brow, his lips compressed, and the long lance held level in both hands as if in the act of charging.

"Catch hold of him!" yelled Grabantak as they flew past. As well might they have tried to catch a comet!

"Steer a little to the left," said Leo in a low tone.

Obedient, on the instant, the girl made a sharp stroke with the oar.

"Steady—so. Now, Oblooria, hold on tight for your life!"

They were going straight at the whale. Leo did not dare to think of the result of his intended attack. He could not guess it. He hoped all would be well. He had no time to think of *pros* and *cons*. They were close to the victim. On it, now, sliding over its back, while the sharp lance entered its body with the full momentum of the charge,—deep down into its vitals! Blood flew out like a waterspout. The lance was torn from Leo's grasp as he fell backwards. Oblooria leaped up, in wild excitement, dropped her oar, and clapped her hands. At that instant the stout traction-line snapped, and the boat remained fast, while the kite descended in a series of helpless gyrations into the sea. Next moment the whale went down in a convulsive struggle, and the boat, with its daring occupants, was whelmed in a whirlpool of blood and foam.

No cry proceeded from the Eskimos during this stupendous attack. They seemed bereft alike of voice and volition, but, on beholding the closing catastrophe, they rushed to the rescue with a united roar.

Before they could gain the spot, Leo was seen to emerge from the deep, dripping with pink and white foam like a very water-god. Oblooria followed instantly, like a piebald water-nymph. The boat had not been upset, though overwhelmed, and they had held on to it with the tenacity of a last hope.

Looking sharply round, as he gasped and swept the water from his eyes, Leo seized the oars, which, being attached to the boat, were still available, and rowed with all his might away from the approaching Eskimos as if he were afraid of being caught by them. They followed with, if possible, increased surprise at this inexplicable conduct. They made up to him; some even shot ahead of him. Poor Leo was not a moment too soon in reaching his kite, for these people were about to transfix it with their whale-harpoons, when he dashed up and ordered them to desist.

Having rescued the miserable-looking thing from the sea and hastily folded it, he placed it in the bow. Then breathing freely, he began to look about him just as the whale came again to the surface in a dying flurry. It so chanced that it came up right under Grabantak's kayak, which it tossed up end over end. This would not have been a serious matter if it had not, the next moment, brought its mighty tail down on the canoe. It then sheered off a hundred yards or so, leaped half its length out of the water, and fell over on its side with a noise like thunder and died.

Every one turned to the place where the chief's kayak lay a complete wreck on the water. Its owner was seen swimming beside it, and was soon hauled into one of the women's oomiaks. Evidently he had been severely hurt, but he would not admit the fact. With characteristic dignity he sternly ordered the fleet to lay hold of the whale and make for the shore.

"Tell him his arm is broken," said Leo that evening to Anders, after examining the chief's hurts in the privacy of his own hut, "and let him know that I am a medicine-man and will try to cure him."

Grabantak received the information with a look of anger.

"Then," said he, "Amalatok must live a little longer, for I cannot fight him with a broken arm. Go," he added, looking full at Leo with something like admiration, "go, you have done well to-day; my young men want to make your nose blue."

The peremptory nature of the chief's command forbade delay. Leo was therefore obliged to creep out of his hut, wondering intensely, and not a little uncomfortably, as to what having his nose made blue could mean.

He was quickly enlightened by Anders, who told him that the most successful harpooner in a whale hunt is looked on as a very great personage indeed, and is invariably decorated with what may be styled the Eskimo order of the Blue Ribbon.

Scarcely had he received this information, when he was seized by the young men and hurried into the midst of an expectant circle, where he submitted with a good grace to the ceremony. A youth advanced to him, made a few complimentary remarks, seized him by the right ear, and, with a little wet paint, drew a broad blue line across his face over the bridge of his nose. He was then informed that he had received the highest honour known to the Eskimos of the far north, and that, among other privileges, it gave him the right of marrying two wives if he felt disposed to do so! Accepting the honour, but declining the privilege, Leo expressed his gratitude for the compliment just paid him in a neat Eskimo speech, and then retired to his hut in search of much-needed repose, not a little comforted by the thought that the chief's broken arm would probably postpone the threatened war for an indefinite period.

That night ridiculous fancies played about his deerskin pillow, for he dreamed of being swallowed by a mad whale, and whisked up to the sky by a kite with a broken arm and a blue stripe across its nose!

Chapter XXVI

TELLS OF A WARLIKE EXPEDITION AND
ITS HAPPY TERMINATION.

While these stirring events were taking place in Flatland, our friends in the Island of Poloe continued to fish and hunt, and keep watch and ward against their expected enemies in the usual fashion; but alas for the poor Englishmen! All the light had gone out of their eyes; all the elasticity had vanished from their spirits. Ah! it is only those who know what it is to lose a dear friend or brother, who can understand the terrible blank which had descended on the lives of our discoverers, rendering them, for the time at least, comparatively indifferent to the events that went on around them, and totally regardless of the great object which had carried them so far into those regions of ice.

They could no longer doubt that Leo and his companions had perished, for they had searched every island of the Poloe group, including that one on which Leo and the Eskimos had found temporary refuge. Here, indeed, a momentary gleam of hope revived, when Alf found the spent cartridge-cases which his brother had thrown down on the occasion of his shooting for the purpose of impressing his captors, and they searched every yard of the island, high and low, for several days, before suffering themselves to relapse into the old state of despair. No evidence whatever remained to mark the visit of the Eskimos, for these wily savages never left anything behind them on their war-expeditions, and the storm had washed away any footprints that might have remained in the hard rocky soil.

Amalatok—who, with his son and his men, sympathised with the Englishmen in their loss, and lent able assistance in the prolonged search—gave the final death-blow to their hopes by his remarks, when Captain Vane suggested that perhaps the lost ones had been blown over the sea to Flatland.

"That is not possible," said Amalatok promptly.

"Why not? The distance is not so very great."

"The distance is not very great, that is true," replied Amalatok. "If Lo had sailed away to Flatland he might have got safely there, but Blackbeard surely forgets that the storm did not last more than a few hours. If Lo had remained even a short time on this island, would not the calm weather which followed the storm have enabled him to paddle back again to Poloe? No, he must have thought the storm was going to be a long one, and thinking that, must have tried, again to face it and paddle against it. In this attempt he has perished. Without doubt Lo and Unders and Oblooria are in the land of spirits."

Eskimos of the far north, unlike the red men of the prairies, are prone to give way to their feelings. At the mention of the timid one's name, Oolichuk covered his face with his hands and wept aloud. Poor Alf and Benjy felt an almost irresistible desire to join him. All the fun and frolic had gone completely out of the latter, and as for Alf, he went about like a man half asleep, with a strange absent look in his eyes and a perfect blank on his expressionless face. No longer did he roam the hills of Poloeland with geological hammer and box. He merely went fishing when advised or asked to do so, or wandered aimlessly on the sea-shore. The Captain and Benjy acted much in the same way. In the extremity of their grief they courted solitude.

The warm hearts of Chingatok and the negro beat strong with sympathy. They longed to speak words of comfort, but at first delicacy of feeling, which is found in all ranks and under every skin, prevented them from intruding on sorrow which they knew not how to assuage.

At last the giant ventured one day to speak to Alf. "Has the Great Spirit no word of comfort for His Kablunet children?" he asked.

"Yes, yes," replied Alf quickly. "He says, 'Call upon me in the time of trouble and I will deliver thee, and thou shalt glorify me.'"

"Have you not called?" asked Chingatok with a slight look of surprise.

"No; I say it to my shame, Chingatok. This blow has so stunned me that I had forgotten my God."

"Call now," said the giant earnestly. "If He is a good and true God, He must keep His promise."

Alf did call, then and there, and the Eskimo stood and listened with bowed head and reverent look, until the poor youth had concluded his prayer with the name of Jesus.

The negro's line of argument with Benjy was different and characteristically lower toned.

"You muss keep up de heart, Massa Benjy. Nobody nebber knows wot may come for to pass. P'r'aps Massa Leo he go to de Nort Pole by hisself. He was allers bery fond o' takin' peepil by surprise. Nebber say die, Massa Benjy, s'long's der's a shot in de locker."

At any other time Benjy would have laughed at the poor cook's efforts to console him, but he only turned away with a sigh.

Two days after that the Eskimos of Poloe were assembled on the beach making preparations to go off on a seal hunt.

"Is that a whale on the horizon or a walrus!" asked the Captain, touching Chingatok on the arm as they stood on the edge of the sea, ready to embark.

"More like a black gull," said Benjy, "or a northern diver."

Chingatok looked long and earnestly at the object in question, and then said with emphasis—"A kayak!"

"One of the young men returning from a hunt, I suppose," said Alf, whose attention was aroused by the interest manifested by the surrounding Eskimos.

"Not so," said Amalatok, who joined the group at the moment, "the man paddles like a man of Flatland."

"What! one of your enemies?" cried the Captain, who, in his then state of depression, would have welcomed a fight as a sort of relief. Evidently Butterface shared his hopes, for he showed the whites of his eyes and grinned amazingly as he clenched his horny hands.

"Yes—our enemies," said Amalatok.

"The advanced guard of the host," said the Captain, heartily; "come, the sooner we get ready for self-defence the better."

"Yis, dat's de word," said the negro, increasing his grin for a moment and then collapsing into sudden solemnity; "we nebber fights 'cep' in self-defence—oh no—*nebber*!"

"They come not to attack," said Chingatok quietly. "Flatlanders never come except in the night when men sleep. This is but one man."

"Perhaps he brings news!" exclaimed Benjy, with a sudden blaze of hope.

"Perhaps," echoed Alf, eagerly.

"It may be so," said Chingatok.

It was not long before the question was set at rest. The approaching kayak came on at racing speed. Its occupant leaped on shore, and, panting from recent exertion, delivered his thrilling message.

"Prisoners in Flatland," said the Captain at the council of war which was immediately summoned, "but alive and well. Let us be thankful for that good news, anyhow; but then, they ask us to help them, *quickly*. That means danger."

"Yes, danger!" shouted Oolichuk, who, at the thought of Oblooria in the hands of his foes, felt an almost irresistible desire to jump at some of the youths of his own tribe, and kill them, by way of relieving his feelings.

"Rest content, Oolichuk," cried Amalatok, with a horrible grinding of his teeth; "we will tear out their hearts, and batter in their skulls, and—"

"But," resumed the Captain hastily, "I do not think the danger so great. All I would urge is that we should not delay going to their rescue—"

"Ho! huk! hi!" interrupted the whole band of assembled warriors, leaping up and going through sundry suggestive actions with knives and spears.

"Does my father wish me to get the kayaks ready?" asked Chingatok, who, as usual, retained his composure.

"Do, my son. Let plenty of blubber be stowed in them, and war-spears," said the old chief; "we will start at once."

The promptitude with which these northern Eskimos prepared for war might be a lesson to the men of civilised communities. We have already said that the sun had by that time begun to set for a few hours each day. Before it had reached the deepest twilight that night a hundred and fifty picked warriors, with their kayaks and war material, were skimming over the sea, led by the fiery old chief and his gigantic but peace-loving son. Of course Captain Vane, Benjy, Alphonse Vandervell, and Butterface accompanied them, but none of the women were allowed to go, as it was expected that the war would be a bloody one. These, therefore, with the children, were left in charge of a small body of the big boys of the tribe, with the old men.

The weather was fine, the sea smooth, and the arms of the invading host strong. It was not long before the sea that separated Poloe Island from Flatland was crossed.

Towards sunset of a calm and beautiful day they sighted land. Gently, with noiseless dip of paddle, they glided onward like a phantom fleet.

That same evening Leo and Oblooria sat by the couch of Grabantak, nursing him. The injury received by the chief from the whale had thrown him into a high fever. The irritation of enforced delay on his fiery spirit had made matters worse, and at times he became delirious. During these paroxysms it required two men to hold him down, while he indulged in wild denunciations of his Poloe foes, with frequent allusions to dread surgical operations to be performed on the body of Amalatok—operations with which the Royal College of Surgeons is probably unacquainted. Leo, whose knowledge of the Eskimo tongue was rapidly extending, sought to counteract the patient's ferocity by preaching forgiveness and patience. Being unsuccessful, he had recourse to a soporific plant which he had recently discovered. To administer an overdose of this was not unnatural, perhaps, in a youthful doctor. Absolute prostration was not the precise result he had hoped for, but it *was* the result, and it had the happy effect of calming the spirit of

Grabantak and rendering him open to conviction.

Fortunately the Flatlanders were on the look-out when the men of Poloe drew near. One of the Flatland braves was returning from a fishing expedition at the time, saw the advancing host while they were yet well out at sea, and came home at racing speed with the news.

"Strange that they should come to attack *us*," said Teyma to Leo at the council of war which was immediately called. "It has always, up to this time, been our custom to attack *them*."

"Not so strange as you think," said Anders, who now, for the first time, mentioned the sending of the message to Poloeland.

Black looks were turned on the interpreter, and several hands wandered towards boots in search of daggers, when the prime minister interfered.

"You did not well, Unders, to act without letting us know," he said with grave severity. "We must now prepare to meet the men of Poloe, whether they come as friends or foes. Let the young men arm. I go to consult with our chief."

"You must not consult with Grabantak," said Leo firmly. "He lies limp. His backbone has no more strength than a piece of walrus line. His son must act for him at present."

"Boo!" exclaimed one of the warriors, with a look of ineffable contempt, "Koyatuk is big enough, but he is brainless. He can bluster and look fierce like the walrus, but he has only the wisdom of an infant puffin. No, we will be led by Teyma."

This sentiment was highly applauded by the entire council, which included the entire army, indeed the whole grown-up male part of the nation; so that Koyatuk was deposed on the spot, as all incompetents ought to be, and one of the best men of Flatland was put in his place.

"But if I am to lead you," said the premier firmly, "it shall be to peace, not to war!"

"Lead us to what you like; you have brains," returned the man who had previously said "boo!" "We know not what is best, but we can trust you."

Again the approval was unanimous.

"Well, then, I accept the command until my chief's health is restored," said Teyma, rising. "Now, the council is at an end. To your huts, warriors, and get your spears ready; and to your lamps, girls. Prepare supper for our warriors, and let the allowance of each be doubled."

This latter command caused no small degree of surprise, but no audible comment was made, and strict obedience was rendered.

Leo returned to Grabantak's hut, where he found that fiery chief as limp as ever, but with some of the old spirit left, for he was feebly making uncomfortable references to the heart, liver, and other vital organs of Amalatok and all his band.

Soon afterwards that band came on in battle array, on murderous deeds intent. The Flatlanders assembled on the beach to receive them.

"Leave your spears on the ground behind you," shouted Teyma to his host; "advance to the water's edge, and at my signal, throw up your arms."

"They have been forewarned," growled Amalatok, grinding his teeth in disappointment, and checking the advance of his fleet by holding up one hand.

"No doubt," said Captain Vane, who, with Benjy, Alf, and Butterface, was close to the Poloe chief in one of the india-rubber boats, "no doubt my young countryman, having sent a message, expected us. Surely—eh! Benjy, is not that Leo standing in front of the rest with another man?"

The Captain applied his binocular telescope to his eyes as he spoke.

"Yes, it's him—thank God! and I see Anders too, quite plainly, and Oblooria!"

"Are they bound hand and foot?" demanded Amalatok, savagely.

"No, they are as free as you are. And the Eskimos are unarmed, apparently."

"Ha! that is their deceit," growled the chief. "The Flatlanders were always sly; but they shall not deceive us. Braves, get ready your spears!"

"May it not be that Leo has influenced them peacefully, my father?" suggested Chingatok.

"Not so, my son," said the chief savagely. "Grabantak was always sly as a white fox, fierce as a walrus, mean as a wolf, greedy as a black gull, contemptible as—"

The catalogue of Grabantak's vices was cut short by the voice of Teyma coming loud and strong over the sea.

"If the men of Poloe come as friends, let them land. The men of Flatland are about to feed, and will share their supper. If the men of Poloe come as foes, still I say let them land. The braves of Flatland have sharpened their spears!"

Teyma threw up both hands as he finished, and all his host followed suit.

For a moment or two the Poloese hesitated. They still feared deception. Then the voice of Leo was heard loud and clear.

"Why do you hesitate? come on, uncle, supper's getting cold. We've been waiting for you a long time, and are all very hungry!"

This was received with a shout of laughter by the Englishmen, high above which rose a wild cheer of joy from Benjy. Amalatok swallowed his warlike spirit, laid aside his spear, and seized his paddle. Chingatok gave the signal to advance, and, a few minutes later, those warriors of the north—those fierce savages who, probably for centuries, had been sworn hereditary foes—were seated round the igloe-lamps, amicably smearing their fingers and faces with fat, as they feasted together on chops of the walrus and cutlets of the polar bear.

Chapter XXVII.

THE GREAT DISCOVERY.

Friendly relations having been established between the Flatlanders and the Poloese, both nations turned their attention to the arts of peace.

Among other things, Captain Vane and his party devoted themselves once more, with renewed energy, to the pursuit of discovery and scientific investigation. An expedition was planned to *Great Isle*, not now for the purpose of consulting Makitok, the oracle, as to the best time for going to war, but to gratify the wishes of Captain Vane, who had the strongest reason for believing that he was in the immediate neighbourhood of the Pole.

"Blackbeard says he must be very near nothing now," observed Chingatok to Anders the day after their arrival.

"Near *nothing*!" exclaimed Teyma, who was sitting close by.

Of course the giant explained, and the premier looked incredulous.

"I wish I had not left my sextant behind me in the hurry of departure," said the Captain that evening to Leo. "But we came off in such hot haste that I forgot it. However, I'll ask Amalatok to send a young man back for it. I'm persuaded we cannot now be more than a few miles distant from our goal."

"I quite agree with you, uncle, for when I looked at the north star last night it seemed to me as directly in the zenith as it was possible to imagine."

"Ay, lad; but the unaided eye is deceptive. A few miles of difference cannot be distinguished by it. When did the Pole star become visible?"

"Only last night; I fancied I had made it out the night before, but was not quite sure, the daylight, even at the darkest hour, being still too intense to let many of the stars be seen."

"Well, we shall see. I am of opinion that we are still between twenty and forty miles south of the Pole. Meanwhile, I'll induce Teyma to get up an expedition to the island of this Maki-what?"

"Tok," said Leo; "Makitok. Everything almost ends in *tok* or *tuk* hereabouts."

"Who, and what, is this man?" asked the Captain.

"No one seems to know precisely. His origin has been lost in the mists of antiquity. His first forefather—so tradition styles him—seems, like Melchisedec, to have had no father or mother, and to have come from no one knows where. Anyhow he founded a colony in *Great Isle*, and Makitok is the present head of all the families."

Leo then explained about the mystery-thing called *buk*, which was wrapped up in innumerable pieces of sealskin.

"Strange," said the Captain, "passing strange. All you tell me makes me the more anxious to visit this man of the valley. You say there is no chance of Grabantak being able to take the reins of government again for a long time?"

"None. He has got a shake that will keep him helpless for some time to come. And this is well, for Teyma will be ready to favour any project that tends towards peace or prosperity."

Now, while preparations for the northern expedition were being made, our friend Oolichuk went a-wooing. And this is the fashion in which he did it.

Arraying himself one day, like any other lovesick swain, in his best, he paid a ceremonial visit to Oblooria, who lived with Merkut, the wife of Grabantak, in a hut at the eastern suburb of the village. Oolichuk's costume was simple, if not elegant. It consisted of an undercoat of bird-skins, with the feathers inwards; bearskin pantaloons with the hair out; an upper coat of the grey seal; dogskin socks and sealskin boots.

That young Eskimo did not visit his bride empty-handed. He carried a bundle containing a gift—skins of the young eider-duck to make an undergarment for his lady-love, two plump little auks with which to gratify her palate, and a bladder of oil to wash them down and cause her heart to rejoice.

Good fortune favoured this brave man, for he met Oblooria at a lonely part of the shore among the boulders.

Romance lies deep in the heart of an Eskimo—
so deep that it is not perceptible to the naked eye.
Whatever the Poloe warrior and maiden felt, they took
care not to express in words. But Oolichuk looked
unutterable things, and invited Oblooria to dine then
and there. The lady at once assented with a bashful
smile, and sat down on a boulder. Oolichuk sat down
beside her, and presented the bundle of under-
clothing.

While the lady was examining this with critical eyes,
the gentleman prepared the food. Taking one of the
auks, he twisted off its head, put his forefinger under
the integuments of the neck, drew the skin down
backwards, and the bird was skinned. Then he ran his
long thumb-nail down the breast and sliced off a lump,
which he presented to the lady with the off-hand air of
one who should say, "If you don't want it you may let
it alone!"

Raw though the morsel was, Oblooria accepted it
with a pleased look, and ate it with relish. She also
accepted the bladder, and, putting it to her lips,
pledged him in a bumper of oil.

Oolichuk continued this process until the first auk
was finished. He then treated the second bird in the
same manner, and assisted his lady-love to consume
it, as well as the remainder of the oil. Conversation
did not flow during the first part of the meal, but,
after having drunk deeply, their lips were opened
and the feast of reason began. It consisted chiefly of
a running commentary by the man on the Kablunets
and their ways, and appreciative giggles on the part

of the woman; but they were interrupted at the very commencement by the sudden appearance of one of the Kablunets sauntering towards them.

They rose instantly and rambled away in opposite directions, absorbed in contemplation—the one of the earth, and the other of the sky.

Three days after that, Captain Vane and his party approached the shores of *Great Isle*. It was low like the other islands of Flatland, but of greater extent, insomuch that its entire circumference could not be seen from its highest central point. Like the other islands it was quite destitute of trees, but the low bush was luxuriantly dense, and filled, they were told, with herds of reindeer and musk-oxen. Myriads of wild-fowl—from the lordly swan to the twittering sandpiper—swarmed among its sedgy lakelets, while grouse and ptarmigan were to be seen in large flocks on its uplands. The land was clothed in mosses and grasses of the richest green, and decked with variegated wild-flowers and berries.

The voyagers were received with deep interest and great hospitality by the inhabitants of the coast, who, it seemed, never quarrelled with the neighbouring islanders or went to war.

Makitok dwelt in the centre of the island. Thither they therefore went the following day.

It was afternoon when they came to the valley in which dwelt the angekok, or, as Red Indians would have styled him, the medicine-man.

It was a peculiar valley. Unlike other vales it had neither outlet or inlet, but was a mere circular basin or depression of vast extent, the lowest part of which was in its centre. The slope towards the centre was so gradual that the descent was hardly perceived, yet Captain Vane could not resist the conviction that the lowest part of the vale must be lower than the surface of the sea.

The rich luxuriance of herbage in Great Isle seemed to culminate in this lovely vale. At the centre and lowest part of the valley, Makitok, or rather Makitok's forefathers, had built their dwelling. It was a hut, resembling the huts of the Eskimos. No other hut was to be seen. The angekok loved solitude.

Beside the hut there stood a small truncated cone about fifteen feet high, on the summit of which sat an old white-bearded man, who intently watched the approaching travellers.

"Behold—Makitok!" said Teyma as they drew near.

The old man did not move. He appeared to be over eighty years of age, and, unlike Eskimos in general, had a bushy snow-white beard. The thin hair on his head was also white, and his features were good.

Our travellers were not disappointed with this strange recluse, who received them with an air of refinement and urbanity so far removed from Eskimo manners and character, that Captain Vane felt convinced he must be descended from some other branch of the human family. Makitok felt and expressed a degree of interest in the objects of the expedition which had not been observed in any Eskimo, except Chingatok, and he was intelligent and quick of perception far before most of those who surrounded him.

"And what have you to say about yourself?" asked the captain that evening, after a long animated conversation on the country and its productions.

"I have little to say," replied the old man, sadly. "There is no mystery about my family except its beginning in the long past."

"But is not *all* mystery in the long past?" asked the Captain.

"True, my son, but there is a difference in *my* mystery. Other Eskimos can trace back from son to father till they get confused and lost, as if surrounded by the winter-fogs. But when I trace back—far back—I come to one man—my *first father*, who had no father, it is said, and who came no one knows from where. My mind is not confused or lost; it is stopped!"

"Might not the mystery-bundle that you call *buk* explain matters?" asked Alf.

When this was translated, the old man for the first time looked troubled.

"I dare not open it," he said in an undertone, as if speaking to himself. "From father to son we have held it sacred. It must grow—ever grow—never diminish!"

"It's a pity he looks at it in that light," remarked Leo to Benjy, as they lay down to sleep that night. "I have no doubt that the man whom he styles first father wrapped up the thing, whatever it is, to keep it safe, not to make a mystery of it, and that his successors, having begun with a mistaken view, have now converted the re-wrapping of the bundle by each successive heir into a sacred obligation. However, we may perhaps succeed in overcoming the old fellow's prejudices. Good-night, Benjy."

A snore from Benjy showed that Leo's words had been thrown away, so, with a light laugh, he turned over, and soon joined his comrade in the land of dreams.

For two weeks the party remained on *Great Isle*, hunting, shooting, fishing, collecting, and investigating; also, we may add, astonishing the natives.

During that period many adventures of a more or less exciting nature befell them, which, however, we must pass over in silence. At the end of that time, the youth who had been sent for the Captain's sextant and other philosophical instruments arrived with them all— thermometers, barometers, chronometers, wind and water gauges, pendulums, etcetera, safe and sound.

As the instruments reached *Cup Valley*, (so Benjy had styled Makitok's home), in the morning, it was too early for taking trustworthy observations. The Captain therefore employed the time in erecting an observatory. For this purpose he selected, with Makitok's permission, the truncated cone close to the recluse's dwelling. Here, after taking formal possession and hoisting the Union Jack, he busied himself, in a state of subdued excitement, preparing for the intended observations.

"I'll fix the latitude and longitude in a few hours," he said. "Meantime, Leo, you and Benjy had better go off with the rifle and fetch us something good for dinner."

Leo and Benjy were always ready to go a-hunting. They required no second bidding, but were soon rambling over the slopes or wading among the marshes of the island in pursuit of game.

Leo carried his repeater; Benjy the shot-gun. Both wore native Eskimo boots as long as the leg, which, being made of untanned hide, are, when soaked, thoroughly waterproof.[1]

Oolichuk and Butterface carried the game-bags, and these were soon filled with such game as was thought best for food. Sending them back to camp with orders to empty the bags and return, Leo and Benjy took to the uplands in search of nobler game. It was not difficult to find. Soon a splendid stag was shot by Leo and a musk-ox by Benjy.

Not long after this, the bag-bearers returned.

"You shoots mos' awful well, Massas," said Butterface; "but it's my 'pinion dat you bof better go home, for Captain Vane he go mad!"

"What d'you mean, Butterface?" asked Leo.

"I mean dat de Capp'n he's hoed mad, or suffin like it, an' Massa Alf not mush better."

A good deal amused and surprised by the negro's statement, the two hunters hastened back to Makitok's hut, where they indeed found Captain Vane in a state of great excitement.

"Well, uncle, what's the news?" asked Leo; "found your latitude higher than you expected?"

"Higher!" exclaimed the Captain, seizing his nephew by both hands and shaking them. "Higher! I should think so—couldn't be *higher*. There's neither

---

1. The writer has often waded knee-deep in such boots, for hours at a time, on the swampy shores of Hudson's Bay, without wetting his feet in the slightest degree.

latitude nor longitude here, my boy! I've found it! Come—come up, and I'll show you the exact spot— the *North Pole itself*!"

He dragged Leo to the top of the truncated cone on which he had pitched his observatory.

"There, look round you," he cried, taking off his hat and wiping the perspiration from his brow.

"Well, uncle, where is it?" asked Leo, half-amused and half-sceptical.

"Where! why, don't you see it? No, of course you don't. You're looking *all round it*, lad. Look down,— down at your feet. Leonard Vandervell," he added, in sudden solemnity, "you're *on it*! you're standing on the North Pole *now*!"

Leo still looked incredulous.

"What you don't believe? Convince him, Alf."

"Indeed it is true," said Alf; "we have been testing and checking our observations in every possible manner, and the result never varies more than a foot or two. The North Pole is at this moment actually under our feet."

As we have now, good reader, at last reached that great *point* of geographical interest which has so long perplexed the world and agitated enterprising man, we deem this the proper place to present you with a map of Captain Vane's discoveries [at right].

"And so," said Benjy with an injured look, "the geography books are right after all; the world *is* 'a little flattened at the Poles like an orange.' Well, I never believed it before, and I don't believe *yet* that it's like an orange."

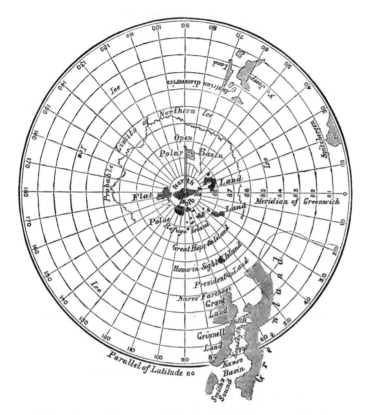

"But it is more than flattened, Benjy," said Leo; "don't you see it is even hollowed out a little, as if the spinning of the world had made a sort of whirlpool at the North Pole, and no doubt there is the same at the South."

Chingatok, who was listening to the conversation, without of course understanding it, and to whom the Captain had made sundry spasmodic remarks during the day in the Eskimo tongue, went that night to

Amalatok, who was sitting in Makitok's hut, and said—

"My father, Blackbeard has found it!"

"Found what, my son?—his nothing—his Nort Pole?"

"Yes, my father, he has found his Nort Pole."

"Is he going to carry it away with him in his soft wind-boat?" asked the old chief with a half-humorous, half-contemptuous leer.

"And," continued Chingatok, who was too earnest about the matter to take notice of his father's levity, "his Nort Pole is *something* after all! It is not nothing, for I heard him say he is standing on it. No man can stand on nothing; therefore his Nort Pole which he stands on must be something."

"He is standing on my outlook. He must not carry *that* away," remarked Makitok with a portentous frown.

"Boh!" exclaimed Amalatok, rising impatiently. "I will not listen to the nonsense of Blackbeard. Have I not heard him say that the world stands on nothing, spins on nothing, and rolls continually round the sun? How can anything spin on nothing? And as to the sun, use your own eyes. Do you not see that for a long time it rolls round the world, for a long time it rolls in a circle above us, and for a long time it rolls away altogether, leaving us all in darkness? My son, these Kablunets are ignorant fools, and you are not much better for believing them. Boo! I have no patience with the nonsense talk of Blackbeard."

The old chief flung angrily out of the hut, leaving his more philosophic son to continue the discussion of the earth's mysteries with Makitok, the reputed wizard of the furthest possible north.

Chapter XXVIII

Soon after this, signs of approaching winter began to make their appearance in the regions of the North Pole. The sun, which at first had been as a familiar friend night and day, had begun to absent himself not only all night, but during a large portion of each day, giving sure though quiet hints of his intention to forsake the region altogether, and leave it to the six months' reign of night. Frost began to render the nights bitterly cold. The birds, having brought forth and brought up their young, were betaking themselves to more temperate regions, leaving only such creatures as bears, seals, walruses, foxes, wolves, and men, to enjoy, or endure, the regions of the frigid zone.

Suddenly there came a day in October when all the elemental fiends and furies of the Arctic circle seemed to be let loose in wildest revelry. It was a turning-point in the Arctic seasons.

By that time Captain Vane and his party had transported all their belongings to Great Isle, where they had taken up their abode beside old Makitok. They had, with that wizard's permission, built to themselves a temporary stone hut, as Benjy Vane facetiously said, "on the very top of the North Pole itself;" that is, on the little mound or truncated cone of rock, in the centre of the Great Isle, on which they had already set up the observatory, and which cone was, in very truth, as nearly as possible the exact position of that long-sought-for imaginary point of earth as could be ascertained by repeated and careful observations, made with the best of scientific instruments by thoroughly capable men.

Chingatok and his father, with a large band of their followers and some of their women, had also encamped, by permission, round the Pole, where, in the intervals of the chase, they watched, with solemn and unflagging interest, the incomprehensible doings of the white men.

The storm referred to began with heavy snow—that slow, quiet, down-floating of great flakes which is so pleasant, even restful, in its effect on the senses. At first it seemed as if a golden haze were mixed with the snowfall, suggesting the idea that the sun's rays were penetrating it.

"Most beautiful!" said Leo, who sat beside the Captain and his friends on the North Pole enjoying the view through the open doorway of the hut, and sipping a cup of coffee.

"It reminds me," said Alf, "of Buzzby's lines:—

"'The snowflakes falling softly
    In the morning's golden prime,
Suggestive of a gentle touch
    And the silent flight of Time.'"

"Behold a more powerful reminder of the flight of Time!" said Benjy, pointing to the aged Makitok, who, with white beard and snow-besprinkled person, came slowly towards them like the living embodiment of "Old Father Christmas."

"Come," said Leo, hastening to assist the old man, "let me help you up the Pole."

Leo, and indeed all the party, had fallen in with Benjy's humour, and habitually referred thus to their mound.

"Why comes the ancient one here through the snow?" said Captain Vane, rising and offering Makitok his seat, which was an empty packing-case. "Surely my friend does not think we would forget him? Does not Benjy always carry him his morning cup of coffee when the weather is too bad for him to come hither?"

"Truly," returned the old man, sitting down with a sigh, "the Kablunets are kind. They never forget. Bunjee never fails to bring the cuffy, though he does sometimes pretend to forget the shoogre, till I have tasted it and made a bad face; then he laughs and remembers that the shoogre is in his pouch. It is his little way. But I come not to-day for cuffy; I come to warn. There is danger in the air. Blackbeard must take his strange things," (thus he referred to the philosophical instruments), "away from here—from—

ha!—from Nort Pole, and put them in my hut, where they will be safe."

The Captain did not at once reply. Turning to his companions he said—

"I see no particular reason to fear this 'danger in the air.' I'll go and consult Chingatok or his father on the point."

"The ancient one, as you call him," said Benjy, "seems to be growing timid with age."

"The youthful one," retorted the Captain, "seems to be growing insolent with age. Go, you scamp, and tell Amalatok I want to speak with him."

Whatever faults our young hero had, disobedience was not one of them. He rose promptly, and soon returned with the chief of Poloeland.

Amalatok confirmed the wizard's opinions, and both opinions were still more powerfully confirmed, while he was speaking, by a gust of wind which suddenly came rushing at them as if from all points of the compass, converging at the Pole and shooting upwards like a whirlwind, carrying several hats of the party with volumes of the now wildly agitated snow up into the sky.

There was no room for further hesitation.

"Why, Massa Bunjay, I thought my woolly scalp he hoed up 'long wid my hat!" cried Butterface, leaping up in obedience to the Captain's hurried order to look sharp and lend a hand.

In a short time all the instruments were removed from the observatory and carefully housed in Makitok's hut. Even while they were thus engaged the storm burst on them with excessive violence. The snow which had been falling so softly, was caught up by the conflicting winds and hurled high into the air, or driven furiously over the valley in all directions, for the gale did not come from any fixed quarter; it rose and swooped and eddied about, driving the snow-drift now here, now there, and shrieking as if in wild delight at the chaotic havoc it was permitted to play.

"Confusion worse confounded!" gasped Leo, as he staggered past Alf with the last load on his shoulder.

"And yet there must be order *everywhere*," observed Chingatok, when, after all were safely housed in Makitok's hut that evening, he heard Leo repeat that sentiment.

"Why do you think so, Chingatok?" asked the Captain with some curiosity.

"Because there is order even in my hut," returned the giant. "Pingasuk, (referring to his wife), keeps all things in perfect order. Is the World-Maker less wise than Pingasuk? Sometimes, no doubt, when Pingasuk is cooking, or arranging, things may seem in disorder to the eye of my little boy Meltik and the small one, (referring to baby), but when Meltik and the small one grow older and wiser, they will see that it is not so."

While Chingatok was speaking, a gust of wind more furious than ever struck the hut and shook it to its foundations. At the same time a loud rumbling sound was heard outside. Most of the men leaped up, caught hold of spears or knives, and rushed out. Through the driving drift they could just see that the observatory, which was a flimsy structure, had been swept clean away, and that the more solid hut was following it. Even as they gazed they saw its roof caught up, and whirled off as if it had been a scroll of paper. The walls fell immediately after, and the stones rolled down the rocky cone with a loud rattling, which was partially drowned by the shrieking of the tempest.

For three days the storm lasted. During that time it was almost impossible to show face in the open air. On the night of the third day the fury of the wind abated. Then it suddenly became calm, but when Butterface opened the door, and attempted to go out, he found himself effectually checked by a wall of snow. The interior of the hut was pitch dark, and it was not until a lamp had been lighted that the party found they were buried alive!

To dig themselves out was not, however, a difficult matter. But what a scene presented itself to their view when they regained the upper air! No metamorphosis conceived by Ovid or achieved by the magic lantern; no pantomimic transformation; no eccentricity of dreamland ever equalled it! When last seen, the valley was clothed in all the rich luxuriance of autumnal tints, and alive with the twitter and plaintive cry of bird-life. Now it was draped in the pure winding-sheet of winter, and silent in the repose of Arctic death. Nothing almost was visible but snow. Everything was whelmed in white. Only here and there a few of the sturdier clumps of bushes held up their loads like gigantic wedding-cakes, and broke the universal sameness of the scene. One raven was the only living representative of the birds that had fled. It soared calmly over the waste, as if it were the wizard who had wrought the change, and was admiring its work.

"Winter is upon us fairly now, friends," said Captain Vane as he surveyed the prospect from the Pole, which was itself all but buried in the universal drift, and capped with the hugest wedding-cake of all; "we shall have to accommodate ourselves to circumstances, and prepare for the campaign."

"I suppose the first thing we shall have to do is to build a snow-house," said Benjy, looking ruefully round, for, as usual, he was depressed by first appearances.

"Just so, Benjy; and the sooner we go to work the better."

Now, the reader must not hastily conclude that we are about to inflict on him or her a detailed narrative of a six months' residence at the North Pole. We have no such fell design. Much though there is to tell,—much of suffering, more of enjoyment, many adventures, numerous stirring incidents, and not a few mishaps— we shall pass over the most of it in total silence, and touch only on those points which are worthy of special notice.

Let us leap, then, into the very middle of the Arctic winter. It is continuously dark now. There is no day at all at the Pole; it is night all round. The last glimmer of the departing sun left them months ago; the next glimmer of his return will not reach them for months to come. The northern Eskimos and their English visitors were well aware of that, nevertheless there was nothing of gloom or depressed spirits among them. They were too busy for that. Had not meat to be procured, and then consumed? Did not the procuring involve the harnessing of dogs in sledges, the trapping of foxes and wolves, the fighting of walruses, the chasing of polar bears; and did not the consuming thereof necessitate much culinary work for the women, much and frequent attention and labour on the part of the whole community, not to mention hours, and sometimes days, of calm repose?

Then, as to light, had they not the Aurora Borealis, that mysterious shimmering in the northern sky which has puzzled philosophers from the beginning of time, and is not unlikely to continue puzzling them to the end? Had they not the moon and the stars, which latter shone with a brilliancy almost indescribable, and among them the now doubly interesting Pole star, right overhead, with several new and gorgeous constellations unknown to southern climes?

Besides all this, had not Captain Vane his scientific investigations, his pendulum experiments, his wind-gauging, his ozone testing, his thermometric, barometric, and chronometric observations, besides what Benjy styled his kiteometric pranks? These last consisted in attempts to bring lightning down from the clouds by means of a kite and cord, and in which effort the Captain managed to knock himself down, and well-nigh shattered the North Pole itself in pieces!

Moreover, had not Leo to act the part of physician and surgeon to the community? a duty which he fulfilled so well that there never had been before that time such a demand for physic in Flatland, and, it is probable, there never will be so many sick people there again. In addition to this, Leo had to exercise his marvellous powers as a huntsman. Benjy, of course, played his wonted *rôle* of mischief-maker and jack-of-all-trades to the entire satisfaction of everybody, especially on that great occasion when he succeeded in killing a polar bear single-handed, and without the aid of gun or spear or any lethal weapon whatever;— of which great event, more hereafter. Anders, the southern Eskimo, made himself generally agreeable, and Butterface became a prime favourite, chiefly because of his inexhaustible fund of fun and good humour, coupled with his fine musical qualities.

We have not said much on this latter point hitherto, because we have been unwilling to overwhelm the reader with too sudden a disclosure of that marvellous magazine of power which was latent in our band of heroes; but we feel it to be our duty now to state that the negro sang his native melodies with such pathos that he frequently reduced, (perhaps we should say elevated), the unsophisticated Eskimos to floods of tears, and sometimes to convulsions of laughter. As, at Benjy's suggestion, he sometimes changed his moods abruptly, the tears often mingled with the convulsions, so as to produce some vivid illustrations of Eskimo hysteria.

But Butterface's strong point was the flute! No one who had not witnessed it could adequately conceive the poutings of thick red lips and general contortions of black visage that seemed necessary in order to draw the tones out of that simple instrument. The agonies of expression, the hissing of wind, and the turning up of whites of large black eyes,—it is past belief! The fruitless efforts of the Eskimos to imitate him were as nothing to the great original, and their delight at the sound was only equalled by their amazement at the sight.

Alf assisted the Captain scientifically and otherwise. Of course he was compelled, during the long winter, to lay aside his geological hammer and botanical box; but, then, had he not the arrangement and naming of his specimens? His chief work, however, was to act the unwonted, and, we may add, unexpected work of a lawgiver.

This duty devolved on him thus:

When Grabantak recovered health—which he was very long in doing—his spirit was so far subdued that he agreed—somewhat sulkily, it is true—to all that his prime minister had done while he held the reins of government. Then he was induced to visit Great Isle, where he was introduced to his mortal foe Amalatok, whom he found to be so much a man after his own heart that he no longer sighed for the extraction of his spinal marrow or the excision of his liver, but became a fast friend, and was persuaded by Alf to agree to a perpetual peace. He also took a great fancy to Chingatok, who begged of Alf to read to the chief of Flatland some of the strange and new ideas contained in his little book.

Alf willingly complied, and for hours these northern savages sat in rapt attention listening to the Bible story.

"My son," said Grabantak one evening to Chingatok, "if we are henceforth to live in peace, why not unite and become one nation?"

"Why not?" echoed Chingatok.

When Amalatok and Makitok heard the question propounded, they also said, "Why not?" and, as nobody objected, the thing was settled off-hand then and there.

"But," said the prime minister of Flatland, starting a difficulty, "who is to be *greatest* chief?"

Amalatok, on whose mind the spirit of Christianity had been gradually making an impression, said promptly, "Let Grabantak be chief. He is wise in council and brave in war."

Grabantak had instantly jumped to the conclusion that *he* ought to be *greatest* chief, and was about to say so, when Amalatok's humility struck him dumb. Recovering himself he replied—

"But there is to be no more war! and I have been a warrior. No, let Amalatok be great chief. He is old, and wisdom lies with age."

"I am not so sure of *that!*" muttered Captain Vane to himself in English; then to the giant in Eskimo, "What says Chingatok?"

"May I speak, my father?" said the giant, dutifully, to Amalatok.

"You may speak, my son."

"Then," continued Chingatok, "I would advise that there should be three chiefs, who shall be equal—my father, Grabantak, and Makitok. Let these consult about our affairs. Let the people appoint twelve men to hold council with them, and what the most of them agree to shall be done."

After some further talk this compromise was agreed to.

"But the laws of Poloeland and those of Flatland are different," said Amalatok, starting another objection. "We must have the same laws."

"My brother chief is wise," said Grabantak. "Let us have new laws, and let that wise young Kablunet, Alf, make them."

"Both my brother chiefs are wise," said Makitok. "Let it be done, and let him take the laws out of the little thing that speaks to him." (Thus they referred to the Bible, having no word in their language by which to name it.)

Great was the surprise of Alf at the honour and labour thus thrust upon him, but he did not shrink from it. On the contrary, he set to work at once with notebook and pencil, and set down the two "Great Commandments:" "Thou shalt love the Lord thy God with all thy heart, and with all thy soul, and with all thy mind;" and, "Thou shalt love thy neighbour as thyself," as the first law in the new code. He set down as the second the golden rule, "Whatsoever ye would that men should do unto you, do ye even so to them."

Proceeding from these as a basis, he worked his way gradually down the code till he had embraced nearly all the possibilities of Eskimo life—a work which kept him busy all the winter, and was not quite finished when "time and tide" obliged him and his companions to quit the land.

Now, not long after this eventful council, Benjy Vane burst rather irreverently into his father's hut with excited looks, holding what looked like an old book in his hand.

"What have you got there, lad?"

"I've got it at last, father! You know I've been trying to wheedle old Makitok into letting me open his mysterious bundle. Well, I prevailed on him to let me do it this afternoon. After unrolling bundle after bundle, I came at last to the centre, and found that it contained nothing whatever but this book, wrapped up in an old cotton pocket-handkerchief. The book is *very* old, father. See, 1611 on the first page. I did not take time to glance at more than that, but brought it straight away to you."

"Hand it over, Benjy," said the Captain eagerly. "This accounts for the mysterious 'buk' that we've heard so much about."

He received the little book with a look of tender curiosity and opened it carefully, while Leo, Alf, and his son looked on over his shoulder.

"1611, sure enough," he said, "though not very legible. The characters are queer, too. Try, Alf, what you can make of it."

Alf took the book. As he did so old Makitok entered, somewhat anxious as to what they were doing with his treasure. Being quieted by the Captain with a draught of cold tea, and made to sit down, the examination of the book proceeded.

"It is much worn, and in places is almost illegible, as might be expected," said Alf. "Let me see. 'Coast of Labrador, (something illegible here), 1611. This day the mutineers took possess ... (can't make out what follows), and put Captain Hudson, with his son, myself, the carpenter, and five sick men into the dinghy, casting us, (blank), with some, (blank), and one cask of water. I begin this diary to-day. It may never be seen by man, but if it does fall into the hands of any one who can read it, he will do a service to ... by conveying ... England.—JOHN MACKINTOSH, *seaman.*'

"Can it be possible?" said Alf, looking up from the relic with an expression of deep solemnity, "that we have found a record of that great Arctic explorer, the unfortunate Henry Hudson?"

"It seems like it, Alf; read on," said Leo, eagerly.

We will not further trouble the reader with Alf's laboured deciphering of this curious and ancient notebook, which was not only stained and worn, but in many places rudely torn, as if its owner had seen much hard service. We will merely run over a few of the chief points which it cleared up. Unfortunately, it threw no additional light on the fate of poor Hudson. Many of the first pages of the book which no doubt treated of that, had been destroyed and the legible portion began in the middle of a record of travelling with a sledge-party of Eskimos to the north of parallel 85° 20 minutes—a higher northern latitude, it will be observed, than had been reached by any subsequent explorer except Captain Vane. No mention being made of English comrades, the presumption remained that they had all been killed or had died—at all events that Mackintosh had been separated from them, and was the only survivor of the party travelling with the Eskimos.

Further on the journal, which was meagre in detail, and kept in the dry form of a log-book, spoke of having reached a far northern settlement. Reference was also made to a wife and family, leading to the conclusion that the seaman had permanently cast in his lot with the savages, and given up all hope of returning to his native land.

One sentence near the end caused a considerable sensation, and opened their eyes to a fact which they might have guessed if they had not been too much taken up with the spelling out of the faded pencilling to think of it at first.

Alf read it with difficulty. It ran thus:—

"Another boy born to-day. His name is Igluk. It is only the eldest boy of a family, in this tribe, who bears his father's surname. My eldest alone goes by the name of Mackintosh. His eldest will bear the same name, and so on. But these Eskimos make a sad mess of it. I doubt if my Scotch kinsmen would recognise us under the name of Makitok which is the nearest—"

"Makitok!" shouted Benjy, gazing open-eyed at the white-bearded wizard, who returned the gaze with some astonishment.

"Why, old boy," cried the boy, jumping up and seizing the wizard's hand, "you're a Scotsman!"

"So he is," said the Captain with a look of profound interest.

"And I say," continued Benjy, in a tone so solemn that the eyes of all the party were turned on him, "we *did* find him *sitting on the North Pole!*"

"And what of that, you excitable goose?" said the Captain.

"Goose, father! Am I a goose for recognising the

fulfilment of an ancient prophecy? Has it not been a familiar saying, ever since I was born, that when the North Pole was discovered, a Scotsman would be found sitting on the top of it?"

"Unfortunately, Ben," returned Alf with a laugh, "the same prophecy exists in other lands. Among the Germans, I believe, it is held that a Bohemian and a Jew will be found on the top of it."

"That only confirms the correctness of prophecy in general," retorted Benjy, "for this man unites all these in his own person. Does not this notebook prove him to be a Scot? Have we not just *found* him? which proves him to be one of a 'lost tribe'—in other words, a Jew; and, surely, you'll admit that, in appearance at least, he is Bohemian enough for the settlement of any disputed question. Yes, he's a Scotch Bohemian Jew, or I'm a Dutchman."

This discovery seemed almost too much for Benjy. He could not think or talk of anything else the remainder of that day.

Among other things he undertook to explain to Makitok something of his origin and antecedents.

"Ancient one," he said earnestly, through the medium of Anders, when he had led the old man aside privately, "you come of a grand nation. They are called Scots, and are said to be remarkably long-headed and wonderfully cautious. Great warriors, but greater at the arts of peace. And the fellow you call your *first father* was a Mackintosh, (probably chief of all the Mackintoshes), who sailed nearly 270 years ago to search for this very 'North Pole' that *we* have got hold of at last. But your first father was not the leader, old boy. He was only a seaman. The leader was Henry Hudson—a man who ranks among the foremost of Arctic explorers. He won't be able to understand what that means, Anders, but no matter—translate it the best way you can. This Henry Hudson was one of the most thorough and extensive searchers of these regions that ever sailed the northern seas. He made many important discoveries, and set out on his last voyage intending to sail right over the North Pole to China, which I daresay he would have done, had not his rascally crew mutinied and cast him and his little son, with seven other men, adrift in a little boat—all of whom perished, no doubt, except your first father, Makitok, my ancient tulip!"

He wound up this summary by grasping and shaking the wizard's hand, and then flung off, to expend his feelings on other members of the community.

Chapter XXIX

A RUNAWAY JOURNEY AND A TREMENDOUS EXPERIMENT.

As winter advanced, Captain Vane continued to keep up the interest of the Eskimos, and to increase their respect for the Kablunets, by gradually unfolding the various sources of power which were at his command.

He did this judiciously, just giving them a taste of the marvellous now and then to whet their appetites. He was particularly careful, however not to practise on their credulity or to pass himself off as a conjuror. He distinctly stated that all his powers were derived from God,—*their* father and *his*,—and that he only excelled them in some matters because of having had better opportunities of acquiring knowledge.

Among other things, he effected an adaptation of his kites which produced results so surprising that we feel bound to describe them particularly.

During the winter he found, as he had expected, that the average temperature at the Pole was not nearly so cold as that experienced in lower latitudes. As far as mere feeling went, indeed, the cold seemed severe enough; nevertheless it was not sufficiently intense to freeze the great ocean, which remained an "open basin" all the year round,—a result which was doubtless owing to the upflow of the warm under-currents from the equator, referred to in a previous chapter.

This, however, did not apply to the waters lying directly around the Poloe and Flatland groups. In these archipelagos the waters being shallow, the frost was quite intense enough to cool them to the bottom. Hence the sea immediately round the islands was covered with a thick coat of solid ice, which resembled in all respects the ordinary Arctic sea-ice, being hummocky in some places, comparatively smooth in others, with a strong iceberg here and there caught and imprisoned amongst it.

As this ice surrounded all the Polar land, and stretched out to sea far beyond the reach of vision, it followed that there was little or no difference between the winter experience of our discoverers and that of all other Arctic voyagers. This realm of what we may style island-ice stretched away, all round, in the direction of the Arctic circle, getting thinner and thinner towards its outer margin, until at last it became sludgy, and, finally, melted away into the open sea. This open sea, in its turn, stretched southward, all round, to the known Arctic regions. Thus the Arctic basin was found to be a zone of open water, surrounded by ice on the south, and with a patch of ice and land in its centre.

Now, it was a strong desire on the part of Captain Vane to visit the southern edge of this central ice-patch on which he dwelt, that induced him to try the kite adaptation before referred to.

"Benjy, my boy," said he, one fine winter day, when the galaxy of stars, the full moon, and an unusually brilliant aurora, diffused a strong light over the undulations of Cup Valley, "I have a notion of taking a trip to the s'uth'ard soon."

"Which s'uth'ard d'you think of going to, father?" asked the boy.

In case any reader should hastily exclaim, "What a ridiculous question; there can be only *one* southward!" we beg leave to point out that at the North Pole *every* direction lies to the southward, and that, as there is necessarily no east or west at all, there is therefore no possibility of stating by compass to what part of the south one intends to go. Of course it was open to the Captain to have said he intended to descend south on one of the degrees of longitude, or between any two of them, and then, immediately on quitting the Pole the old familiar east and west would, as it were, return to him. But he found it more convenient, on the whole, having got beyond all latitude, to indicate his intended route by well-known objects of the land.

"I'm going to steer for the starboard side of Poloeland," he said, "pay a short visit to Grabantak and Amalatok in passing, and then carry on south to the open water."

"It'll be a longish trip, father."

"Not so long as you expect, my boy, for I mean to go by express."

Benjy's eyes twinkled, for he knew that some new device was working in his father's brain, which brain never failed to bring its plans to maturity.

"What is it to be, father?"

"You go and fetch two of the kites, Benjy, and you'll soon find out. Overhaul them well and see that everything is taut and shipshape. Let Butterface help you, and send Alf and Chingatok to me. I suppose Leo is off after musk-oxen, as usual."

"Yes; he pretends that the camp wants a supply of fresh meat. He'd pretend that as an excuse for hunting even if we were all dying of surfeit."

Soon afterwards the Captain was seen, followed by his usual companions and a company of Eskimos, dragging two sledges to the upper ridge of Cup Valley. One sledge was lightly, the other heavily, laden.

"You've brought plenty of supplies, I hope, Alf?" asked the leader.

"Yes, enough for three weeks. Will that do?"

"Quite enough, lad; but it may not be wanted, as I'm going south in a direction we've not yet tried, where I expect to find the open water close to us. It's well, however, to have enough of meat at all times."

"No fear of its being too much, father," said Benjy. "When Butterface goes with us, a three weeks' allowance usually disappears in a fortnight."

"Nebber mind, Massa," said the negro seriously. "You've plenty for tree weeks dis time, 'cause I's off my feed. Got Polar dimspepsy, or suffin' o' dat sort, I tink."

"You've brought the electrical machine, of course, and the dynamite, Alf?" asked the Captain.

"Of course. I never prepare for a trip without these. There's no saying, you see, when we may require them—either to blow up obstructions or astonish the natives."

"The natives are past astonishing now," remarked Benjy; "nothing short of a ten thousand jar battery would astonish Chingatok, and I'm quite sure that you couldn't rouse a sentiment of surprise in Oolichuk, unless you made him swallow a dynamite cartridge, and blew him inside out. But, I say, daddy, how long are you going to keep us in the dark about your plans? Don't you see that we are in agonies of suspense?"

"Only till we gain the ridge, Benjy. It will be down-hill after that, and the snow-crust comparatively smooth as well as hard."

Arrived at the ridge, one of the kites was unfolded and sent up. The breeze was steady, and sufficiently strong. It took twenty Eskimos to hold it when allowed full play, and even these it jerked about in a manner that highly diverted them. These Eskimos were very fond of kite-flying, for its own sake, without reference to utility!

"I knew you were going to try it on the sledge," exclaimed Benjy, with sparkling eyes.

"Why did you ask me about it, then?" returned the Captain.

"Do let *me* make the first trial, father!"

Captain Vane was fastening the drag-line to the fore part of the light sledge, and refused, at first, to listen to the boy's entreaties, fearing that some accident might befall him.

"You know how accustomed I am to manage the kites, father. There's not the least fear; and I'll be superhumanly cautious."

There was no resisting Benjy's tone and eyes. He was allowed to take his place on the sledge as manager. Butterface sat behind to steer. Steering was to be managed by means of a stout pole, pressed varyingly on the snow on either side.

"Don't go more than a mile or so, my boy," said the Captain, in a serious tone. "It's only a trial, you know. If it succeeds, we'll divide the loading of the sledges, and make a fair start in company."

Benjy promised to manipulate the check-string with care. The struggling natives were ordered to let the kite straighten the slack of the line gradually.

"Are you ready, Ben?"

"All right, father."

"Got your hand on the check-string? Mind, it will pull hard. Now—let go!"

The natives obeyed. Benjy at the same instant hauled sharply on the check-string, intending to tilt the kite well forward, and start in a slow, stately manner, but there was a hitch of some sort somewhere, for the string would not act. The kite acted, however, with its full force. Up went the fore part of the sledge as it flew off like an arrow from a bow, causing Butterface to throw a back somersault, and leaving him behind.

Benjy held on to the head of the sledge, and made violent efforts to free the check-string. Fortunately, the surface of the snow was smooth.

"After him, lads," roared the Captain, setting a brave example, and for some time heading the natives in the chase; but a few moments sufficed to prove the hopelessness of the race.

Tug as Benjy would at the regulator, it refused to act. Fortunately, being made of silk, it did not break. By this time the kite had attained its maximum speed, equal, as the Captain said, to a twenty-knot breeze. At first the surface of the snow was so smooth and hard, that Benjy, being busy with the obdurate regulator, did not appreciate the speed.

When he gave up his attempts with a sigh of despair, he had leisure to look around him. The sledge was gliding on with railway speed. One or two solitary hummocks that looked like white sentinels on the level plain, went past him with an awful rush, and several undulations caused by snow-drift were crossed in a light leap which he barely felt. Benjy was fully aware of his danger. To meet with a hummock no bigger than a wheelbarrow, would, in the circumstances, have entailed destruction; he therefore seized a pole which formed part of the sledge-gear, and tried steering. It could be done, but with great difficulty, as he had to sit in the front of the sledge to keep it down.

Recklessly jovial though he was, the boy could not contemplate his probable fate without misgiving. Nothing was visible in all the white illimitable plain save a hummock here and there, with a distant berg on the horizon. He could not expect the level character of the ice to extend far. Whither was he going? South he knew; but in that direction, his father had often told him, lay the open sea. The moon seemed to smile on him; the aurora appeared to dance with unwonted vigour, as if in glee; the very stars winked at him!

"What if a chasm or a big hummock should turn up?" thought Benjy.

The thought seemed to produce the dreaded object, for next moment a large hummock appeared right ahead. Far away though it was, the awful pace brought it quickly near. The poor boy struggled—he absolutely agonised—with the pole. His efforts were successful. The hummock went past like a meteor, but it was a horribly close shave, and Benjy felt his very marrow shrink, while he drew himself up into the smallest possible compass to let it go by.

A bump soon after told that the ice was getting more rugged. Then he saw a ridge before him. Was it large or small? Distance, the uncertain light, and imagination, magnified it to a high wall; high as the wall of China. In wild alarm our hero tugged at the regulator, but tugged in vain. The wall of China was upon him—under him. There was a crash. The sledge was in the air. Moments appeared minutes! Had the vehicle been suddenly furnished with wings? No! Another crash, which nearly shut up his spine like a telescope, told him that there were no wings. His teeth came together with a snap. Happily his tongue was not between them! Happily, too, the sledge did not overturn, but continued its furious flight.

"Oh, you villain!" exclaimed Benjy, shaking his fist at the airy monster which was thus dragging him to destruction.

If Benjy had been asked to state the truth just then, he would have found it hard to say whether consternation or delight were uppermost. It *was* such a glorious rush! But then, how was it to end? Well, he did not dare to think of that. Indeed he had not time to think, for troubles came crowding on him. A violent "swish!" and a sudden deluge told him that what he had taken for glassy ice was open water. It was only a shallow pool, however. Next moment he was across it, and bumping violently over a surface of broken ice.

The water suggested the fear that he must be nearing the open sea, and he became supernaturally grave. Fortunately, the last crash had been passed without dislocating the parts of either sledge or rider. A long stretch of smooth ice followed, over which he glided with ever-increasing speed.

Thus he continued to rush over the frozen sea during a considerable part of that night.

Poor Benjy! he became half-mad with excitement at last. The exaltation of his little spirit at the risky neck-or-nothing dash, coupled with horror at the certainty of a terrible climax, was almost too much for him. He gave vent to his feelings in a wild cheer or yell, and, just then, beheld an iceberg of unusual size, looming up on the horizon before him. Knowing by experience that he would soon be up to it, he used his pole with all his might, hoping to steer clear of it. As he drew nearer, he saw a dark line on either side of the berg. A feeling of deadly alarm filled him. It was the open sea! and he had to choose between being plunged into it or dashed against the berg. It occurred to him then, for the first time, that a third resource was open—he might cut the rope, and let the kite go free! Amazed at his stupidity in not thinking of this before, he took out his clasp-knife, but before applying it, made a last effort to move the regulator. Strange to say, the silken cord yielded to the first pull, as if nothing had been wrong with it at all! The head of the runaway kite was thrown forward, and it came wavering down in eccentric gyrations, while the sledge gradually lost way, and came to a standstill not fifty yards from the berg.

Up to this point what may be termed the northern island-ice continued unbroken, but beyond the berg it was broken up into floes, and, not six hundred yards out, it tailed away to the southward in what whalers term stream-ice. The berg itself was obviously aground.

The first object that met Benjy's eyes, after coming to a halt, was an enormous polar bear. This was no strange sight to the boy by that time, but it was awkward in the circumstances, for he had neither gun nor spear. Even if he had possessed the latter he was too young and light to cope successfully with the shaggy white king of Arctic beasts.

From the attitude of the animal it appeared to be watching something. In truth, it was so intently engaged with a sleeping seal that it had not observed the approach of the sledge. Profiting by this, Benjy quietly moved away round a colossal buttress of the berg, and took refuge in an ice-cave. But such refuge, he knew, could avail him nothing if the bear should scent him out and search for him. Looking hastily round and up into the dark blue cavern, he espied a projecting ledge of ice about thirteen feet above the level of the floor. On this he resolved to perch himself.

His first care was to examine the contents of the sledge. We have said it had been lightly laden at starting, which was the reason of the tremendous pace at which it travelled. Although there was neither spear nor gun, the anxious boy was somewhat comforted to find an axe strapped in its accustomed place; also a blanket, sleeping-bag, and musk-ox skin, besides a mass of frozen blubber, but there was nothing else of an eatable nature. There was, however, a box containing the captain's sextant, the electrical machine, and a packet of dynamite cartridges.

Regarding these latter objects with a sigh of disappointment, Benjy seized the axe and hastened towards the ledge of ice, muttering to himself in a confidential tone—

"You see, old boy, if that bear takes a fancy to call on you, it will be as well to be able to say, 'Not at home,' for he could make short work of you, much though you think of yourself. Yes, this ledge is high enough to bid you defiance, mister bear, and it's long and broad enough to hold me and my belongings. The knobs by which to climb to it, too, are easy—too easy—but I'll soon rectify that. Now, then, look alive, Benjy, boy, for if that bear don't catch that seal he'll be sure to look you up."

Ceasing to speak, he actively conveyed the contents of the sledge to his shelf of refuge. Then he cut away the knobs by which he climbed to it, until there was barely sufficient for his own tiny toes to rest on. That done, he went to the mouth of the cavern to look about him.

What he saw there may be guessed from the fact that he returned next moment, running at full speed, stumbling over ice lumps, bumping his shins and knees, dropping his axe, and lacerating his knuckles. He had met the bear! Need we add that he gained his perch with the agility of a tree-squirrel!

The bear, surprised, no doubt, but obviously sulky from the loss of the seal, entered the cave sedately with an inquiring look. It saw Benjy at once, and made prodigious efforts to get at him. As the monster rose on its hind legs and reached its paws towards his shelf, the poor boy's spirit seemed to melt, indeed his whole interior felt as if reduced to a warm fluid, while a prickly heat broke out at his extremities, perspiration beaded his brow, and his heart appeared to have settled permanently in his throat.

These distressing symptoms did not, however, last long, for he quickly perceived that the bear's utmost stretch did not reach nearer than three or four feet of him. Some of the alarm returned, however, when the creature attempted to climb up by his own ladder. Seven or eight times it made the attempt, while the boy watched in breathless anxiety, but each time it slipped when half-way up, and fell with a soft heavy thud on the ice below, which caused it to gasp and cough. Then it sat down on its haunches and gazed at its little foe malignantly.

"Bah! you brute!" exclaimed Benjy, whose courage was returning, "I'm not a bit afraid of you!" He leant against the wall of his refuge, notwithstanding this boast, and licked the ice to moisten his parched lips.

After a rest the bear made another trial, and twice it succeeded in planting the claws of one huge paw on the edge of the shelf, but Benjy placed his heel against the claws, thrust them off, and sent the bear down each time howling with disappointment.

Sailing softly among the constellations in the aurora-lighted sky, the moon sent a bright ray into the cavern, which gleamed on the monster's wicked eyes and glistening teeth; but Benjy had begun to feel comparatively safe by that time, and was becoming "himself again."

"Don't you wish you may get me?" he asked in a desperately facetious spirit.

The bear made no reply, but turned to examine the contents of the ice-cave. First he went to the hatchet and smelt it. In doing so he cut his nose. With a growl he gave the weapon an angry pat, and in so doing cut his toes. We fear that Benjy rejoiced at the sight of blood, for he chuckled and made the sarcastic remark, "That comes of losing your temper, old fellow!"

That bear either understood English, or the very sound of the human voice caused it irritation, for it turned and rushed at the ice-ledge with such fury that Benjy's heart again leaped into his throat. He had, however, recovered sufficiently to enable him to act with promptitude and discretion. Sitting down with his right foot ready, and his hands resting firmly on the ice behind him, he prepared to receive the charge in the only available manner. So fierce was the onset that the monster ran up the ice-cliff like a cat, and succeeded in fixing the terrible claws of both feet on the edge of the shelf, but the boy delivered his right heel with such force that the left paw slipped off. The left heel followed like lightning, and the right paw also slipped, letting the bear again fall heavily on the ice below.

This was more than even a bear could bear. He rushed savagely about the cavern, growling hideously, dashing the sledge about as if it had been a mere toy, and doing all the mischief he could, yet always avoiding the axe with particular care—thus showing that polar bears, not less than men, are quite awake to personal danger, even when supposed to be blind with rage! At last he lay down to recover himself, and lick his bloody nose and paw.

While Benjy sat contemplating this creature, and wondering what was to be the end of it all, a bright idea occurred to him. He rose quickly, took the electrical machine out of its box, and happily found it to be in good working order—thanks to Alf, who had special charge of the scientific instruments, and prided himself on the care with which he attended to them. The bear watched him narrowly with its wicked little eyes, though it did not see fit to cease its paw-licking.

Having arranged the machine, Benjy took the

two handles in his left hand, pressed his knee on the board of the instrument to hold it steady, and with his right hand caused it to revolve. Then he held down the handles as if inviting the bear to come and take them.

The challenge was accepted at once. Bruin cantered up, rose on his hind legs, and stretched his neck to its utmost, but could not reach the handles, though the boy stretched downward as far as possible to accommodate him. The dirty-white monster whined and snickered with intense feeling at thus finding itself so near, and yet so far, from the attainment of its object.

Sympathising with its desires, Benjy changed his posture, and managed just to touch the nose of his enemy. The bear shrank back with a sort of gasp, appalled—at least shocked—by the result! After a little, not feeling much the worse for it, the brute returned as if to invite another electric shock—perhaps with some sinister design in view. But another and a brighter idea had entered Benjy's brain. Instead of giving the bear a shock, he tore off a small bit of seal-blubber from the mass at his side, which he dropped into its mouth. It swallowed that morsel with satisfaction, and waited for more. Benjy gave it more. Still it wanted more.

"You shall have it, my boy," said Benjy, whose eyes assumed that peculiar glare of glee which always presaged some desperate intention.

He opened another small box, and found what he wanted. It was a small object scarcely a couple of inches in length. He fastened the wires of the electric machine quickly to it, and then imbedded it in a small piece of blubber which he lowered, as before, to the bear.

"You'll probably break the wires or smash the machine, but I'll risk that," muttered Benjy through his set teeth. "I only hope you won't chew it, because dynamite mayn't be palatable. There—down with it!"

The bear happily bolted the morsel. The wires seemed to perplex him a little, but before he had time to examine the mystery, the boy gave the instrument a furious turn.

Instantly there was a stupendous crash like a very thunderbolt. The bear burst like an overcharged cannon! Benjy and the berg collided, and at that moment everything seemed to the former to vanish away in smoke, leaving not even a wrack behind!

Chapter XXX

LEO IN DANGER NEXT! A NOVEL MODE OF RESCUE.

When the catastrophe described in the last chapter occurred, Captain Vane and his friends, following hard on the heels of the runaway, chanced to be within two miles of the berg in the bosom of which Benjy had found refuge.

"There he is!" shouted the Captain joyfully, as the flash of the explosion reached his eyes and the roar of the report his ears. "Blessed evidence! He's up to mischief of some sort still, and that's proof positive that he's alive."

"But he may have perished in this piece of mischief," said Alf, anxiously glancing up at the kite, which was dragging the heavily-laden sledge rather slowly over the rough ice.

"I hope not, Alf. Shake the regulator, Butterface, and see that it's clear."

"All right, Massa. Steam's on de berry strongest what's possible."

"Heave some o' the cargo overboard, Alf. We must make haste. Not the meat, lad, not the meat; everything else before that. So. Mind your helm, Chingatok; she'll steer wildish when lightened."

Captain Vane was right. When Alf had tumbled some of the heavier portions of lading off the sledge, it burst away like a wild-horse let go free, rendering it difficult at first for Chingatok to steady it. In a few minutes, however, he had it again under control, and they soon reached the berg.

"The dynamite must have gone off by accident," said the Captain to Alf, as they stumbled over masses of ice which the explosion had brought down from the roof of the cavern. "It's lucky it didn't happen in summer, else the berg might have been blown to atoms. Hallo! what's this? Bits of a polar bear, I do believe—and— what! not Benjy!"

It was indeed Benjy, flat on his back like a spread-eagle, and covered with blood and brains; but his appearance was the worst of his case, though it took a considerable time to convince his horrified friends of that fact.

"I tell you I'm all right, father," said the poor boy, on recovering from the state of insensibility into which his fall had thrown him.

"But you're covered from head to foot with blood," exclaimed the anxious father, examining him all over, "though I can't find a cut of any sort about you—only one or two bruises."

"You'll find a bump on the top of my head, father, the size of a cocoa-nut. That's what knocked the senses out o' me, but the blood and brains belong to the bear. I lay no claim to them."

"Where *is* the bear?" asked Alf, looking round.

"Where is he?" echoed Benjy, bursting into a wild laugh.

"Oh! Massa Benjy, don't laugh," said Butterface solemnly; "you hab no notion wot a awful look you got when you laugh wid sitch a bloody face."

This made Benjy laugh more than ever. His mirth became catching, and the negro's solemn visage relaxed into an irrepressible grin.

"Oh, you!" cried Benjy, "you should have seen that bear go off—with such a crack too! I only wish I'd been able to hold up for two seconds longer to see it properly, but my shelf went down, and I had to go along with it. Blown to bits! No—he was blown to a thousand atoms! Count 'em if you can."

Again Benjy burst into uproarious laughter.

There was indeed some ground for the boy's way of putting the case. The colossal creature had been so terribly shattered by the dynamite cartridge, that there was scarcely a piece of him larger than a man's hand left to tell the tale.

"Well, well," said the Captain, assisting his son to rise, "I'm thankful it's no worse."

"Worse, father! why, it *couldn't* be worse, unless, indeed, his spirit were brought alive again and allowed to contemplate the humbling condition of his body."

"I don't refer to the bear, Benjy, but to yourself,

lad. You might have been killed, you know, and I'm very thankful you were not—though you half-deserve to be. But come, we must encamp here for the night and return home to-morrow, for the wind has been shifting a little, and will be favourable, I think, in the morning."

The wind was indeed favourable next morning, we may say almost too favourable, for it blew a stiff breeze from the south, which steadily increased to a gale during the day. Afterwards the sky became overcast and the darkness intense, rendering it necessary to attend to the kite's regulator with the utmost care, and advance with the greatest caution.

Now, while the Captain and his friends were struggling back to their Polar home, Leo Vandervell happened to be caught by the same gale when out hunting. Being of a bold, sanguine, and somewhat reckless disposition, this Nimrod of the party paid little attention to the weather until it became difficult to walk and next to impossible to see. Then, having shot nothing that day, he turned towards the Pole with a feeling of disappointment.

But when the gale increased so that he could hardly face it, and the sky became obliterated by falling and drifting snow, disappointment gave place to anxiety, and he soon realised the fact that he had lost his direction. To advance in such circumstances was out of the question, he therefore set about building a miniature hut of snow. Being by that time expert at such masonry, he soon erected a dome-shaped shelter, in which he sat down on his empty game-bag after closing the entrance with a block of hard snow.

The position of our hunter was not enviable. The hut was barely high enough to let him sit up, and long enough to let him lie down—not to stretch out. The small allowance of pemmican with which he had set out had long ago been consumed. It was so dark that he could not see his hand when close before his eyes. He was somewhat fatigued and rather cold, and had no water to drink. It was depressing to think of going to bed in such circumstances with the yelling of an Arctic storm for a lullaby.

However, Leo had a buoyant spirit, and resolved to "make the best of it." First of all he groped in his game-bag for a small stove lamp, which he set up before him, and arranged blubber and a wick in it, using the sense of touch in default of sight. Then he struck a light, but not with matches. The Englishmen's small stock of congreves had long since been exhausted, and they were obliged to procure fire by the Eskimo method, namely, a little piece of wood worked like a drill, with a thong of leather, against another piece of wood until the friction produced fire. When a light had been thus laboriously obtained, he applied it to the wick of his lamp, and wished fervently for something to cook.

It is proverbial that wishing does not usually achieve much. After a deep sigh, therefore, Leo turned his wallet inside out. Besides a few crumbs, it contained a small lump of narwhal blubber and a little packet. The former, in its frozen state, somewhat resembled hard butter. The latter contained a little coffee—not the genuine article, however. That, like the matches, had long ago been used up, and our discoverers were reduced to roasted biscuit-crumbs. The substitute was not bad! Inside of the coffee-packet was a smaller packet of brown sugar, but it had burst and allowed its contents to mingle with the coffee.

Rejoiced to find even a little food where he had thought there was none, Leo filled his pannikin with snow, melted it, emptied into it the compound of coffee and sugar, put it on the lamp to boil, and sat down to watch, while he slowly consumed the narwhal butter, listening the while to the simmering of the pannikin and the roaring of the gale.

After his meagre meal he wrapped himself in his blanket, and went to sleep.

This was all very well as long as it lasted, but he cooled during the night, and, on awaking in the morning, found that keen frost penetrated every fibre of his garments and every pore of his skin. The storm, however, was over; the moon and stars were shining in a clear sky, and the aurora was dancing merrily. Rising at once he bundled up his traps, threw the line of his small hand-sledge over his shoulder, and stepped out for home. But cold and want of food had been telling on him. He soon experienced an unwonted sense of fatigue, then a drowsy sensation came over him.

Leo was well aware of the danger of giving way to drowsiness in such circumstances, yet, strange to say, he was not in the least afraid of being overcome. He would sit down to rest, just for two minutes, and then push on. He smiled, as he sat down in the crevice of a hummock, to think of the frequent and needless cautions which his uncle had given him against this very thing. The smile was still on his lips when his head drooped on a piece of ice, and he sank into a deep slumber.

Ah, Leonard Vandervell! ill would it have been for thee if thou hadst been left to thyself that day; but sharp eyes and anxious hearts were out on the icy waste in search of thee!

On arriving at his winter quarters, and learning that Leo had not yet returned, Captain Vane at once organised an elaborate search-expedition. The man who found him at last was Butterface.

"Oh, Massa Leo!" exclaimed that sable creature on beholding the youth seated, white and cold, on the hummock; but he said no more, being fully alive to the danger of the situation.

Rushing at Leo, he seized and shook him violently, as if he had been his bitterest foe. There was no response from the sleeping man. The negro therefore began to chafe, shake, and kick him; even to slap his face, and yell into his ears in a way that an ignorant observer would have styled brutal. At last there was a symptom of returning vitality in the poor youth's frame, and the negro redoubled his efforts.

"Ho! hallo! Massa Leo, wake up! You's dyin', you is!"

"Why—what's—the—matter—Butterf—" muttered Leo, and dropped his head again.

"Hi! hello! ho–o–o!" yelled Butterface, renewing the rough treatment, and finally hitting the youth a sounding slap on the ear.

"Ha! I be tink dat vakes you up."

It certainly did wake him up. A burst of indignation within seemed to do more for him than the outward buffetings. He shut his fist and hit Butterface a weak but well intended right-hander on the nose. The negro replied with a sounding slap on the other ear, which induced Leo to grasp him in his arms and try to throw him. Butterface returned the grasp with interest, and soon quite an interesting wrestling match began, the only witness of which sat on a neighbouring hummock in the form of a melancholy Arctic fox.

"Hi! hold on, Massa Leo! Don't kill me altogidder," shouted Butterface, as he fell beneath his adversary. "You's a'most right now."

"Almost right! what do you mean?"

"I mean dat you's bin a'most froze to deaf, but I's melted you down to life agin."

The truth at last began to dawn on the young hunter. After a brief explanation, he and the negro walked home together in perfect harmony.

Chapter XXXI

THE LAST.

In course of time the long and dreary winter passed away, and signs of the coming spring began to manifest themselves to the dwellers in the Polar lands.

Chief and most musical among these signs were the almost forgotten sounds of dropping water, and tinkling rills. One day in April the thermometer suddenly rose to eighteen above the freezing-point of Fahrenheit. Captain Vane came from the observatory, his face blazing with excitement and oily with heat, to announce the fact.

"That accounts for it feeling so like summer," said Benjy.

"Summer, boy, it's like India," returned the Captain, puffing and fanning himself with his cap. "We'll begin this very day to make arrangements for returning home."

It was on the evening of that day that they heard the first droppings of the melting snow. Long before that, however, the sun had come back to gladden the Polar regions, and break up the reign of ancient night. His departure in autumn had been so gradual, that it was difficult to say when night began to overcome the day. So, in like manner, his return was gradual. It was not until Captain Vane observed stars of the sixth magnitude shining out at noon in November, that he had admitted the total absence of day; and when spring returned, it was not until he could read the smallest print at midnight in June that he admitted there was "no night there."

But neither the continual day of summer, nor the perpetual night of winter, made so deep an impression on our explorers as the gushing advent of spring. That season did not come gradually back like the light, but rushed upon them suddenly with a warm embrace, like an enthusiastic friend after a long absence. It plunged, as it were, upon the region, and overwhelmed it. Gushing waters thrilled the ears with the sweetness of an old familiar song. Exhalations from the moistened earth, and, soon after, the scent of awakening vegetation, filled the nostrils with delicious fragrance. In May, the willow-stems were green and fresh with flowing sap. Flowers began to bud modestly, as if half afraid of having come too soon. But there was no cause to fear that. The glorious sun was strong in his might, and, like his Maker, warmed the northern world into exuberant life. Mosses, poppies, saxifrages, cochlearia, and other hardy plants began to sprout, and migratory birds innumerable—screaming terns, cackling duck, piping plover, auks in dense clouds with loudly whirring wings, trumpeting geese, eider-ducks, burgomasters, etcetera, began to return with all the noisy bustle and joyous excitement of a family on its annual visit to much-loved summer quarters.

But here we must note a difference between the experience of our explorers and that of all others. These myriads of happy creatures—and many others that we have not space to name—did not pass from the south onward to a still remoter north, but came up from all round the horizon,—up all the meridians of longitude, as on so many railway lines converging at the Pole, and settling down for a prolonged residence in garrulous felicity among the swamps and hills and vales of Flatland.

Truly it was a most enjoyable season and experience, but there is no joy without its alley here below—not even at the North Pole!

The alloy came in the form of a low fever which smote down the stalwart Leo, reduced his great strength seriously, and confined him for many weeks to a couch in their little stone hut, and, of course, the power of sympathy robbed his companions of much of that exuberant joy which they shared with the lower animals at the advent of beautiful spring.

During the period of his illness Leo's chief nurse, comforter, and philosophical companion, was the giant of the North. And one of the subjects which occupied their minds most frequently was the Word of God. In the days of weakness and suffering Leo took to that great source of comfort with thirsting avidity, and intense was his gratification at the eager desire expressed by the giant to hear and understand what it contained.

Of course Alf, and Benjy, and the Captain, and Butterface, as well as Grabantak, Makitok, and Amalatok, with others of the Eskimos, were frequently by his side, but the giant never left him for more than a brief period, night or day.

"Ah! Chingatok," said Leo one day, when the returning spring had begun to revive his strength, "I never felt such a love for God's Book when I was well and strong as I feel for it now that I am ill, and I little thought that I should find out so much of its value while talking about it to an Eskimo. I shall be sorry to leave you, Chingatok—very sorry."

"The young Kablunet is not yet going to die," said the giant in a soft voice.

"I did not mean that," replied Leo, with the ghost of his former hearty laugh; "I mean that I shall be obliged to leave Flatland and to return to my own home as soon as the season permits. Captain Vane has been talking to me about it. He is anxious now to depart, yet sorry to leave his kind and hospitable friends."

"I, too, am sorry," returned Chingatok sadly. "No more shall I hear from your lips the sweet words of my Great Father—the story of Jesus. You will take your book away with you."

"That is true, my friend; and it would be useless to leave my Bible with you, as you could not read it, but the *truth* will remain with you, Chingatok."

"Yes," replied the giant with a significant smile, "you cannot take *that* away. It is here—and here." He touched his forehead and breast as he spoke. Then he continued:—

"These strange things that Alf has been trying to teach me during the long nights I have learned—I understand."

He referred here to a syllabic alphabet which Alf had invented, and which he had amused himself by teaching to some of the natives, so that they might write down and read those few words and messages in their own tongue which formerly they had been wont to convey to each other by means of signs and rude drawings—after the manner of most savages.

"Well, what about that?" asked Leo, as his companion paused.

"Could not my friend," replied Chingatok, "change some of the words of his book into the language of the Eskimo and mark them down?"

Leo at once jumped at the idea. Afterwards he spoke to Alf about it, and the two set to work to translate some of the most important passages of Scripture, and write them down in the syllable alphabet. For this purpose they converted a sealskin into pretty fair parchment, and wrote with the ink which Captain Vane had brought with him and carefully husbanded. The occupation proved a beneficial stimulus to the invalid, who soon recovered much of his wonted health, and even began again to wander about with his old companion the repeating rifle.

The last event of interest which occurred at the

North Pole, before the departure of our explorers, was the marriage of Oolichuk with Oblooria. The ceremony was very simple. It consisted in the bridegroom dressing in his best and going to the tent of his father-in-law with a gift, which he laid at his feet. He then paid some endearing Eskimo attentions to his mother-in-law, one of which was to present her with a raw duck, cleaned and dismembered for immediate consumption. He even assisted that pleased lady immediately to consume the duck, and wound up by taking timid little Oblooria's hand and leading her away to a hut of his own, which he had specially built and decorated for the occasion.

As Amalatok had arrived that very day on a visit from Poloeland with his prime minister and several chiefs, and Grabantak was residing on the spot, with a number of chiefs from the surrounding islands, who had come to behold the famous Kablunets, there was a sort of impromptu gathering of the northern clans which lent appropriate dignity to the wedding.

After the preliminary feast of the occasion was over, Captain Vane was requested to exhibit some of his wonderful powers for the benefit of a strange chief who had recently arrived from a distant island. Of course our good-natured Captain complied.

"Get out the boats and kites, Benjy, boy," he said; "we must go through our performances to please 'em. I feel as if we were a regular company of play-actors now."

"Won't you give them a blow-up first, father?"

"No, Benjy, no. Never put your best foot foremost.

The proverb is a false one—as many proverbs are. We will dynamite them afterwards, and electrify them last of all. Go, look sharp."

So the Captain first amazed the visitor with the kites and india-rubber boats; then he horrified him by blowing a small iceberg of some thousands of tons into millions of atoms; after which he convulsed him and made him "jump."

The latter experiment was the one to which the enlightened Eskimos looked forward with the most excited and hopeful anticipations, for it was that which gratified best their feeling of mischievous joviality.

When the sedate and dignified chief was led, all ignorant of his fate, to the mysterious mat, and stood thereon with grave demeanour, the surrounding natives bent their knees, drew up elbows, expanded fingers, and glared in expectancy. When the dignified chief experienced a tremor of the frame and looked surprised, they grinned with satisfaction; when he quivered convulsively they also quivered with suppressed emotion. Ah! Benjy had learned by that time from experience to graduate very delicately his shocking scale, and thus lead his victim step by step from bad to worse, so as to squeeze the utmost amount of fun out of him, before inducing that galvanic war-dance which usually terminated the scene and threw his audience into fits of ecstatic laughter.

These were the final rejoicings of the wedding day—if we except a dance in which every man did what seemed best in his own eyes, and Butterface played reels on the flute with admirable incapacity.

But there came a day, at last, when the inhabitants of Flatland were far indeed removed from the spirit of merriment.

It was the height of the Arctic summer-time, when the crashing of the great glaciers and the gleaming of the melting bergs told of rapid dissolution, and the sleepless sun was circling its day-and-nightly course in the ever-bright blue sky. The population of Flatland was assembled on the beach of their native isle—the men with downcast looks, the women with sad and tearful eyes. Two india-rubber boats were on the shore. Two kites were flying overhead. The third boat and kite had been damaged beyond repair, but the two left were sufficient. The Englishmen were about to depart, and the Eskimos were inconsolable.

> "My boat is on the shore,"

said Benjy, quoting Byron, as he shook old Makitok by the hand—

> "And my kite is in the sky,
> But before I go, of more,
> I will—bid you—all—good-b—"

Benjy broke down at this point. The feeble attempt to be facetious to the last utterly failed.

Turning abruptly on his heel he stepped into the *Faith* and took his seat in the stern. It was the *Hope* which had been destroyed. The *Faith* and *Charity* still remained to them.

We must draw a curtain over that parting scene. Never before in human experience had such a display of kindly feeling and profound regret been witnessed in similar circumstances.

"Let go the tail-ropes!" said Captain Vane in a husky tone.

"Let go de ropes," echoed Butterface in a broken voice.

The ropes were let go. The kites soared, and the boats rushed swiftly over the calm and glittering sea.

On nearing one of the outer islands the voyagers knew that their tiny boats would soon be shut out from view, and they rose to wave a last farewell. The salute was returned by the Eskimos—with especial fervour by Chingatok, who stood high above his fellows on a promontory, and waved the parchment roll of texts which he grasped in his huge right hand.

Long after the boats had disappeared, the kites could still be seen among the gorgeous clouds. Smaller and smaller they became in their flight to the mysterious south, until at last they seemed undistinguishable specks on the horizon, and then vanished altogether from view.

One by one the Eskimos retired to their homes— slowly and sadly, as if loath to part from the scene where the word farewell had been spoken. At last all were gone save Chingatok, who still stood for hours on the promontory, pressing the scroll to his heaving chest, and gazing intently at the place on the horizon where his friends had disappeared.

There was no night to bring his vigil or his meditations to a close, but time wore him out at last. With a sigh, amounting almost to a groan, he turned and walked slowly away, and did not stop until he stood upon the Pole, where he sat down on one of the Captain's stools, and gazed mournfully at the remains of the dismantled observatory. There he was found by old Makitok, and for some time the giant and the wizard held converse together.

"I love these Kablunets," said Chingatok.

"They are a strange race," returned the wizard. "They mingle much folly with their wisdom. They come here to find this Nort Pole, this nothing, and they find it. Then they go away and leave it! What good has it done them?"

"I know not," replied Chingatok humbly, "but I know not everything. They have showed me much. One thing they have showed me—that behind all *things* there is something else which I do not see. The Kablunets are wonderful men. Yet I pity them. As Blackbeard has said, some of them are too fond of killing themselves, and some are too fond of killing each other. I wish they would come here—the whole nation of them—and learn how to live in peace and be happy among the Eskimos. But they will not come. Only a few of their best men venture to come, and I should not wonder if their countrymen refused to believe the half of what they tell them when they get home."

Old Makitok made no reply. He was puzzled, and when puzzled he usually retired to his hut and went to bed. Doing so on the present occasion he left his companion alone.

"Poor, poor Kablunets," murmured Chingatok,

descending from his position, and wandering away towards the outskirts of the village. "You are very clever, but you are somewhat foolish. I pity you, but I also love you well."

With his grand head down, his arms crossed, and the scroll of texts pressed to his broad bosom, the Giant of the North wandered away, and finally disappeared among the flowering and rocky uplands of the interior.

THE END